Also by Sarah Morgan

A Merry Little Lie
Other People's Summers
The Holiday Cottage
The Summer Swap
The Book Club Hotel
The Island Villa
Snowed In for Christmas
Beach House Summer
The Christmas Escape
The Summer Seekers
One More for Christmas
Family for Beginners
A Wedding in December
One Summer in Paris
The Christmas Sisters
How to Keep a Secret

For additional books by Sarah Morgan, visit her website, sarahmorgan.com.

Also by Sarah Morgan

FIVE-STAR SUMMER

SARAH MORGAN

MIRA

MIRA™

Recycling programs for this product may not exist in your area.

ISBN-13: 978-1-335-01323-1

Five-Star Summer

For questions and comments about the quality of this book, please contact us at CustomerService@Harlequin.com.

TM is a trademark of Harlequin Enterprises ULC.

MIRA
22 Adelaide St. West, 41st Floor
Toronto, Ontario M5H 4E3, Canada
MIRABooks.com

HarperCollins Publishers
Macken House, 39/40 Mayor Street Upper
Dublin 1, D01 C9W8, Ireland
www.HarperCollins.com

Printed in U.S.A.

26 27 28 29 30 LBC 5 4 3 2 1

FIVE-STAR SUMMER

PROLOGUE

It was a place of beauty, where sheer towering cliffs plunged into the wild Atlantic Ocean below. A place of myth and legend, steeped in tales of wizards and knights, of mermaids and witchcraft.

The hotel had stood on the headland for over a century, a witness to wind and tide, to storms and shipwrecks and all manner of human behaviour.

Within its walls there had been life and death and everything in between. Love, excitement, celebration, disappointment, pain and betrayal.

Especially betrayal.

A hotel keeps its secrets. People, however, were not so reliable.

1

★★★★★

Evie

Take your career to the next level . . .

Evie stared at the screen. She definitely needed the next level because the current level wasn't working out for her. An upscale hotel in London known for its luxurious accommodation and impeccable customer service had a vacancy. She should apply.

London. Busy. Anonymous. She'd be able to walk down a street without everyone stopping her to catch up with gossip. No one would notice or care if she arrived home early in the morning wearing the same clothes she'd left the house in the night before. She wouldn't be greeted by winks and knowing looks from the locals or asked for regular updates. She wouldn't have to drive to the next town to find a pharmacist who hadn't known her since she was a baby. A fresh start. *A new life.*

A new job, where her colleagues wouldn't include people who used to babysit her.

The team members beaming at her from the website seemed happy. Their careers were obviously going well. Unlike hers.

A big red button encouraged her to "apply here." Her finger hovered for a moment and then she sat back with a sigh.

Why was she so indecisive? Why was she finding it impossible to make the decision when it was obviously the right thing to do, particularly given the current situation?

Maybe she was having a crisis of confidence, which wasn't surprising in the circumstances.

How was she going to sell herself? How did she gloss over the fact that the hotel where she'd worked since she'd graduated was basically falling apart under her watch? Admittedly she'd only been in this role for a short time, but knowing that none of this was her fault didn't make her feel better.

She opened a document on her screen and started to draft a few lines.

"I am a passionate professional—no, that doesn't sound right." Evie deleted the words and tried again, staring at the words on the screen. "I am an *experienced* hospitality professional—yes, that's better—dedicated to delivering the highest standards of guest relations. I pride myself on offering an unforgettable and curated experience to each—"

"Evie?"

Donna, one of the receptionists, appeared in the doorway and Evie slammed her laptop shut and picked up the cup of coffee that had been growing cold on her desk.

"Hi. Everything okay?"

"Not really. I need to talk to you." Donna leaned against the door-frame and grinned at her. "You should see your face! Picture of guilt. What are you doing on that laptop of yours that's so secretive? I hope it's something that could get you arrested. Your life is much too clean and wholesome."

"Nothing."

Preparing to apply for new jobs, because we're all about to lose the one we currently have.

She felt a flash of guilt. Should she be sharing her fears with the staff? No. That wouldn't be fair. They'd been through enough lately what with Gerald, the general manager, being unwell and it wasn't as if she had any real evidence to support her fears. No one from head office had actually *said* they were going to be closed down or put up for sale. But it seemed the obvious path to her. The rest of the staff were carrying on as normal, cheerfully oblivious to the economic realities of running a hotel.

And it was frustrating because she truly believed she could change things. She was brimming with ideas, but the way things were currently it was impossible to put them into practice.

"Have you joined one of those dating sites?" Donna wasn't easily deflected. "Because I said to Molly last week, I can't remember when our Evie last had sex with anyone. She should join one of those sites. But Molly pointed out that one of the disadvantages of living in a small village is that you already know all the eligible men of the right age on account of having been born here, and if you were going to get together with them it would already have happened. You need to spread your net a bit wider. How would you feel about someone older? Edward Barnes is a nice man."

"Edward Barnes?" Evie spilled coffee on her desk. "Are you talking about Mr Barnes the butcher? Mr Barnes who is retiring next year? He's more than thirty years older than me." She snatched a bunch of tissues and soaked up the liquid before it could do any damage.

"He's seasoned, that's true, and his hips are giving him problems but he has a gentle personality and he knows a nice piece of sirloin when he sees it . . ." Donna's voice trailed off and she laughed. "Just kidding. Sort of. Unless you—"

"Enough!" She'd never again be able to walk into the butcher and buy a decent steak. She'd have to order online for the rest of her life.

This whole exchange should make her feel better about being forced to move away from an area she'd lived in all her life and loved. She'd be with people who hadn't known her since birth. People who wouldn't take such an active interest in her sex life.

It might even be possible to *have* a sex life. Which would be a refreshing change.

So why was she feeling conflicted?

"I don't have time for sex, Donna."

"Are you listening to yourself? That's tragic. And don't tell me you don't have time. There's always your lunch hour. We could cover for you while you have a quickie in the laundry room."

"If you could say that a little louder, Donna—I think the kitchen staff possibly didn't hear you."

"Oh, I think they probably did." The deep male voice came from the doorway, and she glanced up and met the laughing gaze of Luca, her new head chef.

There was no point in wondering if he'd overheard, because clearly he had.

She didn't know whether to kill Donna or bash her head on the desk.

"Luca."

Recruiting Luca was one of the few things she'd done right recently, partly because he was an excellent chef, but also because he was one of the few people working here who hadn't known her since she was a baby. Until thirty seconds ago she'd had an appropriately professional relationship with him, which had been a novelty.

Unfortunately, that professional relationship was now a thing of the past.

She'd never felt this embarrassed in her life, a feeling intensified by the fact he didn't seem embarrassed at all. Judging from the smile on his face, he found the situation hilarious.

Or maybe it was the thought of someone wanting her badly enough to have a quickie against a stack of freshly laundered sheets and towels that he found hilarious.

Either way, it was going to be a while until she could have a conversation with him without thinking of laundry cupboards.

Determined not to allow this to become awkward she looked him straight in the eye, trying not to think of him naked.

That part wasn't easy because as well as producing sublime food, Luca was undoubtedly easy on the eye.

He was above average height and beneath the traditional chef whites his shoulders were wide and powerful. She didn't know whether his physique was the result of a serious gym habit or if he'd been lifting a lot of heavy pans. Maybe that was it. Every time she tried to heave her cast iron casserole out of the oven she promised herself that she was going to start going to the gym.

She gave what she hoped passed for a professional, detached smile. "Did you need something, Luca?"

Still laughing, he stepped forward and placed a file on her desk. "The new menu designs. I know which one I prefer, but I'd like your opinion."

Someone wanted her opinion. Someone actually thought she might have something to contribute.

The wilting shoots of her confidence sprang back to life.

"Great. I'll take a look and let you know what I think."

Donna frowned. "What's wrong with the current menu design? Gerald approved it."

Luca transferred his gaze from Evie to Donna. "We're updating the restaurant. We'll be offering a smaller, seasonal menu and we need the design to reflect that. I'm sure Gerald would agree."

Evie almost groaned. She could predict what was coming next. *We've always done it this way . . .*

Donna drew breath. "We've always—"

"Thank you, Donna," Evie interrupted hastily. She didn't want anyone stifling Luca's creativity or he'd end up as exhausted and disillusioned as she was. She patted the file and smiled at him. "I'll take a look at this and get back to you. Great job, Luca."

"And I had some ideas for redesigning the restaurant. We're not making the most of the views."

"Agreed. Let's arrange a time to talk about that."

She waited until he left the room and closed her eyes. "He heard you. This is terrible."

"Terrible? It's not terrible," Donna said, "it's brilliant. Luca! Why didn't we think of him? We need to add him to our list. True, he's changing things that don't need changing which isn't great, but he is the hottest guy we've had around here in a long time. And talking of hot, your cheeks are flaming. I could fry an egg on them."

"Thanks to you, I already have egg on my face. I don't need more. And what is this list you're talking about?"

"The list of potential men you could date. We spent an hour on it last night when we were in the Smuggler's Inn."

Evie was appalled. "You were discussing my sex life in the pub? What if the people at the next table heard you?"

"Funny you should say that because they did. It was Anthony and Jeff. They were out celebrating the fourth anniversary of the gallery, but they happily joined in."

"Joined in?"

"We had quite a large group on it in the end. The more the merrier, I always say."

"Oh well, that's great then. Maybe you could have opened

it up to the whole pub. Fixing my love life is more entertaining than quiz night, I'm sure." *This* was why she should be applying for that job. "Don't you have more important things to talk about?"

"More important than you? No. We all care about you."

"Well, that's nice, obviously, but I can handle my own romantic life, and right now dating is not a priority. And I'm especially not dating someone I work with."

"Why not? That man is hotter than a chilli pepper, and it's convenient that he works here. It means that a rendezvous in the laundry room is a definite possibility. Or one of the empty bedrooms."

And there were far too many of those.

"Stop!" Evie held up a hand. "You have to stop."

"I'll stop if you tell me what secretive thing you're doing on that laptop of yours. And don't say nothing because I know you well enough to know when you're hiding something."

"It's nothing of interest, really." Seeing the speculation on Donna's face, Evie wished she was a better liar. "You said you wanted to talk to me?"

"Is it Pat's anniversary you're planning?" Donna was still peering at Evie's laptop, as if it held the clues to the universe. "Can you believe she has worked here for twenty-five years?"

Yes, she could believe that. She also believed that Pat probably should have moved on to other things at least twenty years ago when she was still feeling fresh and enthusiastic.

"We have a loyal staff," Evie said. And that, of course, was part of the problem. They'd been here for so long they were set in their ways and refused to change. And she had no idea how to motivate them to do things differently.

She adored Gerald, who had been the general manager for the past fifteen years, but after his heart attack she'd stepped up into the GM role in the hotel and what she'd discovered had almost given her a heart attack, too.

How could he have let things get so bad? The whole place was a disaster.

For the first month she'd worked eighteen-hour days trying to get a full picture, and once she'd got the full picture she'd spent a few more days in full panic mode before sitting down and trying to form a workable plan to save the place. But her plan required everyone to join together and change the way they did things. Unfortunately, most of the staff, though lovely and loyal, liked the way things were done and weren't prepared to change anything bigger than a lightbulb.

She didn't have a fraction of Gerald's experience, but even she could see it was only a matter of time until head office made the decision to intervene in a big way. She knew a developer was interested in the site. He'd had the audacity to spend three nights at the hotel, during which he'd poked his thin hooked nose into every corner and asked intrusive questions. He reminded Evie of a weasel. She'd managed to resist the urge to give him scratchy sheets or feed him dodgy seafood. What was the point? What difference would it make? The ship was sinking and she was trying to bail it out by herself with a teaspoon.

All she could do was grab herself a lifebelt, which was why she really should be applying for jobs. This was the push she'd needed to do what she probably should have done a long time ago.

Maybe calling herself "an experienced hospitality professional" was pushing it. If she was being honest she should probably be describing herself as "burned out, disillusioned and hopeless at establishing boundaries with the staff." She'd thought that over time they'd start to respect her experience but that wasn't happening. And maybe it was unrealistic to expect it. To some of them she was still the child who had sat on their laps and watched TV with a glass of milk.

She felt a pang, because there were some things she'd miss, of course.

She woke every morning to the sound of waves crashing onto the rocks and the shriek of seagulls. She ran on the beach and the coast path and bought her fish straight from the boats that landed on the quay.

But she kept those thoughts to herself and tried again to make Donna focus on work. "You came in here to talk to me about something."

"Did I? Oh yes—" Donna nodded. "I'd forgotten for a moment. Mrs Dodds is refusing to pay in full because she says she asked for hypoallergenic bedding and she was given feathers. She hasn't had a wink of sleep for three nights because her airways have closed up."

"But she always has hypoallergenic bedding. It's on the computer system."

"Mandy hates the computer system. And I know we also keep cards for each guest, but I think she forgot to look at it. Anyway, Mrs Dodds didn't get hypoallergenic bedding. I've told her it was the highest quality down and feathers but that didn't soothe her. She said when this happened last time Gerald comped the whole stay."

"He didn't charge her at all? For the whole week?"

"That's right."

And *that*, Evie thought wearily, was just one of the reasons the hotel was in trouble.

"All right. I'll deal with this. How bad is it? Should we offer to make her a doctor's appointment?"

"I don't think she wants that. I told her it was a mix-up and that we're sorry, but she seems to want financial compensation. And one of our branded waffle bathrobes."

One of the disadvantages of being a five-star hotel and providing top quality bathroom products was that guests tended to walk off with them.

"I'll talk to Mrs Dodds right now, then I need to see Mandy."

Mandy was the head housekeeper. Evie had tried to persuade her to use the computer system that automatically flagged guest preferences, but she was scared of it and preferred to check the old-fashioned card system that had been in place for decades.

"Go easy on her," Donna said. "She's already upset because Mrs Dodds shouted. Honestly, it's not that big a deal. I'm sure she'll stop sneezing if she goes for a walk on the beach. Fresh air, that's what she needs. And maybe antihistamine."

"Donna, it's a big deal," Evie said. "Firstly, because we have an unhappy guest, which means we've failed at our job. Secondly, because it is much easier to keep guests than it is to cultivate new ones, so losing a guest is bad news. And thirdly, as well as losing money by compensating her, we risk a bad review and bad reviews put people off staying here. And they also affect our SEO ranking and—"

"Our what?"

"Never mind. I'll handle it, Donna."

"Right—before you do that, I wanted to ask if I could leave early today. I need to take my mother to a hospital appointment and the journey takes forever at this time of year. I know it's not great timing—"

That was true. They were already short-staffed, but what could she say? She knew how hard it was for Donna, caring for her elderly mother at the same time as raising her family and working.

"Of course. How is she?"

"Frail. She seemed to give up after Dad died. Anyway, such is life. All you can do is carry on carrying on. Thanks, Evie."

Evie wondered if she dared ask Donna to come in early tomorrow to make up the time, but then remembered she had to drop her youngest at school.

Unable to see a solution, she stood up and followed Donna to the front desk where Mrs Dodds was making her discontent known to anyone who would listen and a great number of other people who would probably rather have not listened. Her face was red and blotchy and her tirade was punctuated by sneezing.

Her mouth tightened when she saw Evie. "I have been staying at The Alexandra, Cornwall for—"

"The past ten years. I know, Mrs Dodds, and you're a special and valued guest. I'm extremely sorry this happened. It was a genuine mistake and I assure you it will never happen again." She smoothed and soothed, ignoring the inner voice telling her that the way things were at that moment, it probably would happen again.

"What are you going to do about it? Gerald would have offered me my next holiday free of charge."

"Last night will be complimentary, and we are going to offer you a special discounted rate for your booking next year." She was determined not to give away an entire stay.

"I've been rethinking my booking for next year. I'm not sure I'll be able to look forward to it after what has happened. How can you be sure it won't happen again?"

Good question.

"Because I am personally going to look into it and will be doing some intensive staff training." Which, she could safely predict, would make absolutely no difference at all to the level of service delivered.

It didn't really matter what she promised because she

couldn't shake the nagging feeling that The Alexandra wouldn't be in business next year. It would have been closed or sold off to someone who would probably turn it into holiday homes which would remain empty for eleven months of the year. The thought depressed her. She couldn't imagine strolling through the village and not seeing the hotel nestled in the dip on the headland.

Having pacified Mrs Dodds and offered medical assistance (which was refused), she returned to her office and Mandy appeared a few minutes later.

Evie knew this wasn't going to be an easy conversation.

"Mandy, why don't you take a seat and—"

"You look exhausted, Evie. You're the one who should be taking a seat, you poor lamb. I still can't believe you're all grown up and in charge."

How was she supposed to exert authority when the staff treated her like a favourite pet?

"I'm fine, really. But, Mandy, I need to speak to you about Mrs Dodds."

"Don't you worry your head about that. No one likes to be yelled at and I was upset by the things she said, that's true, but I'm over it. I'm not one to hold grudges. I'm sure she didn't mean to shout at me the way she did. She obviously woke up in a bad mood."

Evie opened her mouth to say that Mrs Dodds had woken up surrounded by feathers which might have explained her less than sunny disposition, but Mandy was still talking.

"When did you last eat something, Evie? You're always working, that's your problem. Morning, noon and night you're in this office slogging away. And you're so serious. You used to laugh all the time. You've always been a smiler. I remember your dad pushing you through the village when you were two years old and you were waving your chubby little legs and beaming at everyone. Every trip took him twice as long because we all wanted to cuddle you."

"I'm just trying to do my job, and—"

"You need to be easier on yourself," Mandy said, "or you'll go the same way as Gerald, God bless him."

Evie was fond of Gerald, who was kind and avuncular and had ultimately carried the responsibility for the success or failure of the hotel. But he'd let things slide and it wasn't until he'd collapsed on that horrible day a couple of months ago that she'd realised how bad things were.

In a way this whole situation was his fault, she thought, although she would never dare to voice that opinion out loud.

She'd panicked and sent an email to head office, directed to the guy in charge of UK operations. When she'd had no reply, she'd sent another one, assuming her first email must have gone into spam.

When there had been no reply to that either, she'd left a voicemail and then given up.

Perhaps they didn't want to help. Perhaps they'd already sold the hotel and hadn't got round to telling the staff.

She sat up straighter. There was no evidence for any of the grim thoughts she was having. She was overthinking things.

"I hope I'm in better health than Gerald," she said, "and I'm younger. You don't need to worry."

"But it's a slippery slope. We all think you've been working too hard. So hard you've forgotten what day it is."

Evie stared at her. "What day is it?"

But Mandy already had her head out of the door and was gesturing to whoever was outside.

A moment later her office was full of people. At a rough count it seemed like the entire staff, including Edward, her dad, who had been working as concierge for three decades. He was the longest-serving member of staff and definitely the most knowledgeable.

Emotion filled her and she felt her throat thicken.

If the hotel was sold, her dad would lose his job and that would be terrible. This place was like a home to him, and the team a family.

None of them seemed to have any idea how bad things were. They'd trusted Gerald completely.

And now they were all smiling as they produced a large cake with eight candles blazing.

"Today is the eighth anniversary of the day you started working at the hotel," Mandy said, "I mean full-time—I'm not counting all the hours you put in here as a teenager. You're so busy holding the fort you've forgotten. And look at you! Sitting in the boss's chair. We can't believe our little Evie is all grown up."

"Well, I—thanks." The fact that she was sitting in the boss's chair didn't seem to have any impact on the way they saw her.

"We made your favourite cake, Evie. Chocolate sponge with chocolate icing, topped with chocolate buttons. I remember making something similar for your fifth birthday. Most of it ended up on your face. I have a photo somewhere. I should try and find it."

"Please don't." Evie stood up and blew out the candles before they could set off the smoke alarm. "How thoughtful of you all. Thank you. Er—who is on reception while you're all in here?"

"No one, but if someone comes, they can wait for five minutes."

"It's important to greet guests immediately when they arrive, and—"

"Gerald always believed it was important that the staff were relaxed. It makes us seem more welcoming."

"But if no one is manning the desk then it won't be welcoming, and—"

"Stop stressing. You put such pressure on yourself. No wonder you look tired. Now—" Mandy wielded a large knife "—large slice or small slice?"

"Small is—oh, you're going for large. Right. Thanks." She took the slice of cake. It was bigger than her head. She was starting to understand why Gerald had suffered a heart attack. "I might save it until later and have it with a cup of tea."

"We can make you tea. Or something stronger? You look wrung out."

And this was the problem of course. They were nice people. Generous and kind. Occasionally they were even reasonable at their jobs, but occasionally reasonable wasn't enough to give the hotel the occupancy they needed or the reviews. And every time she tried to address some aspect of improving the guest experience, they either reminded her that their approach had worked fine for Gerald, or they mentioned some time in her childhood when she'd committed some hilarious infraction she'd been trying to escape ever since.

Maybe it would be easier if she had a peer she could talk to, but there was no one.

She was on her own with this. She had to keep going. Keep trying.

Or get out.

"While I have you all here it's the perfect time to remind everyone of the importance of keeping accurate guest records." She tried to sound firm and managerial. "We keep meticulous and detailed records on every guest so that we can make sure we deliver exactly the experience they're looking for, and more. These should be reviewed every evening when we're preparing for the following day's arrivals. One of the many advantages of having such a long-established staff is that we have the privilege of getting to know guests over a period of many years. We are more than hotel staff, we are friends and we pride ourselves on the personal touch."

"Don't worry about that now, pet. Eat your cake."

Cake wasn't going to solve her problems, but they weren't going to leave her office until she'd eaten it.

"Just a little taste, and I'll save the rest for later—" Because they were all watching her expectantly she dug her fork into it and ate a small piece. It was heavenly. The flavour. The texture. The softness of the sponge against the creamy filling. It didn't just taste delicious, it actually made her feel better about her life. "Oh . . ." She closed her eyes. "This is—who made this?"

Luca emerged from the back of the crowd. "That would be me."

The laughter in his eyes and the way his cheeks creased when he smiled made her wish she'd done more than simply pull her hair into a scrunchie that morning.

Thanks to Donna she couldn't stop thinking of the laundry cupboard.

She blanked that thought. Who cared that he was hotter than a chilli pepper? What really mattered was that he was an excellent chef. He was so talented that she was afraid that once he discovered the truth about the establishment he'd joined, he might be on the first train back to London.

Still, until that happened, she was going to make the most of eating well.

During his interview he'd produced several dishes for her to taste. She'd nibbled her way through tiny strips of seared venison in a blackberry sauce. She'd eaten broccoli that tasted nothing like any broccoli she'd ever cooked at home. By the time she'd sampled his crème brûlée she'd been ready to beg him to take the job.

He'd taken it, and the restaurant had been transformed into

an almost overnight success. They even had a waiting list for some evenings.

But it wouldn't be enough, would it? It was too little, too late.

No matter how hard she tried to remain optimistic, it didn't change the fact that the hotel was in trouble. And it also didn't change the fact that no matter what she did, people were always going to see her as "our Evie." She had so much more to give! So much more that she could be contributing. So many ideas. She wanted a chance to prove herself.

She waited until they all finally left the room and opened her laptop again.

With one eye on the door, she finished filling out the application.

Feeling like a traitor, she hit the button and submitted it without allowing herself time to do any more thinking.

There. Done.

And she had no reason to feel guilty. It was obvious that head office had no plans to sell or they would have been in touch. Things would carry on the way they always had, with or without her.

Everything was going to be fine.

2

★★★★★

Abby

They were going to have to sell, that much was obvious. But before that conclusion was reached, she was required to present her findings to the board. And that, Abby thought, was something she wasn't looking forward to.

Being the daughter of the boss should have come with advantages, but most days Abby saw nothing but disadvantages. Like today, for example.

Others on the team had wanted to lead this project, including Jack the UK manager, but Abby had been chosen, which felt both exhilarating and awkward. It was fair to assume her presentation would be given against a background of silent but ill-disguised resentment. She was used to it, but being unpopular didn't get easier with time, nor did the stress of knowing they were waiting for her to fail. Not just waiting for it. Hoping.

They never took her seriously. They saw her as her mother's daughter and nothing else.

I can do this, she told herself silently. *I may be the daughter of the boss, but that doesn't mean I'm not good at my job. I don't need their validation.*

She'd done the work she needed to do, then she'd checked it and checked it again because she couldn't allow herself to make a mistake. She'd spent so long staring at spreadsheets her vision had started to blur and she'd gone to bed still seeing squares and numbers. She'd looked at it from all angles, making sure she'd missed nothing. She'd anticipated every question she could be asked.

She couldn't see how it could go wrong, although anything was possible.

Looking at her colleagues, gathered around the water cooler like a pride of lions waiting for the kill, Abby was reminded of a lecture she'd attended in college on how to handle difficult people. The way not to be intimidated, she'd been told, was to imagine yourself as the predator, not the prey. The problem was that lions didn't have many predators. The biggest threat to their existence was probably a human.

She empathised.

She stood up straighter, ignored the knot of tension in her stomach and pushed through the doors to join them. When it came to hiding her feelings, she'd had the best teacher. Her mother was skilled at hiding her emotions to the point that Abby sometimes wondered whether she experienced them in the same way other people did. She never seemed to be hurt or offended. She didn't get angry, and Abby had never seen her cry. Appearances suggested she felt nothing.

Abby, on the other hand, felt everything but disguised it. She'd learned the hard way that any display of doubt or suggestion of vulnerability on her part simply fed into her colleagues' belief that she didn't deserve to be here. She'd long since accepted that the only way to win their trust was to earn it and she was going to keep trying to do that however long it took, and however hard she had to work.

She was hoping today would be that day, although it didn't seem to be starting well.

You have as much right to be here as anyone, she reminded herself. *You have earned your place in this room.*

Conversation stopped as she walked towards them, but that wasn't unusual. Everyone was guarded around her because they didn't trust her not to pass on what was said to her mother. Which showed how little they knew about the boss. Alexandra Strong was interested in facts and numbers. Profit and loss. She considered gossip to be as much a waste of her time as watching TV.

Still, people kept a wary distance from Abby, and it had been that way since she'd started working for the company right out of college. It didn't matter that she'd started at the bottom and rotated through all the different hotel departments, gaining experience in the day-to-day operations. No matter what she did or how much experience she gained or what she achieved, her presence was tolerated rather than welcomed, her ideas listened to politely rather than embraced.

It was exhausting.

"Hi everyone, good weekend?" She behaved as if she was one of them, as if she was going to be welcomed into their space even though she could *feel* the barrier between them. Did people have limits? She was starting to think she might be reaching hers.

"The weekend was fine, thanks. Yours?" Katya, VP of sales, filled her cup with water. Her tone was civil. She was far too experienced and professional to ever cross the line. But she wasn't friendly.

Abby ignored that reality and behaved as if she was friendly.

"My weekend was busy," she said brightly. "I spent most of

it preparing for today's meeting." Why had she said that? She sounded needy.

Tim, head of guest relations for the group, headed for the door. "I need to pick up some documents before the meeting. See you all in a minute."

A couple of other people followed him and Abby watched them go, a hollow feeling inside her.

She worked hard. Most of the time it felt that was all she did. And for what? Eventually, if she proved herself, she'd take over the company. Her mother had been telling her that since she was old enough to have the conversation.

But was this the price she was going to have to pay? What if she didn't want to pay that price?

The rebellious thought crept into her brain from nowhere and shocked her. Of course she wanted that. Why was she even doubting herself?

She remembered sitting at her mother's desk aged seven, watching as her mother dealt with problem after problem. By ten, her mother was asking her opinion on things and discussing her answers. Sometimes it felt as if the company was the only thing they talked about.

One day this will be yours. It's never too soon to learn.

It was just the two of them. It had always been the two of them because Abby's father had died before she was born. There was no extended family. No network of loving grandparents or fun cousins. Just her and her mother, and the successful hotel group she'd built from the one hotel Abby's father had left her.

On a few occasions she'd tried to ask her mother about her childhood, but her mother always shut her down and Abby had to respect that choice, but it left her with frustratingly little knowledge of her past. She sometimes felt as if the two of them existed in a bubble.

Katya glanced at the time. "I need to get to the meeting room and set up. We both know the boss doesn't tolerate lateness."

Abby almost apologised for it, even though she could hardly be blamed for the boss's obsession with precise timekeeping.

One by one they melted away until she was left standing alone.

"Great to see you, Abby," she muttered under her breath as she tucked the files under her arm and filled a cup with water. "You worked all weekend on the report? You must be exhausted. The company is lucky to have you. Can't wait to hear your recommendations. Your analysis is always insightful and your solutions inspired."

In her dreams.

Since when had any of them taken her seriously? Never. Since when had any of them thought she might have something to say that was worth listening to? Also, never. Or maybe it was more that they were jealous of her perceived privileges.

Whatever the cause, it made for a hideously lonely existence at work.

But it was fine. She was used to it.

She paused. In fact, it wasn't fine at all, and she would never get used to it, but she'd learned to live with it. Fortunately for her she loved the work itself. She enjoyed the varied challenges she faced, and the creativity involved in finding solutions. She had a natural talent for spotting how improvements could be made, how guest service could be improved and profits increased. It was a busy, stimulating job and in the end that was what mattered. She could survive without having friends at work. But she would have liked their respect. Whatever she did, they resented her. They thought she was given preferential treatment, and that there were others more deserving of the opportunities that came her way. What they didn't understand was that she'd been shadowing her mother since she was old enough to walk.

Balancing her laptop and the water, she headed to the meeting room where everyone was already gathered.

Abby distributed the reports she'd had printed, settled herself at the table and waited.

Beyond the huge glass windows of the corporate office the sun blazed, light shimmering across Boston Bay. On the streets far below people were out enjoying the glorious summer weather, taking long lunches in outdoor cafés, strolling along the cobbled streets, or heading out onto the water.

She felt a pang of envy. They probably didn't have indigestion from stress, or a headache from working into the night and then being unable to sleep.

She reminded herself that she was doing something she loved. This was what she'd been working towards since she'd graduated college and even before that. *I built this for you*, her mother would say as she took ten-year-old Abby through her plans for developing a hotel on the beautiful Oregon coast. *For us. No one can take it away.*

Abby had felt a responsibility to take seriously what she'd been given. To that end she'd let friendships lapse, she hadn't had a full night's sleep in as long as she could remember and her last relationship—and it was stretching credulity to describe it as that—had been over a year ago. But she wouldn't change a thing. *Would she?*

She jumped as the door opened and the boss strode in.

It was precisely two o'clock.

Abby felt tension grip her muscles. It was true that she occasionally felt intimidated by her colleagues, but it was also true that the person who intimidated her most was her own mother.

Alexandra sat down at the head of the table and raised an eyebrow. "Abby?"

That was it.

No small talk. No pleasantries. Nothing that wasted time. That was her mother.

Her expertly coloured hair framed her face in a precision cut and she was wearing a cream silk shirt with a tailored skirt and high heels. Understated. Elegant. In charge.

And waiting.

Abby released her death grip on her chair and stood up. No matter what people might think, at work their relationship earned her no favours. If anything, her mother was harder on her than anyone else.

She'd woken early and done her usual thirty lengths of the pool in her apartment building, and now she felt exhausted and was starting to wish she'd prioritised sleep over exercise and checking the numbers one more time. She'd wanted to impress her colleagues, but really their opinion didn't matter. The Alexandra Hotel Group was a privately owned company. In the end there was only one person she needed to impress, and that was the woman seated at the head of the table.

And in a way this felt like a waste of time. She already knew what the outcome of this presentation would be. Her mother wasn't sentimental. She'd want to sell.

This presentation was almost a formality. For a moment she wondered what it would be like to work in a place where her opinion on something had an impact. *Let's ask Abby* . . .

She flicked to the first slide. "The Alexandra, Cornwall."

She started with a photograph of the hotel, which might have been a mistake because there were murmurings around the table of how stunning the coastline was and how incredible the views.

Abby's mind drifted for a moment, imagining herself sitting with a book, enjoying that view. It had been a long time since she'd had a vacation. And yes, there was work pressure, but also she wondered if the appeal of a vacation was less if you were taking it alone. Was dinner for one at a resort in Bali really that different to having dinner alone in her apartment in Boston? The view would be better. And there was always the possibility of meeting someone. Maybe that was why people travelled. For possibilities.

Hearing the impatient tap of her mother's foot on the floor, she snapped back to the present.

When she'd been pulling together the presentation she'd wondered if focusing on this particular hotel would give her mother a moment of nostalgia given that this was the first place she'd owned, but there was no sign of anything other than professional interest.

"I've done a full, detailed analysis and by almost every measure, The Alexandra, Cornwall has been underperforming. Revenue has been down for the past four quarters, and that includes a summer season. We're barely covering operating costs. If you turn to page two of the document in front of you, you'll see the summary." She focused on facts. That was what her mother had taught her. *Never bring your emotions to work, Abby.*

She didn't allow herself to think about the people currently working at The Alexandra whose futures were in jeopardy. Instead, she talked about the key performance indicators, detailing the occupancy rate, revenue and guest satisfaction scores. She talked about the local market, about seasonality and economic pressures. She showed the impact of interest rates and rising costs on their profits.

Her comments on staffing were equally factual. "The general manager had a heart attack two months ago, however revenue was declining before he became ill."

She continued talking and by the time she finally sat down her head was throbbing. She allowed herself a sip of water.

Everyone looked at the boss, waiting for her usual prompt response but for once the boss said nothing.

She was staring at a single page of the report.

Abby slowly lowered the glass to the table. She craned her neck, trying to see which page exactly her mother was looking at. It would be finances, obviously. With her mother it was always finances.

Had she found a mistake?

Please don't let me have made a mistake.

The finance director cleared his throat.

"It's obvious that it's time to sell. As I mentioned at the last meeting, we've had a generous offer from the developer who contacted us. Generous enough that to begin with I was suspicious. I ran a few checks, but he's legitimate. The company is Howard Developments. He sees the potential in the site and wants to demolish the original building and build a block of holiday homes. He seems to want it no matter the cost. Maybe there's buried treasure that we don't know about." His joke fell flat and he cleared his throat. "Maybe it's just the position. It's extraordinary, as you can see from the photographs. At the price he's offering, we'd be fools not to sell. We'll need a more detailed analysis of course, and a conversation with the lawyers, but selling fits with our long-term strategic goals. The next stage is for him to have a meeting with you."

Abby waited for her mother to agree, but still she said nothing, her gaze fixed on the same page of the report.

The silence lengthened. Abby's breathing quickened along with her pulse.

She must have missed something. But what? She was sure she'd covered every possible angle.

She braced herself for a question she hadn't anticipated. She turned hot and then cold.

Despite the air conditioning, she was sweating.

Finally, her mother looked up. "How is the general manager's health now?"

There was a shocked silence. Alexandra Strong wasn't given to enquiring after anyone's well-being and no one would have predicted that question.

Fortunately, those facts were on record, and Abby had memorized them.

"He is still on sick leave," Abby said. "He had a triple bypass, but there were complications. I don't get the impression he'll be returning to work anytime soon. We need to consider the fact that he won't return at all."

"And who is the acting general manager?"

"Her name is Evie Hamilton." Abby didn't even need to check her notes. "She stepped up and has been covering since the GM went off sick. This is her first senior leadership role and she's young, but she has worked in the hotel for her whole career and she knows the business well." She studied her mother's face, trying to understand what she was thinking.

She'd started this meeting sure of the outcome.

The Alexandra, Cornwall would be sold. Financially it made sense.

Her mother was nothing if not decisive. Abby had expected the decision to be final within a few minutes of her finishing her presentation.

The finance director tapped his fingers on the table. "The developer would ideally like to meet in Cornwall, but he understands your schedule might make that challenging and he's willing to fly to Boston. I can arrange a meeting as early as next week. Then we can at least get the ball rolling."

Abby had a disturbing vision of a massive ball rolling along the picturesque clifftop and crushing The Alexandra and everyone in it.

Her mother transferred her gaze from the report to the finance director's drumming fingers.

He stopped drumming and shifted in his chair. "If that works for you."

There was a long pause and then finally her mother spoke.

"It doesn't." Her voice sounded strange, as if her throat had been rubbed by sandpaper.

Abby frowned. Was her mother ill? Something was wrong, she sensed it.

Everyone was looking at the woman at the head of the table. The finance director was sweating through his shirt.

"No? You mean no to a meeting next week? The developer felt—"

"His feelings are of no interest to me. And neither is his offer. I won't sell to him."

There was a stunned silence around the table.

"But his offer is—"

"I don't care what he offers. We will not be selling."

"You're not even willing to hear what he has to say?" The finance director shuffled the papers in front of him. "I got the impression he might be prepared to go even higher. If you want, I could—"

"What I want is more information on the hotel." Her voice was steady now. Sure and certain.

More information? Something fluttered inside her. Panic? Abby was sure she'd covered everything. What had she missed? What more information did her mother need?

She sat up a little straighter to get a better look, but she still couldn't figure out which page her mother had been studying so closely.

"If there are some numbers or data you think—"

"I don't need data. The report gives us a full picture of the current financial situation. What it doesn't tell us is why. And before I make any final decisions on the future of our hotel in Cornwall, I want to understand why." Alexandra closed the report in front of her. "The location is perfect, which is why people are scrambling to buy it from us. The building is sound. The staff are loyal, long-term employees. If it's not working, then we need to identify why and make some changes."

Miranda, head of people and development, scribbled a note to herself on the pad in front of her. "I can arrange individual interviews with key staff members. We can do it remotely."

"I want it to be in person."

There was an uncomfortable pause as everyone anticipated a sudden and unwelcome increase in their work volume.

"I should be able to clear my schedule and head over there in the next couple of weeks. I can ask a few questions. Dig a little deeper." Jack, who was the UK manager, picked up his phone and checked his schedule.

Alexandra studied him for a moment, her lips pursed. "Did you visit after the general manager had his heart attack?"

"Visit? You mean in hospital?" Jack sat up straighter. "No—er—we sent flowers and a card, I believe."

"I was asking when you last visited the hotel."

"Ah. I'd have to check." Jack ran his finger round the neck of his shirt. "As you know, most of my focus in recent months has been on The Alexandra, Loch Lomond. Since it opened a year ago the growth has been astonishing. It has become *the* place for weddings. We are fully booked for the next two years."

Everyone knew that Jack's interest in the hotel was driven by his ongoing affair with the wedding and events manager.

"You last visited Cornwall in November last year." Alexandra's gaze didn't shift from his face. "So you're not in a position to offer any insight into the present situation."

Jack looked uncomfortable. "Well, I—"

"It wasn't a question."

"I'll set up a visit." Jack's face was scarlet. "As a priority."

"No," Alexandra said. "Someone will go over and work with the team for the summer."

"The summer?" Miranda gaped at her. "The whole summer?"

"Yes. The busiest season. It's the perfect time to observe how the hotel operates under pressure."

Abby said nothing. She was as surprised as the rest of the team by her mother's unexpected response.

Something still didn't feel right about this. The offer from the developer was surely too good to refuse. And yet her mother was refusing it.

Miranda was still frantically scribbling.

The finance director was sweating. "I do feel a responsibility to suggest that you at least take a meeting with the developer. Listen to what he has to say, that's all. You might change your mind."

Tension rippled around the table and Abby braced herself.

"Change my mind?" Alexandra's voice was gentle and pleasant. "Are you suggesting that I don't know my own mind?"

Here we go, Abby thought.

The man coloured deeply, squirming in his seat. "No, but—"

"In the time you have worked for me, have you known me to be indecisive?"

"No."

Alexandra nodded. "Then I'm sure I don't need to repeat what I said a few moments ago." She spoke so softly that everyone had to stay absolutely still in order to hear her. "I will not, under any circumstances, be selling. And because

I don't believe in wasting people's time, I won't be taking a meeting."

Abby might have had sympathy for the finance director, but he'd worked for the company for five years. Surely he should know by now that when her mother made a decision she never faltered. Nor did she allow herself to be intimidated by any person or situation. She had nerves of steel.

And she was still talking.

"I want someone I can trust embedded in the hotel. I want them to integrate and work closely with all departments. Become one of the team. I want regular reports, and an informed analysis of what has gone wrong here and recommendations of how to fix it. Once we have a summary of all the options, I will decide next steps."

Miranda, who had regrouped while Jack was in the spotlight, glanced up from the notes she'd made. "I've been thinking about this, and I suggest we send—"

"Abby will go."

Everyone was visibly shocked, Abby included.

Her mother wanted her to spend the summer at The Alexandra, Cornwall? The whole summer? Why? What was going on? And how would getting to know the staff change anything?

Her mother wasn't a people person. She wasn't touchy-feely. She was a numbers woman. Her interest was balance sheets. She focused on profit and loss and ultimately the success of the company. And Abby understood why. Her mother had grown up with no financial security. She'd been a young single mother with no family support. She'd had no choice but to step up and provide for both of them. There was no room for emotion when you were fighting to survive. She made decisions that were right for the business.

So why this sudden urge to dig deeper into why The Alexandra, Cornwall was failing?

Deep down she was as perplexed as the finance director.

Miranda inhaled. “Right. But I think perhaps we should—”

“Abby has worked in every area and all the key departments. She understands our business better than anyone.”

Jack looked panicked. “But I’m the one who knows the hotel. I should do it. Maybe not the whole summer, that’s a big ask, but I could check in weekly—”

“I want someone there for the whole summer. And that someone will be Abby. Abby?”

“Of course.” You didn’t argue with the boss, even when you could feel the resentment wafting across the table like a noxious gas. “I’ll contact the staff and let them know I’m coming.”

“Miranda will do that. You’ll be under-cover.”

“Under-cover?” Abby stared. “You mean—not tell them who I am?”

“If they know who you are, you won’t be able to get a true picture of the situation. They’ll hide things from you, stop conversations when you walk into a room, exclude you.”

It sounded like an average working day to Abby.

“You’ll join as a member of staff,” the boss was saying. “Miranda will make the arrangements. Let the acting GM know we’re sending someone experienced to help her out in whichever area of the hotel she feels is the priority. You’ll be flexible, helpful and most of all observant. You’ll send me regular reports and we’ll speak weekly.”

Miranda looked thrown. “You want me to—what exactly? Create a fake identity? Is that even legal?”

“I’m leaving the details to you. I’m confident that you’ll find a solution.”

The usually unflappable and competent Miranda didn’t seem to share that confidence, but she nodded. “I’ll get right on it.”

Under-cover?

Abby didn’t like the idea any more than Miranda, but she

knew her feelings on the subject were irrelevant. Her mother had made up her mind, and nothing anyone said would shift it. Also, there was logic behind the proposal. If they knew who she was, she wouldn't get a true picture although why that picture was needed she had no idea.

Either way, she would be spending her summer in Cornwall. Incognito.

And she had to admit the idea had some appeal. It would be blissful to escape from the office for a couple of months and to not have people judging her before she even walked into a room.

The more she thought about it, the more she saw possibilities.

This would be a chance to reinvent herself. If she was "undercover," she wouldn't be "the boss's daughter." She wouldn't have to watch her back the whole time. And hopefully the acting general manager would be relieved to have support, and not resentful.

And yes, she was uncomfortable with the idea of not being honest about her true role in the company but if she was careful there was no reason, no reason at all, why anyone should find out who she really was.

3

★★★★★

Alexandra

Later that evening in her townhouse in historic Beacon Hill, Alexandra poured herself a glass of wine. A few drops fell onto the marble counter-top and she mopped them up, relieved no one was there to witness her hand shaking. She knew how people saw her. As a robot. Someone with no emotions. Someone who felt nothing.

They'd be shocked if they could see her now.

She picked up the glass and walked through the open French doors to the pretty garden courtyard that was both a suntrap and a haven.

Climbing hydrangea clung to the walls, peonies added a splash of colour to the borders and the soothing sound of bubbling water from the fountain created a serene, tranquil space.

It was her sanctuary. One of the few places she could truly relax. A place she found comfort, and she'd never needed that comfort as much as she did this evening.

She was still wearing the tailored skirt she'd chosen for the meeting along with the ivory silk shirt, but she'd undone a few of the buttons and her feet were bare.

Beyond her garden lay the charms of Beacon Hill with its tree-lined cobblestone streets and charming boutique stores, but here behind these walls she had privacy and right now she was glad of it because the meeting had unsettled her more than she'd imagined possible.

Who would have thought her emotions would be this churned up over something that happened years ago?

She'd blocked it all out. Put it behind her. Left it in her past. But now all those feelings were back, as fresh and real as the day she'd left Cornwall for Boston and a new life.

She was angry, of course. Furious. But behind that heated burn of emotion lay something else. Something insidious and unwanted. Doubt? Regret?

She held on to the anger because anger was easier to deal with than the other more complicated emotions that swirled inside her.

In her head she'd divided her life into two parts—before and after.

No one knew all the details of her "before." Not even her own daughter. From the moment she'd discovered she was pregnant all those years ago, she'd been determined that her daughter's life wouldn't be like hers. Alexandra's entire mission had been to protect her from it and that was going to continue. She would not allow the past to intrude on the present.

She breathed and ran her hand over the back of her neck.

It was fine. Everything was fine. The people in that meeting would have had no insight into her true thoughts and feelings. She hid herself behind silk and success. They thought she was ruthless and ambitious, and they weren't wrong. But it wasn't ambition or the promise of success that had brought her to Boston. It was cowardice.

She'd been running away.

The sound of the doorbell startled her, but it shouldn't have done because a glance at her watch told her it was 7 p.m. and her daughter was never late.

She would have liked a little more time to compose herself, but that wasn't an option. Fortunately, she'd had decades of experience making sure the way she looked didn't reflect the way she felt. She knew how to appear cool and collected even when on the inside she was fierce and fighting.

Alexandra put her glass down carefully, took a moment to smooth her hair and steady herself before sliding her feet back into her shoes and walking through the house to open the door.

Abby stood there and Alexandra felt emotion tighten in her chest.

Her daughter. Her family.

Looking at her now she felt not one single regret about the decisions she'd made. She'd given none of her baggage to her daughter. She'd left it behind and built a new life.

Abby had changed into a white linen dress, and she was clutching a bottle of wine and a small white box tied with a blue bow.

She looked poised and elegant and thankfully untouched by the grimmer side of life.

"It feels strange doing this on a Monday when our usual routine is Friday. As it's going to be our last evening together for a while before I head off to Cornwall for the summer, I brought wine and dessert." Abby stepped inside and sniffed the air. "Something smells good. You've been cooking."

Occasionally they went out for dinner, but tonight Alexandra hadn't been able to trust her emotions sufficiently to step out in public. She'd needed the sanctuary of her own home and garden.

"It's just chicken." Just chicken, but the herbs were fresh from her garden, and the olive oil and garlic had come from her favourite Italian store two blocks away. Normally cooking soothed her, but this evening she barely remembered throwing it all together. It had done nothing for her stress levels. "I have to mix a dressing and then we can eat."

"I'll mix the dressing. You've been working all day too, you shouldn't do all the cooking."

Abby took the wine and the box through to the kitchen and pulled out plates and cutlery.

Then she rooted through the cupboards and found what she needed for a dressing.

They worked together seamlessly, as they had for all the years Abby had lived at home. It was a familiar routine, and one Alexandra still missed even though Abby had been living in her own apartment for years.

Abby mixed oil and vinegar, added a little mustard and ground pepper. "I must admit I was shocked when you decided to send me to Cornwall. I never would have expected you to go in that direction. I thought you'd sell. I'd love you to talk me through your thinking."

Alexandra reached for water glasses from the cupboard.

Invariably during the evenings they spent together they talked about work, but tonight she didn't want to. She had no intention of explaining her decision.

"The hotel is in the perfect location." She put water glasses on a tray and added napkins. "If I was looking at it now, I'd consider it a perfect addition to our portfolio. I think the disappointing performance of the last few years merits further investigation. And you're the person to do it."

"Thank you. I'm excited." Abby dipped a salad leaf into

the dressing and tasted it. "Tell me everything. The more detail the better."

Alexandra's mouth dried. "Everything? I'm not sure I know what you mean."

"Weather, what clothes I should pack, what the people are like, any strange local customs I need to know about—"

Alexandra relaxed slightly. Abby was asking her about the place, not the past.

Since when had she been this jumpy?

"The weather is changeable so pack layers. And as for customs—remember jam, then cream."

"Excuse me?"

"A Cornish cream tea. A fresh scone, sliced in half and topped with jam and then clotted cream. The order matters."

She tipped olives into a bowl and added the bowl to the tray.

"You remember that detail from when you were there?"

"I served hundreds of cream teas to guests over the summers I worked at the hotel. Probably thousands." She'd had blisters on her feet from walking at speed between the sunny sea view terrace and the kitchen. She'd done battle with wasps who were attracted to the jam, and squirming toddlers bored from sitting. Her face had ached from smiling. Her head had ached from lack of sleep because she'd been working three jobs at the time. Her stomach had ached from anxiety and stress and beneath it all had been anger.

She'd buried it deep, but it had never completely gone away.

Abby glanced at her. "I can't imagine you at eighteen serving cream teas."

Sixteen, Alexandra thought. She'd been sixteen. And she'd been working in the hotel for four years by then, rushing home from school and then rushing out again to clean. She'd lied about her age so that they'd let her work more hours, but it had been a punishing schedule. She'd been exhausted and on at least one occasion she'd fallen asleep in the laundry room.

"I've done most of the jobs in the hotel at some point in my life," she said. "There is no better way to get to know the business. It's the reason I've encouraged you to do the same."

The difference was that her daughter's need to work in the hotel hadn't been driven by desperation.

"Was it tough?" Abby stole an olive from the bowl. "I always forget that you started out working there. You never talk about it."

"It was a long time ago," Alexandra said. "Nothing to talk about."

"Jam, then cream. Got it. Anything else?"

"Be mindful of the tides if you're walking on the beach." Her heart bumped against her chest as she remembered one particular night. *One particular man.*

"Mom? Are you okay?"

Alexandra dragged herself back to the present. "Yes. I was thinking which information might be useful for you. The coastline can be dangerous. I know how much you love to swim but be careful. There are rip currents."

"I'll be working. I doubt I'll have much time for swimming in the sea."

"Do you mind going?" Only now did it occur to her that by sending her daughter to Cornwall she was depriving herself of her company for the whole summer.

She enjoyed the time they spent together. It was the closest she ever came to relaxing in another person's company.

"I don't mind. You raised me to be adaptable." Abby poured the dressing over the salad and tossed it. "It will be interesting, I'm sure."

Her daughter would be in Cornwall, walking where Alexandra

had walked. Seeing the views Alexandra had seen and working in the same hotel.

It was unsettling. It made her feel vulnerable and she hated that feeling.

She had an unusual urge to hug her daughter. To hold her close and be comforted by her presence.

Alarmed by that feeling, she picked up the tray.

Since when had she needed a hug from anyone to make herself feel better? She made herself feel better. That was what she did. She didn't lean on people, not even her own daughter. And she could imagine Abby's reaction if her mother had suddenly hugged her. She'd be shocked. And worried. Alexandra knew all too well how it felt to worry yourself sick about a parent and she didn't want to burden her daughter with that.

They didn't have a tactile relationship, but it was a good one, nonetheless.

Her greatest achievement, in her opinion, wasn't the company she'd built, but the childhood she'd managed to give her daughter. Stable. Secure. Nothing like her own chaotic and stressful childhood. Abby was independent, and able to support herself without relying on anyone. She'd never find herself vulnerable.

True, Abby had never had a father around, but in Alexandra's opinion that came with benefits. She'd protected Abby from emotional and financial instability. Her daughter had never lain awake at night crushed by responsibility, worrying about how she was going to pay the bills, how she was going to afford her mother's care, how she was going to feed both of them. Her daughter had never had to lie about her age in order to get a job she desperately needed. Her daughter had never clung to the flapping edges of her father's coat, frantic to stop him walking out of her life.

Shaken by memories she'd buried deep, Alexandra carried the tray outside, relieved she was good at hiding her emotions.

They settled themselves at the wrought iron table Alexandra had found on a trip to Italy.

She poured wine for both of them.

"Is everything all right?" Abby glanced at her quizzically. "You seem a little tense."

So maybe she wasn't as good at hiding her emotions as she'd thought.

"I have things on my mind, that's all," she said. "I've found a hotel in Maine I think might be a perfect addition to our collection. The position is excellent. I'm going to look at it next week."

"Let me know how that goes." Abby helped herself to chicken and salad. "Can I ask you something?"

Alexandra tightened her fingers on her glass. "Of course."

"In that meeting today you spent ages studying one particular page of the report and I couldn't figure out which one it was."

"I don't recall." The lie came easily. "Why are you asking?"

"Because I'm trying to understand your decision not to sell when you're sitting on such a generous offer. I like to think I know exactly what you would do in any given situation, but not this time it seems." Abby nibbled a piece of chicken. "I wondered if it had anything to do with the fact that The Alexandra, Cornwall was your first hotel. Or that it was left to you by my father when he died." She said it hesitantly, aware that she was treading on sensitive territory. It was something they rarely talked about, and with good reason.

Alexandra picked at her salad. "Have you ever known me to allow sentiment to influence a business decision?"

"Never."

"The hotel is in a prime position. You won't find anything

better in that area. It was the reason I knew I could make it successful all those years ago. That hasn't changed. Everything I have started with that hotel. You're going to find out exactly what is going on. Flag anything that seems unusual to you." She shifted the conversation away from the past to the present.

"Unusual?"

"Anything out of the ordinary."

"Like what?" Abby's eyes narrowed. "You suspect something is going on? With the staff? Fraud or something?"

"No. But I'd like you to go in with open eyes and an open mind."

"All right." Abby nodded. "You never considered selling it? Not even in the beginning when things were hard?"

"I couldn't afford to sell. I was nineteen and pregnant with you. I had no support. I had to find a way. The hotel was in trouble and selling would have left me in more debt. I knew I could capitalise on the position. I knew I could turn it around." She skilfully steered the conversation away from the past. Away from the personal.

"I've never been there, obviously, but it looks stunning. The coastline of North Cornwall reminds me a little of parts of Oregon."

"And some of the beaches are more like the Caribbean, without the weather of course." Alexandra speared a slice of seared chicken. She had no appetite, but not eating would draw attention. "But you'll be able to judge for yourself and let me know."

"Our usual Friday evenings, only over video conference?"

"Sounds good."

"I'll miss your cooking. This is delicious." Abby finished her chicken and helped herself to more salad. "I'm not entirely comfortable joining the team under-cover. Do you think it's necessary?"

Alexandra knew she had to be careful how she answered that. "I think," she said slowly, "there are occasions when the end justifies the means."

"And this is one of those occasions?"

"How else are you going to get a true picture of what's going on? If they know you're part of the senior management team, they will edit what they tell you."

It wasn't the only reason of course, but it was the one she was prepared to share.

Abby put her fork down. "It's true that people will open up and talk more freely to me if they don't know of my connection to you. But how do I make that happen? What name do I use?"

"Your own." She'd thought it through carefully. Weighed up the likelihood of anyone knowing. Remembering. She'd decided the chances of that were slim. "Abby is your middle name. If they search your name, I doubt they will find you." She knew, because she'd checked.

"I hadn't thought of that." Abby picked up her wine. "No one calls me Madeleine except the doctor and dentist."

"And you have a different surname."

"True." Abby leaned forward. "I know you changed your surname to Strong when you moved to Boston, and I understand why—you wanted a fresh start—but did you not think of changing mine too?"

"I was creating a new life for myself—a new identity in every sense. I wanted to leave the past behind. Alexandra Strong was the name I chose." And when she'd felt out of her depth and doubted her abilities, which in the beginning had happened frequently, the name served as a reminder of the person she wanted to be. Strong. "My mother was Madeleine Jones. I wanted you to keep that name. Your grandmother was a special person. Also, I always hoped and intended for you to work in the business, and I thought it might be easier if we had different names."

"Given that everyone knows who I am anyway, it hasn't made much difference." Abby smiled. "But maybe it will now. It will certainly make it less likely that people will make a connection."

"Exactly. And of course you won't mention your relationship to me."

Abby frowned. "But if they ask about my family?"

"Be vague. Deflect. I doubt they'll ask. In my experience people are usually more focused on themselves." She studied Abby's troubled expression. Her daughter was straightforward and honest, with a strong belief in fairness and justice. She was also kind. "I can see you're still uncomfortable with it."

Abby stared at her wine glass for a moment. Alexandra could almost feel her brain working as she tried to align the task ahead with her values.

"No." She looked up and smiled. "I understand why it needs to be this way. I want to do this. I won't let you down."

Alexandra felt pressure in her chest.

"Your experience will be invaluable to them."

Abby nodded. "And if they see me as one of them, one of the team, they're more likely to talk to me. If they know who I am then they won't tell me anything. The conversation will shut off the moment I walk into a room, the same way it does at—" She broke off, but Alexandra didn't need her to complete the sentence.

"The same way it does at the moment. They still exclude you?"

Abby's smile didn't slip. "It's more that they're careful. And I understand."

Alexandra felt an unusual urge to comfort her. To reassure her and tell her everything was going to be all right.

But she didn't do that. She'd made a point of not being overly protective, even when she badly wanted to. Handling life's challenges created resilience. She wanted her daughter to be resilient. In her opinion being self-sufficient and having confidence in your ability to deal with whatever life threw at you was an important survival mechanism. And a parent should give a child survival skills. She'd been forced to develop her own and it had been a brutal journey. In the end it was easier to handle loneliness than to lean on people and be disappointed.

"If they were a bit more open-minded they'd discover they could learn a great deal from you," she said. "You did well today."

Abby looked startled by the praise. "It was an interesting project. And the next part will be even more interesting. Thank you for choosing to send me to Cornwall."

"I'm sending you because you're the best person for the job."

In fact, she was the only person for the job. It was the perfect solution to a problem, but that was because the problem wasn't entirely as it seemed.

Dusk fell over the pretty garden and Alexandra lit a couple of candles.

Abby finished her wine and put her glass down. "What was the hotel in Cornwall like when you first worked there?"

It was an innocent enough question. A simple question on the surface, but one that didn't have a simple answer.

It wasn't Abby's fault that it was a question Alexandra would rather have not answered.

What was it like?

When she looked back now she saw only the darker elements but of course her relationship with the hotel was more complex than that.

It had been a lifesaver when she was desperate, a sanctuary when she'd needed to escape the misery and pressures of home as a child—and she had been little more than a child the first time she'd talked her way into a job there. It was the place where she'd fallen in love for the first time, and the place that had confirmed to her what she'd always suspected—that people were often disappointing and that love, while occasionally romantic and wonderful, was more often brutal and heartbreaking. It wasn't something you wished for, it was something you survived.

Abby didn't need to know any of that. Her own path through life had been much smoother. Alexandra had made sure of it.

She blew out the flame of the match she was still holding. "What was the hotel like? It was tired and run-down." They'd had that in common, she thought. Both she and the hotel had been struggling to survive in a world where everything seemed to be against them.

It had been the scene of her greatest happiness, and also her greatest unhappiness.

Back then she'd had no interest in the hotel itself. Her desire for it to succeed had stemmed purely from a need to build a life for her daughter.

And she'd been angry. Furiously angry. That anger had fuelled her through the long days and nights she'd spent trying to rescue the place.

"But you knew you could turn it around. And you were so *young*. You didn't have any experience of running a hotel."

"Young, yes, but I'd been working there for years, and I was familiar with all the different areas of the hotel." And it was surprising the skills you could find when you were desperate.

"Are you not interested in seeing it again yourself after all this time?" Abby toyed with her wine glass. "I don't only mean the hotel, but also your old home. The place where you grew up."

"I doubt it even still exists." Her mouth was dry and she could barely speak. "It was a long time ago. It will have been knocked down and replaced by a new build."

"You could come over for a visit while I'm there."

A visit?

She'd left it all behind. Stepped out of her old life and into the new. She hadn't looked back, and the only reason she was looking back now was because it was no longer possible to ignore it.

"My summer schedule is already planned."

It was true, and she had no regrets about that. But even if it hadn't been true, she would not be going back.

There was nothing left for her there and no part of her past that she wished to revisit.

4

★★★★★

Evie

Evie slotted her headphones into her ears, selected her favourite playlist and headed off along the coast path. It wound along the top of steep cliffs, undulating gently for a long section before plunging steeply into a tiny cove and rising up again on the other side.

She ran easily, long-limbed and relaxed, her strides eating up the ground. Her head was throbbing and her brain was circling around all the problems she was facing and the decisions she had to make.

But she wasn't going to think about those now. She was going to take a moment to herself and hope that fresh air and exercise would both improve her mood and clear her head.

She'd discovered long ago that running was the best way to blow off steam after a stressful day. It was impossible to feel tension when your feet were pounding the path, the breeze was blowing in your face and the ocean stretched far into the distance. She preferred to run alone, just her and the rhythmic pounding of the soundtrack she'd chosen.

Far below, the sea sparkled. Those same foamy white waves that in winter could lash the rocks with terrifying force seemed almost benign today, lapping the coastline gently.

The evening sun warmed her face and beneath her feet the ground was firm. They'd had so much rain during the winter she'd had to run on roads but now the weather was heating up she spent every spare minute on the coast path or the beach itself.

She ran quickly up the steep section, her lungs screaming for air as she pushed herself. At the top she paused to catch her breath and the moment she stopped moving the thoughts rushed back at her again.

Now that she'd pressed Send on her application she felt guilty, as if she was somehow abandoning everyone.

Maybe the hotel wasn't going to be sold, but there was no escaping the fact that it was in trouble. Something had to change.

She felt disloyal for even contemplating leaving. What if she left and then the worst actually happened?

All those jobs, she thought, rubbing her face with her hand. What would Donna do if the hotel closed? She needed not only the money, but also the warmth and support of her coworkers. Then there was Pat, who had lost her husband six months ago. She'd admitted to Evie on more than one occasion that it was coming to work that had kept her going.

And then there was her dad, who definitely didn't want to retire yet. He was the longest-serving member of staff. He'd worked at the hotel for most of his working life. He loved the job and he was brilliant at it. Maybe another hotel would snap him up. But what if they didn't? Plenty of people valued youth over experience.

These people had all been there for her since childhood and

she was going to abandon them instead of working to protect their jobs.

But what could she do, really? Her title was acting general manager, but all she was really managing was the mess Gerald had left. No one saw her as anything other than "our Evie." Two weeks into the job once the full horror of what she was dealing with became clear, she'd sent everyone a memo outlining the changes she thought they should be making. She'd talked about the importance of great customer service, the impact of good reviews, the importance of trying to maximise revenue by upselling, whether it was upgrading rooms or spa treatments. She'd had loads of ideas that would have increased both occupancy and profits, but in the end none of them had been implemented. People carried on doing things the way they'd always done them when Gerald was running the show.

If she left and they appointed a new general manager, that person might actually be able to turn the place around. The staff might take seriously someone who had come in from the outside. They wouldn't have to throw off decades of history. And that would be good. In the end she'd be saving their jobs by leaving.

She probably should have left long ago, but it had never felt like the right time. Family was important to her. Was that pathetic? Did it make her boring? Some people lived on the other side of the world and saw their family only occasionally in person and relied on video calls for connection. Evie couldn't imagine that. She'd appreciated being able to spend so much time with her grandmother growing up. She'd been there for Evie, and later on as her grandmother had needed more help herself, Evie had been there for her. When she or her father had needed help there had been at least a dozen people they could call on. There was a saying that it takes a village to raise a child and sometimes she felt as if that summed up her childhood. She really had been raised by the village. She'd felt loved and safe and never lonely. She had connections with everyone here, and those connections were hard to break.

It was a community in the true sense of the word and Evie had never had the slightest urge to leave. Until now.

Lately she'd felt restless. A little trapped. She felt stifled in her job and unable to progress.

It was time to spread her wings.

She tried to justify it to herself but her head spun with pros and cons, doubts and uncertainty.

Did she really want to move away? She tried to imagine how it would feel not to look at this view or hear the sounds of the sea when she woke up in the morning. She screwed her eyes tightly shut and tried to picture London. Street noise, the rumble of trains, buildings fighting for limited space, expensive stores with glossy windows and intimidating staff whose make-up was always perfect. And people, people everywhere.

But also life. A different life. A different experience. And how did you know what you really wanted if you never tried anything else?

She wished there was someone she could talk to about it, but there was no one who wouldn't be impacted by her decision. Technically she was the boss, even though no one treated her that way.

She pushed a strand of sweaty hair away from her face.

This was ridiculous. She probably wouldn't even get an interview for the job she'd applied for, in which case nothing would change.

Feeling tired and a little defeated, she turned round and jogged back the way she'd come.

She ran through the village, slowing her pace to accommodate the throng of tourists gathered around the entrance of the small harbour. They milled around the narrow streets, cooing over quaint cottages, wandering into gift shops and spilling out of the pub. She breathed in the salty tang of sea air and gave a wide berth to a seagull who was watching a tourist with an ice cream.

Waving a quick hello to Thea who ran a local book group in the winter, Evie ducked into a narrow cobbled street and paused outside a row of pastel cottages. She dug her hand into her pocket for her key and let herself in to the one with the pale pink door.

Home.

She knew how lucky she was to have this place. Many of the locals had been driven out by the high prices and some of the cottages were now second homes and lay empty for much of the year, waiting for their owners to arrive, usually from London or the surrounding counties. This cottage had belonged to her grandmother and when she'd died, instead of selling it, her father had rented it to a local family. They'd moved out two years before and Evie had moved in. Much as she'd loved living with her father, she was grateful to have her own place. The fact that it was next door was a bonus in her opinion. She could still see her dad regularly, while enjoying her independence.

Having to leave this place would be one of the biggest disadvantages of moving to London. She wouldn't sell it, of course. She'd rent it so that she always had the option of coming back.

It was an old fisherman's cottage, tight on space, but full of charm and character with beams and flagstones and sash windows that flooded the rooms with light. There were views of the harbour and cliffs, and a small cottage garden that was crowded with colourful blooms that she was mostly too busy to tend.

She tossed her keys onto the table, slid off her running shoes and headed straight to the bathroom. She'd painted it a pretty ocean blue and added a few nautical touches that reflected its coastal position.

She stepped into the shower and closed her eyes as the sharp sting of water washed away the cares of the day.

Then she dried her hair, pulled on a pair of shorts and a pale pink linen shirt, and headed downstairs.

She poured herself a glass of wine and was about to take a sip when there was a knock on the door. She wasn't in the mood for company and was relieved to see it was her dad.

He eyed the glass in her hand. "I hope you're not calling that dinner."

"Are you judging me?"

"No. I'm worrying about you. Father's prerogative. Have you eaten?"

"No. Haven't got as far as thinking of food. I'll probably have cheese and crackers." Did she have cheese? She couldn't remember. The contents of her fridge had been right at the bottom of her priority list for the past few weeks. Usually she loved cooking but since she'd had to step into Gerald's job she never seemed to find the time to create anything elaborate. She opened the door wider. "Do you want to come in? There's more wine where this came from. I might get fish and chips from Meg's. You could join me?"

He pulled a disapproving face. "Cheese and crackers are not dinner, and fish and chips from Meg's is delicious but I happen to know that's what you ate last night."

"Are you spying on me?"

"No, but I was told by at least two people in the village that last night you ordered small chips and medium cod."

She sighed. This, she thought, was why she'd finally submitted her application. In London, she'd be able to eat junk food without being judged.

"We're the only village in the South West that doesn't need CCTV."

"Look on the bright side—if you slip and knock your head someone will know and your body will be discovered within seconds. There might even be time to resuscitate you before the ambulance arrives."

She laughed. "That is a comfort I suppose."

"Talking of comfort, I have a lasagne in the oven, and I picked fresh salad from the garden. I can bring it round if you want to work. Or you can come round to mine to eat it and tell me why you've been looking exhausted and beaten all day."

She'd looked exhausted and beaten?

"It was a long one, that's all."

He gave her a keen look. "You're not afraid of hard work, so it's not that. If you don't want to talk about it that's fine, but at least you should eat. We can sit in silence if you prefer."

And this was just one of the reasons she loved him. He never pushed. Never overstepped. But he was always there for her.

She thought about the application she'd submitted and felt a stab of guilt. She should tell him. She really should.

But what was the point in telling him? She probably wouldn't hear back from them, and then she would have worried her father for nothing.

Evie's mother had died a few days after she was born. Her father had raised her alone, although his mother—Evie's grandmother—who had lived next door had helped on plenty of occasions. But mostly it had been just her and her father. That was one reason they were close, the other being that her dad was an all-around good person.

If she refused the offer of dinner he'd worry, and she didn't want him to worry. Also, she loved his lasagne. Which was probably why he'd made it. He wasn't above being manipulative.

She put her wine glass down and picked up her keys.

"I can't say no to your lasagne."

She followed him to the house next door that had been her home for so many years of her life.

Stepping through the door gave her a feeling of warmth and comfort. There was the wonky pot she'd made for her dad when she was eight which still had pride of place on one of his shelves, and a photo of her dad with her mother, sitting on the beach at sunset, laughing together. It was her favourite. She had the same photo in her own cottage.

She settled herself at the table in the kitchen and glanced out of the window at the red-streaked sky.

"Amazing sunset." She'd spent hours at this table doing her homework.

"Yes, looks as if it's going to be another hot day tomorrow. How was your run?"

"Glorious." She didn't add that for once she'd been too stressed to enjoy it.

He put a large dish of lasagne in the centre of the table, golden on top and still bubbling from the oven.

"That smells good." She served him and then herself, and then did the same with the salad. "Thank you for this."

"Anytime."

They ate in a companiable silence and she had second helpings, even though she'd promised herself that she wouldn't.

"It's delicious."

"You can thank your mother for that. She was the one who taught me to make it, as you know."

She did know. She had a notebook in her kitchen full of recipes that her mother had written out in her neat handwriting.

"I should make it myself, but somehow I prefer eating yours. It's the perfect comfort food."

"And do you need comfort?"

He always knew. He always saw. She wondered sometimes

if it was because he looked harder than other people. He paid attention.

She resisted the temptation to pour out her problems. She wanted people to treat her as an adult at work and the first step towards that was surely behaving like an adult. She couldn't lean on her dad every time she had a problem. She needed to handle this by herself. He couldn't make decisions for her.

He put a coffee down in front of her but before she could take a sip her phone rang.

She had no intention of answering it because her father had a strict rule about no phones at mealtimes, but she couldn't resist glancing at the screen and was immediately filled with panic.

"Boston." She snatched the phone up. "Head office."

Her stomach quaked. Was this it? Was he about to tell her they were going to be closed down?

She sent her father a look of apology.

"Take it," he said gruffly and carried his coffee into the living room, closing the door behind him.

She answered her phone, palms sweating, a hundred bad scenarios spinning through her head. Her heart was pounding. She was afraid she was about to have a heart attack and end up in hospital next to Gerald.

The call lasted ten minutes and when she eventually put the phone down she felt dazed.

"Well?" Her father came back into the room. "Was it something important?"

"Oh—no, nothing major. Why do you ask?"

Her father transferred the remains of the now cool lasagne to a smaller dish and covered it. "Because that white-haired man with eyes like a weasel who stayed at the hotel last month wasn't enjoying a mini break. He was doing a valuation and looking for commercial opportunities."

She gaped at him. "You knew that?"

"Of course I knew that." He put the lasagne in the fridge and the other dish in the sink to soak. "It's my job to know about the people staying in my hotel."

She felt a rush of emotion. He'd noticed, but he hadn't said anything to her. The fact that her father thought of it as "his" hotel did nothing to reduce the feeling of pressure.

"You didn't mention it. Does anyone else know?"

He shrugged. "They knew he wasn't who he said he was, but whether they've drawn conclusions from that—I don't know. I haven't heard any gossip, so possibly not. What's happening? What was the phone call about?"

"They're sending someone to help me. Someone experienced who can work in most areas of the business." She was still absorbing the information. Was the call a result of the memo she'd sent? When she'd had no response, she'd assumed no one had read it. "Miranda—she's the global head of talent or some other lofty title—said that they understand it has been difficult since Gerald was taken ill. The executive team had a meeting about it and decided we need support. They know about the staffing problems. They didn't mention anyone looking around the hotel." And that had to be good news, surely?

"So we're getting a new team member?"

"Yes. That's great, isn't it?" She forced a smile. "Having someone with experience will be good. It's not as if she's taking over or anything. They said she'll be able to support me wherever she's most needed."

It bruised her ego of course, but she was willing to take a little punch to her self-esteem if it meant protecting everyone's jobs. And it was further confirmation that they weren't thinking of closing the place down. She'd been wrong about that. If they'd wanted to, they would have done it. And that was good. One less thing for her to feel bad about if she managed to get herself a new job.

Her father drank his coffee and then put the cup down slowly. "So when is this person arriving and who is she?"

"It's a woman, and she's arriving the day after tomorrow."

"That soon?"

"Yes. I'm to arrange accommodation. Someone called Abby I think, but they're sending me through details later."

"She'll use the rooms at the Smuggler's Inn?"

"The Lookout? I suppose so. I'd better call and warn Tristan." The pub held one room for them for new staff members, to give them time to find more permanent accommodation. The lack of affordable places to stay was one of the reasons they had problems recruiting. "This will be good for everyone."

"So you keep saying."

"You were the one who taught me to be positive in any situation." She stood up and loaded the plates and cups into the dishwasher. "Dinner was delicious. Thanks, Dad. You're a lifesaver."

"You're doing a good job, Evie." He helped her finish the job. "Don't doubt it. I'm proud of you."

She leaned her head against his shoulder. "You don't think you might be biased?"

"You're good at what you do, and you've been handling a tough situation. And you've already had a positive impact on the place."

"Like what?"

"For a start, you recruited Luca, and the restaurant is fully booked for what feels like most of the summer. We're having to turn people away. And he's a good guy."

She stepped back and looked at him properly. There was a twinkle in his eyes. "Did you happen to speak to Donna today by any chance?"

"Maybe. I speak to most of the staff at one point or another, you know that."

She did know that. Her father was always the centre of everything, which was why he was her first point of contact when she wanted to know something.

"And did she happen to tell you that she was discussing my sex life when he walked in?"

"She might have mentioned it, although the way she told it the subject under discussion was the lack of a sex life."

She gave him a stern look. "I hope you told her that my love life is my business."

"This is a small village and you've lived here your whole life. You should know by now that your love life is everyone's business."

"But not yours. You're not like that." She felt the need to remind him. "You are a hands-off parent who always encourages me to make my own decisions in life. You don't believe in interfering."

He wiped the table. "You're my daughter. According to Marie, it's my job to interfere and I'm falling down on it. So here I am, stirring the pot a little. You've avoided romance since Martin. I know you were hurt, but you can't let that stop you trying again."

"Really? This from you who never married after Mum died?"

His hand stilled for a moment and then he carried on wiping. "That's different. And anyway, I've had relationships."

"But nothing serious, and—" She paused. "Wait—Marie? You've been talking to Marie?"

Marie owned the ice cream shop on the quay.

"And if I have?"

"Were you buying ice cream at the time?" She planted her hands on her hips and gave him a severe look. "The doctor told you to lower your saturated fat intake."

"Are you nagging me? I thought you were supposed to be a hands-off daughter who always encourages me to make my own decisions in life?"

She kissed him on the cheek. "It seems our relationship has taken a new turn. Which one did you have? Don't tell me it was vanilla and honeycomb."

"It was vanilla and honeycomb."

She drooled. "How can she own an ice cream shop and stay slim? If that place was mine, I'd eat all the goods before breakfast and be so full of ice cream I'd be attacked by seagulls the moment I stepped out of the shop. Are you and Marie close now? Is there romance in the air as well as chocolate sprinkles?"

He sent her a look and she shrugged.

"What? If you're going to meddle with my love life, I can meddle with yours."

"I'm happy as I am, thank you. I'm too tied up with my parental responsibilities to have time to date."

"Yes?" She grinned. "Is that daughter of yours causing trouble?"

"She's a handful."

"I can't believe everyone is talking about my sex life. I should move to London." She said it casually. "At least there I'd be anonymous."

"You'd hate London."

Her heart thudded. This would be the perfect time to tell him she'd applied for a job. "Maybe I wouldn't. And for the record the only thing that interests me about Luca is his crème brûlée."

"His crème brûlée?"

"Absolutely. And possibly his sticky duck recipe."

"I'm not interfering. I want to see you happy, that's all."

"I'm happy! See this smile?" She produced one. "Have you ever seen anything bigger?"

"No. Nor anything faker."

She switched off the smile. "I'm happy. Tired, that's all. But that's going to change now they're sending help. It will be great, won't it? Absolutely great. Lucky me."

She was going to treat it as a positive thing and not overthink it.

They wanted to be supportive.

And she'd be working with someone who hadn't known her since she was a baby. That had to be a step up.

5

★★★★★

Abby

The heels were a mistake, she thought as she stepped out of the taxi onto the sweeping gravel driveway and had her first proper look at the hotel that was going to be her home for the summer.

It was every bit as idyllic as the photos had suggested. The place looked more like a large English country house than a hotel.

They'd offered to send a car to collect her from the railway station, but she'd chosen to travel independently. After a drive along narrow, twisting lanes framed by hedges and trees she'd finally reached her destination, arriving unannounced and a little early in order to give herself time to linger over first impressions.

And her first impressions were good.

The hotel nestled in a dip on the headland, an unusually sheltered position that offered endless views of dramatic cliffs and sparkling ocean. A narrow path snaked away from the hotel, winding through mature trees and dropping out of sight near the cliff edge. She knew from her intensive study of the place that it led down to a small sandy cove popular with surfers and more adventurous bathers and that descending it required a scramble at some points. Those with small children or less nerve and agility could drive further along the coast and use one of the more easily accessible beaches.

The village with its famous harbour was a thirty-minute walk away down a steep hill.

The sun blazed but the gentle breeze meant that the temperature was perfect.

After a long and tiring journey she wanted to kick off her shoes and walk barefoot through the soft grass and wild flowers that framed the approach to the hotel, but she reminded herself that she wasn't here to rest or enjoy a vacation. She was here to do a job, and that job started right away.

She felt a flicker of nerves. She was still uncomfortable with the idea of concealing her identity, but up until this point she'd also been excited at the prospect of being anonymous. She'd thought it would make it easier to build relationships and a rapport with the staff, but what if it didn't? What if she wasn't capable of it? She wouldn't be able to blame it on her links with her mother.

She pushed that thought away. She just had to get on with it.

With that in mind, she dictated a few thoughts into her phone.

First impressions are good. The buildings are impressive—I feel as if I've stepped onto a movie set. Maybe Jane Austen. The views are incredible, although I have the advantage of seeing it for the first time on a sunny day with clear blue skies. The gardens are well-tended and inviting with plenty of places to sit and enjoy the spectacular view.

"Good morning. Can I help you?"

A man approached across the manicured lawn. His smile was

warm and welcoming, his appearance smart and professional. She guessed him to be in his mid fifties, although he looked younger possibly because his hair was thick and dark, showing only the occasional hint of silver.

This would be Edward, she thought. The concierge and longest-serving member of staff.

She knew from studying the staff members in depth that he was also the father of Evie, the acting manager.

She wondered if that was awkward, and if Evie found working with a parent as challenging as she did. Not that it was a question she'd be able to ask. She wouldn't be making any reference to her mother while she was here.

"Abby Jones, I assume." He extended a hand. "Welcome. I'll let Evie know you're here."

She shook his hand. "How do you know who I am?"

"It's my job to recognise the people coming in and out of the hotel. I know you're not a current guest. You could be coming for lunch, but your dress is a little formal for that." His gaze swept over her. "You look businesslike. And the fact that you were making a few notes about the hotel was a giveaway."

She'd been indiscreet, she could see that now. Five minutes into this assignment and already she'd almost blown it. She needed to be careful, particularly around Edward who was clearly observant.

"It helps me form an impression of a place. Get a sense of what it offers the guests. It's a habit of mine."

"We all have them." He reached for her luggage and she stopped him.

"Thanks, but I can manage."

"I'm sure you can, but here at The Alexandra we pride ourselves on our level of service. We like to spoil our guests."

"I'm not a guest."

"You're not expected until 4 p.m. Until then you're a guest."

"My journey was quicker than I'd imagined." She had a feeling he knew that she'd arrived early intentionally, a feeling that intensified as his smile widened.

"That's the best way for a journey to be. But I'm sure you're ready for a drink in the garden. I reserved a table in the shade for you and Evie so you can talk. I'll let her know you're here. I know she's looking forward to meeting you."

Was she? All she knew about Evie Hamilton was what she'd read about her as part of her research into the hotel. She knew nothing about her as a person and it had crossed her mind that far from being relieved to have help, she might resent it. Abby was used to being resented and treated with suspicion so the prospect of that didn't worry her, but she knew that it would be easier to gain an accurate picture of what was going on in the hotel if she could form some kind of bond with the staff, particularly the acting general manager. And that worried her. She hadn't managed to bond with any of her colleagues in the office, and she'd tried everything. Maybe she wasn't the sort of person people warmed to. Maybe it was all her.

Hopefully it would lessen the feelings of resentment if Abby made it clear from the beginning that although she was another experienced pair of hands, Evie was still in charge.

She walked with him towards the main entrance, trying not to twist her ankle as she trundled her small suitcase over the gravel.

What had possessed her to wear these shoes?

"Edward!" A woman with a small dog on a lead waved to them from a path that led from the gardens. "I was hoping to see you before we went off for the afternoon."

"Mrs Charles. And Tiddly." Edward bent and made a fuss of the dog, a gesture that earned him a beaming smile from the dog's owner. "How was lunch in the garden?"

"Delicious. I had the monkfish, as you suggested. And

now Tiddly and I are going on a little trip to see the ruins at Tintagel. After all the stories you told us, we thought we should see it for ourselves. We're hoping to catch a glimpse of Merlin's cave."

"Enjoy, but be careful on the paths and the rocks, Mrs Charles. It can be slippery underfoot. And keep Tiddly on a lead."

"Is it too late for me to book a table for dinner? I asked in the restaurant and they said they were full."

"Leave it with me," he said smoothly. "I'll sort something out."

"You're a treasure, Edward."

They exchanged a few more words and then Mrs Charles and the dog headed off for their adventure.

Abby watched her go. "Is she a regular guest?"

"Yes. She's staying in The Stables. Those are our dog-friendly rooms."

Abby gazed around her. "This is a beautiful place."

"It is. I'm sure Evie will give you a tour later."

"And Mrs Charles has been coming for a few years?"

"Ten years. Originally with her husband, but alone since her husband died five years ago. She was nervous to be travelling solo, so Gerald contacted her personally and told her how much the team were hoping she'd return and assured her that she would be surrounded by friends."

"Smart move," Abby said. "Guest retention is important and far more cost-effective than trying to attract new people. Losing customers means losing revenue."

He gave her a curious look. "Yes, although I don't think Gerald was thinking of profitability or revenue when he made that call. He was thinking of an elderly woman who had lost her life partner and was feeling alone and afraid."

"Of course." It was on the tip of Abby's tongue to say that it was obvious from the numbers that Gerald hadn't spent anywhere near enough time thinking about profitability, but something in the way this man was looking at her made her swallow the words. Embarrassment crawled over her. Her mother had drilled into her that emotion shouldn't play a part in decisions affecting the business and that sounded logical when you were sitting in a glass office staring at spreadsheets, but something close to inhumane when you were face-to-face with the people who were potentially impacted by your decisions.

She reminded herself that it was her job to maximise profit for the company. In doing so she was protecting the future of the hotels, and by extension protecting jobs. They were a commercial organisation, not a charity. The Alexandra, Cornwall had existed for so long precisely because it had been treated as a business.

Hopefully, with her help, it would continue to exist.

Her first instinct when she'd stepped onto the gravel driveway and had her first proper look at the hotel had been that if they couldn't make a place like this profitable they might as well give up and go home, but her mother wasn't interested in instincts. She wanted facts, and Abby's job was to produce those facts. She needed to maintain an element of detachment if she were to do her job properly.

Edward stood to one side and she walked through the doorway and into the hotel.

She glanced around her, and noticed that some of the flowers in the large display on the reception desk were past their best. "You've worked here for a long time. Has it changed much over the years?"

"A great deal, but that's to be expected. In my experience nothing in life stays the same however much we would like it to."

"And your experience must be invaluable. I'm sure you know many of the hotel's secrets."

His gaze settled on hers. "I know a few of them."

Something about the way he was looking at her made her feel faintly uneasy. She'd made a casual comment. Small talk to shift the conversation away from the uncomfortable topic of profits. She hadn't thought for a moment that this place had secrets. Occupancy challenges, yes. Staffing issues, definitely. Secrets?

She decided to keep it light. "Are you about to tell me the place is haunted? Should I be on the lookout for ghosts?"

He smiled. "We hide our ghosts and I like to think that all secrets are safe here. Discretion is an essential feature of all good hotels, don't you agree? If you're worried your deepest secrets will be revealed, Ms Jones, don't be."

"Call me Abby. And I don't have secrets." That wasn't strictly true, of course. Guilt nibbled at the edges of her conscience. She should never have agreed to do this job under-cover. She wasn't built for subterfuge. She should have insisted on being honest about who she was right from the start and if that meant it was harder to get to the bottom of how the place was run, so be it.

He studied her for a moment. "Everyone has secrets, Ms Jones." He walked to the reception desk which was unmanned and helped himself to a key. "I'm going to store your luggage for now and give Evie a call."

"You don't have a receptionist?"

"We do, but she may have accompanied a guest to a room." He took her case from her, unlocked a door behind the reception desk and stowed her case safely.

"I know you've had staffing issues."

"The entire hospitality sector has staffing issues," Edward said, "but it's particularly bad here."

"And why do you think that is?"

He glanced at her keenly and she silently berated herself for moving too quickly. She needed to be careful with her questions. Ultimately, she intended to speak to everyone of course, but she needed to do that in a low-key, organic way. She didn't want anyone suspecting that there was more to her presence here than simply another pair of hands.

"I'm no expert," he said, "but I would have thought it was a combination of factors, not least the competition from other hospitality establishments, and the challenges of finding accommodation locally."

She wanted to ask him what he thought could be done about it, but she stopped herself. There was time. Plenty of time. She was here for the whole summer.

"Obviously I'm willing to step in wherever I'm needed."

They thought she was an extra pair of hands. She needed to remember that and be more subtle in her questioning.

Edward walked to the reception desk, reached for the phone and dialled.

While he was doing that, she glanced around, finally seeing in person what she'd previously only seen in photographs.

Knowing that an important cause of guest dissatisfaction was arriving in a place and finding that it didn't match expectations, she pulled up the website on her phone and quickly flicked through the photographs.

There were several external photos of the hotel, all taken on a perfect summer's day.

Satisfied that they matched the picture she'd had when she'd driven up to the entrance, Abby scrolled on.

She glanced up as she heard footsteps.

"Abby?" A woman approached. There was a bounce in her step and her smile was wide and warm. Her choppy blonde hair ended somewhere between her chin and her shoulders and her nose was dusted with freckles. "I'm Evie. It's good to meet you."

Evie Hamilton, Abby thought. *Age 30 and has worked in the hotel for eight years full-time, and before that during holidays.*

They shook hands.

"I'm early, I know," Abby said. "I'm happy to wait in the gardens until you're ready to show me around. I'm sure you're busy."

"We are busy—which is great, and also why I'm keen to show you around as soon as possible so you can get started! But first we'll have tea in the garden." Evie glanced at Edward, who nodded.

"All arranged. Sea view table. I'll ask Chef to make tea."

"Super. Scones, obviously." Evie eyed Abby. "I always think it's helpful for the staff to experience what the guest experiences. Or maybe you don't eat carbs?"

"It was a long journey. I'm more than happy to eat every carb you can produce."

"Excellent." Evie frowned at the flowers and then at Edward. "Where are the fresh flowers?"

"The florist called this morning. They were having a crisis. They'll be here tomorrow."

"Okay. But in the meantime could you ask Donna to refresh these please?" Evie removed a couple of drooping roses. "Half of them are past it, and we don't want guests thinking that we let things die on our watch. It will make them nervous."

"I'll talk to Donna and I'll deal with those." Edward took the roses from her and Evie led Abby out of the hotel and towards the gardens that led down to the edge of the cliff.

"So you've already met Edward, and he's a key member of staff. He knows everything about the hotel and the area, so if you have questions he's a great place to start. He's also friendly and approachable and a good person, and I'm not saying that because he's my father and I'm biased."

Abby felt a flash of kinship. "Working together must have its challenges."

"Not at all. If anything it's easier because he knows me, and I know him." Evie waved cheerfully to a guest who was carrying a toddler and wrangling a little girl towards the hotel. "Need any help there, Chrissy?"

"We're fine, thanks." The woman was sweating. "Just trying to persuade the girls it's naptime."

Evie grinned. "Good luck with that. Holly's not looking particularly sleepy." She gestured to a table with a perfect view of the sea. "This is us."

Abby watched as the woman disappeared into the hotel. "You know all the guests by name?"

"I try to. It's the job, isn't it? To make people's stay personal. Chrissy and her girls are here for a month. Her husband is something important in the city and joins them for weekends. She orders a lot of room service. Also sends back a lot of room service because Holly is a fussy eater."

Abby sat down and gazed at the view. "This is spectacular."

"I know. I never tire of looking at our cliffs. It's the reason many of our guests like to eat outdoors. On warmer evenings we can open up the side of the restaurant so that even those indoors can enjoy the sound of the ocean."

"How many of the people using your restaurant are residents?"

"It varies." Evie sat down opposite her. "At this time of year a lot of people come here for a cream tea. It's tradition, and of course they enjoy the views. The evening clientele is a little different. We've had problems filling the restaurant, but that has changed since our new chef arrived. Word has spread quickly and we're fully booked for most of the summer, although we always keep a couple of tables back for residents."

"Your new chef is Luca?" Abby delved into the information she'd memorised.

She knew he'd previously worked in London, and before that in a five-star establishment on Lake Como.

Evie's eyes widened. "How do you know his name?"

"Oh—" She realised that she was coming across as far too

well-informed for someone who was simply here to bolster staff numbers. "I read a bit about the hotel. Also, I'm a foodie. I often pick my holiday destinations based on restaurant recommendations."

"In that case you won't be disappointed by Luca. His *gnocchi con parmigiano* is the ultimate comfort food. Although you may not have much time to sample his skills. You're going to be busy." Evie sat back as their tea was delivered. "Tell me everything about yourself. All head office told me was that you're experienced, and you've worked in most areas of the hotel."

"Yes. I travel around a lot. The last place I worked was The Alexandra, Cape Cod." That was true. They'd been having problems with a new guest booking system and Abby had spent a month helping out.

"You don't know Cornwall at all?"

"No. And I'm looking forward to exploring." She wanted to do more than explore the local area. She wanted to see the place her mother had lived as a child. Where *she'd* lived, because she'd been born here. Abby had been four when they'd moved, but she had no memory of it. All she'd ever known was Boston.

She wanted to see if she could find out more about her family history.

It was an urge that had crept up on her slowly. A desire to fill in the blanks. To understand.

Her mother had shared little about her childhood growing up in Cornwall. All Abby knew was that life had been hard for her. Her mother's father had left when she was eleven leaving Alexandra to help care for her mother who had been seriously injured in a car accident the year before. She'd died when Alexandra was eighteen and that same year her mother had met Abby's father and within months she was pregnant. Tragically he'd died before Abby was born and a few years after that her mother had moved to Boston.

That decision made perfect sense. She'd wanted to leave the past and all that grief behind.

It also explained why she was reluctant to talk about it.

But Abby was hoping that while she was here she might be able to find out more about her family history, and her father especially, without having to press her mother for more. She felt frustrated that she knew so little, while at the same time sympathising with her mother's wish not to talk about what had clearly been a traumatic time of her life.

"If you have any questions, ask me." Evie poured tea for both of them. "I was born here. Lived here all my life apart from a few years in college."

Abby already knew those details, but she nodded as if she was hearing them for the first time.

"These look amazing." She reached out and took a scone. It was still warm from the oven and when she sliced it in half the texture was soft and fluffy.

In front of her was a small bowl of thick clotted cream, and another of homemade strawberry jam.

She tried to remember what her mother had told her. Cream, then jam? Jam, then cream?

Did it even matter?

Evie read her mind. "Cornish tradition says jam first then cream, but I always think that once it's in your mouth the order doesn't matter."

Abby copied Evie and took a bite. "Oh—"

"I know." Evie grinned at her. "Incredible, isn't it?"

"It really is." Abby found herself smiling back. "You eat this every day?"

"If I ate this every day I'd have blocked arteries. I do eat it occasionally, and then I double my morning run along the cliff path to make up for it."

Abby laughed. "I might have to join you." She froze. Why

had she said that? She knew better than to try and build a social connection with colleagues, particularly one she'd only met moments before. What had come over her? Braced for a chilly rebuff, she tried to rescue the situation. "I was joking, obviously."

"Why are you joking? I think that would be great. It would be the perfect way to show you the area and I'd love to have your company."

"You would?" Abby was conscious that she'd put Evie in an awkward position. "Because you really don't have to—"

"I'm not being polite, if that was what you were going to say. I think it would be great. Aren't you going to finish your scone?"

Telling herself that she could always find a way to excuse herself from the run later, Abby finished the scone and nodded. "Delicious. It's great to have this experience. You must tell me how I can be of most help. It must have been hard for you having to take on all that extra responsibility when Gerald became ill."

Evie put the spoon back in the jam. "You know about Gerald?"

"I was briefed," Abby said. "It's important to know anything that might have an impact on the staff."

"It has been hard, not least because everyone adores Gerald so they were all a bit distracted and anxious. Once he was out of danger things improved of course, but there is no doubt it has affected everyone. Gerald was the backbone of this place."

And Evie had stepped in.

"That must have been particularly difficult, taking on that responsibility when everyone was shaken up." Abby could immediately see the challenges she would have faced.

"Yes. And I was worried about him, too. Gerald was my mentor. I've known him since I was a toddler. The guests adore him, as do the staff. In fact, most of them—" She hesitated and then drew a breath and smiled. "Let's just say his were big shoes to step into. And we're still not sure he'll be coming back."

Abby wondered about that moment of hesitation. There was something going on beneath the surface, and not that far beneath the surface. She sensed that Evie was putting on her brightest face to cover up the fact she was struggling to hold everything together.

Abby knew that feeling. "What can I do?"

"I've been thinking about that." Evie sat back in her chair. "I think the best thing is if you shadow me for the first few days, and then we can figure out where your skills will be most useful. How does that sound?"

"It sounds good."

"Is there anything you don't do? Any part of the hotel you'd rather not work in?"

"I'll work anywhere. And I've done everything in my time," Abby said truthfully.

"Great. I'll give you a tour after we've had our tea, then I'll take you down to the village and get you settled in your new home."

"I'm not staying in the hotel?"

"That was the plan originally. We have a small loft room we keep for staff in emergency situations, but we had a leak in the roof a few weeks ago that still hasn't been fixed so you're using the apartment in the Smuggler's Inn that we also reserve for staff. It's small, but the views are great and you're right in the village so you can take advantage of all the amenities."

It hadn't occurred to her that she wouldn't be staying in the hotel itself. Was that good or bad?

Good, she decided. It might be easier to keep a little distance if she wasn't on the premises all the time. And she could write up her reports and contact her mother without worrying about someone overhearing.

"It sounds perfect. Thank you for arranging that."

"I'm glad you're here. And if you see things you think we need to improve you're to tell me right away. Don't spare my feelings. This place is important to me. I *really* want it to do well."

It wasn't the response she'd expected. She'd never met anyone as open and enthusiastic as Evie.

She knew more experienced managers than Evie who would have done anything to avoid asking for feedback.

"How is the hotel doing generally?" Abby didn't reveal that she already knew the answer to that question.

"It's great," Evie said brightly. "Super. We have a few little staffing issues of course, but so does everyone in the hospitality industry. And costs are soaring, which isn't easy to handle. But I'm confident that everything is going to be fine. Totally fine. Especially now you're here. I'm glad head office sent you—it's supportive of them, and that's good to see. A relief, in fact, after—" Her voice tailed off and her smile dimmed a little. "Actually, things haven't been that great, to be honest. Lately I've had a bad feeling. Not sure if I'm being paranoid."

Abby waited. Her first assessment of Evie had been wrong, she could see that. She'd thought she was bright and breezy and she was, but she was also weighed down and worried. And good at hiding it.

Evie hesitated and then glanced at her. "We've had this man poking around the place and it freaked me out a bit. I first saw him a month ago, when he checked in for a few days. He reminded me of a weasel."

"A weasel?"

"He was behaving furtively. Several of the guests commented on the fact that they'd seen him loitering in the corridors behaving suspiciously. Every time I saw him he looked guilty and stopped what he was doing."

Abby frowned. "And what was he doing?"

"Different things." Evie shrugged. "Measuring doorways and corridors. Staring out of windows. Tapping walls. And he even asked Mrs Masters, one of our long-term guests, for a look inside the King Arthur suite. Fortunately, she isn't afraid to speak her mind and told him exactly where to put his tape measure, but it left me with a bad feeling. I've been waiting for the phone to ring and someone in head office to tell us they were selling The Alexandra, Cornwall to a grasping developer. I imagined this place being renamed Weasel Towers. When they called and told me they were sending you, I breathed a sigh of relief. I'm sure they wouldn't have done that if they were thinking of selling." Evie batted a wasp away from the table. "Which is good. I had a bad feeling about him."

Abby had a bad feeling, too. "What was his name?"

"Well, *that's* the annoying thing. Or one of them. When he checked in he said he was Nicholas Glyn. I happened to be helping behind the desk on that day and something about him didn't seem right to me, so I kept an eye on him. He didn't behave like someone on holiday. He didn't visit anywhere. And he asked for his room not to be touched during his stay which normally we would respect, but we had a leak in one of the bedrooms above and I had to access his bedroom and that's when I saw the plans."

"Plans?"

"Building plans. They were spread out over every surface. Turns out he works for a company called Howard Developments. Known for buying land and building holiday homes, although not in Cornwall. That seems to be a first. I did an internet search—there have been a lot of complaints about the quality of his buildings."

Howard Developments.

Abby felt a flicker of annoyance and made a note to mention it to her mother. She was confident no one had given him permission to look around the hotel.

"And this was a month ago?"

"Yes. I didn't mention it to anyone because—well, I didn't have any actual facts. Just a bad feeling. As a manager you can't dump suspicions on people, can you? But he was back here last week lurking in the grounds. Phillip, our head gardener, saw him and challenged him."

"Last week? You're sure?" Abby mulled over the timing. That didn't make sense, because her mother had turned his offer down before that. Why was he persisting? Perhaps he thought her mother was using a negotiation tactic.

"Yes." Evie watched her and nodded. "Do you think I'm overreacting? I sometimes do, I know that. I'm a bit of an all-or-nothing person. I consciously have to rein myself in and focus on facts, not feelings."

Abby wasn't sure how to respond. Evie was obviously relieved to be able to share the stress of it, and she wanted to reassure her.

But something didn't feel right to her, either.

"I think it's good to be observant, and I think if you have a bad feeling about something," she said slowly, "then it's worth paying attention to that."

"Yeah, but it's not as if I can contact head office and say hey, there's a suspicious man poking around the hotel and by the way are you planning on selling it? But it's good to know you agree with me that it was weasel-like behaviour." She took a sip of her tea and then put her cup down. "It is *such* a relief to be able to talk about it with someone. I hadn't realised until this moment how isolated I've been feeling. Before I stepped in to cover Gerald I used to be able to talk to everyone, you know? Never had to watch what I said. Didn't give it a second thought. I miss that camaraderie. It's pretty lonely. It's hard to explain. I don't expect you to understand."

She understood. She was used to feeling lonely at work. It was the only thing she knew. And it wasn't a good feeling. It was hard when you couldn't share your thoughts and your anxieties. When you had to choose every word carefully and conceal everything you were feeling.

People at work didn't confide in her, but Evie had confided in her.

A warmth spread through her and she felt a connection she wasn't used to feeling.

"I do understand." She almost told Evie exactly how well she understood, but she stopped herself. She couldn't do that without revealing things about herself that she didn't want to reveal.

"I probably shouldn't have said anything to you, but as you've been parachuted in from the outside it's a bit different."

"I'm pleased you told me."

"It's funny how talking something through with someone can help. And do you know what I'm most annoyed about?" Evie leaned forward. "I don't think he even checked in under his real name. It was a fake identity. I mean, who does that? It's dishonest."

Abby's warm feeling evaporated. She wondered if her guilt showed on her face. She would have made a terrible spy.

"Maybe he had a good reason."

"He had a reason, but it wasn't a good one. He didn't want us to know who he was. He wanted us to trust him. He wanted us to answer his questions. But I hope he never joins the CIA or MI5 or whatever because honestly, I'd make a better under-cover agent than him. He was hopeless. He asked a lot of questions about the people in head office, none of which I could answer of course because I don't know any of them." Evie lathered jam and cream onto the other half of her scone and then topped up Abby's tea. "I feel better just having talked it through with you. You have no idea how many times I wanted to go into the staff room and sob on someone's shoulder. I refrained, but I have been eating too much cake to compensate. And the odd glass of wine in the evening. And since then I've just been working as hard as I can to make the place profitable."

"I'll do anything and everything I can to help you." Abby kept her voice casual. "What sort of questions did he ask about head office? What exactly did he want to know?"

Evie put the teapot down and shrugged. "A few things. Was anyone from head office likely to visit soon, that kind of thing. As if they're just going to show up here unannounced. I had a feeling he was hoping to ambush them."

"And what did you say?"

"I said it was none of his business, and before you judge me I should say in my own defence that it takes great provocation for me to be anything other than polite and willing, but as he'd already lied about who he was I didn't think he deserved that courtesy. I can't stand people who lie to me." Evie lifted the scone and then paused. "Are you okay? Your face is red. We can move into the shade if you're too hot. I don't want you to burn."

"I'm fine. I like the sun."

"That's because you have dark hair. You probably don't burn the way I do. I have to virtually bathe in sunscreen every morning and I still wake up with new freckles." Evie took a bite of her scone and then put it back down on her plate. She chewed for a moment. "Forget I said anything. I'm hoping Mr Weasel is history. But now you know it all. Welcome to the team, Abby. To The Alexandra, Cornwall." She raised her cup. "Long may she stay as she is. I really want this place to be excellent and I'm happy you're here to help me."

Abby lifted her cup, mirroring Evie's gesture, and managed what she hoped was a convincing smile.

She was here to gather information, and she'd just learned several things.

Firstly, that Evie, despite her sweet smile and warm, friendly nature, was clearly no fool. She knew the place was in trouble. Secondly, that the developer, despite being told no, hadn't backed off. And thirdly, that joining the team undercover had definitely been a mistake. A big mistake.

Evie hated people who lied. Ironically, so did Abby. And yet here she was . . .

It was too late to unravel it now. She just had to hope that her skills at subterfuge improved.

Evie

Abby wasn't what she'd expected.

Evie sneaked a look at her as they walked back to the hotel.

How did she walk in those shoes? If Evie had worn something similar she would have twisted her ankle and ended up using crutches. Abby seemed to have no problems. She was long-limbed and elegant, like a gazelle. Next to her Evie felt like an overenthusiastic labrador.

She started to smooth her hair but then gave up. It didn't matter what she did, she was never going to look as poised and elegant as Abby.

If Evie had just stepped off a long flight followed by a train and car journey, she would have been a crumpled mess, but she was willing to bet that Abby had never been crumpled in her life.

Her make-up was subtle, her hair twisted into an elaborate

knot on the back of her head. Her white shirt was perfectly cut and pristine. Everything about her suggested discipline and control. She'd said she'd worked in all the different areas of hotels, but Evie was struggling to picture her cleaning a toilet.

She might have felt intimidated, but then she remembered that little bonding moment over the scone when they'd laughed together. There had been nothing distant about Abby at that moment, which was presumably why Evie had suddenly opened up and spilled all her worries. And to be fair Abby had listened attentively. She'd seemed almost as annoyed as Evie that a stranger had been poking around the hotel.

She really seemed to care, and for the first time since Evie had taken over the job from Gerald, she felt as if she had someone in her corner.

Talking to Abby had lifted her mood a little and Evie felt more cheerful as she showed her round the hotel, introducing her to staff members, who were universally welcoming.

Fortunately, there seemed to be no disasters ongoing at that particular moment. No pipes had burst. No guests were complaining. None of the staff were asking to leave early to handle a family crisis. No one was taking an elongated lunch break.

Abby herself was reserved, greeting people politely but formally, listening while they explained their role in the hotel.

Evie was impressed by the interest she showed and the questions she asked. Most of the staff just took care of their role (and sometimes not even that!) and didn't worry about the rest of it. Abby was interested in all of it. Interested and engaged.

"Ooh, it will be good for our Evie to have reinforcements," Pat said cheerfully. "You're very welcome here. We're a friendly bunch, so don't hesitate to ask us anything. Where will you be staying while you're here?"

"We've booked her into the Lookout at the Smuggler's Inn," Evie said. "I'm taking her over there when I've finished the tour."

"Lucky you." Pat winked at her. "If I were twenty years younger I'd be booking myself in there, too. And maybe doing a little sleepwalking and finding myself in the landlord's apartment."

"Thank you, Pat." Mortified, Evie moved on hastily. "Now I'll show you the kitchens."

Abby glanced over her shoulder and watched Pat vanish down the corridor. "What did she mean by that?"

"Nothing. Nothing at all. Ignore her." She should have gathered the staff together and given them a talk on appropriate behaviour.

"But why would she want to find herself in the landlord's apartment?"

Evie sighed. She should probably be honest. Abby had a right to know what she was dealing with. "Because Tristan, the landlord, is single and particularly good-looking, and because everyone in this village is obsessed with meddling with other people's love lives. Please ignore it. That's what I try and do."

Abby gave her a curious look. "They meddle with your love life?"

"Oh yes. You get used to it." That wasn't exactly true of course because she'd never got used to it. "It's particularly bad in your teenage years when you're gawky and uncertain about who you are and everyone has an opinion. For example, my first kiss was round the back of the pub and I thought we'd been discreet. Then the next day four different people told me they didn't think he was right for me, and they also told my dad."

Abby laughed. "That must have been a little limiting."

"Very limiting. And it still happens." She thought of Martin, and then pushed the thought aside. She wasn't going to let Martin ruin what was otherwise a perfectly good day.

"I can't imagine living in a place where everyone knows everyone else."

"Well, it's heaven or hell, depending on your taste. It's impossible to keep secrets in this place. On the other hand if you want everyone in the village to know something you don't have to waste time or money on a mailing. Just tell Marie in the ice cream shop. And while you're there order a scoop of her vanilla and honeycomb." She pushed open the doors that led to the kitchen.

Every surface gleamed and the staff were in the process of prepping for the evening.

There was no sign of Luca but Evie made a mental note to thank him for organising his domain so well.

"This is where the magic happens." Evie paused as Alina, one of the receptionists, stuck her head around the door.

"Evie! There you are. The Hunters just checked out. They were complaining that their breakfast was cold so I removed it from their bill and offered them a free night next time they're staying."

Evie felt a ripple of frustration and resisted the urge to bang her head against the wall. They couldn't afford to overcompensate. "Did they complain about their breakfast at the time?"

"I—I don't know."

"I did a walk-around this morning and all they said to me was 'good morning.' We encourage guests to tell us right away if they encounter anything during their stay that falls below the standard they were expecting. We can't fix something at the end."

"Right." Alina looked confused. "I thought our aim was to have happy guests."

"It is, but we need to do that while keeping an eye on our profit. It isn't all about discounts. Sometimes we just need to do better."

Alina nodded. "It's just that Gerald always—"

"I know," Evie interrupted quickly, conscious that Abby was listening, "but next time there's a problem give me a call and I'll talk to them."

"Okay. I'll do that."

Alina left and Evie led Abby back to the office. She wished Abby hadn't witnessed that. It was mortifying. She'd wanted to impress Abby, and instead that encounter had been a demonstration of staff inexperience and her own ineptitude as a manager. Abby wasn't to know how hard Evie had worked to try and change things. She was probably wondering what sort of outfit she'd joined.

Her mood deflating again, she grabbed her bag from her desk. She hoped the Hunters weren't going to leave a bad review. It was true that Gerald probably would have offered them a big discount, but she was fast becoming aware that his misplaced generosity (or maybe it was his aversion to conflict) was one of the reasons the hotel was losing money.

Pushing that aside, she smiled at Abby as if nothing was amiss. "I'm going to take you down to the village now and get you settled in your new home. I can show you around so that you can orientate yourself."

They walked to the back of the hotel where Evie's car was parked and loaded Abby's luggage into the back.

"It's stunning," Abby said as they drove back along the coast. "And it's such a pretty day."

"Yes, you timed it well. Which is good. I want you to see it at its best. Hopefully it will stop you wanting to run away from us."

"Why would I run away?"

Because this place is slowly collapsing and you don't want to be buried under the rubble.

Evie concentrated on the road. It had been easy to tell Abby about the weasel and her concerns for the future of the hotel. Not so easy to confess that she was struggling to manage the staff. That felt too personal.

"I'm really pleased you're here, that's all. Relieved. I'm sure you're in demand and I don't want head office to snatch you away and put you elsewhere yet. I've been desperate for help."

Abby was silent for a moment. "So you don't mind that head office sent me?"

"Are you kidding? I could hug them." Evie waited for a gap in the traffic and turned into a narrow road that led steeply down towards the harbour. "I'd been telling them for a while that it would be helpful to have a conversation about the way things are." She slowed down to allow a mother with a toddler to cross the road safely.

"You contacted them? And what did they say?"

"Nothing. They didn't respond."

"So did you try again?"

"A couple of times, but after that I stopped. I didn't want to be a bother. I assumed they were busy." And Evie knew that feeling. "They're expanding a lot so we're not a priority."

"Every hotel is important. I'm sorry you had that experience."

"You have no reason to be sorry. It's not your fault! You're a worker bee like the rest of us." Evie shot her a brief smile. "Anyway, everything is good now. And they sent me you, so I'll forgive them."

"You'd better get to know me before you form a judgement."

"I know enough. From the moment you set foot inside the hotel you've been asking sharp, pertinent questions. I can tell you're exactly the person I need to help me get everything back on track. Dare I ask what your first impressions are?"

Abby looked thrown by the question. "I—the position is exceptional of course. The staff approachable and friendly. From what I've seen so far you seem to be a close-knit group. Supportive."

A little too close-knit on occasions, but that wasn't something Evie was ready to discuss.

The road narrowed still further and Evie swung into a parking space. "This is my space. Can't go further into the village or we'll be stuck. Tourists do it sometimes of course. They ignore all the massive notices and try and park on the quay when the tide is out. Then the tide comes in and they're annoyed that their car is filled with seawater. They seem to think we put the warning signs there for our own entertainment."

Abby undid her seat belt. "You said no one in head office replied to you. Who did you contact?"

"Do you know them all?" Had she been indiscreet? Yes, she probably had. She didn't want to get anyone into trouble. "Forget I said anything. It was unprofessional of me."

"Not at all. You were being honest, and honesty is essential if a business is to run smoothly."

"My email probably went into spam or something." She didn't mention that she'd emailed more than once and left a voicemail. "Between you and me, I haven't had much to do with anyone at head office. They've pretty much left us to get on with things ourselves, which is a compliment, obviously. They must have been happy with the way things were or they would have said so."

"But you would have liked more support."

"After Gerald collapsed, it would have been helpful. Everyone was in a bit of a state—everyone loves Gerald, you see. I have to be sensitive about suggesting any changes. Gerald had his own way of doing things and the staff feel it's disloyal to do things differently."

"But there are changes you would make?"

"Some, yes." Evie grabbed Abby's luggage from the car. "Lately I've been feeling as if the place needed a bit of a change in strategy, you know? And I'm only acting general manager, obviously. I didn't want to overstep my remit, although I'm not entirely sure what my remit is. A bit of everything, I think. I even wrote a memo outlining what I thought we could do to improve things and make more money—we're missing opportunities—but I don't think anyone bothered to read it."

"Did you talk to them about it in person?"

"No. I didn't want to hear all the reasons why my ideas wouldn't work. I thought it was easier to send a memo." She paused, wondering how honest to be. "I'm not great with conflict. Particularly when it's people I've known forever. How about you?"

"I think there are situations where being direct is appropriate, and I don't usually have a problem with that."

"You don't worry about it damaging relationships?"

Abby gave a faint smile. "No," she said. "That concern isn't generally top of my list. But I probably don't have the same close relationships at work that you do."

"I suppose that's inevitable as you move around a lot."

And Abby wasn't a manager, Evie thought. It was different.

"That memo you sent—I'd like to read it if you'd be willing to share it."

"You would?"

"Yes. It's your vision for the hotel, and I'm going to be part of the hotel."

If only her permanent staff were as interested. "I'll send it to you. The woman who called was a bit vague, but she said you were a sort of trouble-shooter—that you go wherever you're needed? That must be fun. You can find yourself doing pretty much anything?"

"Yes." Abby took the case from her with a smile of thanks. "My role is varied. It's interesting."

"And you get to see a lot of hotels, which means you can take the best of what you see and apply it elsewhere." Evie gestured to a steep, narrow street. "We have to go this way. It's a bit uneven underfoot. Forget vicious rocks and dangerous tides—I always thought that this street was probably the biggest hazard the smugglers faced. Imagine walking up this after a bottle of rum or two. They probably all had broken noses. Will you be okay in those shoes?"

"I'll be fine."

They walked together down the steep, narrow lane, the wheels of Abby's case bouncing over the cobbles.

"It's not for everyone but I love this place. In summer it's swollen with tourists, but in winter it's mostly locals with a few hardy long-term visitors." Evie paused outside her cottage. "This is where I live. My dad is right next door. If you need anything at any time, day or night, just call me or knock on one of our doors. We're here to help."

Abby studied the cottages. "You live next door to your father?"

"Yes. My cottage used to belong to my grandmother, although I've gradually done it up to suit my taste. I adored Granny, but not her interior design choices. She had a thing for porcelain cats."

Abby gave a wistful smile. "You're close to your dad."

"Yes. My mother died when I was born, so it has always been the two of us."

"Oh, I'm sorry."

"Thanks. Dad and I are close and I have what feels like a million proxy mothers in the village. How about you? Family? I assume you're not married."

"Not married," Abby said. "So far I haven't met anyone that makes me want to rethink my workaholic lifestyle."

Evie laughed. "Well, don't tell anyone you're available or they will set you up with every single man in the village. We'd better pretend you're married with seven children. The pub is just down there—" She gestured. "It overlooks the harbour."

As they reached the main street the crowds thickened. There were people wearing shorts and T-shirts, their faces red from too much sun and not enough sunscreen. Fractious toddlers whined, and dogs pulled at their leads and panted in the heat.

"At five in the morning, this place is deserted." Evie led Abby round to the back entrance of the Smuggler's Inn and opened the door. "Tristan?" She yelled his name. "Are you there or have you been trampled by tourists? He's probably down in the cellar."

Abby held back. "You don't knock or ring the bell or something?"

"I've known Tristan since I was five years old. His mother used to plait my hair because my dad always struggled with it. So no, I don't knock or ring the bell. Tristan can be a bit gruff but don't be daunted. He's a big old softie really." Evie yelled again. "Tris?"

"I can hear you. The whole county can hear you. And of course I'm here. Where else would I be?" Tristan emerged from the cellar carrying two large boxes. He dumped them on the floor and rubbed his biceps. There was a streak of dirt on his cheek and his dark hair was in a state of disarray.

Evie stepped forward and hugged him. "I thought you might have escaped this place and be sunning yourself on an island in the Caribbean and drinking rum from a coconut. I've brought you a new guest—this is Abby. She's going to be helping me at the hotel."

Tristan wiped his hands on his trousers. "I wasn't expecting company. I've been sorting out the cellar." He nodded to Abby. "Tristan Penrose. You'd probably rather I didn't shake your hand given what I've been hauling around down there."

Evie felt guilty for not having called to warn him that they were on their way. "Shall I grab the key and take her up? We don't need to bother you."

He scowled at her. "I'm the landlord, Ev. It's my job to make guests welcome."

"Well, currently you're wearing your grumpy face, so you might want to rethink your approach to customer relations."

He ran his hand over the back of his neck and breathed out. "Long day and we still have the evening to go. You know what it's like at this time of year."

That wasn't it. She knew that wasn't it. She'd known him long enough to know when something was wrong.

"How's your dad?"

"Doing fine, thanks." He disappeared through a door that led to the bar and returned a moment later holding a key. "I'll get Matt to take your luggage up."

"No need," Abby said smoothly. "I can handle it, thank you."

Evie saw Tristan's gaze travel from Abby's face to her shoes. To his credit, his expression didn't change.

"If you're sure." He gave a nod. "Settle in and then come and find me. There's a small kitchen in the Lookout, but it's not great for cooking anything substantial. I'll arrange for you to have something to eat in the pub."

"Thanks, but that won't be necessary." Abby was close to frosty and Evie didn't blame her.

Tristan wasn't exactly giving her a warm welcome. What was wrong with him? She wanted Abby to feel comfortable and at home. Right now she was neither. She was wary and distant and nothing like the woman who had been laughing over a scone in the garden and listening carefully to Evie's work issues.

Evie felt a flash of sympathy. It must be daunting coming to a strange place where you knew no one. She was probably missing her friends, colleagues and family back home and Tristan being all growly and broody wasn't exactly going to make her feel welcome.

Evie decided a rethink was necessary.

"If you have the energy when you've unpacked and settled in you could just come round to mine. It will probably be pizza and salad, but you're welcome." Her plans for a long soak in the bath and an hour in the garden with her book vanished into the ether, but she reminded herself that she could do that any night. The priority right now was to make sure Abby felt at home.

"That's a kind offer," Abby said, "but it has been a long day and I'll probably just take a shower and collapse into bed."

"You definitely need to eat something before you do that," Evie said. "The food here is amazing. I recommend the fish pie. If you're tired, Tristan can bring it up to your room, can't you, Tris?"

He looked at Evie and there was a gleam of something in his eyes. "If you want the room to smell of fish, sure."

Abby gave him a cool smile. "I don't eat much in the evenings. Usually just an apple."

Tristan raised an eyebrow. "An apple?"

"An apple?" Evie echoed him, appalled. "I'd die if all I ate was an apple." She decided this conversation had gone on long enough and grabbed the key from Tristan. "Thanks for this. You're obviously busy. We'll let you get on with things."

And scowl at someone else.

Without waiting for Tristan to respond, she headed inside

the inn and up a narrow flight of stairs. The walls were covered in black-and-white photos of boats. Fishing boats. Sail-boats. A lifeboat and crew.

At the top of the stairs she opened a door and took another short flight of stairs up to the Lookout.

"How old is this place?" Abby was staring at one of the photos on the walls.

"Old. Seventeenth century, I think. Maybe older. The cellars were used by smugglers. Some of the rooms still have trapdoors and hidden cupboards. They were good at hiding contraband. Sometimes they sank it in the harbour. This room—" she fiddled with the key and managed to unlock the door "—was used as a lookout. Hence the name."

"What were they looking out for?"

"Ships? Excise officers? Jealous wives and girlfriends?" She shouldered the door open. "You won't find any alcohol hidden under the bed though. These days if you want brandy you just phone down to the bar. Here you go. This is it. Home. It's not exactly spacious, but it's cosy."

Abby followed her into the room and Evie saw surprise on her face.

"It's gorgeous. I expected something dark and—I'm not sure—sinister?"

The late-day sunlight sent a rosy glow over the room, bouncing across the wooden floors. There was a desk beneath a large window that overlooked the harbour and the cliffs, and a comfortable armchair.

"The bathroom is through here—" Evie pushed open the door and saw with relief that it was gleaming and that there were fresh towels. Whatever was wrong with Tristan and his team, at least he hadn't fallen down on the job. "I know it's not big, but—"

"It's perfect." Abby walked to the window and stared out over the cliffs. "Thank you." She turned. "You've been kind. You should go home and relax. You've earned it."

She'd thought she wanted to do just that, but there was something about Abby that made her hesitate. She seemed—vulnerable? No. Not that. She'd had no trouble putting moody Tristan in his place and she was clearly independent and used to looking after herself.

What then?

Evie couldn't put her finger on it. Maybe she just needed a friend. "Are you sure I can't tempt you to join me for a glass of wine in my garden? It goes well with apple."

Abby laughed. "Maybe another night. But thank you."

"If you're sure." Comforting herself with the fact that she'd tried, Evie handed over the key and headed back to the door. "If you need anything call me. Or Tristan. Despite appearances, he's very approachable. I know he seemed a bit moody, but it's not personal. Things have been tough for him lately. His dad fell down the steps in the cellar a few months ago and he broke more bones than I can bear to think about. Tristan has had to step in, and that hasn't been easy for either of them."

She closed the door behind her, headed downstairs and found Tristan behind the bar, serving customers.

Evie stepped behind the bar and stood at his elbow so he couldn't ignore her.

"Okay, sunshine. Tell me what's wrong."

"Nothing is wrong. In case you hadn't noticed, I'm working." He handed over two glasses of wine to the man hovering at the bar and took payment.

"We can talk about it here if you like. I'm sure your customers would all have an opinion on it."

He gave her an exasperated look and then glanced at Matt, who was working alongside him. "I'll be five minutes."

"No worries, boss."

Tristan followed her out to the back of the pub. They stepped onto the street and he leaned against the wall and looked at her.

"Whatever it is you want to say, say it quickly. It's hot out here and sweating and burning in the sun isn't going to make me less grumpy."

"It's gorgeous." She shaded her eyes from the sun. "It's a perfect day. Don't you remember those horrible rainy days in January and February? This is blissful—"

"Ev, there's only so much of your relentless cheerfulness I can handle in one day. Get to the point."

She let her hand drop. "Tell me what's wrong."

"Nothing's wrong. I'm a grumpy person and you need to accept that."

She pulled him into a small patch of shade and linked her arm with his. "You're not a grumpy person. You're grumpy today, and I want to know why. What happened? Is it your dad?"

It was a moment before he answered. "We had a conversation five minutes before you arrived. Bad timing, that's all."

"And how is he?"

"Frustrated by his lack of ability to move around as freely as he used to, but still well enough to point out in detail all the things I'm doing wrong. Every conversation is a joy, particularly when you're in the middle of hauling heavy weights around a cellar."

She knew how conflicted he was about the situation.

"It's hard for both of you. It must be frustrating for him not being able to do all the things he did before the accident. He's having to adjust to a new normal."

"We're all having to adjust. What I don't understand is why

he can't let me get on with it my way." He looked down at her. "Why are you smiling?"

"Because it's obvious." She squeezed his arm. "He's trying to stay involved, Tris. This place was his life. Letting go of that is a process. Telling you where you're going wrong is probably what's keeping him going."

"Maybe. But you'd think he'd be happier that I'm back, seeing as this is what he always wanted. Instead, everything I do irritates him."

Her heart ached for her friend. "He wanted you to be running it together. And has it ever occurred to you that he might be irritable because he feels guilty?"

"Guilty?"

"Yes. Because he knows this wasn't what you wanted and yet here you are. He feels bad."

There was a long silence.

He eased his arm away from hers. "Do you always have to be so insightful? It can be annoying."

"Because you want to be left to sulk in peace, you mean?"

"Something like that." He ran his hand over his face. "I hate to admit it, but I know you're right. It's tough for him. I should be more patient."

"It's tough for you, too. You're allowed to be occasionally grumpy."

"We should probably clarify this. How many hours each day am I allowed to be grumpy?"

"You're allowed five minutes, morning and evening. But not when my guest is around. I've told her you're approachable, so you need to be approachable. No glaring. No sighing. No muttering. And no looking at her shoes while doing that whole raised eyebrow thing you do."

He glanced at her, curious. "Who is she exactly? Apart from

someone who has no idea what shoes to wear in a Cornish fishing village. She's going to break her ankle. Shouldn't someone tell her?"

"No. We're going to treat her like an adult and let her figure it out for herself," Evie said, "and hope that happens before she breaks her ankle. And to answer your question, she's an extra pair of hands. Head office arranged for her to come and help out."

"Doing what? I can't see her scrubbing a bathroom. She seems more like the type who spends her time at a computer."

"Stop making assumptions. You don't know anything about her."

"Neither do you."

"No, but I know better than to judge a person by what I see on the surface," Evie said firmly, ignoring the fact that she'd had the same thought as him. "You don't know what's going on in someone's life. I like to give people the benefit of the doubt."

"I know. It's a terrible flaw."

She laughed and poked him in the chest. "Take you for example. People could think you were just a grumpy, scary person by nature, but I knew immediately when I saw you that you'd probably just come off the phone from your father."

"Stop telling me I'm grumpy. It makes me grumpy."

"I adore you, you know that. All I'm saying is that there are a million reasons why human beings behave the way they do. That's what makes them fascinating."

"That's what makes them annoying. And your new friend wasn't exactly warm, either. If my ice machine breaks, I know where to go."

"Give her a chance." Trying a different approach, she gave him her pleading look. "Do it for me."

"Why would I do it for you?"

"Because you love me really. As a friend, obviously. Deep down."

"Do I?" But there was humour in his eyes so she pushed ahead.

"She's probably tired. Long journey. Probably feeling a bit lost. And then you gave her the chilliest welcome since Scott arrived in Antarctica. You're the one who froze her. Promise me you'll smile next time you see her. No more frowning."

He leaned against the wall. "Do I have to promise?"

"Yes." She gave him a stern look and he sighed.

"Fine. I'll take food up to her. I'll even polish the apple. If you prefer, I could turn it into humble pie. Why are you smiling?"

"Because you're funny when you're grumpy."

"Do you always have to be so damn cheerful?"

She shrugged. "I like being cheerful."

"Maybe, but right now you're doing it to annoy me."

She beamed at him. "You're right, I am. Is it working?"

"It's working. You always know how to wind me up, and not in a good way. No wonder we only went on one date." He eased away from the wall. "Don't worry, I promise to keep an eye on your city princess."

"You're doing it again. Judging."

"Okay. But can I at least say 'I told you so' when she twists her ankle?"

"No, if that happens, you'll say 'oh you poor thing, let me take you to hospital.' I'm serious. I need her to like it here. Things aren't great at work. I think she might be able to help."

He gave her a sympathetic look. "Everyone still trying to do things the Gerald way?"

"They are. I've tried everything. I've tried sweeping everyone along on the tide of my enthusiasm. I've written a memo.

I shower everyone with enthusiasm. Nothing works. If I hear 'but Gerald did it this way' again I might scream."

"Yeah?" He gave a half-smile. "I'd drag myself up from the cellar to witness that."

She ignored that comment. "I'm hoping Abby is going to help me turn things around if only because she doesn't know Gerald."

"You don't think your expectations might be a little high?"

"I'm an optimist."

"I know. It's your second biggest flaw." He brushed her cheek with his fingers. "Okay. I'll be approachable, whatever that means. I'll smile when I deliver the apple. I'll make sure it isn't poisoned. And in return you're going to be a bit wary for once in your life. Until you get to know her better."

"You see? You do care about me."

"Not really. I just don't want to have to witness your heartbreak when it all goes wrong. It was bad enough after—" He stopped and she shrugged.

"After Martin. I know. It was a hideous time and you were brilliant. It was lucky for me you happened to be home at the time. But I can't go into every relationship assuming someone is going to stab me in the back. It's just not me. And why would I be wary? She's here to help, after all."

He watched her for a moment. "Right. It's just that she doesn't seem—"

"Doesn't seem what? Frazzled, like me? She's groomed and poised but I'm sure that after an hour working at the hotel she'll look as stressed out as the rest of us. Now go." She gave him a little push. "You have tourists waiting to coo over your quaint little inn, with its handsome landlord. Talking of which, I hear Linda Porter made a pass at you when she was drunk the other night."

"Where did you hear that?"

"I always protect my sources. But basically from everyone in the village. Saskia happened to be leaving the gallery at the precise moment you kissed Linda in the doorway."

"She kissed *me* in the doorway. Saskia needs to get her facts straight."

"She didn't hang around to see what happened next."

"What happened next was that I carefully unravelled myself and told her that I'm not in the market for a relationship."

"That part didn't make it into the gossip machine." She gave his arm an affectionate squeeze. "You're due a little fun, my friend."

He rolled his eyes. "Talking of which, how is it going with your hot chef?"

"How is what going?"

"Your romance."

"There is no romance. Who told you there was a romance?"

"Probably the same people that told you about Linda," he said. "But from what I hear, it sounds like a perfect match."

"What makes you say that?"

"Because he will cook for you, and you love good food."

She sighed. "He's cute, that's true, but most of all he's brilliant at what he does and the restaurant is fully booked. As an experiment we're doing two sittings from next week. It's the only bit of work that is going well."

"Right. So your interest in him is purely professional. You're not interested in him bringing you breakfast in bed."

She grinned at him. "He does have lovely dark eyes and an appealing smile. But like you, I'm too busy for a relationship. But hopefully Abby is going to help with that."

His smile vanished. "I hope so. Keep me updated on that."

He was suspicious of Abby, and she had no idea why.

What exactly did he think was going to happen? That Abby was going to steal the toilet rolls?

It was true that Abby had told her little about herself, but that didn't mean she was hiding anything.

Evie was looking forward to getting to know her. And looking forward to proving Tristan wrong.

7

★★★★★

Abby

Abby stared out of the window, watching as Evie headed back up the street towards her cottage. It took her a while because she stopped to greet at least five people on the way, her smile visible even from Abby's lofty position.

She'd never met anyone quite so cheerful and positive, but she was sure that some of it was a front. A defence mechanism. Abby did the same herself, sometimes.

I can't stand people who lie to me.

Abby turned away from the window, swamped with guilt. Ironically enough she felt the same way. And yet here she was, lying.

This wasn't going to work, and she was going to tell her mother that.

She should never have agreed to it. She hadn't even started work yet and already she felt like a traitor. It might have been easier to justify if she'd understood what was going on in her mother's head.

What was she going to do with the information Abby gleaned from her clandestine observations? Was she using it to justify closing the hotel? Looking for ways to reinvigorate it? Abby had no idea. She knew the team she worked with back in the office imagined her sitting with her mother while she confided all her hopes, plans and fears but her mother had never been like that. She made her own decisions and rarely shared the thinking that had led to those decisions, even with Abby.

Abby worked hard to please her mother and deliver what she wanted, but in this case it was hard to deliver something when she didn't really understand the end objective. And when you weren't comfortable with the requested methods.

She pulled her laptop out of her bag and put it on the little table by the window.

She'd work with the staff, deliver a report, but no more subterfuge.

Tomorrow she was going to walk into the hotel and confess to Evie who she was.

She slid off her shoes, stripped off her clothes and stepped into the shower, trying to figure out the best way to have that conversation.

Before today The Alexandra, Cornwall had been all about data. She could recite everything from occupancy rates to revenue performance metrics. She knew the names of every member of staff, including their age, experience and the length of time they'd been working at the hotel.

Until today they'd been names on a list in the report she'd compiled. But now?

She reached for the shampoo and lathered her hair.

Now, the hotel was more than a pretty photograph, it was a place. And the staff were more than names. They were people.

Evie was a good example. Abby had known the basic facts about her, but even after spending one afternoon with her, she could see that the situation was more complicated than she'd first imagined and that the facts at her disposal didn't tell the full story.

Most surprising of all was that Evie had felt comfortable enough with Abby to talk to her honestly. She'd felt able to open up, and people didn't usually open up with Abby. On the contrary they shut down, and sometimes even left the room.

And the fact that Evie had trusted her with information she hadn't shared with anyone else gave Abby a deep sense of responsibility.

Yes, she was here for her mother, but she was determined to help Evie, too.

She'd done extensive research into the hotel as part of her report but nothing had suggested that Evie herself was concerned about the way the place was being run, or that she had fears of it closing.

Most importantly of all, her research hadn't flagged the fact that Evie had already contacted head office to discuss the situation.

Abby rinsed her hair. What had happened to the emails Evie had sent? Who had she contacted?

Jack, presumably. That needed to be handled, as did the fact that the UK general manager clearly hadn't spent any time at all at their Cornish hotel in recent months despite Gerald's situation.

Was that why Jack had been resistant to her spending the summer here? Had he been afraid of what she might discover?

Abby turned off the shower and reached for a towel.

The truth was that although she was deeply uncomfortable with the idea of being "under-cover," it was unlikely that Evie would have revealed any of those facts had she known who Abby was.

Evie had seemed relieved to have the opportunity to talk to someone from the outside. Someone who wasn't already part of the close-knit team she worked with every day. If Abby told her the truth she'd hold back. She'd be wary.

In order to produce a fair analysis, Abby needed access to all the facts and Evie was only going to confide in her if she trusted her.

Which proved that, as usual, her mother was right.

She pulled on the robe that had been left for her along with the towels.

She didn't love being "under-cover" but she'd keep it going for now and once she had a clearer picture of how the hotel was operating, she'd consider how best to deal with it. And in the meantime, it was important that she didn't get emotionally attached. Not that such a thing was likely to happen. Her mother had drilled that into her from an early age.

Once your emotions are involved, you cease to make the right decisions for the business.

She dried her hair quickly, switched the robe for a white linen shirt that had been washed to a state of delicious softness and fell to mid thigh. Then she sat down at the little table by the window and opened her laptop. She was tired, but she knew she wouldn't sleep and if she wasn't going to sleep she might as well work.

First she dealt with her emails. Then she typed up her notes, leaving nothing out. She described the gardens, the food, the way she'd felt as she'd walked into the hotel for the first time. She mentioned each member of staff that she'd met, and her first impressions.

When she'd finished, she opened a new document and picked out the key points that would impact the business. Her mother wouldn't be interested in the smoothness of the clotted cream, or the sweetness of the jam that Evie had told her was made in their own kitchens from strawberries grown in the hotel gardens. She wouldn't care about the wild flowers on the cliffs or the way the sun had sparkled on the sea.

She wouldn't care that Abby and Evie had laughed together, that Evie had confided in her and that Abby had found herself hoping they would be friends. In fact, an admission like that would probably horrify her.

Abby pulled herself together.

Her mother would care about how the hotel was operating. Facts.

The acting general manager Evie is motivated and bright. It's clear that the sudden departure of the manager Gerald had a significant emotional impact on the team. He was well-liked by everyone—

She paused, then deleted that last sentence. Her mother wouldn't care whether the staff loved him or hated him. She only cared about outcomes.

She carried on typing.

Of note is the fact that Evie reached out to head office several times but received no response. We need to review the systems we have in place for offering support during potentially challenging periods, but particularly when requested.

She stared at the page. That observation pointed the finger directly at Jack and wasn't going to win her any friends, but she was used to that. And it didn't matter. She was here to do what was best for the business, not what was best for her own relationships.

Jack would no doubt be defensive, but his feelings weren't her problem to deal with.

Evie had done the right thing and her actions should be on the record. Abby felt strongly that people should be given the tools and the support to do the job they were hired to do. Clearly that hadn't happened in this case.

She stood up and grabbed a bottle of water from the fridge. Her neck ached and her head throbbed.

The sun dipped behind the horizon and she flicked on the table lamp.

She was about to finish her report when there was a knock on the door.

Abby closed her laptop quickly and opened the door.

Tristan stood there holding a tray. "I brought you a peace offering."

He seemed a lot taller than he had downstairs, but then she realised it was because she'd taken off her shoes.

She glanced at the tray. "An apple?"

"You said you wanted an apple. I took you literally."

"That's thoughtful of you. Thank you."

"I also brought a small taster portion of fish pie, in case you decided you wanted something more substantial. Evie said you took an overnight flight and have been travelling for most of the day. You should eat something." His voice was gruff. "It will help you sleep."

"You're worried about the state of my health?"

"Not really, but I'm worried about the state of my own health if Evie thinks I haven't been looking after you." His smile was a surprise. "And I owe you an apology for being grumpy earlier. You caught me at a bad moment."

"It's not a problem. You and Evie are clearly close."

"I've known her for a long time. She's a good person. I look out for her." Something in his tone made her wonder if he saw her as some kind of threat to Evie's well-being. Was he giving her a warning?

"Don't tell me—she's the little sister you never had?"

"No. I have a little sister, although she'd floor me for describing her that way. Evie is a friend." His gaze held hers, unflinching. "A good friend."

Definitely a warning there.

"I'm looking forward to working with her." She went to take the tray. "Thank you for this."

He nodded and handed it over. "You look different without the armour."

"Armour?"

"Heels. Suit. Pristine white shirt. Regimented hair. The intimidating corporate look. That's what it is, isn't it? Armour? You're still wearing the shirt, of course, but this version is more casual."

She realised that she was so tired she was only wearing the shirt she'd pulled on after her shower. Fortunately, it was decent, but less formal than she would have liked given her present company.

"It's called dressing for work."

He nodded. "Armour." His blue gaze was so intense it was like being interrogated.

"Thank you for the food, Mr Penrose."

"Call me Tristan, or Tris. We're pretty informal around here." He leaned against the door-frame. "So what is your role, exactly?"

Her conscience tingled and she had a desperate urge to glance over her shoulder to check she'd closed her laptop.

"I have amassed considerable experience working in hotels over the course of my career. I'm here to help." It wasn't a lie. She did intend to help.

"Right. So you're not Gerald's replacement. You're not here to take Evie's job? Because you have no idea how much she loves that place and how much it means to her."

It was obvious that he'd step in front of a bus to protect Evie.

"What does it mean to her?" She was here to get information. The perspective of an outsider might be interesting and possibly relevant.

"She virtually grew up in that hotel. Her father raised her alone so occasionally he had to take her to work with him. Evie learned to walk along those corridors. The staff took turns to babysit her. The moment she was old enough, she took a job there. Weekends. Summer holidays. Plenty of the kids around here did the same."

And so did she. It was almost as if he'd been describing her childhood, except that in her case she'd moved from hotel to hotel as her mother had gradually built up her business.

Unsettled by the similarities between her and Evie, she dragged herself back to the present.

"Did you work at the hotel, too?"

"No. I worked for my dad in this place." He studied her. "Evie's dream was to run the hotel one day. When she was ten she used to play 'hotels.' She made herself a sign that said Evie Hamilton—General Manager, and she made people come to her with problems. She'd kill me for telling you that."

"I'm glad you did," Abby said. "I see now how important this is to her."

"She's brimming with ideas. She used to talk about what she'd do differently if she was ever promoted. It didn't happen quite the way she was hoping it would."

"I can see that." And it would have been a tricky situation to handle.

"She stepped up in a crisis, so there was no celebration. Her title is 'acting' general manager. Which means, I assume, that sooner or later the company will be appointing a permanent general manager. It should be her."

She felt a flicker of envy.

Evie was lucky to have someone looking out for her. And it wasn't even a romantic relationship. It was a friendship.

Abby cast her mind over her acquaintances and tried to think of one who might go out on a limb for her. She came up blank.

Unsettled, she pushed that thought aside. "I'm not Gerald's replacement. And my intention is to support Evie. And if the time comes when the company needs to appoint a permanent general manager, it won't be me making the decision."

He watched her for a moment. "You don't give much away, do you?"

"Discretion is important in the hotel business."

"Discretion. If that's important to you then you're going to have a problem living here." He smiled. "This is a small village where everyone knows everyone. Don't be fooled by the number of tourists. Discretion isn't a word you hear a lot, and you see it in practice even less."

Having lived most of her life in a big city, Abby didn't really understand what he was talking about, and she didn't see the relevance for her.

She was going to be spending her time in the hotel, not the village. And she was here for the summer, not for the rest of her life.

"Thanks for the information. And the food." She looked at him and tension pulsed between them.

He cleared his throat. "If you don't want to eat alone you could come downstairs and join me in the pub. There's a table by the window. Good views. Or we could sit outside."

She reminded herself that the invitation wasn't personal.

A pub was a social hub, and he was the landlord. In a place like this the pub was, in all likelihood, the heart of the community. He probably felt a responsibility towards his guests. Either that or he was trying to compensate for his less than warm welcome earlier.

"Thank you for the offer, but I'll be fine here. And don't worry—I'll be sure to give you a glowing reference when I talk to Evie."

"Good. Because she can be scary." He didn't move from the

doorway. "If you need anything else, let me know. And leave the tray outside your door when you're done. That way your room won't smell of fish."

"Thank you. I appreciate the food. It was thoughtful of you." It was, although she had a feeling that his attention had more to do with him keeping an eye on her than delivering good hospitality.

She carried the tray back into the room and was relieved to hear him close the door behind her.

Either way, she would be keeping as much distance from him as possible.

Her stomach growled and she picked up a fork, intending to sample the fish pie.

Five minutes later she'd eaten the entire thing and was staring at an empty bowl. Evie was right. It was incredible.

She ate the apple, then put the tray outside her room.

She could hear the muffled sounds of conversation and laughter coming from the pub far beneath her, but there was no sign of Tristan.

The familiar feeling of loneliness crept over her and for a moment she wished she'd accepted Evie's invitation to join her for something to eat.

But it was too late for regrets, so she did what she always did when she felt alone. She took refuge in her work.

Closing the door to her room, she walked back to the little desk, picked up her phone and braced herself to call her mother.

8

★★★★★

Evie

The room was a mess, thanks to the out-of-control partying of a couple celebrating a milestone birthday. Every surface was covered in half-empty wine glasses, bottles and half-eaten plates of food. Someone had spilled a bottle of red wine on the duvet, there was broken glass on the carpet, and the place was littered with party poppers and burst balloons.

"I don't believe this." Evie stared at it, appalled. "Is this the way they behave in their own homes?"

Abby glanced around her. "It must have been quite a party. Does this happen often?"

"Hardly ever. We've been lucky that way. Some guests are untidier than others, but we have little actual damage." Evie grabbed a lone balloon that had wrapped itself around a light fitting.

This was the last thing they needed.

It was part of running a hotel, of course, but it was bad timing.

She'd already had one of the housekeeping staff call in sick that morning, so things were stretched.

It was Abby's first day and she'd offered to help wherever she was needed but it didn't seem fair to start her with this job.

"The Grangers are due to check in here this afternoon." Mandy surveyed the scene with weary acceptance as Abby went to check the bathroom. "We're going to have to move them to another room. There's no way we'll be able to turn this room around in time, especially with Tilda off sick. We're going to need to have the carpet professionally cleaned for a start. This is why I prefer the rooms in the stable wing. They have those beautiful slate floors."

Evie retrieved a cushion from the floor. She'd forgotten about the Grangers. "They requested this room specifically because it's their anniversary and they stayed here on their honeymoon." She sighed. "I'll call them myself and break the bad news."

"Wow, they clearly partied in here, too." Abby's voice came from the bathroom. "What *is* that on the mirror? Is it lipstick? Was the woman kissing her own reflection or something? What time are the Grangers arriving?"

"Check-in is from four o'clock. Why?"

"Because I'm sure we can rescue the room by then." Abby walked back into the bedroom, all business. "I worked in a hotel in San Diego a couple of years ago where two of us managed to turn around a totally trashed room in six hours, and that included having the bathroom door replaced. And this isn't as bad. There doesn't seem to be any physical damage, apart from the bedcover and that mark on the carpet. No holes in woodwork or broken drawers."

She bent to make a closer examination of the stained carpet. "This will come out. If not, we can put a rug over it." She stood up. "Where do you think we should start, Mandy?"

Mandy stared at her. "Me?"

"You're the expert so I'll follow your lead but I'm sure that between us we can turn this around in time for the Grangers to check in and have their special stay, aren't you?"

Mandy glanced around the room, looking doubtful. "Well—"

"It obviously means such a lot to them. It would be great to make this happen so that they can have the special celebration they're hoping for, don't you think? I'll do whatever you tell me to do. Where shall we start?"

Evie was mute with admiration. Whenever she'd had to ask staff members to go above and beyond she usually found herself prostrating herself. *Would you mind awfully? . . .* or *I'd be massively grateful if you could . . .*

She virtually begged, and most of the time it didn't work.

Abby hadn't given Mandy a choice. And that approach seemed to be working.

Mandy straightened her shoulders.

"The Grangers are nice people. You're right, it would be good to do this for them. Make it special. Okay, where would I start—" She surveyed the room, suddenly businesslike. "I'd pull on a pair of gloves and clear all the rubbish and also bag up any bedding or cushions that are ruined." She eyed Abby, gauging if that was the right answer. "Then I'd take it a step at a time."

"Sounds good. And you'll want me to make a note of anything that's broken or damaged beyond repair. I'll do that, and I'll take a few photos right now so that we have that on record. You can leave this to us, Evie." Abby was already pulling on gloves from Mandy's trolley. "If in a few hours we don't think we can do it, we'll let you know and you can call the Grangers. Mandy and I have got this."

Evie admired Abby's optimism and enthusiasm (and also the

way she'd skilfully managed Mandy), but despite her obvious willingness to get her hands dirty Evie doubted they'd be able to turn the room around in that time and not only because of the enormity of the task. Mandy loved to chat, and Abby presented her with a whole new audience. That would slow the pace of things considerably.

Still, the room needed to be dealt with either way, so she left them to it and went to handle the next problem, which was a long line at the reception desk.

She worked there until the line was cleared, then headed back to her office to deal with all the paperwork that was mounting up.

A few hours passed before she even lifted her head to check the time and when she did she discovered it was lunchtime. She couldn't put the moment off any longer. She was going to have to call the Grangers and work out a way to make it up to them. Whatever she offered would eat into the hotel's profits, but she didn't see an alternative.

She closed her laptop and walked through the hotel greeting staff and guests, quietly observing everything before ending up back at the room Abby and Mandy were turning over.

She opened the door with her key.

Two large black bin bags leaned against the wall, both stuffed to the brim.

She heard laughter and Mandy's voice.

"So she said to him, *listen, sunshine, I'm old enough to be your mother*, and that's when he told her!"

"You're kidding." Abby was laughing so hard she could barely speak. "I'm convinced you're making this up. Grab the end of this, Mandy, and we'll give it a shake."

"Every word is the truth. He said *you are my mother*, and can you imagine her response?"

"Honestly? No, I can't. I wish I'd been there to see it for myself. That's the best story ever. Throw me that pillow, will you?"

Evie paused in the doorway. She hadn't expected this to be a fun task, but they were both laughing like old friends. Abby hadn't struck her as the talkative sort, but it seemed she was as chatty as Mandy. Which was good on one level, but presumably meant they hadn't made much progress.

Resigned to making that phone call, Evie stepped into the room.

"How are you doing here? It's lunchtime, and you should—" She stopped, stunned.

If she hadn't seen them both standing there, she wouldn't have known it was the same room.

The rubbish had been removed, every surface shone and the carpet had been returned to its previously pristine state. The bed was freshly made, the white linens displaying not a single crease. The bed looked so inviting Evie was tempted to lie down on it herself.

"How did you do this?"

"Mandy is brilliant," Abby said. "Just brilliant."

"We worked hard." Mandy patted the last pillow and placed it carefully on the bed. "And it helped that Abby is a genius with stains and blobs. Also full of great stories. When you have a moment you have to ask her about the mess she had to clean up at a hotel in Cape Cod last year. It involves guests who decided to barbecue fish on their balcony, the fire service and a dramatic rescue of a dog who shouldn't have been in the room in the first place." Mandy smiled at Abby. "Hilarious."

"We made a note of the damage, but there's nothing too dramatic. I'll email you the list," Abby said. "Apart from needing to replace one cushion from the sofa, and the pretty one with the sea-bird that was on the bed, this room is ready to welcome the Grangers."

"Thank you." Evie felt weak with relief. "You've both done a great job. I'll get those cushions and sort out a welcome basket and some fresh flowers."

"I can do both those things," Mandy said. "I'm about to dispose of the rubbish so I'll do that afterwards."

Evie wondered if she'd noticed the time. "It's lunch—"

"Oh, we already agreed that we're not going for lunch until we've finished here," Abby said. "You're okay with that, aren't you, Mandy?"

"Definitely." Mandy nodded and patted Abby on the shoulder. "Please tell me you're going to be working in housekeeping the whole time you're here. I hope I didn't bore you with all my stories about how the hotel used to be when I first joined. It was a real trip down memory lane."

"I loved hearing about it. This whole thing ended up being so much fun." Abby frowned, as if that was surprising.

"It's important to be able to have a laugh at work," Mandy said. She gave the room one last look. "We're done here. Where would you like me next, Evie? What's the priority?"

Evie was still digesting the fact that Mandy had agreed to delay her lunch break. Whenever she gently suggested something similar she was always told that there was nothing that couldn't wait until after lunch.

She pushed that aside and focused on Mandy's question. "Connie is in the process of setting up one of our function rooms for a children's party this afternoon. We're expecting a balloon delivery any moment."

"You want help with that? Point me in the right direction."

"That would be great, thanks. And then I thought you might want to work alongside Edward this afternoon. He knows the hotel better than anyone, and you'll pick up some useful information about the local area, so if a guest happens to ask you something at least you will have had some preparation."

"That sounds like a good idea." Abby followed Evie out of the room. "Did things change for you with the staff when you were promoted?"

"Change? You mean our relationship? No, not at all. And that's good and bad I suppose. They treat me exactly the same way they always have. Although I wasn't exactly promoted in the traditional sense. It wasn't a case of *hey, Evie, we think you're brilliant so we're giving you the big job*. It was more *hey, Evie, we're desperate so you're in charge of the ship for now and please don't sink it*."

And it was sinking. And it didn't matter that she wasn't responsible for how they arrived at this point. She was responsible for what happened next.

"But they must have thought you were capable of doing the job."

Evie shrugged. "I was the obvious person. The only person. There wasn't anyone else on the team with the same experience." Was that a bit too honest? "I'm happy, obviously. I'm lucky to have been given this chance. But my position is temporary. I'm a caretaker."

Abby angled her head. "Do you think Gerald will be back?"

It was a question that plagued her daily.

"I don't know. I went to see him at home a couple of weeks ago and he didn't look that well. Rhoda—that's his wife—said he'd been sleeping a lot. He asked about the hotel. He's worried about the place and Rhoda was frustrated that he couldn't switch off."

Would he come back? She didn't know. And what would happen to her job if he did?

Would she really be able to step back into her old role, knowing what she now knew?

There were things she'd want to challenge him on, and she

wouldn't feel able to. She wouldn't know how to. But holding it all in and carrying on as normal would be hard.

Still, there was no point in worrying about that now.

"That's tough on you," Abby said. "I guess you don't really know where you stand. You probably don't feel you can make the job your own because it doesn't feel as if it is your own. You have lots of ideas, but can't make major changes in case Gerald does come back. And you must be wondering what your role will be if that happens."

How did she know all that?

Since stepping into this job Evie had felt completely alone, unable to share her thoughts with anyone apart from her dad and the occasional indiscreet moment when she'd confided in Tristan. She hadn't even talked to colleagues she'd been fairly close to before her promotion. They'd all be horrified if they knew she was contemplating leaving. They wouldn't understand. She knew they had no idea how she was feeling or what she was dealing with.

But Abby knew. Abby had seen it instantly. Abby understood.

Grateful for whichever lucky star had brought Abby into her life, she cleared her throat. "That's it exactly."

"Your position isn't easy, I can see that. We should talk about it more. Come up with some solutions."

Evie was touched. "Don't worry about it. There's nothing you can do. There aren't any solutions. Believe me, I've looked for them. All I can do is carry on doing the best I can and see what happens. And in the meantime I now have you, which is brilliant on many levels. You have no idea how good it is to talk to someone about it. I hope you don't think I'm unprofessional, but it's not as if you're a permanent member of staff. Talking of which, I don't suppose you'd like a permanent job? I'm kidding. I know you like to move around. I'll try and be grateful that at least we have you for the summer. You're completely brilliant. I'm sure you've heard that a million times."

"I—no. In fact, I haven't." Abby seemed a bit surprised by the praise which Evie thought was a bit strange.

Or maybe she'd been too effusive. She had a tendency to express her emotions freely and some people found that a little uncomfortable. Abby seemed like the reserved type. The sort of person who thought carefully before speaking and only revealed exactly what she'd chosen to reveal. On the other hand she'd tucked into scones with the same enthusiasm as Evie and had laughed out loud while working with Mandy. She'd been having fun and seemed almost surprised to be made welcome by everyone.

She remembered Tristan's warning that she should be careful around Abby and felt a flicker of irritation with him for planting thoughts in her head. The whole point of Abby being here was to offer support and help. She had plenty of experience. More importantly, her experience had been gained from working in different hotels and that gave her an advantage over Evie who had only ever worked in this one place. Abby must have seen both good and bad in her time. Evie might be able to tap into some of that experience and improve the way things were running. But she wasn't going to be able to do that by holding back and not being honest.

She wasn't by nature a suspicious person and it felt uncomfortable behaving that way particularly given that Abby seemed really eager to get to know everyone and was interested and engaged.

And besides, she liked Abby. She hoped head office wouldn't move her on too quickly because she could picture them becoming friends.

"Thanks for listening. It helps to talk things through with someone who understands."

"You don't talk to your dad?"

"About business? Rarely."

Abby gave her a curious look. "But you work in the same place. In the same business. And your father has worked here for a long time. He must be a mine of information."

"He is, but we generally talk about other things when we're together."

"Was it awkward when you were promoted? Technically you're now his boss."

Evie smiled. "He would say I've been his boss since the moment I learned to talk. It's not awkward. I suppose we're both used to it. He's been here for his whole career, so there's not much he hasn't seen and done. Before Gerald there was a manager who was determined to shake everything up and do things differently. Half the staff left, but it was less of an issue back then because we didn't have the recruitment challenges we have now." She checked the time. "I'm interviewing a couple of people in ten minutes. If you could help with party prep now, and then go for lunch, that should work. Get someone to show you where the staff room is."

"I will." Abby's gaze slid to the door, where balloons were already being unloaded. A strange expression crossed her face.

"What's wrong?"

Abby frowned and shook her head. "Nothing. Seeing those balloons made me think—I had a flashback to being at a party when I was young—"

"It's weird when that happens. I used to hate balloons when I was little. Anyway, come and find me when you're done here and you've finished lunch and I'll take you to Edward for the afternoon . . . Abby?"

Abby was still staring at the balloons and gave a start. "Yes. Sorry." She looked at Evie. "You don't have to take me to Edward.

You have enough to do. I can find my own way. Good luck with those interviews. Hope you find someone good."

"Thanks." What Evie really wanted was to find someone like Abby. Someone calm, competent and uncomplaining. Someone who saw what needed to be done and did it. She'd hire a million Abbys given the chance, but right now she was appreciating the one she had. "I'm *so* happy head office chose to send you here. You're a lifesaver. Or at least a hotel saver. Between us we're going to make a difference, I can feel it. I'll see you later."

She took one step and then stopped. "If you feel like fresh air after your first day you could join me on my run this evening?"

Abby stared at her. "Me?"

"Yes. We talked about it yesterday."

"Oh, I didn't mean—you really don't have to do that." She looked so thrown by the invitation that Evie wondered if she'd made a mistake by suggesting it.

"If running isn't your thing, we could go for a walk. But it will be beautiful on the coast path and I can show you some of the local area. And then you could come back to mine for something to eat. It would be fun."

"That's generous of you." Abby was hesitant. "I probably shouldn't—I mean, I'm sure you have better things to do than babysit me—"

"I'd love to have your company." Or maybe Abby didn't want to spend an evening with her. "Unless you've had enough of me for one day. I know I talk a lot. Tristan says I'm exhausting. You'd probably rather sit quietly with a book, or generally chill out after your first day. That's fine, honestly, I'll see you tom—"

"I'd like to. If you're sure." Abby spoke quickly. "I don't have plans. Thank you. What time?"

Evie hadn't thought that far ahead, but clearly Abby was a planner so she thought about all the work she had to do and did some mental calculations. "I'll pick you up from the pub at seven, if that works for you?"

"That works."

"Great. I'll see you later. And good luck with those balloons."

Evie headed down the corridor to her office, feeling lighter. Abby was insightful. She'd instantly seen the challenges Evie was facing without Evie having to spell them out. It was refreshing to feel understood and she was looking forward to the evening.

She pushed open the door of her office and stopped.

Luca was transferring a plate of sandwiches from the tray to her desk. "There you are. I thought I was going to have to take these away again and put them in the fridge." He straightened and gave a nod of approval. "You look happy. That's good. Yesterday you weren't smiling. I was worried."

"Yesterday I was surrounded by people trying to manipulate my life, although your chocolate cake was a high point." She concentrated on the food to stop herself looking at his biceps. "You brought me lunch?"

"Yesterday all you ate at work was the chocolate cake. The day before, two cups of coffee. You need to eat."

He'd made her lunch.

No one ever made her lunch. Sometimes, when she remembered, she grabbed one of the staff sandwiches from the fridge in the kitchen, but usually she was too busy rushing from one task to the next. No one noticed. But Luca had noticed.

The gesture made her feel ridiculously emotional. "You didn't need to do that."

"What would you have eaten if I hadn't?"

"I don't know," she said. "I haven't thought about it. A chocolate bar?"

Luca looked pained. "And where's the nutrition in that?"

"I was going more for comfort and energy than nutrition."

"Sit down—" He gestured to the small table in the corner of her office where she sometimes held meetings.

"Luca, this is kind of you, but you really didn't have to—"

"Five minutes. That's all it will take to eat what I've made you and you'll thank me."

She eyed the stack of messages on her desk. "I really should—"

"Consider it work. It's a sample of our new afternoon tea menu which I'd like you to approve. I've kept it fairly traditional because that's what my research suggests people want. Mini quiches, smoked salmon on freshly baked rye bread, chicken and tarragon—have a taste. Also, I have included my special cannoli for you to try. I thought it would be fun to add a Sicilian twist to your traditional afternoon tea. I'd appreciate your feedback."

"Is that true? Or do you just want me to eat?"

"Both." He smiled, and she felt emotion threaten to swamp her.

She *had* to pull herself together. It was a bit unsettling that all it took for her to feel like sobbing was for someone to be kind enough to make her a sandwich. What was wrong with her? Was she really that close to the edge? She needed to pull herself together.

She sat down at the table and reached for a sandwich. "Thanks, Luca. I'm starving." She'd left the house without eating breakfast and she hadn't given a thought to lunch. "They're a work of art. How do you do that?"

"It's my job. Appearance matters, but taste is more important. So taste it."

She reached out and selected chicken, feeling self-conscious. "I feel weird eating alone with you watching."

"In that case, how does seven thirty tomorrow work for you?"

She glanced up at him. "For what?"

"Eating together. I've booked a table. There's a restaurant half an hour from here I'd like to try. Here's the address." He put a piece of paper in front of her. "You'll probably want to drive separately to reduce the chance of gossip. I know you hate that, and I don't want to make things difficult for you."

She put the sandwich down untouched. There was a strange fluttering in her stomach. "Are you asking me to dinner?"

"I didn't make that clear?"

A date. He was asking her on a date. "Are you sure?"

He raised an eyebrow. "I'm sure. Why would you doubt it?"

"Oh, you know—" she was flustered "—because there are a million reasons why that would be a bad idea."

"Unless one of those reasons is 'I don't like you, Luca, and the last thing I want to do is spend an evening with you', I'm going to object to your reasons."

"That's because you're new around here and you don't know how things work. Whichever restaurant we choose, someone will see us."

"And that matters because?"

He had no idea. And why would he? "You're relaxed about it now, but that's because you haven't been on the sharp end of gossip and speculation." She could imagine what would happen if they were seen out together. Donna would be booking the church and buying a hat. "If we go out to dinner together you won't be able to walk through the village without people nudging, winking, and asking you inappropriate and probing questions. Pretty soon you'll wish you'd never asked me, and then you'll start avoiding me, which will be awkward for both of us. Trust me, it's not worth it." *She'd been there.*

"I'll be the judge of that." He sat down opposite her, his gaze fixed on her face. "I wouldn't have come to a small town if I couldn't handle gossip and speculation. It doesn't worry me. I was raised in a village in Sicily where the local community look out for each other."

"There's a difference between people looking out for you and people looking at you."

"So? If it bothers you, we'll tell them we were scoping out the competition. That's if anyone sees us. Which I doubt they will."

She wished she could be as relaxed. "It isn't only other people that are the problem. We're colleagues. It could be awkward."

"We work in the same hotel, but not the same area. Technically we're separate. I don't see how it will be awkward. If it turns out we bore each other, it's not going to affect our work. Enough excuses. Try the sandwich. You're hungry. No one can make good decisions when they're hungry."

She bit into the chicken and closed her eyes. Everything he made tasted better than the last thing. "This is incredible."

"I know. It's my grandmother's recipe. It has a secret ingredient. Say yes to dinner and I'll consider sharing the secret with you."

"I'd rather you made it for me." She finished the sandwich and immediately ate another. "Your grandmother taught you to cook?"

She realised she knew virtually nothing about him apart from his professional credentials.

He smiled and stood up. "I only answer personal questions away from the workplace. I'll see you at seven thirty tomorrow."

He said it as if it was a sure thing and she felt her willpower melt away under the warmth of his gaze. "All right. But just this once. And don't say I didn't warn you."

His smile widened. "Life is no fun if you don't take a few risks. It's important to live in the moment. And talking of moments, try the prawn and lemon next." He pushed the plate closer to her and his fingertips brushed hers. "You can let me know what you think tomorrow night. Seven thirty. Don't be late, and don't waste the rest of the day thinking of reasons why you should cancel because I'm going to be there anyway, and you don't want to stand me up."

She watched him go, rubbed the edge of her fingertips where he'd touched them, and then ate the prawn and lemon. It was every bit as delicious as the chicken.

What did she think? That the man was a genius in the kitchen. Also fun. And cute, obviously. That part went without saying. And she wasn't going to deny there was chemistry, although if Donna or Mandy had been standing in the room she absolutely would have denied it, just as she would have denied the fact that she felt all fluttery inside when he smiled at her.

Tomorrow she was having dinner with Luca, and tonight she was going for a run with Abby.

She ate the last sandwich and reached for the cannoli.

A new friend and a flirtation. Maybe life was looking up.

9

★★★★★

Abby

She'd had the best day at work she could ever remember having. And she could see the funny side of that because her best day had been spent clearing up someone else's mess, mopping stains the origin of which she didn't want to think about, and picking shards of glass out of soft furnishings. It had been surprisingly satisfying, transforming mess into order. And then there had been the children's party, which meant transforming more mess into order. And that had been satisfying, too. It had also felt a bit unsettling because being in that room with all those balloons had triggered a hazy memory which she couldn't pin down.

Had she been to a party here when she'd lived here as a young child?

Yet another question that only her mother could answer.

And even with that weird flashback that she didn't understand, it had been a good day.

Her head was buzzing. Her back ached and her arms ached from the physical demands of the job, and her ribs ached from laughing at Mandy's outrageous stories.

She'd never felt like part of a team before, but today she'd felt like part of a team. They'd treated her as if she was one of them. Mandy had talked freely and painted an interesting picture of the changes in the hotel over the years. The team running the children's party had made her laugh with their stories, none of which had encouraged her to apply for a job as a children's party planner.

And then there was Edward, who had been generous with his advice and help.

Would they have been so warm and welcoming if they knew who she really was?

Probably not. In that respect she was no better than the man Evie called the weasel.

Unsettled, she walked to the window of her room. She'd kept it open from the moment she'd arrived. The air was clean and smelled of salt and sea, and she enjoyed listening to the sounds. She'd woken that morning to the call of seagulls, the clink of masts, and the shouts of fishermen as they hauled in their catch at dawn.

Now she watched the tourists milling on the cobbled street below, gazing into shop windows and taking photos of the quaint cottages and the boats in the harbour. Everywhere you looked there was potential for the perfect photo. Flowers spilled from window boxes, baskets of seashells gleamed in shop windows, fishing nets and plastic swords were stacked in colourful buckets by doorways to entice children inside to spend money. The place was almost too pretty.

Edward had told her something of its history, from the smugglers centuries ago to more recent stories of daring lifeboat rescues. She'd been captivated, as were the guests he'd talked to as she'd worked alongside him.

She'd spent the afternoon with him, watching in awe as he'd devoted his time and attention to making sure everyone had the perfect stay. He'd entertained children with his stories of magicians and dragons, suggested a hiking route to a couple from Germany, and booked a restaurant for a woman travelling alone. The demands were endless and varied and he dealt with them all with the same impressive depth of knowledge and good-humoured patience. There seemed to be nothing he didn't know, and nothing he wasn't prepared to try and source if it meant keeping a guest happy.

Abby couldn't remember enjoying an afternoon more.

There had been a couple of awkward moments when one of the staff had asked her something personal about herself and she'd found it difficult to formulate a response that wouldn't reveal too much. Each time it had happened she gave the briefest of answers and shifted the subject. Those moments were a stark reminder that although they made her feel like a member of their team, she wasn't one and never would be. Every conversation she had was threaded with the knowledge that she wasn't who they thought she was.

With a sigh, she turned away from the window.

This should have been an easy job for her—spending her summer in this special place with a brief simply to help and observe, but she knew it wasn't going to be easy.

The fact that she wasn't being honest about who she was and why she was here weighed on her.

And why was she here? She still didn't know, not really.

She'd thought it would be easy enough to stay detached because that was how she lived her life, but now she realised that the reason she lived that way was because the people around her had made it easy, and gradually it had become a habit. When she was working in the office people kept their distance and her social life—such as it was—involved snatched catch-ups with a couple of college friends who were equally focused on their jobs, and the occasional unsatisfactory date.

She was so used to being alone, to feeling like an outsider, that it wasn't something she thought about. But she was thinking about it now.

Not for a moment had she anticipated that anyone from work would invite her to join them socially. She knew that some of the team back in Boston were friendly outside the office. They met for drinks. They went to concerts and walked together at the weekend. Abby was never invited to join them. And she was mostly fine with that. She told herself she was too busy anyway. But occasionally she'd see them laughing together as they left the office to hang out in a wine bar, or sample a local tapas bar, and she'd feel a pang of something.

She never reached out to anyone at work because she assumed she'd be rebuffed. She took no emotional risks. She never would have invited anyone at work to join her on her run. And yet Evie had invited her without hesitation. She'd taken more emotional risks in that one conversation than Abby had taken in a lifetime.

She'd been in the village for little more than twenty-four hours and instead of spending an evening alone as anticipated, she was going for a run on the coast path and then dinner in Evie's garden.

And she was looking forward to it.

Not because it would give her a chance to learn more about the hotel and Evie, which was what she'd been sent here to do, but because she was looking forward to spending time with Evie.

Was that wrong?

Deep down, she knew it probably was. Evie was warm and friendly, but that friendliness would vanish in a moment if she knew who Abby was—if she knew that, far from sharing her problems with an impartial outsider, she was sharing them with someone from head office. Someone who had the ear of the boss.

She should probably cancel. That would be the right thing to do in the circumstances. It was bad enough being "under-cover" at work. Being under-cover socially was plain wrong. But she'd felt a kinship she didn't usually feel with people. Evie had been so open with her. It had made her feel—warm. Connected.

And it had felt good.

Abby rubbed her fingers over her forehead and contemplated her options. If she cancelled, it would be awkward. Evie would wonder why, and it would possibly hurt her feelings and that Abby didn't want.

She'd go, but she'd keep the conversation light. She'd ask no questions about the hotel. Not tonight. Not when they were technically off duty.

Satisfied with her decision, she changed quickly, secured her hair in a ponytail and grabbed a baseball cap.

She headed down the stairs and heard laughter and singing coming from the bar. And the sound of a piano.

Intrigued, she stepped through the door straight into Tristan who was on his way out.

It was like walking into the wall. He was big and solid and she put her hand on his chest to steady herself. "Sorry!" Her heart thudded out of control. "I wasn't looking where I was going."

"That's obvious. Did you need something?"

She stepped back. She felt flustered, probably because she was remembering his warning about not hurting Evie and only a few moments ago she'd been worrying about the same thing herself. "No. I'm meeting Evie in five minutes. I heard the piano—" She noticed that the sleeves of his shirt were rolled up to the elbows and his forearms were tanned and strong. She shifted her gaze back to the bar and the crowd of people gathered round singing. "You have a music night?"

He followed her gaze. "The singing is impromptu, but yes, we have music nights. In the winter months it's mostly the locals flexing their vocal cords with friends, but in summer we're a little more organised. The tourists like it. It brings in business, and business is always welcome."

She listened as the man at the piano shifted from folk to jazz. "He's good."

"Ray? Don't tell him that. He'll put his prices up. You play?"

"I used to. I started when I was six and had lessons until I was eighteen." Every Tuesday and Friday. Her mother had been big on routine.

His blue eyes were fixed on her face. "Don't tell me—Chopin, Rachmaninov—some Mozart."

"You can tell that by looking at me?"

"You seem the type. Serious. Dedicated. The type that would devote an hour a day to piano practice."

Two hours, she thought. *Sometimes three.*

But she didn't tell him that. She didn't want to give him the satisfaction of being right. She didn't want him to feel he knew her.

"Maybe I'm not what you think I am."

"Maybe you're not. But then again maybe you're exactly who I think you are." His gaze moved slowly from her face to her running shoes. "I gather you're not planning to spend the evening singing round the piano."

"No, which is probably lucky for you. I'm going for a run. Evie is going to show me something of the local area."

"How was your first day at work?"

She was still figuring out how to answer that when his phone rang.

He swore softly and dug it out of his pocket. "I have to take this."

"Of course."

She didn't know whether to feel relieved or disappointed. All she knew was that the knot of tension in her stomach eased slightly as he turned away. She had a feeling he was a human lie detector.

"Dad? Is everything okay?"

She walked to the door that led to the street, trying not to listen.

Yes, I know that . . . yes, you told me that already . . . I've got it covered . . .

His voice was gruff and low but surprisingly patient.

She stepped out onto the street into evening sunshine, feeling sympathy. She knew what it was like constantly trying to please a parent. To live up to high standards. It was tiring.

She frowned, wondering where that thought had come from. It was true that her mother had high standards and expected a lot from her, but Abby knew it came from a place of love and caring. Her mother had faced tough challenges during her life. She'd done everything she could to ensure Abby's future was as secure as possible and Abby was grateful for that.

Still, she was feeling increasingly frustrated that there were big gaps in her past she knew nothing about. Maybe it was being here that was making her more aware of it. Making her ask questions. Her mother had lived here. *She'd* lived here. And she didn't even know where. Had they had a house? Had her mother lived in the hotel? She understood why her mother was reluctant to talk about the loss she'd experienced, but surely something as simple as a place of residence shouldn't be a no-go area?

"Abby!"

She looked up and saw Evie weaving between tourists, a pink hat jammed onto her head. She waved at Abby, dodged a couple with a toddler, narrowly avoided tripping over a dog's lead, and arrived breathless and smiling.

"Sorry, am I late? It's about five minutes to my house from here but always takes much longer."

"Because of the crowds?"

"Partly, but mostly because I keep meeting people I know—"

"Evie!"

"You see what I mean?" Evie grinned at Abby and then stepped forward to hug the woman who had called her name. "Gayle. How are you doing? I tried calling you yesterday."

"I know. I got your message. I was at the hospital having a follow-up. All good, touch wood. The chicken was delicious. How you had time to make that when you're working full-time I have no idea."

"It's one of my signature dishes. I could make it with my eyes shut, except then I'd probably burn myself. Dad used to make it for me when I was sick and it was so comforting it was one of the first things I learned to cook for myself. I lived on it when I was at college. It was how I made friends."

Abby didn't believe that for a moment. Evie seemed the type that would pick up friends the way sticky tape picked up dust.

"You might have saved my life." Gayle glanced curiously at Abby. "Hi there. I'm Gayle. I work in the dental surgery at the top of the hill."

"This is Abby," Evie introduced her. "She's helping me out at the hotel."

"Oh fun. Enjoy. Well, I should go, and thank you again, Evie. See you soon."

Evie watched her go. "She's had such a rough time. Life can be like that, can't it? Sometimes things are steady and then other times life pummels you. Right. Let's go. We'll walk through the harbour because we don't have much choice about that with this number of people, but the moment we hit that hill—" she pointed to the road rising up in the distance "—we'll pick up the pace. The coast path heads off to the right. It will only take us a couple of minutes to get there and then the crowds disappear. Most people stay within a few steps of the harbour. Have you seen Tristan? I forgot to ask you earlier."

"I bumped into him a few minutes ago, but he had to take a call from his dad."

"Poor thing. His father is finding it difficult relinquishing control. Understandable I suppose, when you've built a business from the ground up. The pub was in a state when he took it over. Dark and dingy. Not exactly welcoming. Tristan's dad transformed it. Now it's the place everyone likes to hang out in the winter. They hold the book group there, and quiz night, and singing night, although they pay me not to go to that because I have a voice like a strangled seagull."

It took more than a couple of minutes to reach the other side of the harbour because Evie stopped to pet dogs, hug children and laugh with their parents. She knew every third person she passed and seemed up-to-date on all their lives.

Did you try that book?

What happened about your car? Did they find the person who did it?

When are you going to Majorca?

Did Lissy pass her driving test? She did? Yay! I'll be sure to look an extra time before I cross the road.

It was pretty clear to Abby that Evie wasn't just well-known in the community, she was central to it. And she could also see that being part of a close-knit community must bring added pressures. Everything you did came under scrutiny. If you failed at something, everyone knew. That had to be hard.

She tried, and failed, to picture her mother here, living as part of this small community, exchanging small talk about small details.

What had she been like back then? Her childhood had been tough, Abby knew that. Her father, Abby's grandfather, had walked out when she was eleven, leaving his only child to care for her ailing mother who had died when Alexandra was eighteen. At eighteen she'd fallen in love with a man only to lose him before Abby was even born.

Whenever Abby thought of it her chest ached. Her mother had suffered so much tragedy by an age where most people were simply focusing on where to go to college.

Had she had the support of this community? What had happened exactly?

Abby assumed she'd never let herself love again, although it wasn't something her mother would ever discuss. Her one attempt to ask her mother about her love life had been greeted with a frown.

Even when she asked about her father, her mother would say little.

You have to understand it was a painful and difficult time for me. But I had my business, and I had you.

Abby dodged a child on a scooter, wondering why she was thinking about her mother's childhood now. It was so far in the past it had no relevance. Even if she did locate the house where her mother had lived, it wouldn't answer any of her questions.

Eventually they made it down to the quaint harbour. They ran past boats, lobster pots stacked haphazardly against a wall, fishing nets drying in the sun. Evie yelled a cheerful greeting to a man tinkering with a boat and then they headed up the hill. Although it was late the sun was still hot, and Abby was sweating by the time they turned onto the coast path.

Ahead of them the sea sparkled, a vast ocean of turquoise and aquamarine against a perfect blue sky.

"Brilliant, isn't it?" Evie paused to take a gulp of water and admire the view. "This is my favourite route. No matter how crowded it is in the harbour, it's never crowded up here. By the way, do you see that gorgeous sandy beach down below? Don't get too close to the edge!" She grabbed Abby's arm as she stepped forward to get a better look.

"It is gorgeous, you're right."

"You can access it at low tide from the harbour. Otherwise the only way onto it is a steep path from the top."

"Do you swim there?"

"People do, but I'm more of a runner. I like routine, and if you swim that's dictated by the tides."

"You run every day?"

"Yes, whenever I can. This is the reason I can eat my dad's lasagne and the cinnamon buns from the bakery." Evie clipped the lid back on her bottle. "I need to show you where that is. You'll thank me."

"I'm already thanking you." Abby gazed at the view. "This is spectacular." She dug her phone out of her pocket and took a few photos.

Rugged cliffs plunged steeply into the sparkling sea, calm now but she could imagine how wild it could get when the weather changed.

The cliffs were jagged and unforgiving, the channel into the harbour narrow and curved.

"Were there many shipwrecks around here?"

"Oh yes, plenty. It's a diver's paradise. The views are even better from the top."

Abby followed Evie along the trail that hugged the coastline, mindful of the steep drop to her right. The path wound through long grasses, through carpets of wild flowers shading the cliffs purple and pink.

They passed a couple of other people but apart from that

their only company on the cliffs were sea-birds and butterflies. They ran to a viewpoint high on a headland where Evie stopped to take a breath.

"You get a good view of the beach from here—" She gestured to a smooth crescent of creamy sand far below them. "The tide can come in fast, and there are sometimes rip currents, so you need to be careful. I'll take you there at the weekend if you like. Do you swim?"

"I love to swim, although normally it's laps of the pool where I live or whichever hotel I'm staying in."

Evie sat down on the grass, keeping a respectful distance from the edge of the cliff. "So how does that work? You travel a lot?"

"Not always. Sometimes I'm in one place for a while. It's the way I like it."

"You don't want to put down roots?" Evie took another glug of water. "Settle somewhere?"

"Home is Boston. I have an apartment."

"But you don't want to take a job where you're in one place? Travelling must be fun, but also exhausting. I'm not sure it would work for me." She pulled off her hat and ran her fingers through her damp hair. "Do you have family in Boston?"

Abby was beginning to wish they hadn't stopped for a rest. "My mother."

"That's nice. You see a lot of each other?"

Most days at work.

"We often meet up on Friday nights. Dinner." That was true, after all.

"That's great. I meet up with Edward—I mean Dad—" She grinned. "Sorry, even I get mixed up sometimes, particularly after a long working day. It's complicated working with a parent!"

Tell me about it, Abby thought. She almost acknowledged how hard it was but managed to stop herself in time.

"You see each other a lot, I guess."

"Yes, but we're a bit more spontaneous than you and your mother. It's easier to be spontaneous when you live next door."

Her mother was the least spontaneous person she knew, but Abby was keen to move away from that topic of conversation.

"You did a lot to the house when you moved in?"

"I lived in it for six months without changing a thing because I felt guilty about erasing my grandmother from a place she'd lived all her life. But then I pulled myself together and gutted it. New kitchen. New bathroom. French doors onto the garden."

"You did it yourself?"

"Mostly, although people dropped by to help me. And I don't touch electrics, so Jay did that for me. He lives in the village. Everyone uses him. And there's my dad of course. He can do everything. I try to be an adult and handle things that go wrong in the house, but I admit that sometimes I cave in and call him."

Abby relaxed a little. This topic of conversation was much easier to navigate. "He seems like a capable man."

"He's great. How about you? Is your dad in your life?"

"He died before I was born." She hadn't intended to reveal anything personal, but she couldn't see a way not to answer that question. And part of her wanted to, particularly knowing that Evie had also never known her mother. They'd both been raised by one parent. They had that in common.

Evie pulled a face. "Sorry to hear that. Your mother didn't marry again?"

"No." Talking about her father had felt natural, but talking about her mother? That was different. Heat prickled her skin. Her mother wasn't some third party, removed from all this. She was part of it. Any moment now Evie would be asking what job her mother did and Abby would have failed in her task less than forty-eight hours into the job. Hoping to head off those questions, she stood up and stretched. "What next? I'm pretty hungry."

"Me, too." Evie crammed the hat back on her head. "Let's go back. We can eat in the garden."

They ran back towards the village, Abby relieved at having managed to cut the conversation off and rehearsing future conversation topics in her head. She'd talk about the house, about the garden. She'd ask questions about the village, about the fishermen, about shipwrecks. Maybe she'd ask a question or two about Tristan.

Anything, as long as they kept away from the personal. Her family. Her history.

It would be fine.

Her optimism lasted as long as it took Evie to put the key into the door of her pretty cottage.

"So you grew up without a dad and I grew up without a mum. That sort of makes us tragedy sisters, doesn't it? Although I had my grandmother too, and obviously everyone in the village." She stepped into the house and dropped her keys onto the little table by the front door. "How about you? Did you have extended family? How did your mother manage? Come through to the kitchen and I'll make us both a drink."

"No extended family. It was just the two of us."

"No grandparents?"

"My grandfather walked out when my mother was eleven, and my grandmother died when my mother was eighteen. It's not something my mother ever talks about much." Abby followed Evie through the house, noting the pretty yellow walls and the splashes of blue in the form of quirky pots and cushions. There were photos of sea-birds and boats, and the evening light flooded through the windows and bounced off the white painted floor. Her gaze rested on a photo on a bookcase, a man and a woman laughing together.

Evie followed her gaze. "That's my mum."

"You look like her."

"So everyone tells me. I like to keep photos of her around. It makes me feel as if she's with me. Are you the same?"

"I—er—no. It was a difficult time. My mother preferred to put it behind her." That, at least, was the truth.

"Sounds as if your mum had a tough time. What does she do?"

Abby's mouth was dry. "She's a businesswoman. She has her own business."

"Successful?"

"Yes."

"Well, good for her. You must be proud. And she must be proud of you."

Fortunately, that was a statement, not a question, so Abby didn't have to answer but the words disturbed something inside her.

She watched as Evie opened the fridge. Was her mother proud? There was no evidence to suggest it.

"It's weird," Evie said, "because although I didn't know my mother, I feel as if I do. My dad talks about her all the time, and so do other people. I've sort of formed a picture of her over the years. I expect you're the same. You build your own impression of someone."

Abby managed to nod, signifying that she knew what Evie meant.

In fact she had no idea what Evie meant.

She had no impression of her father. He was a ghost. Nothing more than a name.

Evie pulled out a jug of lemonade. "I bought too many lemons by accident so I made lemonade. That sounds like one of those annoying sayings, doesn't it? Don't be impressed. Usually when I have too many lemons I don't make lemonade—I forget about them and they go mouldy in the fruit bowl."

She put ice into two tall glasses and topped them up with the cold lemonade. She handed a glass to Abby.

"Are you hungry? We can eat in the garden. It's such a warm evening it's a shame to be indoors." She drank the lemonade and put the glass down. "I have fresh mackerel which I picked up this morning, and salad. Is that okay?"

"It sounds more than okay." Abby was relieved that the conversation had moved on from the personal. "What can I do?"

"You could mix up a salad while I fry the fish. It came straight off the boat so it won't take much cooking." She pulled the fish from the fridge, picked up a sharp knife and filleted it like a pro. Then she seasoned it with sea salt and black pepper.

"Where did you learn to do that?" Abby poked around in the fridge for salad ingredients.

"My dad. We used to go mackerel fishing when I was little. Then we'd cook whatever we caught." She heated oil in a heavy-based pan. "When the fish is this fresh you don't have to do much with it. Sometimes we used to barbecue it on the beach. Can you make a lemon dressing? It will go perfectly with this, and it will also use up the last of the lemons which will make me feel virtuous and stop me hearing my grandmother's voice scolding me. She hated waste."

Talk of family peppered Evie's conversation. Even gone, they were still part of her life. And she seemed to know everything about them. All Abby knew about her grandmother was that she'd been hit by a car when she was thirty-eight and the resulting injuries had left her in need of almost constant care. Abby's grandfather had walked out, leaving responsibility for that care on the shoulders of eleven-year-old Alexandra.

Pulling herself back to the present, she picked up her phone and searched for a recipe for lemon dressing.

The fish sizzled in the pan and after a couple of minutes Evie flipped it over.

While it finished cooking, she grabbed a couple of large plates. They were a summery shade of blue with a border of sea-birds.

"Those are pretty." Abby took them from her. "Unusual."

"I bought them from Harbour Pottery last summer. A birthday present to myself. Do you remember Mia? We ran past her on the other side of the harbour. She was carrying a bucket and spade and gripping the hand of a sandy, cross toddler."

"I think so." They'd met so many people it was hard to remember each individual. "Short dark hair?"

"That's the one." Evie dressed the salad, served it onto the plates and added the fresh mackerel. "She's a local artist. She paints, too. Mostly seascapes. I have one in my bedroom. But she is best known for her range of gorgeous ocean-themed kitchenware. I thought it was perfect for my cottage. She sells a ton to tourists and I often wonder how it looks when they get it home to a city. Is there a place for sea-birds in Shoreditch? I have no idea. Bread? It's fresh from the bakery." Without waiting for Abby's response she cut a couple of thick chunks and added a wedge of butter. "I'm telling myself we ran off the calories earlier."

Despite a busy day Evie seemed to have boundless energy. She bounced from one task to the next, chatting the whole time. What did Abby think about this? About that?

Abby found her enthusiasm infectious. "You seem more upbeat than you did earlier."

"Yes." She handed Abby a plate. "That's down to you."

"Me?"

"Yes, talking everything through made me feel better. It gave me some clarity. You're a good listener, so thanks for that."

They settled themselves in Evie's pretty garden and Abby tasted the fish.

Evie watched her expectantly. "It's good, isn't it?"

"It's delicious."

"But you have seafood in Boston?"

"Yes. We have excellent seafood."

"But you don't spend a lot of time there because you're always travelling and working in new places? Did you know that The Alexandra, Cornwall is the oldest hotel in the group?" Evie spread butter thickly on her bread, not waiting for an answer to her first question before she asked a second.

"I—yes, I did know that."

"A staff perk is to get a discount on other hotels in the group. I was thinking of having a few days in Scotland at some point but now I'm wondering if that's sad and unadventurous. Which hotel have you liked best out of all the ones in the group? The one in Cape Cod where you worked last—is that good?"

"It's beautiful. Sandy beaches, dunes and whale watching."

"And what was the best thing you ate when you were there?"

"Probably fried clams." Abby put her fork down and admired the garden. "Are you a keen gardener?"

"No. I'm a terrible gardener, but it was my grandmother's pride and joy so I feel compelled to try and keep things alive. Dad helps me sometimes. A coastal garden isn't easy, particularly here on the north coast. Plants have to be able to withstand howling Atlantic winds. So do the locals. We're hardy specimens." Evie's dimples showed as she smiled. "So it's mostly perennials—are you impressed that I know what those are? Sage, rosemary and lavender." She waved a hand vaguely at the tumbling garden. "That one by the wall is Rosa Rugosa—my grandmother used to make rose hip syrup. Do you have a garden?"

"No. I live in an apartment, but I can see Boston harbour and the skyline."

"Sounds amazing. I could come and stay with you, and you could show me around. That would be fun. A girls' weekend."

"Yes." For a moment she allowed herself to imagine that scenario. Showing Evie Boston. She'd take her on a whale watching cruise. Walk the Freedom Trail, take her to the MFA. Perhaps they could do a day trip to Martha's Vineyard. It *would* be fun. Two friends, exploring each other's hometowns.

But it was never going to happen. The moment Evie found out that Abby hadn't been honest with her, that would be it.

Anticipating that moment killed the rest of her appetite and she put her fork down. "Has your dad always worked in hotels? What did he do before he started working at The Alexandra?"

"He trained as a history teacher. Are you eating your bread? Because if you're not, I'll eat it. I'm so hungry I could eat a camel." Evie's hand hovered and when Abby nodded she scooped it up. "Anyway, he didn't love teaching. He said it was more about discipline and psychology. No one seemed that interested in listening or learning. Then I came along. My mother died right after I was born—it must have been horrible for Dad. I try not to think about how hard it must have been because it chokes me up. You're probably the same."

"I—"

"But you keep going, don't you? When life knocks you to the ground, you get up and keep going. And Dad kept going. Of course everyone in the village helped. The interfering can be annoying, but it can also be a lifesaver and on that occasion, it was a lifesaver. Do you want a slice of lemon tart? It's left over from yesterday. We can share it."

Abby raised her hand and shook her head. She had a growing respect for Evie's appetite. "Thanks, but I couldn't eat another thing. You were telling me how your dad started working at the hotel."

"Oh yes. The school he was teaching at was almost an hour away along roads that were busy in tourist season. He needed to be closer to home, so when he saw that the hotel was recruiting a concierge, he decided to apply. They wanted someone who knew the local area well, but also knew local history and legend. There's lots of that around here. Magicians, witches, dragons—you name it. No one knows more about that than Dad, and he thought it would be nice to chat to people who were interested. He had an interview, and he got the job. That was thirty years ago and he's still going strong. Loves his job."

Thirty years? No, that couldn't be right.

Her mother would have been at the hotel still, and she hadn't mentioned ever meeting any of the current staff.

She cast her mind back to Edward's file. It had said twenty-eight years, she was sure of it. He'd arrived after her mother had moved to Boston. Evie must have that wrong.

She wanted to ask a few more questions but she couldn't find a way to do that without arousing suspicion, so she simply listened as Evie talked, enjoying the scent of the garden and watching as the sun streaked the sky with orange and shades of pink.

Evie made coffee and put a slice of lemon tart in the middle of the table. "Two forks. In case I can tempt you. Can I ask you something? But first you have to promise not to mention it to anyone at work. At least, for now. It isn't easy to keep secrets around here."

"Of course." She was already keeping so many secrets that one more was hardly going to make a difference.

Evie dug her fork into the lemon tart. "So I'm having dinner with Luca tomorrow." Something about her ultra-casual tone caught Abby's attention.

"Luca?"

"Yes, Luca. Our Luca. At first I said no because to be honest I'm a bit off dating after my last experience, but then he fed me this sandwich and I thought, why not?"

"A sandwich? I don't understand why that would change your mind."

"That's because you haven't tasted this particular sandwich. Chicken. The flavours were incredible—a touch of lemon made it sharp, but it was also creamy and smooth with just enough bite."

"A man made you a sandwich and now you want to go on a date?"

Evie sighed. "There was the cannoli too, but yes, it started with the sandwich. It was his grandmother's recipe. Turns out I may have a thing for hot guys who love their grandmothers." She fiddled with the slender bracelet on her wrist. "Okay, it's more than that. He made me lunch. He noticed I hadn't eaten, and he wanted me to eat. Nobody notices things like that."

This wasn't casual to her at all, Abby thought. It was a big deal.

"That was thoughtful of him."

"Yes. Deliciously so." The bracelet was still under attack. "I confess I'm nervous."

Abby smiled. "I'm getting that. Presumably that's because you really like him?"

"Yes. I haven't gone on a date in a while. I almost wish I'd said no. The thought of it is giving me butterflies. I have no idea what to wear. Casual? A bit more dressy?"

Abby waited. "Are you asking me?"

"Yes. All advice gratefully received." Evie picked up her fork and dug it into her slice of tart. "I don't exactly know if this is a date *as such*, although it's just the two of us and he picked a place half an hour away in the hope we might have more privacy—" She put her fork down. "I don't want to overdress and I don't want to underdress. Clothes send a message, don't they? So what do you think?"

"I don't think I'm an expert on clothes, at least not for dating."

Evie tilted her head. "What did you wear on the last date you went on?"

Todd Tremain, Abby thought. A lawyer who worked for one of the big Boston firms.

"I wore a silk dress, but it wouldn't have mattered what I was wearing because he spent most of dinner checking out his own reflection in the mirror behind me. Evidently, he preferred his own appearance to mine."

Evie choked with laughter. "So it went well then."

Abby laughed too, mostly because Evie's laughter was infectious. "It was a disaster." And it felt really good to tell someone and laugh about it. At the time she'd felt annoyed and a little insecure.

"He doesn't sound like a man who loved his grandmother."

"I doubt he would even have noticed his grandmother if she'd walked into the room. He was too busy looking at himself."

"Sounds as if you had a lucky escape. The sex would have been terrible. He would have been wondering how he looked all the time. Do you want any of this tart?" Evie hovered her fork over the last piece. "Because if you don't speak now, I'm going to finish it."

"You go ahead."

Evie speared the last piece. "How did you meet him, Mr I'm-in-love-with-my-own-reflection?"

"He was the colleague of a friend of mine who thought we'd be perfect for each other."

"You're kidding." Evie shook her head. "She doesn't know you that well, then."

"No," Abby said slowly. "I don't think she does."

She'd never even thought about it before, but now she was thinking about it.

When did she ever sit with a friend and talk like this? Laugh like this?

Having demolished the tart, Evie picked up her coffee. "As a matter of interest, what exactly did she think would bond you?"

"She said we were both focused on work so neither of us would be annoyed if the other was never around."

"Wow." Evie put her cup down. "That's a low bar for a relationship. Also sad. I assume your friend is single."

"In fact, she is."

"Okay, forget that particular date. What did you wear on the last date where you had fun?"

"I went to the opera with a guy who owned a tech startup—Boston is full of them—and he spent the whole night doing something on his phone and being hissed at by the people around us."

"I said the last date where you had fun."

"I did have fun. The opera was great, and I ended up going for a late drink with the guy sitting to my left."

"Oh, respect!" Evie studied her. "And what did tech guy have to say about that?"

"Nothing at all. I don't think he noticed I'd gone. He was too busy trying to take over the universe. But I think I've proved that I'm not the person to ask for recommendations on clothing that might enhance your sex life. I can't remember what I was wearing but I think it's safe to say it didn't capture his attention."

"Mm. Maybe I should be the one giving you tips. I thought my dating history was sad, but yours is pitiful."

"You're right." She wanted to ask Evie why her dating history was sad but wasn't sure that would be appropriate. She didn't have conversations like this with people. It was whole new territory. Presumably if Evie wanted to talk about it, she'd talk. She didn't seem to be holding back on other things.

Evie sat back in her chair. "Okay, we're going to spice up your love life while you're here, but first we're going to focus on me because my situation is the more urgent. I have a blue linen dress that's pretty. Cute and summery. I was thinking of wearing that. Creases like mad of course, so option one is to hang it in the back of the car and drive naked. Change in the car park."

Abby laughed. "What's option two?"

"You could drive me, and I could lie flat on the back seat. That would have the added advantage of making sure no locals see me. It would be like driving a getaway car. Also, if it goes badly and I literally want to get away, you'd be there with the engine running. Sounds exciting, don't you think?"

"It sounds unsafe and not eco-friendly. Is it that important that no one sees you?"

"Yes." Evie's smile dimmed. "That's been a problem for me in the past. I'll tell you about it sometime, but not now or I'll talk myself out of going."

"Right." Abby moved the subject along. "But what does a getaway driver normally do while they're killing time and you're deciding if you want to get away or not?"

"You act as a lookout and message me if someone we know arrives in the car park."

"The problem with that is that I know very few people and you know everyone."

"Yes. That's my problem, right there." Evie shrugged. "I'm

kidding, obviously. I'll arrive creased. Or try and sit like a plank in the driver's seat. The creases are always worse when you bend in the middle."

"Which road will you be taking? Just so I can make sure I'm nowhere near your route."

Evie stood up. "Come up to my bedroom and I can show you a few more options."

"I—now?"

"Yes, we can pull out everything I own and you can say yes or no. I don't have that many options, so it won't take long."

"What do you want this outfit to achieve?"

"You mean do I want it to lead to a night of hot sex?" Evie gathered up the plates and pondered. "Probably not. It's a bit soon. It's not only about physical chemistry, is it? I want to know if we have other things in common."

"Given your appetite and his cooking skills I'd say you were a perfect match."

"Tris said the same thing."

"You two are close."

"Yes, we are, but as friends. Nothing more. He's a sweetheart when you get to know him. I can see from your face you don't believe me. But he's had a lot to adjust to lately. He was a mountain guide, you know. Serious stuff in the Himalayas and the Alps. Led a pretty nomadic lifestyle so being trapped in one place, even a place like this, is a struggle for him. That's why I give him a free pass when he's grumpy. He came home to support family. That tells you everything you need to know about him in my book." She walked back to the house. "How about a glass of wine? We can take it upstairs while we're going through the contents of my wardrobe."

"Sure. Why not. A small one."

Abby scooped up the rest of the plates and followed Evie back into the house.

She should have said no, of course. She should have thanked her for inviting her on the run, and for the food, and then made a rapid exit before Evie could spill any more intimacies and secrets. But Abby didn't want to. She was enjoying herself too much. It felt good to make a friend, to chat and joke about normal things, to laugh with someone about the terrible dates she'd had.

Just this one evening, she promised herself, and then she'd find a way to put some distance.

Her phone pinged and she checked it quickly while Evie was raiding the fridge for wine.

It was an email from her mother.

Her finger hovered, ready to open it.

"You take the wine, I'll bring the glasses." Evie held the bottle out to her and Abby took it and shut her phone off.

She'd answer the email later.

Right now she had to help Evie choose a dress.

10

★★★★★

Evie

"This place has a great view." Evie sat down at the table overlooking the sea and smoothed her dress. She was jumpy and on edge and really wishing she'd said no when he'd invited her to dinner. Better to imagine the romance they could have had than actually have one and live through another painful and awkward ending. Not only that, but this time they'd have to carry on working together.

Still, it had been a while since she'd given the village entertainment, so at least someone would benefit.

She was going to enjoy herself and not spend the evening glancing around her to check she didn't know anyone else in the restaurant. She was going to stop thinking about what had happened the last time she'd dated someone.

Luca had arrived moments before her, so she hadn't had time to check her reflection in the mirror, smooth her hair or reapply her lipstick. Abby had talked her out of the linen dress and had also talked her out of wearing something understated so that she was less likely to be noticed. What had she said? *You're dating a hot guy so you should look hot.* Which was why Evie was now sitting here in her hot-pink dress, wearing a matching hot-pink lipstick.

Thanks, Abby.

Wishing she'd had something beige and nondescript in her wardrobe, she cast a single look over his shoulder.

"Is the coast clear?" Luca was watching her with laughter in his eyes and she felt bad.

He had the kind of face most women would happily gaze at all day.

And she was looking over his shoulder.

"Sorry. It's a reflex. I can't help it. If I suddenly dive under the table don't take it personally."

"You don't think that would draw attention?"

"I don't know, and if I'm under the table I won't be able to see it." The glass doors were open and she could smell the sea. "This place is brilliant. Have you been here before?"

"It's my first time. You?"

"My first time, too. It's been a while since I've been on a date. Not that I'm saying this is a date," she said hastily, "obviously I'm here because I need your grandmother's recipe for chicken. And you're probably here because I'm the only single woman under the age of thirty-five in the village."

"That's not why I'm here. And my grandmother's recipe for chicken is a closely guarded secret." His gaze lingered on hers for a moment and then he glanced at the menu. "Shall we go for their set menu?"

"You mean so you can sample as many dishes as possible and work out which ones you're going to modify and use at The Alexandra? Go for it. I'm up for the challenge."

They ordered and Evie forced herself to relax and keep her eyes on him and not on the door of the restaurant. It was such a long time since she'd been on a date she'd forgotten how to do small talk. Was she supposed to flirt? Entertain him with her witty conversation?

She didn't usually find herself short of words, but it had been a while since she'd been on her own with a man as attractive as Luca. After Martin she'd felt too raw and vulnerable to even consider dating again. She'd focused on herself, throwing herself into her hobbies, her work, her friendships. In the five years since that relationship had crashed and burned, no one had given her a reason to rethink that approach. Until now.

"Do you miss London?"

"What a question to ask when we're sitting in front of a view like this." He glanced at the ocean, lapping at the sand below the restaurant. "No, I don't miss it. It was the right thing to do at the time, and great experience, but it was never my long-term goal. I wanted more control. I wanted to create my own menus, have a chance to implement my own ideas. Experiment. And I want to attract real foodies."

"You couldn't do that in London?"

"To an extent, but it's hard to stand out in London and often the people who eat there aren't even noticing the food. They choose a place because they read a review online, or a celebrity has been spotted there and suddenly it's the place to be seen, and then they pick at their food and send most of it back to the kitchen. You could argue that as long as they've paid, it doesn't matter. But it matters to me."

"Of course it matters. When you care passionately about something, it matters. I can't imagine anyone sending back food you've made. Clearly they need major help. I'm more likely to be thrown out for licking my plate clean."

He laughed. "Have you ever thought of being a food critic? *I licked the plate clean* is probably the dream review for most chefs."

"It's a bit basic though, isn't it?" She felt herself start to relax. "Aren't you supposed to rabbit on about a fusion of flavours and textures?"

"Probably. But in the end the only thing that matters is that the diner leaves feeling they've eaten the best meal of their life. I want them to be so focused on the food they don't notice the celebrity at the next table."

The way he was smiling at her made her insides flutter.

"The Alexandra is lucky to have you."

"Maybe. Time will tell." He shrugged. "They're certainly lucky to have you."

"Me? I'm not sure about that." His comment flustered her. "I'm different from Gerald."

"I never met Gerald, but unless he has blond hair and looks good in hot pink, I can imagine you *are* different."

She laughed. "He's late fifties and he doesn't have much hair at all. But I meant in management style. And experience. I don't have a lot of experience, but I do have tons of enthusiasm. I'm not sure if that counts for much."

"It counts for a lot." He put his glass down. "It's an appealing trait."

"It is? Usually it annoys people. Mandy says it's like having an out-of-control labrador puppy in the room. And the problem is that I have ideas, but experienced people kill them all the time. *We tried that back in 1998 and it didn't work*. Or, more often, *Gerald always did it this way*." She hadn't intended to confide, but he seemed to understand in the same way that Abby did. He saw the bigger picture. He saw *her*.

"That must be frustrating."

"Occasionally it is."

"And yet still you smile."

"On the outside, yes. Sometimes on the inside I'm screaming."

"That's why I made you lunch. Good food is a way of calming inside screaming."

How did he know her so well? "Am I that easy to read?"

"No. But I've been paying attention."

She swallowed. "You do that with people?"

"Not generally."

But he did it with her. He'd paid attention to her.

She felt warm inside and the way he was looking at her took her breath away. "The hotel has definitely improved since you turned up."

"Ah, the hotel." He smiled, as if he'd actually forgotten about the hotel. "Do you see yourself staying long-term? What do you want?"

She wanted the same thing he wanted. More control. The opportunity to implement her own ideas. The chance to experiment. When she'd been asked to step up and be acting general manager she'd thought maybe this was her chance, but it hadn't turned out the way she'd planned.

She was little more than a caretaker.

But that was far too much information to share with someone who was essentially a colleague.

"I want to be able to make a difference. The way you feel about your restaurant is the way I feel about the hotel," she said. "I want guests to leave feeling as if it was the best stay they've ever had anywhere. If we get a bad review, I'm heartbroken. I spend hours figuring out what we could have done differently for that person. It takes me weeks to recover from it."

"Because your feelings are hurt?"

"What? No! Because someone didn't have a great holiday. Holidays are precious, aren't they? I don't want people feeling disappointed when they leave. If that happens then I basically haven't done my job well, and I very much want to. This place means a lot to me."

"You never thought about moving away?"

Not until recently.

She thought about the email that had been waiting for her in her inbox that morning.

She'd be invited for an interview the following week. And it would be virtual, so she wouldn't have to make up excuses for disappearing for a day.

She'd told no one, of course. There seemed no point at this stage. She probably wouldn't get the job. Her experience was limited to this one hotel which she knew might put her at a disadvantage. She was tempted to discuss it with Luca. He'd worked in a London hotel. It would have been useful to talk through his experience and see what she could learn.

But it was unfair to put him in that position. The moment any of the staff got wind of the fact she was considering leaving, things would be awkward.

The only person she might be able to tell would be Abby. Not because she wasn't a permanent member of the team and therefore telling her didn't have the same implications, but because she always gave thoughtful, measured answers to problems. She'd be telling her as a friend, not a colleague.

Maybe she'd do that. Or maybe she'd wait to see what happened after the first interview.

And in the meantime, Luca was waiting for an answer.

"The Alexandra feels like home to me." It was true. It did feel like home. At certain points in her life she'd spent more time in the hotel than her actual home. But people left home, didn't they? They didn't stay forever.

How would she feel about leaving this place?

She gazed out across the ocean. She'd lived right beside it all her life. She couldn't imagine being immersed in city life, her view all steel and glass. But the hotel she'd applied to was perched on the edge of one of London's most famous parks, so she'd have plenty of green space.

Their food arrived, course after delicious course, and they ate their way through a delicate crab tart, monkfish, and a pumpkin and sage ravioli.

Luca dissected everything, examined it carefully, made a few comments about it needing more of something and less of something else.

She was fascinated. "Do you ever just eat and not think about how it was made?"

"No." He frowned down at the food on his plate. "There is an ingredient in this I can't quite figure out. Star anise, maybe. No." He shook his head and took another mouthful.

"It tastes like—" She broke off as two women walked into the restaurant. Her heart pounded as she saw the blonde hair. "Oh no—is that? No, it's not." She breathed out. "Sorry. For a moment I thought it was Kristina from Guest Services."

He put his fork down. "And would that really matter?"

"No." She looked at him. "Yes. Maybe. A little." It would matter a lot. Particularly if it turned out she liked him as much as she thought she probably did.

He reached across the table and took her hand, his fingers closing over hers. "Why do you worry so much about other people? Are you ashamed to be seen with me?"

He was holding her hand. On top of the table. Where anyone and everyone could see.

The seductive stroke of his finger sent electric currents under her skin.

"Ashamed? No! Of course not. You're smoking hot, you have to know that, I mean part of me wants to draw attention just to make sure everyone has seen who I'm on a date with because it's good for my credibility—" She saw amusement in his eyes and stopped talking. "And now I've gone too far the other way. It's not you, Luca. It's me. For me, dating hasn't been a particularly happy experience. It's complicated, that's all."

"We are two people having dinner. How is that complicated?"

His eyes were like rich dark chocolate and the way he was looking at her made it hard to concentrate.

"Right now, it's not. And maybe this is just dinner, and we'll enjoy a nice evening and that will be it. Or maybe we'll decide we had a good time and we're going to do it again. Maybe we'll even manage to find some quiet restaurants, sneak out of a few windows before dawn and keep it to ourselves. But eventually people will find out and soon it stops being our relationship and becomes everyone's relationship. And that changes everything."

"Why?" He looked puzzled. "It would still be our relationship."

"It wouldn't feel that way. People would be telling you every single thing about me."

"And that's a bad thing?"

"If I was trying to impress you, then yes. I'd be working hard to show you only the good things about me, and they'd give you examples of all the times I've messed up. You'd laugh, because there are plenty of examples. They'd take that as encouragement. Next, they'd be showing you my baby photos—"

"Okay, now I'm interested. Who exactly has these baby photos and how much do I have to pay to see them?"

He had such a great smile. Looking at him made her want to smile too and she realised this was the first time she'd been able to laugh about it for a long time.

Martin hadn't found it funny at all, and because he'd been stressed about it, she'd been stressed.

"It doesn't seem like much, but when you've got the whole village watching you, and commenting on your every move, it feels like a lot of pressure. And when it goes wrong, it can feel awkward. I get it." And it wasn't only dating, of course. It applied to every area of her life. If she failed at work she'd be letting people down, and these were people she'd known for most of her life.

The pressure felt crushing.

His hand was still on hers. "Who was this man who found it awkward?"

It wasn't something she talked about. Since it happened, she'd made a point of being her usual smiley self and not sharing the depth of her pain.

But she hadn't dated anyone since.

"Martin. We were in the same year at school, so I'd known him for ages before we got together. Which gave them twice as much to gossip about, of course. I reminded them once that they didn't need to tell me what age he was when his voice broke because I was at school with him so I already knew, but they did it anyway. It drove him insane. He found it tougher than I did, probably because he wasn't born here. His parents moved here when he was a teenager. It wasn't a great time," she admitted. "And if dating under a microscope is hard, breaking up is even harder. Which is why I prefer to keep things under the radar so that when it all blows up I don't have everyone asking me if I'm okay and leaving cakes on my doorstep."

"Cakes?" He raised an eyebrow. "Were they good cakes?"

She laughed. "Delicious. Okay, maybe I don't mind the cake part. Especially if it's chocolate. But I don't like the scrutiny. It makes me feel like a failure. Also, these people genuinely love me so when I'm upset, they worry and the fact that they're worrying puts more pressure on me to be okay. It's tiring. Sometimes when life is crappy all you want is to lie in bed with a box of chocolates and not have half the village hammering on your front door to check you're not contemplating jumping out of the window."

Luca nodded. "Tell me about him."

"Not much to tell." She pulled her hand away. Part of her was tempted to shut down the conversation, but another part thought she might as well be straight with him so that he could walk away now. "We'd known each other since school. We were friends. I'd always had a thing for him, which unfortunately people noticed because I'm not great at hiding my feelings."

He smiled. "I like that about you."

"Really? There are times when I'd like to be better at hiding my feelings. Anyway, according to everyone, we were perfect for each other. They'd been trying to set us up for ages. And eventually it happened. We dated for a year. Every time we bumped into someone in the village, it would be the same—winks, knowing smiles, *when are you two going to make it official.* Martin hated it. He wasn't used to it, of course. He hadn't grown up with it. And to be fair it isn't always easy for outsiders, and I think that was how he felt. He said it was my fault for being so embedded in the community. He told me I should keep to myself more."

"He didn't just roll his eyes and laugh it off?"

"No. He suggested moving away, but I didn't want to do that. My family is here. My whole life." And yet she was thinking of doing exactly that now. Moving away. Leaving. "He ended it. And everyone kept asking him why he'd ended it when I'm 'such a lovely girl' and he seemed to think I was behind it and that I was turning him into the bad guy and somehow trying to manipulate him into getting back together. He made a scene in the pub. He'd drunk too much of course, and it was all very upsetting. People stepped in, because that's what happens around here. He resigned from his job the next day and moved to France. No one has seen Martin since. So you see?" She looked at him and shrugged. "People have a relationship with me and then they have to blow up their lives and move away. Be warned. Stick around and you might find yourself heading for Argentina."

The waiter delivered another course and Luca waited until he'd left before speaking.

"And you really think this is why the relationship ended? Because of other people?"

For a while she'd thought that. She'd never really focused on people's meddling because she'd considered it good-natured and part of village life, but because Martin was sensitive to it, she became sensitive, too. It had changed her relationship with people. Before Martin she'd loved being part of the community. She'd seen them as her extended family and he'd tainted that. He'd made her wary.

She gazed at the tiny pieces of chicken on her plate and then at him. "He didn't like being in a place where everyone knows everyone. I was part of that."

He shook his head. "How could anyone think he was the right person for you?"

She'd thought it.

She'd enjoyed the chemistry, and being in a relationship with someone. She'd focused on what they had in common. She hadn't considered their differences. Hadn't realised they might be an obstacle. She'd had the optimism of youth and the naïve belief that love could conquer everything.

Unprepared, she'd been devastated when he'd ended it. And the fact that the whole thing had played out in public had made it much harder to deal with.

She hadn't had a relationship since.

Luca was looking at her, waiting, and she realised she hadn't answered his question.

"Why did they think Martin was the right person? Well, he was single and didn't have any obviously unfortunate habits.

There is a limited pool to fish in around here. If you're single, you get pushed together. That made him the right person. And it gave everyone a purpose for a while. They focused their attention on fixing me up with someone else." She finished her food. "That was delicious, but nowhere near as delicious as that salmon dish you make with lemongrass and fresh ginger. When you go out to restaurants don't you ever think *I could have cooked better at home*?"

"Sometimes, but not tonight." His gaze lingered on her face and she put her fork down, her heart thumping.

"What's different about tonight?"

"The company. I'm not here for the food. I'm here because I want to spend time with you." He spoke softly. "And I don't care who's watching." The look in his eyes made her feel breathless.

"Why do you want to spend time with me?"

"Where do I start?" His gaze was warm. "You're fun. I like you. I'm drawn to your energy and enthusiasm. You're an all-or-nothing person. I love the way you look in that hot-pink dress. I love the way you love food."

She swallowed. "All or nothing?"

"You love something, or you hate it. You feel things deeply. You're happy or you're sad. There is no flat middle ground. And you care about people. You're loyal. I see it all the time. The way you handle the staff. The way you are flexible when they have problems. I hear them say 'talk to Evie, and she will help.' They're lucky to have you as a boss, and they know it."

She shifted uncomfortably. "Because I'm a total pushover."

He looked at her thoughtfully. "I don't think that's it. And I like the way you see solutions, not problems. You have high standards. If something isn't right, you try and fix it."

She thought about all the things she wanted to do with the hotel. "I don't usually succeed."

"But you keep trying. You will never be satisfied with mediocre." He gave a slight shrug. "I'm the same. I want passionate people in my kitchen. People who care deeply about what they do, and who want to do it to the best of their ability whether it's making a complicated sauce or peeling a carrot. I want the food to be the best it can be. And I am clear about that with people who work with me. We have to share the same goal and be going in the same direction. And it's my job to be clear about what that direction is."

Was she clear about the direction? About her goals for the hotel?

Maybe not.

She thought again about how direct Abby had been in her dealings with Mandy. *This is what we want to achieve.*

She was far too focused on asking nicely and tiptoeing around people to avoid upsetting someone.

And she realised that she was drawn to Luca not only because he was attractive, or even because he was skilled at what he did, but because he cared deeply.

He would never be satisfied with mediocre either.

"Is that why you picked this particular restaurant? To check your food is the best in the area?"

"No. I picked this restaurant because I knew that if I booked a table somewhere locally you wouldn't come." His gaze was dark and disturbingly intense. "Would you?"

"Probably not."

He smiled. "Exactly. And now I understand why. But let me make something clear—wherever this goes, or doesn't go, the reaction of people around us will have no impact at all." He stabbed a piece of chicken with his fork and held it out to her. "Now stop worrying about everyone else and try this. It's good and I'd hate you to miss out."

She leaned forward and ate the food from his fork.

He was right. The chicken was delicious. But so was being with him.

Their conversation felt like foreplay, and she knew that this evening wasn't going to be a one-off. He would want to see her again, and she wanted that, too.

And he was right that other people's opinions shouldn't matter at all.

Martin had made her feel awful about the way their relationship had played out, as if the curiosity of everyone around them was somehow her fault. And because he'd blamed her, she'd blamed herself. And she'd blamed the close-knit community she lived in.

But she could see now that they hadn't been responsible for the end of her relationship any more than she had.

Her relationship hadn't ended because everyone in the local community had meddled and interfered. It had ended because Martin had wanted it to end. And he'd moved away because he'd felt guilty about hurting her.

Why hadn't she seen that before?

The door to the restaurant opened again but this time she didn't even glance across to see if it was anyone she knew.

Instead she leaned forward.

"Tell me about your grandmother. And then tell me, in detail, exactly what I have to do to persuade you to hand over that chicken recipe."

11

Alexandra

Abby had missed their meeting.

Alexandra tapped her fingers on her desk and checked the time again.

It was five minutes after the time they'd arranged, which in itself was enough to annoy her because she valued punctuality, but given all the other things that had happened over the past few weeks, annoyance was warring with concern.

Three weeks had passed since Abby had arrived in Cornwall and during the first few days everything had appeared normal. She'd sent daily reports, each one detailing the current situation in the hotel in a factual, logical manner.

Alexandra had filed each one carefully.

It was during the second week that things had started to change. Abby had been increasingly slow to answer emails, and she'd rearranged their regular meeting twice.

Her reports were less frequent and the last one she'd sent, a few days before, had been glowing and effusive, so much so that Alexandra had wondered whether her daughter's email might have been hacked. It didn't read like anything her daughter would have produced.

Abby was analytical. She focused on facts. Her first couple of reports had done exactly that and Alexandra had found them interesting and useful reading. But something had changed, not least her daughter's devotion to punctuality.

She was about to give up when her phone rang.

It was Abby.

She answered the call expecting to see Abby at her desk. Instead the background was blue skies with a few wispy clouds.

Her face was pink and she was smiling. "Hi, Mom. I'm sorry! I lost track of time."

Lost track of time?

She happened to know that Abby scheduled her time down to the minute, at least when she was working. She was ruthlessly organised and efficient.

But not today apparently.

"Where are you?"

"I'm on the cliff." She sounded out of breath. "I went for a run with Evie—she's gone now. I'm on my own. It's stunning here! Let me show you what I'm looking at." She reversed the camera and Alexandra saw those familiar cliffs, the sparkle of sea and a carpet of wild flowers.

Her mouth dried. She knew those cliffs. She'd once walked them in an agony of indecision, her turmoil as great as the sea that had thrashed at the rocks far beneath. It was a reminder she hadn't wanted or needed.

Shaken by the memory, she forced herself back to the present. "Evie. Evie Hamilton, the acting general manager?"

"Yes, she has been so welcoming and friendly. Everyone has. She's the daughter of Edward, the concierge. He's amazing."

Abby didn't use words like "amazing." Abby used factual terms. *He can secure a table at any restaurant in the area. He is well versed in local history. He's always punctual. He builds a rapport with the guests.* Observations that were measurable.

"It sounds as if you've successfully developed relationships."

"We've been spending time together. I've written a detailed update. I'll email it to you when I get home. Evie has plenty of great ideas."

"Does she have what it takes to run the hotel successfully? Because current numbers would suggest not."

"The short answer is yes, definitely, but it's complicated. I think there are decisions to be made. I've put more in the report. It doesn't help that her position is temporary. I think that's something we need to look at urgently."

"But you feel the place is viable."

"Yes. More than that. I think it has the potential to be one of the most important hotels in the group. Mandy said yesterday that—"

"Mandy?"

"She's the head housekeeper. She has been here a long time. We were turning over a room together and she was telling me that she remembers a time when the hotel had close to a hundred percent occupancy over the summer months. Extraordinary. I think we can achieve that again. Luca is doing excellent things with the restaurant. If they're not drawn in by the views and the charm of the village, the food should do it. We have to persuade people that dining in the restaurant is more pleasurable if you treat yourself to a night in the hotel afterwards. It was Evie's idea. I think it's a good one." She was breathless, almost babbling as ideas tumbled out of her.

Alexandra was struggling to keep up. "Luca is the new chef?"

"Not so new. He's been here for a few months now and he's particularly good at harnessing commercial opportunities.

Afternoon tea is almost a religion here. He's embracing the potential of that and also revitalising the evening menu in the restaurant. It's innovative, and he's keeping the focus on locally sourced produce. I think we should extend that ethos throughout the hotel. Sylvie, who deals with all the procurement, was telling me about a local company that make organic soaps and shampoos—we're going to source samples and if they're good I think we should consider offering them to guests."

"We use the same brand across the whole hotel group."

"But maybe we should rethink that. As Evie said, guests come here to experience all that Cornwall has to offer. We should be giving them that."

Evie, Edward, Mandy, Donna, Sylvie, Kristina, Luca—Abby dropped names into conversation as if they were old friends. Alexandra had rarely seen her daughter so energised. And rarely heard her talk about individuals with such passion.

Clearly she'd started to form relationships with them.

Alexandra hoped that wasn't going to cause her a problem.

"Draw up a plan and send me your recommendations."

"I intend to, although I still have weeks to go of course. It would help if I knew exactly what you're looking for. What your long-term intentions are."

Alexandra ignored that question. "These people that you describe in such detail—do they know who you are?"

Abby's smile faded. "No, not yet. And I'm still not comfortable with that. We've become friends, and—well, I need to find a way to tell them. Obviously that part won't be easy, particularly as I've almost been here for a month."

"Don't do it yet." She didn't want to complicate things. And she knew, without a doubt, that if they knew who Abby was, it would complicate things.

"But—"

"It's important to me that you stay under-cover."

"All right." Abby said it grudgingly. "I have a day off tomorrow. I thought I might go and see the house where you grew up."

Alexandra kept her expression neutral. "I doubt it even still exists. There has been a lot of development around that area. It was a long time ago."

"Talking of a long time ago—I wanted to ask you something. Is it possible that you were at the hotel at the same time as Edward, the concierge? Evie mentioned that he'd worked there for thirty years, but I don't think that's right. Our records show twenty-eight. But I'm wondering if they're wrong."

An email pinged into her inbox. A name she didn't want to see.

A name that made her hands shake.

It was a good thing she was sitting down because she knew without testing them that her knees felt like water.

"Mom?"

She stared at the email without opening it. She was a grown woman. It was ridiculous that she should react like this. She could handle it. She *would* handle it.

Panic ripped through her, together with emotions that she'd not felt in a long time. It was like being back there again and she was feeling all the same things.

Her heart was hammering. Her skin felt clammy. Was it her heart? It felt like something terrible was happening.

"Mom?"

Abby's voice cut through the clouds in her head and somehow she managed to answer.

"I have a work issue I need to deal with urgently. I didn't expect this meeting to overrun."

"It's my fault, I know, for keeping you waiting. Again, I apologise. But before you go do you remember—"

"I'll speak to you next week. Keep sending those reports."

"But—"

Alexandra cut the connection and closed her eyes. The pain in her chest grew worse. Breathe. Breathe. Everything was fine. It wasn't her heart, at least not in a physical sense. It was panic. And she was mortified that her mind and body could betray her like this.

She'd really hoped this wouldn't happen. She'd told herself that it wouldn't. Forced herself to think positive thoughts. She'd constructed a good life for herself, one she controlled.

But she'd forgotten that life had a nasty habit of waiting until everything seemed calm and well before punching you in the face.

She opened her eyes and stared at the email again.

Her finger hovered and then she deleted it, the way she'd deleted all the others.

She hoped it would be enough.

12

★★★★★

Abby

Abby took a shower, pulled on a clean linen shirt and a pair of jeans, and slammed the door to her room behind her.

Her mother had hung up on her. She'd actually hung up on her. Who did that?

Her insides were churned up, her emotions boiling. She'd tried breathing. Mindfulness. A few bars of Mozart on her headphones. So far nothing had worked. She had no idea how to calm herself, so she'd settled for an evening walk around the village.

On her way out she heard laughter and conversation coming from the bar and paused, torn between the lure of cobbled streets and sea air and a crisp, cold glass of wine.

It wasn't even a contest. She'd never before used alcohol as a comfort or a crutch, but right now wine felt more appealing than a walk.

She headed back to the bar.

The outdoor garden with its tables overlooking the harbour was packed with people and inside was equally busy and no less full of charm. With its low beam ceiling and flagstone floor, the bar appeared to have changed little over the centuries, but although the bones of the place were cemented in tradition, there were stylish, modern touches. The whitewashed walls in this part of the bar were covered in framed prints—antique maps of Cornwall, black-and-white photos of fishing boats, nautical charts. The chalkboard above the bar listed all the different local ales and craft beers, along with cider and wine.

There was something comforting about gathering in a place that people had been drinking in for centuries.

Tristan was serving, which almost made her spin around and take the evening walk option instead, but she decided she wanted the wine more than she wanted to avoid him. And it wasn't as if he'd been rude to her over the past few weeks. More wary and a little detached, as if he still didn't quite trust her. And his concerns were justified, she thought grimly, given that she wasn't exactly who she was pretending to be. Which made him a man of good judgement.

If she was lucky, it would be Matt with his easy smile and affable nature who served her.

She wasn't lucky.

Tristan was laughing with a couple of locals at the far end of the bar but made his excuses when he caught sight of her.

"What can I get you?" He looked at her with those sharp blue eyes that always saw more than she wanted to reveal.

Before she could answer a young woman sprinted up to the bar. "Hey, Tris! I was hoping you'd be here tonight. I got back a few hours ago so I wanted to say hi!"

He dragged his gaze from Abby and smiled.

"Vicky." He leaned forward and kissed her on both cheeks,

which was presumably what she'd wanted given that she was all but sprawled across the bar. "You back for the summer?"

"Yep. I'm here for the next month. So if you want to get together and catch up, or something—" her cheeks dimpled and her eyes were all invitation in case he was in any doubt what the "or something" might be "—give me a call. My number hasn't changed."

"I'll remember that."

She hovered, hopeful. "Are you due a break? Because we could—"

"We're short-staffed tonight, Vick. No break. But we'll catch up at some point, I'm sure. Give my best to your dad."

"I will." Her smile dimmed a little, then she straightened her shoulders and gave Tristan a final wistful look before weaving her way through the crowd to the door.

"You could have taken a break, boss." Matt reached for a bottle of whisky and winked at Tristan. "Made a girl's dreams come true."

"Don't you have customers down the other end of the bar?"

"Serving them right now and thankfully for us, they have fat wallets."

"Then go and relieve them of the weight of all that money before they decide to take it elsewhere." He turned back to Abby. "Sorry about that."

"No problem. White wine, please."

Tristan studied her face. "Do you want to be more specific?"

"No. You choose."

"We have a delicious local white. Crisp and delicate. Light citrus notes with hints of honey . . ." His voice trailed off and his gaze held hers. "I thought you were the type who might care about that, but judging from your expression I got that wrong."

"It would be great if you could stop judging me, just for this evening. In fact it would be good if people could stop judging me, full stop." She wasn't in the mood for it, not after that phone call with her mother.

She was impossible to talk to. Impossible.

She thought about the easy relationship Evie had with her dad. Even Tristan and his father communicated, even if the relationship seemed to be on the volatile side. At least there was interaction.

What did she have with her mother? She wasn't even able to describe it.

The tension was getting worse, throbbing at her temples and stiffening her shoulders.

Maybe she should have gone for a swim in icy water.

"Okay, clearly I hit a nerve there. One glass of white coming up, no questions asked." Tristan turned away and took a bottle from the fridge.

"Large glass please."

He reached for a glass and raised an eyebrow. "Bad day?"

"The day was fine until the last hour when it plunged downwards faster than a seagull swooping for an ice cream." She sighed. "Is it that obvious? I like to think I'm inscrutable."

"You are. But a customer asking for a large glass of anything is usually a clue. As a landlord I'm supposed to pay attention." He poured her a large glass. "Also, you've been here for three weeks and this is the first time you've come here alone for a drink. Or looked remotely ruffled."

She frowned. "I look ruffled?"

"Physically, no. Psychologically? Yes. Which shows you're human so don't go beating yourself up." He pushed the glass towards her. "Do you want to talk about it?"

"No, thanks." Part of her did, but she wouldn't know where to start. She'd never discussed her relationship with her mother with anyone. And she couldn't do it here, because she wasn't supposed to tell anyone who her mother was. "The wine is all the therapy I need." She held out her credit card but he shook his head.

"On the house."

"That's generous, but shouldn't you be trying to relieve me of the weight of all my money?"

He laughed. "Another time, definitely. But tonight it's on me." His gaze lingered on hers for a moment and then he turned to Matt who was now at the far end of the bar. "I'm taking five, Matt. You're in charge."

"No worries, boss." Matt glanced curiously at Abby, then handed two bottled beers to the young guys standing at the bar. "Take your time."

Tristan snagged a beer from the fridge and gestured to the door. "Let's go."

Abby opened her mouth to ask where they were going, but he was already walking out of the door and she had no choice but to follow him.

"I thought you weren't taking a break tonight."

"That was before you ordered a large glass of wine."

"Are you a psychologist now?"

"A landlord is expected to be many things, and psychologist is probably among them," he said. "Maybe tonight I'm trying to be a friend." He stopped and she was so startled by his words she almost walked right into him.

"Why?"

"Because you look as if you need one." His gaze hovered on hers for a moment and then he pushed through a gate and took her into a little private garden that overlooked the harbour.

The air was filled with the sweet scent of honeysuckle and rose. The place seemed to be a haven for wildlife.

Her stress levels receded. "I didn't know this existed."

"It's my secret hideaway. It's a good place to unwind, and

you look as if you need that as much as that glass of wine." He put his beer on the table and sat down.

There was room to sit next to him but she chose to sit opposite.

She hadn't expected company, and now she was going to have to make small talk.

She grasped at something. "She seemed pretty keen on you. Vicky."

"Yes, that part is unfortunate."

"You had a thing?"

"Only in her mind. But that doesn't seem to make a difference. It's the way of the world, isn't it? People falling for the wrong people. I suppose it wouldn't be life if it wasn't complicated." He watched her. "I saw you running past with Evie earlier, on your usual route. You were laughing. What happened?"

Her usual route.

She'd been here a little over three weeks, but she'd developed a routine. It was funny how quickly that had happened.

Usually the run was the perfect end to her day, and it had been tonight until that phone call.

"I spoke to my mother."

He picked up his beer. "That explains why you needed a large glass of wine."

"It does? How?" She took a sip of the wine. It was cold, dry and exactly what she needed.

"I'm going on personal experience. Speaking to my father has the same effect on me." He gave a humourous laugh and lifted the bottle to his lips. "Frustrating, isn't it? Filial duty. There are times when you want to walk away from it, but loyalty and love keep you coming back for more."

Loyalty and love.

He was right. He was so right.

And she always made excuses for her mother. She'd had a tough time growing up. She was focused on the business. She was putting pressure on Abby because she wanted her to be the best she could be.

"She never answers my questions!" Abby blurted the words out. "I do everything I can to please her. I twist myself into a pretzel. I deliver everything she wants, on time and with a smile. I never let her down. Never step out of line. I try and be the perfect daughter, but I ask her one personal question—*just one*—and she cuts me off."

He lowered the bottle to the table. "Why do you have to be the perfect daughter?"

She was thrown. She'd expected him to ask what her question had been.

"Simple answer? My mother is the sort of person you don't want to disappoint. It has always been the two of us—we have no relatives. I admire her, I really do. More than anyone else I know. She's strong, capable and clever and she can be intimidating, but I always remind myself she had a tough time when she was young. What she has achieved is nothing short of incredible." She stopped.

She was doing it again. Justifying. Making excuses. Why did she keep doing that? And she realised with a flash of regret and panic that she'd said far, far too much. Now he was going to start questioning her about her mother's achievements and she was going to have to dodge around the subject the way she did whenever the subject was raised by anyone at the hotel.

Fortunately, he didn't.

"So you're pretty close."

She liked to think she and her mother were close, but were they? Really? It was slowly dawning on her that there was a great deal she didn't know about her mother. She had so many questions but there was no point in asking them because her mother was always evasive.

Whenever she asked about that early period in her mother's life, she brushed the questions aside.

It doesn't matter what went before, she'd always told Abby. *It has no relevance to the present.*

But that wasn't true, was it?

Because she was pretty sure that her presence here had something to do with her mother's past history.

"We're not close in an emotional sense. I don't think my mother is capable of that. And I understand, I really do. Her dad walked out when she was eleven leaving her to care for her sick mother—I mean, what kind of guy does that? And then my dad died before I was born—I think she figured out that it's safer to do things alone. She's never had anyone she can rely on. No one to lean on. I have always felt a responsibility to be reliable and exactly what she wants. I was determined to be the one person who never disappointed her. But she even keeps me at a distance." She thought of her mother saying *rely on yourself, Abby, not other people.* It sounded good in theory, but in practice it was a lonely way to be. She had no family other than her mother and no real friends. Until now. "Sorry, that was far too much information. I'm embarrassed."

"Why?"

"Because you don't need to hear any of this."

"Don't apologise. It's good to know you're human."

"You don't think I'm human?" The tension was slowly releasing its grip on her. She realised she probably should have had something to eat along with the wine, which had already gone to her head. A warm, relaxed feeling was slowly spreading through her body.

"I think you keep yourself hidden," Tristan said slowly. "You're afraid to show who you really are."

Well, *that* was true, she thought. On more than one level. They had no idea who she really was.

Feeling guilty, Abby finished her wine. "That was delicious. I probably drank it too quickly." Her head spun a little but it wasn't an unpleasant feeling. Certainly not enough to make her regret her decision.

"I'll get you another glass." He half rose but she shook her head regretfully.

"Tempting, but no. I only ever drink one glass." Another glass and she might stop hiding who she was and spill the truth.

"One glass? That's it?"

"I have boundless self-discipline. My mother insisted on it. She thinks it's important to always be in full control." She sighed. "Also, I'm working tomorrow."

Tristan sat back down again. "How's that going? You're enjoying it?"

"I'm loving it."

And that was unexpected.

She gazed through the wooden gate to the fishing boats in the harbour.

She'd come here to focus on the business. To learn more about the hotel and the people. To assemble sufficient information to enable her mother to make a decision, whatever that would be.

But this no longer felt like business to Abby. It felt personal. And it was confusing.

There were gaps in what her mother had told her and suddenly the past felt murky and indistinct.

She thought back to the phone call. When she'd asked the question about Edward, her mother had cut her off, saying that she had another commitment. And it was probably true, because her mother never wasted a minute of her day and Abby had been late on the call, but still it felt as if she'd been using it as an excuse to avoid the question. Or was she overthinking it? It would be in character for her mother to be annoyed by her lateness and to cut the meeting off to make a point.

But she wasn't only a member of staff, was she? She was her daughter! She should be allowed to ask questions of a personal nature. And her mother should be asking her personal questions too, not just enquiring about the business.

Frustration simmered inside her.

"I've been here for more than three weeks and she hasn't once asked me if I'm enjoying it. How it feels to be here. My mother doesn't do feelings or emotions. I know that. And this is supposed to be work, after all, although it's interesting that the people I'm working with have asked me more questions in the few weeks I've been here than my mother has asked me in a lifetime. It shouldn't bother me. It doesn't usually bother me." She fiddled with her empty wine glass. "But for some reason tonight it bothered me." She broke off. "Sorry."

"What are you sorry for?"

"For spilling my problems all over you. Anyway, enough of me. Isn't tonight supposed to be piano night? Shouldn't you be in there, revving up the crowd?"

"Yes. Unfortunately Ray is ill, so people are going to have to sing a cappella tonight. No doubt the complaining will start when I go back inside. Which is why I'm lingering out here with you." He finished his beer. "I'm letting Matt take the flak for once."

She decided he really was very attractive and wondered why it had taken a glass of wine to make her see that.

Or maybe it wasn't the wine. Maybe it was because he was smiling at her for the first time.

She wondered how it would feel to kiss him. *Complicated*, she thought. It would feel complicated. And she had all the complicated she could deal with right now.

"I could do it." The words spilled out of her before she had time to overthink it and stop herself. "I can play."

He gave her a curious look. "Do you know any sea shanties?"

"No, but if you have music I can sight-read. And there are other things I can play. Piano rags? Your customers might like those, and if not I can play something else." It had been ages since she'd performed but she remembered that occasionally music had made her forget everything but the moment. If she was lucky, that would happen tonight. She badly needed the escape.

"I thought you were the classical type—Chopin, Beethoven—"

"Maybe I'll surprise you."

"You already have. Have you ever played in a pub before?"

"No." She thought about the concert halls she'd played in as a teenager. The featureless practice rooms. The grand piano in her mother's home. "But a piano is a piano. At least, I assume it is."

"Let's find out." He stood up and picked up his empty bottle. "Thank you. For doing this, I mean. I owe you."

"You'd better wait to hear me play before you thank me." She suddenly realised what she'd committed herself to and her stomach quaked a little. "Are there lots of people in there?"

"It's busy enough. Why? Are you about to suffer from stage fright?"

"I might. Maybe I shouldn't have—"

"Too late. No backing out now. You made a commitment and letting me down would jar with your sense of duty."

"That's probably true." She held out her glass. "But if I'm going to play in public, I'll take that second glass of wine."

He took the glass from her. "Coming right up. Playing the piano in a bar and a second glass of wine. Two firsts in one evening."

She followed him into the pub, wondering why on earth she'd volunteered for this.

She sat down at the piano, trying to pretend she was alone in her mother's drawing room.

"Hey, Tris, you have a new pianist?" A man with a wide smile and an even wider gut beamed at her. "She's a lot better looking than Ray. Can she play?"

"Why don't you listen and find out?" Tristan handed her a brimming glass of wine. "You're allowed to put it on top of the piano."

"Oh, I would never—" But he'd already put it there and walked away before she could ask him what he thought she should play first.

She took a massive gulp of wine and decided it was probably best to dive in. And when they booed her out of the pub she'd take that walk she'd planned earlier. And obviously she'd never be able to show her face in the place again.

She started with Scott Joplin's "Maple Leaf Rag," and wondered from the sudden silence around her if that had been a mistake, but then feet started tapping and there were a couple of whoops from behind her. She played more piano rags, then moved from that to a couple of Irish jigs that had people dancing, and then shifted to a couple of folk songs to give everyone a breather.

When she finally took a break the applause echoed round the old pub.

Embarrassed and pleased in equal measure, she drank the wine Tristan had left her. She'd intended to sip it slowly, but they were encouraging her to play more so she gulped the wine down faster than she should have done and started playing again.

She'd emptied her glass, but when she looked at it again it

was full and she realised Tristan must have brought her a replacement at some point.

When she finally stopped playing her head was spinning and her ears were ringing.

Everyone cheered and clapped and she felt a rush of pleasure.

"When you said you'd step in for Ray I wasn't sure what to expect, but it wasn't that." Tristan leaned on the piano and smiled at her. "You're a revelation. If you ever want to leave the hotel business, you can have a job here."

"Why are they cheering and clapping?"

"Because you're brilliant?"

"Me?" She assumed he was joking, or being polite to get her to play some more, then realised he wasn't smiling. He meant it.

Brilliant.

No one ever told her she was brilliant, even when she'd strained every muscle to earn that level of approval. It had never come. Until now.

Someone she didn't know and would probably never again meet slapped her on the shoulders.

"That was great. Amazing."

She could *feel* their delight and approval. It was like a drug. It made her whole body buzz. "They liked what I played."

"Why so surprised?"

"People don't usually—I'm not used to—" It was dizzying, hearing people applaud and whoop loudly as a gesture of appreciation for something she'd done.

"Is that your first time playing in public?"

"No. I played in concert halls when I was younger."

"And nobody clapped?"

"Yes, they clapped, but in that setting everything is more restrained, even the applause." And that summed up her life, didn't it? Restrained. Careful. No excess. No wild moments of passion. "It's my first time playing in a pub. They're easy to please."

"Don't kid yourself. This is the toughest audience you could ever have." He was smiling at her but that was because he didn't understand. He didn't understand that praise and approval were so rare in her life that when it came she didn't even believe it.

She glanced around and realised the place was packed, to the point that there was barely space between people. "Is it always this busy?"

"No. People heard you playing and came in from the street. We've made more money since you started playing than we have for the whole of the last month. People are dancing and dancing makes them thirsty. When they're thirsty, they drink. What do I owe you?"

"Owe me?" She frowned. "Nothing. I was doing a favour for a friend." And she was wondering if he wasn't the one who had done her a favour.

When had she last enjoyed an evening this much?

She was having fun. So much fun that she was wondering why she'd stopped playing the piano. Why wasn't she doing this every day?

And she realised that the reason she hardly ever touched the piano now was because there was no purpose. No concert to rehearse for. No reason to play it. She never thought to play for her own enjoyment. To please herself.

There was something in his eyes. Something warmer. Something unsettling.

Something that made her think he could read her mind.

"I don't know what's happening to you," he said, "but I like it. And the friend thanks you. Drink your wine. I brought you a fresh glass when you were playing."

She'd forgotten about the wine. "I don't usually—"

"I know. But you've already broken your one-glass rule, so a third one won't count. Billy is going to take a turn on the piano so you can dance. He's not in your league when it comes to playing, but he'll do."

"Dance? I don't—"

"If you're about to tell me you don't usually dance don't bother." He dragged her to her feet and it was so unexpected that she couldn't find her balance and had to grab him to steady herself.

She was dimly aware of Billy taking her place at the piano with a happy grin and then Tristan slipped his arm around her waist, told the crowd to move aside and proceeded to twirl her to the rhythm of the music.

The rest of the evening was a blur of music, more piano playing and probably another glass of wine although at some point she'd lost track.

When Tristan suggested they step outside for a breath of fresh air she was reluctant. She wanted the evening to last forever.

She felt like a different person. A better person. The person she was supposed to be?

"Let's go to the beach!" She grabbed Tristan's hand and tugged him along. It was late now and the narrow labyrinth of streets that wound their way to the harbour was quiet and mostly free of tourists.

"Er—now? It's dark."

"All the better for what I have in mind."

"Now I'm intrigued."

She followed the path that led from the harbour and then fell away gently down to a small local beach. During the day at low tide it was crowded with families with toddlers but now it was empty and the only sounds were the gentle rush of the ocean as it hit the sand.

"Is the tide going to come in and drown us?"

"Not for another few hours."

"That gives us time."

She tugged off her shoes and felt the cool sand under her feet. "Time for what? You haven't told me what you have in mind, but if it's swimming I'm going to stop you."

"It's not swimming." Everything was a little hazy. A little blurry. His face, her feelings, their surroundings. "I'm going to kiss you. Because that's another thing I don't do."

"You don't kiss men?"

"I don't kiss men I don't know well. I definitely don't kiss men who don't like me."

"Who said I didn't like you?"

She undid the shirt that she'd knotted at her waist when she'd started playing. "You took a dislike to me the moment I walked through the door."

"I'm liking you a lot more after this evening."

"Because I'm drunk?"

"No. Because you're finally human. I'm seeing the real you. No more robot girl."

"Robot girl?"

"No emotions."

Was that what he thought? Well, she probably couldn't blame him for that. It was how she felt a lot of the time. She was someone who behaved the way she was expected to. The way she was programmed to.

Except not tonight.

"Just because I don't show my emotions doesn't mean I don't feel them."

"Is that right?"

"It is right—" she might have slurred her words a little "—and I'm going to prove it to you."

"Okay." He stood still, legs spread, solid and strong which

was a good thing because she needed someone to lean on. "Prove it."

She put her hands on his shoulders. Felt the hard swell of muscle under her fingers and the slow heat spread through her body. "I have never kissed someone after three glasses of wine before."

"It's here—" he pointed to his mouth "—in case you need help orientating yourself."

"I don't need any help." She rose on her toes and brushed her lips against his, gently at first, exploring the shape and taste of him. Then he slanted his mouth over hers and excitement rushed over her.

She felt his hands slide down her back and wrap around her, hauling her close. Desire slammed into her, the intensity of it almost knocking her off her feet, but he held her firmly, his hands steadying her against the force they created together.

Her mind emptied and all she could do was feel. The gentle skim of his fingers over her skin, the erotic slide of his tongue, the heat of her own body.

When she finally eased her mouth from his her breathing was shallow and so was his.

They stared at each other for a long moment, both acknowledging the unexpected.

The next step seemed entirely natural to her and she stripped off her shirt and let it drop to the sand.

His gaze slid from her face to the swell of her breasts pressing against her lace bra.

"Abby—"

"I've never done a striptease on a beach before." She dropped her hands to the button at the front of her jeans. "And I've never had a one-night stand."

"That's a lot of first times for one evening, maybe we should—"

"You have far too many clothes on." She started to unbutton his shirt, but his hands closed over hers.

"No." His voice was roughened. "Not now. Not like this."

"You prefer to go back to the pub?" She wasn't sure she could make it that far. Her whole body was alive and on fire. She was pretty sure his was, too. "Is it the sand?"

"No, it's being in a public place. I'd rather not be arrested. I'd never hear the last of it. And also having sex with a woman who has had three large glasses of wine and feeling the effects would be a first for me, and it isn't happening."

"You think I'm feeling the effects?"

"Could you stand up if I wasn't holding you?"

"Let's find out—" She eased away from him and swayed a little. "That's because I'm being blown by the breeze."

"There is no breeze. It's a still night."

It certainly wasn't still inside her head. It felt as if there was a party going on. Every brain cell was dancing.

"Maybe a swim would sober me up."

"I think it's more likely that you'd drown."

The world was going in and out of focus. "I'm a good swimmer. When I do something, I do it really well."

"I can believe that." He sighed. "You should get dressed, before we both do something really well and then regret it afterwards." Jaw clenched, he retrieved her shirt and helped her to put it back on, his movements unsteady and uncoordinated.

She'd imagined him undressing her, not dressing her. She'd imagined his hands on her skin, stroking and seeking, not fumbling with buttons.

She couldn't understand why he was rejecting her but it all felt frustrating and unfair.

"I know exactly what I'm doing."

"Yeah, right, well we can talk about that another time."

"I'll have you know I'm a very controlled person. And careful about my choices." She peered at him. "You look tense. Are you tense?"

"Could you button your shirt please?"

She frowned. "Why? Is that another of your tests? If I can stand on one leg, close one eye and button my shirt I'm sober enough for you to have sex with me?"

"No test. I think it would be a good idea, that's all." With a rough curse he reached out and buttoned her shirt himself and when he'd finished he snatched his hands away as if he'd scalded the tips of his fingers.

She was hurt and a little humiliated and even the wine couldn't entirely numb those feelings.

"Okay, I get it. You don't want me. But I'm not ready to go back yet. It's beautiful out here. You go if you like. I want to stay here for a while." She stared out at the inky blackness of the ocean. "It's beautiful. Isn't it beautiful?"

"Yes, it's a picture. I think we should go back now."

"Why?"

"I think maybe you should go to bed and prepare yourself for your first hangover." He gave a faint smile. "It's not going to be pretty."

"I don't care. That's future me's problem."

"Future you had better have strong painkillers ready for the morning."

The morning. A new day. "What time is it in Boston?"

"Now? I have no idea. Why?"

"I'm going to call my mother."

"Is that a good idea?" He frowned. "Not that it's my place to dictate what you do, but in my experience phone calls after three large glasses of wine—particularly when you haven't built up a tolerance—usually turn out to be a mistake."

"I wouldn't know. I've never drunk three large glasses of wine before. This will be another first. And I think it's a brilliant idea. Possibly one of my best ever." All filters gone, she squinted at her phone and called her mother. "Voicemail. That's typical. She never answers calls unless they're scheduled in. She hangs up when she doesn't want to answer a question. Well, right now I have a few questions of my own. I'm leaving a message." She waited and took a breath. "Hi, Mom, it's me. Abby—we were cut off earlier and there are things I need to say—"

"But not now," Tristan muttered. "Don't say them now." He reached for the phone but she turned away from him and carried on with her message.

"*Don't be a people pleaser*, that's what you always said to me. Don't let other people influence your decisions. But you influence my decisions all the time. Everything I do, I do to please you—"

Tristan closed his eyes. "You should definitely hang up. This is going to end badly—"

She took a few steps away from him and would have lost her balance if Tristan hadn't grabbed her arm and steadied her. "You told me to always challenge things I didn't agree with, so here I am challenging you. I'm not comfortable being under-cover like this. I like these people. I *love* these people. For the first time in my whole working life I feel like a proper member of the team. I laugh at work. Do you know how that feels? To actually *laugh* during your working day? I walk into a room and people include me in the conversation, instead of blocking me out. I have friends! People who care about me. They deserve to know the truth, and that's what I'm going to do. I'm going to tell them who I am. And I'm going to tell them what I know, which isn't much because you refuse to answer my questions." Her head swam and she paused, waiting for her vision to settle. She was starting to feel weird.

She felt Tristan let go of her and she swayed slightly and tried to steady herself.

"I deserve to know the real reason you sent me here, because I know there is something else going on. And in case it's relevant you should know that the weasel man was hanging around the place again the other day. Have you changed your mind about selling to him? Because if you haven't, he doesn't seem to have got the message. Not knowing what is going on is really unsettling." The world spun and she lost the thread of the conversation.

What had she been saying?

Oh yes. "It's making everyone unsettled. Evie is worried, and she shouldn't have to worry. She's brilliant and we should be working out ways to keep her. And while we're talking—well, I'm talking—I really would appreciate it if you could tell me something about your past. Because your past is my past, and sometimes I feel as if I came out of a laboratory or something—"

She was sure there was a whole lot more she'd wanted to say to her mother but suddenly it seemed more important to sleep than to talk.

She stabbed at her phone, trying to end the call, but the characters on the screen were dancing around. Eventually she managed to hit the red button and then promptly dropped her phone in the sand.

"Oops." She bent down and scrabbled around for it, lost her balance and landed hard. "Ouch. I thought sand was supposed to be soft. That's what happens when you let go of me." She felt Tristan's fingers clamp around her wrist and then he was hauling her to her feet.

"Time for you to go to bed."

"Good idea. Best idea you've had all night." She leaned in to kiss him again but he grabbed her arm and propelled her up the beach.

The mood had shifted from playful and romantic to grim, and her spinning brain couldn't quite figure out why.

"Where are we going? You're impatient, which is pretty romantic, but also challenging given that my legs are wobbly." They'd reached the pub and he nudged her through the door and up the stairs, his grip on her making sure she didn't tumble again.

All the giddy euphoria she'd been feeling had drained away and now she felt dazed and desperately tired.

She caught a glimpse of Tristan's serious expression and she giggled.

"You're no fun when you drink. You could at least smile."

She fell face-first onto her bed, closed her eyes and remembered nothing else.

She woke hours later and winced at the light. Where was she? And why was she lying fully clothed on top of the bed?

She started to sit up and then groaned and flopped back down again. It felt as if the entire Boston Symphony Orchestra was performing Beethoven's Ninth in her head. Her mouth was so dry it felt as if she'd swallowed the entire beach.

A shrill sound made her jump and she clamped her hands over her ears, then realised it was her alarm clock.

It was 6 a.m. and she had to get ready for the day. For work.

How was she going to work? She felt as if she'd been trampled by a herd of wild animals. She'd never known pain like it. The whole room was swimming. Her stomach was churning. Her feet hurt. Why did her feet hurt?

Snippets from the night before gradually seeped back into her brain.

The piano. She'd played. And she'd danced. She'd danced

in the bar and—oh God, had she danced on the table? Yes, yes she'd done that. She remembered someone lifting her down, telling her that she might fall.

What then?

The beach. She'd walked to the beach. And she'd kissed Tristan. There was no forgetting that part. And she'd—

With a gasp she sat up, holding the edge of the bed to steady herself. She'd removed her shirt and tried to remove his, but he'd rejected her. Now, *that* was embarrassing. What was she supposed to say when she saw him again?

She was never drinking again, as long as she lived. And judging by the way she felt right at that moment she probably didn't have long to live.

Squinting through her pounding headache she saw a glass of water on the table next to her bed, along with a couple of tablets and a note.

She picked up the note, pain lancing through her eyes as she read it.

Take the tablets and drink the water. Then get to work. And tell them the truth. Or I will.

Tristan, presumably. And presumably it was Tristan who had brought her back from the beach and removed her shoes before she'd collapsed on the bed.

Thoughtful of him to leave tablets and water.

She frowned at the note, the words swimming slightly. Truth about what? What was he talking about?

She picked up her phone and saw that she had five missed calls from her mother.

Her mother never rang her spontaneously. Why would she be calling? Especially when she knew the time difference.

There was a single voicemail and she pressed Play with a growing sense of foreboding.

Abby, I received your message. Please call me back when you're sober.

Message? What message? *Sober?* How did her mother know she'd drunk too much? Did she have someone spying on Abby? Was someone working under-cover, watching her while she was under-cover? That was a lot of under-covers to keep track of.

A memory flickered to life in her brain. Her heart started to race. Her fingers were slippery with sweat.

The night before, had she called her mother? Yes, she had. How could she have forgotten that? And what had she said exactly?

The conversation dripped back into her aching head in horrifying fragments.

She'd spoken her mind. She'd told her mother she was going to tell the team the truth about who she was. And Tristan must have witnessed the entire conversation.

Which explained his note.

Get to work. Tell them the truth. Or I will.

He knew. He knew everything. Well, not everything, because she didn't know everything (and she noticed that her mother still hadn't answered any of the questions she'd asked), but he knew all the worst parts. He knew she'd been lying about who she was.

She sat there, shaking and drenched in panic.

What had she done? *What had she done?*

She'd been having the best time of her life, and now she had to walk in there and confess to all these people that she'd grown to like so much, and who had welcomed her so warmly, that she was a fake. That she'd been lying to them.

Her stomach rolled and she dragged herself off the bed, stumbled across the room trailing sand behind her and just made it to the bathroom in time.

13

★★★★★

Alexandra

It was past midnight in Boston and Alexandra was wide awake. She'd been working late and the desk in her study was covered in spreadsheets and reports, but she'd been unable to concentrate.

Instead, she'd been checking her phone as obsessively as a teenager. She kept checking it was switched on. That the volume was up. That she hadn't missed any calls in the few minutes it had taken her to fetch a glass of water from the kitchen.

There had never been a time when Abby had failed to return one of her calls.

And she couldn't ever remember a time when her daughter had drunk too much. Whatever had possessed her? She'd never heard Abby so emotional. Even allowing for the influence of alcohol, it had been unsettling to hear. Like listening to a stranger.

She was worried. Seriously worried.

She'd called Abby's phone numerous times, and in the end had left a message.

So far, her daughter hadn't called back.

This wasn't good.

Alexandra picked up her phone and for the sixth time that evening replayed the message Abby had left

I deserve to know the real reason you sent me here . . . and later . . . *I really would appreciate it if you could tell me something about your past. Because your past is my past.*

Alexandra put her phone down. Would Abby have forgotten the message when she sobered up (and what, exactly, had made her drink so much)? Would she even remember she'd made that call?

She had to assume Abby would call her back, and when she did Alexandra needed to decide what answer to give.

She had to decide what to do next.

She prided herself on being able to handle any situation, but for once her confidence in herself was draining away. She didn't feel at all in control. Far from it.

She had a feeling that the life she'd constructed for herself was about to come tumbling down.

14

Evie

Evie was sifting through applications, feeling despondent. Why was it so hard to find good people?

Everyone fell short when compared with Abby.

She wondered if there was any way she could persuade Abby to take a permanent job.

That would at least solve some of her problems.

Tristan's slightly cynical attitude had made her wary at first. As a result, she'd kept her expectations low when it came to Abby, but within hours she'd proved herself to be nothing short of an asset. And now, a little over three weeks later, it felt as if she'd always been here. Evie felt a little smug that her initial instincts had been correct. She needed to remember to point that out to Tristan next time she saw him, as he was always accusing her of being naïve and far too trusting.

Not only had Abby proved to be a hard worker who was willing to throw herself into anything and go wherever she was needed, she did it without moaning or whingeing. Nor did she insist on doing things the way Gerald had always done them.

And Abby seemed to have inside knowledge about everything. She knew how to remove stubborn stains from carpets, she could fix a dripping tap without needing to call the maintenance team, and she was able to work at speed.

Evie usually allowed double the necessary time for jobs to be completed because the staff chatted as they worked. Abby somehow managed to be friendly but still complete a job in under the time allocated. And she had a keen eye for detail. She noticed the slightest mark on a pillow, or a sticky fingerprint on a cupboard door. She had an excellent memory for names, and greeted all the guests personally.

When Donna's mother had fallen and she'd had to take her to the hospital Abby had stepped in and worked the reception desk, charming all the guests and impressing everyone with her knowledge.

And she was becoming a good friend.

Evie smiled to herself. Yesterday on their run she'd confessed to her developing relationship with Luca. Part of her was worried about talking about it in case she jinxed it, but she was falling hard for him and was desperate to confide in someone.

Abby had proved to be the perfect audience. Receptive and excited in equal measure.

When Evie had told her that she'd finally spent the night at Luca's apartment, Abby had hugged her. His apartment was slightly out of town, so Evie had decided that the chances of bumping into anyone she knew were vastly reduced. Not that Luca seemed to care.

Abby had wanted to know all the details and had seemed as happy about it as Evie was.

But at work she was the soul of discretion.

It was good to have a friend who hadn't grown up here. Who hadn't watched her grow from child to adult and didn't feel the need to comment on the process. And maybe their friendship had extra depth because they shared a similar background. They'd each grown up with one parent. They'd suffered a similar loss and that gave them a connection.

For the first time since she'd stepped into Gerald's shoes, Evie was starting to enjoy coming to work.

She eyed the email in her inbox. She'd now had two interviews with the hotel in London and really liked the people. She was waiting to hear if she was through to the final stage, which would be an in-person interview in London.

What would she do if that happened?

Finding time to go up to London without everyone asking awkward questions wouldn't be easy. What would she say to people?

And there was an emotional element, too. Throughout this process she'd been telling herself she was testing the waters, but a final in-person interview felt like commitment. What would happen to her relationship with Luca if she left?

She glanced at the clock. She was seeing him again tonight and she couldn't wait. Never had time moved so slowly. She was amazed no one else had noticed and said something because she was struggling to behave normally around him. Even that morning when he'd come to her office first thing to discuss menus, she found herself distracted by his eyelashes. They were long and thick and he had a way of looking at her as if—

"Evie!" Donna burst into her office. "Have you heard about last night?"

Last night? She hadn't seen Luca, so that couldn't be it.

"What happened last night? Have you seen Abby, by the

way? She's late, and that's not like her." Evie checked her phone in case there was a message. "Should I call?"

Donna grinned. "So you *haven't* heard."

"Heard what?"

"She led quite the party in the pub last night. Oh, by the way, Mr and Mrs Spencer have cancelled tonight, but I've told them there's no charge."

"No charge?" Evie forced Luca and his long eyelashes out of her head and focused on work. "We have a cancellation policy."

"I know, but Gerald never charges loyal guests, even if we don't manage to rebook the room. Anyway, and more importantly, it turns out that our Abby plays the piano. According to Nick Holland, who heard it from Steve Mathews who was actually there, she had everyone on their feet dancing."

Evie made a mental note to review the cancellation policy and talk to staff.

No wonder their profits were down. They might as well let everyone stay free.

She tried to focus on what Donna was saying.

"Abby played the piano?"

"Yes. And she hasn't mentioned it once in all these weeks we've been working together."

"But I saw her last night. We went for a run. I left her on the cliff because she had to call someone in Boston. She didn't mention playing in the pub."

"From what I could gather it was a spontaneous thing. Ray went down with something and called in sick. She stood in for him. And after she'd finished playing, she and Tristan were dancing together."

Evie tried to picture it. "Tristan? Dancing? Are you sure?"

"Yes. I would have given a lot to see that, too. And at one point Abby was dancing on the table. Ask anyone who was there and you'll get the picture. But I was thinking that seeing as she's such a good piano player, maybe we ought to make use of her talents here. Get a piano in the bar. Liven up the evenings."

"There is no way Abby would have danced on the table! She's far too dignified."

"Not last night she wasn't. There's obviously another side to her."

Evie wished she'd been there to see it. "You're sure it was Abby?"

"Oh yes." Donna winked at her. "There are photos doing the rounds. You just have to ask the right people."

"But—" Evie broke off as Abby walked into the office. "Hi there! I was starting to worry about you. Is everything okay?"

"Yes. I'm sorry I'm late." She walked carefully, as if every step was painful. Her face was a sickly colour, and she had black smudges under her eyes that make-up hadn't managed to conceal.

"You look terrible. Are you ill?" Concerned, Evie stood up quickly. "Sit down."

Abby grabbed the back of the chair, her knuckles whitening. "I can't apologise enough."

"Really, it's fine. Why are you even here? You should have called in sick."

"I'm not sick. Not exactly. And I'll make up the time, obviously."

"Abby, it doesn't matter. And from what I've heard, you earned that lie-in. Rumours about your amazing piano playing have spread through the village. And your dancing. You should have called me! I love dancing."

Abby winced and rubbed her forehead with her fingers. "It was all a bit spontaneous. Ray was sick. I played a few pieces. People seemed to like it."

"From what I've heard, you were a hit." She was dying to ask how Abby had come to be dancing with Tristan, but she was going to wait until they were alone together because Abby was unlikely to reveal anything with Donna in the room.

"I really am sorry I'm late. I've never been late to work in my life."

"Well, I'm sure you—" Evie broke off as she saw Abby's expression. "Never?"

"Never."

"Not even five minutes when the traffic was bad?"

"No. I always leave enough time for the unexpected. This is a first for me. There have been a lot of those since yesterday." She fumbled for her bag and poked inside for a moment before giving up and closing her eyes briefly. "Do we have a first aid kit? I could use some painkillers."

"That would be the third glass of wine you had. Large glasses, from what I heard." Donna patted her on the shoulder. "I know exactly what you need. Painkillers, a bacon sandwich and a strong black coffee. Leave it with me."

"I really couldn't eat—" Abby began but Donna had gone. "I'm sorry, Evie. You have every right to be angry."

Evie grinned. "I'm angry that you didn't invite me. It sounds like a great evening. You had three glasses of wine?"

"Please don't remind me. I only ever have one, but when I offered to play piano and realised how many people would be watching—well, I thought a second one might be a good idea. And maybe that would have been okay but then Tristan brought me a third one." Abby rubbed her fingers across her forehead. "Drinking that was a bad decision. One of many that I made last night."

"Ooh—" Evie leaned forward "—please tell me one of those bad decisions involved Tristan."

Abby swallowed. "Evie, I have to talk to you. There's something I have to—need to tell you."

Evie decided the day was getting better by the minute. "Did you have sex with him? You need to tell me everything that happened. I want all the details. I promise I will not tell a *soul*."

"No, we didn't have sex! Although I think I might have tried. But—that's not it. I—" Abby rubbed her forehead. "I don't even know how to say this. I don't know where to start."

"Just tell me." Evie was desperate to know everything. It would be great if something was developing between Abby and Tristan. "I know we've only known each other a short time, but already our friendship feels special. You can talk to me about anything! You've listened to me for hours while I've been going on about Luca. Honestly, I was thinking this morning how much fun life is since you came. I've been plotting how I can persuade you to stay forever." She pushed aside thoughts of the two interviews she'd had.

Abby opened her mouth to speak, but before she could say a word Donna crashed back into the room carrying a loaded tray.

"I explained our problem to Luscious Luca," she said, winking at Evie, "and he put together what he calls the perfect hangover breakfast. He was muttering something about hydration and nutrients. So here's the result."

"Thanks, Donna." Evie ignored the *luscious Luca* reference.

Donna put the tray on Evie's meeting table. "Sourdough toast, poached egg and avocado, black coffee and freshly squeezed orange juice. Also water and painkillers."

Abby took the painkillers with the water but ignored everything else.

Evie was impatient to hear whatever it was that Abby wanted to tell her, but she obviously wasn't going to say it with Donna in the room.

"That's great, Donna. I know you have a lot of guests checking in today, so I won't keep you any longer."

Fortunately, Donna took the hint for once and left the room, closing the door behind her.

"Right. Time to talk." Evie joined Abby at the table and helped herself to coffee. "Donna's probably right. You should eat something."

"I couldn't eat a thing."

"It might settle your stomach. At least nibble a piece of toast." She sliced off the corner and put it on a plate for Abby. She held it out. "Here. You should—"

"I'm not who you think I am." Abby blurted out the words and Evie stared at her, the plate still in her hand.

"What?"

"I'm—" Abby closed her eyes briefly. "I'm not some random summer employee. I'm a member of the senior management team. I'm based in head office in Boston, although I do spend a lot of time on the road and in hotels and it's true that I've worked in almost every role during my time. I'm not only here as an extra pair of hands for the summer. I'm in charge of special projects. I was sent here to help out for the summer, that's true, but also to give the board a full and honest picture of how the hotel is functioning."

Evie put the plate down. Slowly she picked through what Abby had just told her. "I don't understand. What do you mean 'a full and honest picture'?"

"The hotel is not performing as well as it should, but you already know that."

"Yes, I do. I've been worried that—"

"And you were right to worry."

Evie felt as if the ground had shifted beneath her feet. Panic gripped her with icy fingers. "What are you saying? Are they going to sell us? Are we all going to lose our jobs?"

"No! I—" Abby rubbed her hand over her face again. "Honestly? I don't know what she's planning."

"She?"

"Alexandra Strong." Abby swallowed. "My mother."

"Your *mother*?" Evie stared at her. She knew who Alexandra Strong was, of course. The woman was a legend. She'd started the company from nothing and now she ran a thriving hotel group (although The Alexandra, Cornwall wasn't so much thriving as barely surviving). But she'd never met her, of course. To Evie and the rest of the staff, she was nothing more than the person behind the name of the hotel. And talking of names . . . "But you're not Strong. You're Jones. Abby Jones. Did you use a fake name?"

"No. My mother changed her name to Strong when we moved to Boston. It was important to her. A statement. I think it was all part of leaving her past behind, but it's not something she talks about in any depth. She wanted me to keep her mother's name, as a tribute. My grandmother. She was Madeleine Jones. I'm Madeleine Abigail Jones. Known as Abby. As well as being a reminder of her mother, her goal was always for me to work in the company and she thought it would be easier for me to be accepted if I wasn't immediately recognised as her daughter. So at work I'm Abby Jones. Sometimes I use—"

"Stop. Enough. It doesn't matter." Her heart thumping, Evie cut her off. "I don't care what you call yourself. The only thing that matters is the reason you're here. And it seems you're here to spy on us." She couldn't sit for another moment. Stressed and shaken, she sprang from her chair and walked across her office to the window, trying to hold it together. Trying to figure out the implications of what she'd just learned. Tristan had warned her, hadn't he? He'd said that she was too trusting, and he'd been right.

Tears of fury and misery stung the back of her eyes.

She felt stupid.

Panic rippled again. What exactly had she said? What had she told her?

So much.

Too much.

"Evie." Abby's voice was quiet. "I know you're upset and I don't blame you."

"Why didn't you tell me the truth?" Evie turned to face her. "I don't understand how you could do such a thing. We ran together. You sat in my garden and we talked. And you never once even hinted—" She swallowed. "Why?"

"The theory was that if I was under-cover I would be able to do a more accurate assessment of the situation. If the team had known I was from head office, they wouldn't have been so open."

"And you were okay with that?"

"No, I wasn't." Abby looked so wan and miserable that Evie almost felt sorry for her.

"So why not tell her that?"

"Because my mother is persuasive, and I spend my life trying to please her. And despite my aversion to the idea of not revealing who I was, I could see the logic of what she was saying."

It was too much to take in. Evie couldn't believe anyone would do such a thing.

"I let you into my life." Overwhelmed by the enormity of it, she took a breath. "I invited you to my home. Introduced you to the people in the village. I told you things."

Abby held her gaze without flinching. "Yes."

"*Anything you say is just between us*—that's what you said to me."

"I know. I didn't expect you to reveal so much of a personal nature—"

"That's who I am. I did that because I liked you! And I trusted you. And that probably makes me a terrible judge of character. You lied, Abby."

"I didn't exactly—" Abby stopped and her shoulders sagged. "You're right, I did lie. I don't blame you for being angry. But you should know that I really did believe that everything I was doing would lead to a better outcome."

"A better outcome? You mean for the company."

"I mean for the company and the employees. For you. Would you have told me the truth about how things were if you'd known I was from head office?"

"Yes! I have been trying to talk to someone from head office for a while. I told you I emailed and I had no response."

"That's right. But when you didn't get a response, did you go higher up the chain? Did you try again with someone more senior?"

Evie frowned. "No, but—" She paused, forced to admit the truth. "I didn't want to get anyone into trouble. And also it felt safer to keep my head down and not draw attention. I had this vague hope people might not have noticed our numbers."

"They noticed. There was an offer from a developer—"

"Mr Weasel." Evie felt a rush of anger. "I knew it."

"Yes, I suspect it was your Mr Weasel. But his offer was rejected."

"Did anyone tell him that? Because he was spotted having tea in the gardens a couple of days ago." She saw Abby nod.

"I know. And I told my mother that."

"And what did she say?"

Abby turned scarlet. "I don't know. We haven't had a conversation. I left her a message last night."

"After you'd had three glasses of wine?"

"Yes. But the fact that I'd drunk a little too much didn't make the content of the message any less pertinent. I don't know why that man keeps showing up."

"Maybe he happens to love our afternoon tea, but somehow I doubt it. So if he increases his offer will your mother sell the place?"

"No." Abby's answer was immediate. "She was adamant that she wouldn't sell and she doesn't change her mind about things. But there is something strange about this whole situation. Something specific to this hotel and I don't know what it is—it all started here, of course, but my mother isn't the sentimental type so I'm not sure what's going on in her head."

"Why don't you ask her?" Evie snapped out the words and then regretted it. "Look, I don't mean to be rude, and obviously I'm far too trusting, but I'm not a pushover. To you this is another of your hotels. An 'asset', is that what you'd call it? But to me, and all the people who work here, it's like home. And yes, sometimes the staff can be frustrating, especially when they insist on doing things the way they've always been done, but they're loyal and great and decent people. I love them. I will fight to the end for them."

But maybe this was the end, she thought. Maybe this was it.

And what could she do about it really? She had no power at all. No say in anything.

Maybe they'd be better off without her. She knew they had a big problem, but she hadn't been able to turn it around. Maybe someone else would have more success. Someone more experienced. Someone the staff took seriously.

She thought about the job application she had sent off.

It would feel as if she was abandoning the sinking ship. *But what if she was the one driving the ship onto the rocks?*

"You're a good manager, Evie. The staff are lucky to have you."

Evie straightened her shoulders. "No, I'm not a good manager. No one takes me seriously around here because they've known me since I learned to tie my own shoelaces. People do things the way they've always done things, and I can't get them to change. I don't have the authority to change anything because I'm just covering while Gerald is ill." And no doubt Abby had already briefed her mother on Evie's inadequacies.

"That's one of many things that need to be resolved," Abby said. "You *are* a good manager. And you need to be given the tools to do the job."

"Or maybe you need to appoint an experienced general manager to cover until the situation with Gerald is resolved. I'll step down if that would help. You could take over. How long do we have before your mother decides our fate? I'm not good with tension and suspense. It makes my stomach hurt."

"No one is stepping down, Evie." Abby's tone was urgent. "I admit that I don't really have a full picture of what's going on here. If I did, I would share it with you."

"You said you were supposed to give the board a full and honest picture." Evie folded her arms. "So what form does that take?"

"I send reports directly to the boss."

"The boss who is also your mother. I'd like to see those reports," Evie said. "I have a right to know what you've been saying about us."

Her insides quaked a little. Did she really want to read what Abby had written about her? About the whole team? Presumably it wouldn't make easy reading. Still, she might learn something about herself, and it was important to take on feedback, even negative feedback.

Abby hesitated and then nodded. "Yes, of course. I'll forward the emails to you."

"And now that you've finally been honest with me, what

does that mean? Are you no longer working here?" Something tapped at the edges of Evie's brain. "Wait a minute. You were supposed to be here for the whole summer. Two months, that woman from head office said. So why are you telling me this now? Today? You're not even halfway through your assignment."

"Because last night when I called my mother and left the message, Tristan overheard me talking." Abby reached for the glass of water and drank.

"And he made you promise to tell me the truth today."

"Yes, but I was going to anyway." Abby put the glass down. "I don't expect you to believe me, but that's why I called my mother. To tell her I wasn't going to stay under-cover any longer."

"But the fact that you thought better of it doesn't really change anything, does it? Do you know what hurts most?" Evie gave up trying to sound professional and distant. "The fact that you were great to be around. When you first arrived I wasn't sure—you were distant and a little intimidating, but then you threw yourself into work and opened up. I don't really have anyone I can talk to here—they all see me as 'little Evie' or 'our Evie.' I'm not Evie the manager, and never Evie the colleague we should listen to because she has great ideas. But you—" she felt her voice crack and hated herself for not being able to hold it together "—we talked about everything. And I couldn't believe how lucky I was having you working with us, even if it was only for the summer. I felt as if we were friends. Real friends. You ate in my kitchen. You sat in my garden and listened to me spill my fears and worries. You encouraged me to open up, and I did. I thought you were interested. I thought you liked me. But the whole time we were together, you were mining for information that you could use against us."

Abby swallowed. "That isn't—"

"But it is though, isn't it?" Suddenly she felt exhausted. Betrayed. "I'd tell you to go home, but we're short-staffed so I can't afford to do that. You can join the housekeeping team for the day. We'll talk later."

Abby stood up but she didn't make a move to the door. "Before I leave, there's something else I need to say to you."

Evie wasn't sure she wanted to hear anything else. She felt as if her emotions had been rubbed raw with sandpaper. "As I say, we can talk later." She needed time to think things through. To work out what to do for the team.

"I need to say this." Abby gripped the back of the chair. "You were right when you said I could have said no to my mother. I could have refused to be under-cover. And I didn't do that, and it's true that part of the reason was because my mother isn't an easy person to say no to—when she has made up her mind about something, she's hard to shift. And it's also true that I could see the benefit of being able to observe without people knowing who I was. But that wasn't the only reason I agreed to do it."

Evie's head was throbbing. "What then?"

Abby's fingers were white on the chair. "I don't have a close relationship with my colleagues in Boston. They don't trust me."

"If you lie to them the way you lied to me, then that doesn't surprise me."

Abby flinched. "This was a one-off. They don't trust me because of who I am. I've never been part of a team before, not really. When I walk into a room, people stop talking. When people go for drinks after work, I'm never invited. I work twice as hard as most people, but it makes no difference—people still assume I'm only where I am because of my mother. Nepotism. It's fine, but—" She paused and gave a faltering smile. "Actually, it's not fine. I tell myself it's fine because there's nothing I can do about it, but it's pretty lonely. Sometimes I feel as if I'm back at school with no friends in the playground. When I was asked to work here under-cover, I saw a chance to reinvent myself for a short time. To be someone other than me. To be judged for what I do, and not who my mother is."

Evie felt a spasm of sympathy and squashed it down. She didn't want to feel sympathy! She needed to toughen up.

Channelling her tough side, she scowled. "Are you trying to make me feel sorry for you?"

"No." Abby shook her head. "I'm trying to explain why I agreed to it. Yes, I was uncomfortable with the principle of being under-cover, but the chance to work in a place where people weren't prejudging me was appealing."

Evie didn't understand the point she was making. "Why are you telling me this?"

Abby swallowed. "Because I want you to know that the past few weeks have been the best of my whole working life. The moment I walked into this place, you've all treated me as if I'm one of the team, you especially. You've included me in the conversation. People laugh with me, instead of making me the butt of the joke. You've all made me feel as if I belong, and I've never had that before. I didn't actually know it was possible to feel this happy at work." Her voice wasn't quite steady. "And those things you said just now—you've been a real friend, Evie. Part of me doesn't even understand it, because I don't find it easy to get close to people and yet I felt close to you in a way I've never felt before. As if we had a bond. A connection. It felt special, and I never meant to damage that."

Evie felt something tighten in her chest. Why did she suddenly want to hug Abby? She should be mad with her. *Furious.*

Abby's deception at work was inexcusable, but Evie knew

that the real reason she was so upset was personal. She'd enjoyed Abby's company. She thought she'd made a friend. Deep down she knew that the prime reason she was feeling terrible wasn't because of the work implications, although that was bad enough, but because she'd thought Abby was a friend. She'd assumed she could be trusted.

This wasn't only a business betrayal, it was a personal betrayal.

But that wasn't what mattered right now. Her own feelings, her personal feelings about having made and lost a friend, were going to have to wait.

"I—what you did was wrong."

"Yes, it was. And I don't expect you to forgive me."

"I need—" Evie broke off as the door to her office flew open.

"SOS from Tilda! The Seashore room is in a state. Is Abby available?"

"I'm available." Abby walked across the room gingerly, as if every step was an effort. She held on to the door and glanced back at Evie. "I'll send you those emails as soon as I've done the room."

Evie wasn't sure she'd have the courage to read them.

"Right. Good." She wasn't going to feel sorry for Abby. She wasn't.

But she did. She felt sorry for Abby and sorry for herself.

She had things to do but she felt drained after everything that had happened. She flopped down onto the chair and ate a piece of toast from Abby's plate.

Her eyes stung and she felt as if there was a lump in her chest.

Her office door opened again and Evie quickly brushed her palm over her cheeks. Why couldn't people leave her alone? There was no such thing as privacy in this place. Maybe she should lock herself in the laundry cupboard.

Donna walked in and closed the door behind her.

"Okay. Tell me everything."

"What?"

"Don't play that game with me. I held your hand when you learned to walk. I know when you're upset. I'm not sure who looked worse a moment ago. You or Abby. Have you had a fight? And don't lie to me because I always know. You once tried telling me you hadn't eaten the last chocolate biscuit. You were about twelve at the time. You were doing your homework in one of the bedrooms and I was watching you for your dad. Of course the chocolate round your mouth was a giveaway, but I would have known anyway."

"We haven't had a fight. At least, not in the way you mean—" Evie rubbed her forehead. For a moment she felt like a child again and she longed to spill everything out, but she couldn't do that. "It's fine, Donna. It's kind of you to check on me but I need five minutes to get my thoughts straight. It's a work thing."

"Look at you! All grown up and serious. Everything's going to be okay." It was her most maternal voice and it was the final straw.

"I am grown up. *I am grown up!*" Something burst inside Evie. "And everything is not going to be okay. Not until all of you stop treating me like a child and take me seriously. Yes, I grew up here. Yes, I learned to walk in these corridors, but I've learned a lot of other things since then, too. I've learned about balance sheets, and SEO, and the importance of upselling. And I've learned that sometimes things have to change, no matter how much we'd like to stay stuck in the past." She took a deep breath. "And I've learned that I'm not great at managing people because I have no idea how to motivate them to do what I want them to do. This place is in trouble—it has been in trouble for a while, and unless things change around here fast, I'm not at all confident the hotel has a future."

Donna stood in stunned silence and Evie felt an immediate wash of remorse.

"I'm sorry. I didn't mean to snap or be rude. Ignore me. I'm having a bad day. Leave me alone for ten minutes and I'll pull myself together."

But Donna didn't leave.

Instead, she walked across to the table and sat down. "I'm the one who is sorry. I didn't know I made you feel that way. I love you like my own child." She gave a rueful smile. "And that's the problem, isn't it? You're not my child, you're my boss."

Evie felt an ache behind her ribs. "Donna—"

"Is it true that we're in trouble? Is that what you were discussing with Abby? Are they going to close us down? Sell us to that weasel man who is always hanging around? Why didn't you say something?"

Evie looked at her, eaten up by guilt. "I didn't have facts. Only suspicions. And I don't know what's going on. But I do know it's not good. We need to think more about how we can increase our profits."

"Gerald didn't like to—" Donna stopped, cutting off her own sentence midway through. "But Gerald isn't here now, and if what you're saying is true then it seems his approach didn't work."

"I'm not talking about exploiting or taking advantage—I'm talking about making the most of opportunities. If we have a better room available then instead of giving it away as a goodwill gesture, we should ask the guest if they'd like to upgrade for a small charge—still less than it would have cost them to book that room to start with. They get a bargain, and we get money for an empty room. Try and encourage them to book spa treatments, and to treat themselves to afternoon tea—"

"What can I do? And what does all this have to do with Abby?" Her voice was gentle and kind and Evie felt emotion bubble up inside her. She'd been horribly rude and she didn't deserve kindness.

"It turns out that Abby isn't who she said she was. I mean, she is in a way—it's true that she works in all departments, but she's based in head office and her mother is the boss. She wasn't supposed to tell us that."

"The boss. You mean the actual boss? The elusive Alexandra?"

"Yes. Her."

"So Abby was sort of spying."

"I suppose so."

"Mm. For a spy she was remarkably good at clearing up mess. You should have seen the bathroom she did in the Merlin suite last week. Pat said the two of them almost needed hazmat suits but Abby got stuck right in." Donna thought for a moment. "You're saying she was finding out what's going on here and reporting back to her mother?"

"Apparently."

"Which means her mother takes notice of what she says."

Evie had no idea where this was going. "I suppose so."

"Well then, maybe we can turn that to our advantage."

"How?"

"Abby's a decent person. She made a bad choice, but I suppose it's not much of a choice if the boss is also your mother. She could have resigned on principle I suppose, but this is her mother so that's going to mean a lot of awkward Sunday lunches. The way I see it, if she's feeding stuff to her mother, we need to make sure she's feeding the right things."

"It's too late for that. She's already sent feedback," Evie said. "And I feel bad. This is all my fault. Or at least, a large part of it is my fault."

"Why do you think that?"

"Because I'm the acting general manager. I saw how things

were from the first day I took over, but I haven't managed to turn things around. I've let you all down."

"That's not true."

"It is true. I thought it would be great stepping up and managing this place. It's what I've always wanted. I had loads of ideas at the beginning, but I have totally failed to put any of them into practice. I wrote a memo and no one even read it, and that's on me. Her report will probably say that I don't know how to get people to take me seriously, and an effective general manager needs the respect of the staff. And she's right. Someone more experienced should step into the role and I should move aside. That would be best for everyone."

There was a long pause and then Donna stood up. "I'm glad you told me this. I wish you'd told me sooner. I remember the memo, but I thought they were just ideas you'd been having. I didn't understand what was at stake. I'm pretty sure the others didn't understand either. That's on us."

No, Evie thought, it was on her. She hadn't been direct enough, she saw that now.

She'd sent the memo because it had seemed easier to email people. She'd been afraid to act like the boss, always conscious that most of the staff were older than her and had known her forever. It felt like overstepping. She'd had no idea how to handle her new position or them, but instead of learning and dealing with it, she'd hidden away. She'd addressed things in a roundabout way and hadn't been direct. She'd hoped that by sending the memo it might be enough to persuade people to change what they were doing. But it had been a type of avoidance. She should have done it in person. She should have been straight with them. That's what a leader would do, and she was supposed to be a leader.

"Donna?" She stopped her colleague before she could reach

the door. "Ask everyone to come to the conference room at midday. I'm going to talk to them."

Donna nodded approval. "Good plan. I'll do that."

She turned and left the room, leaving Evie feeling overwhelmed by a sense of responsibility.

15

Abby

She'd ruined everything.

On balance maybe it was better not to care about your colleagues, because then when things went wrong it didn't hurt so much.

Abby sat in her room staring at the wall. She had no idea how she'd made it through the day. She'd felt terrible physically, and even worse emotionally.

The conversation with Evie had left her drained and exhausted. She'd been unable to defend herself because everything Evie had said had been true up to a point. She'd been unable to make excuses because there weren't any. They thought she was a liar, and she was. She deserved every accusation they'd thrown at her. They despised her, which wasn't a surprise.

She could justify her choices in any number of ways, but in the end there was no escaping the truth.

She was thirty-two years old and still trying to please her mother.

Pathetic. Also, a thankless task because there was no pleasing her mother.

The heat in the attic room was oppressive and she ran her hand over the back of her neck, freeing her damp hair, but there was no relief to be found. For the first time since she'd arrived in Cornwall she wished she was back in Boston, in her own apartment. She longed for the frigid air conditioning, and also the anonymity. There, the atmosphere was so sterile she frequently forgot she had neighbours. She'd met the woman who lived next door on one occasion since she'd moved in the year before and that was when a fire alarm had sounded in the middle of the night, causing them both to collide in the corridor. Other than that, she might as well have been the sole person on a planet.

But here in the Smuggler's Inn? The whole place was alive. Laughter floated up from the street and trickled through the windows. She heard the sound of seagulls and the tinkle of masts. And she heard sounds coming from the pub below. The occasional thud, the waft of laughter from the bar far beneath her and occasionally Tristan's deep voice communicating with someone outside.

She longed to go for a walk, if not for fresh air (it was stifling!) then at least to clear her head, but she was too afraid of bumping into someone who would berate her.

She should be used to it, shouldn't she? She should be used to being unpopular. Not one of the cool girls. The outsider. The one left alone in the playground. She'd made peace with that. She'd learned to distance herself. She'd reminded herself that they were just being mean and she didn't deserve it.

But this time she deserved it.

Why did it bother her? Why was the approval of this particular group of people so important to her?

The answer was simple, of course. Because she'd grown to like them. Respect them. And they'd made her part of their team. She'd worked with close-knit groups before, but she'd always been on the outside. No one had ever let her in.

Until now.

She cared about their opinion of her, which was a shame because their opinion of her couldn't sink any lower.

What they probably didn't know was that she despised herself more than they did.

Her head was throbbing and she stood up and found some tablets tucked into the back of her suitcase which she washed down with a glass of water.

Now what? What was she supposed to do next?

She'd already forwarded the emails to Evie, as promised. And now she should be updating her mother. She was waiting for Abby to call back, but so far she hadn't been able to face that conversation. No doubt she'd be less than impressed that Abby had got herself into this position.

Abby didn't care. Her main concern was how she was ever going to redeem herself with Evie and the team. Edward, Mandy, Donna, Luca, Kristina—all of them. How could she make it up to them?

She finished the water but her head still throbbed. If only the weather would break. What they needed was rain.

And what she needed was to escape from here. She needed to get out of this room. She needed to lower her stress levels and think calmly.

At home she'd go for a swim in the pool in her apartment block.

She stared at the window for a moment. There was a pool at the hotel, of course, but there was no way she could use that. The staff would probably drown her, and she wouldn't blame them.

But she didn't need a pool, did she?

She was a stone's throw from the Atlantic Ocean. The tide was out. She could walk around the headland to access the beach closest to the harbour and she'd try not to think of the drunken striptease she'd done the night before.

Without giving herself time to plan what she was going to say if she met someone she knew, she stuffed a towel, a sweatshirt and a drink into a bag, pulled a baseball cap over her eyes, and threw her phone onto the bed.

If it rang she'd feel obliged to answer it, and she didn't want to answer it.

She headed out of the pub and into the crowded street.

She kept her head down and kept walking, past the harbour and then down onto the sand.

The beach was quiet, with just a couple of families at the far end and a couple of teenagers with bodyboards.

At the water's edge a mother was holding a baby, occasionally lowering her and dipping her little feet in the water. Her other child, a little girl about five years old wearing a vibrant pink dress, was building a sandcastle a short distance away, cramming sand into a bucket and plopping it out. Her mother kept glancing in her direction to check on her, shouting encouraging words while the baby in her arms kicked its legs and giggled.

Abby stripped down to her swimsuit, watching the young family. It was no picnic trying to watch two young children by yourself. The woman looked familiar, but she couldn't place her.

Admiring the mother for handling it on her own, she walked across the damp sand to the edge of the sea. The tide had started to turn and the waves were picking up, but didn't look too scary apart from the area near the rocks. She'd avoid that.

It was past 6 p.m. and there were no lifeguards on the beach, but that didn't worry her. She was a strong swimmer, and she had no intention of going far.

She waded into the sea, the water icy cold against her heated skin. She could hear the little girl laughing with happiness and she smiled at the sound as she plunged into the water and started to swim, the water muting sound.

It was bliss to be in the water and to wash off some of the stress. She swam with strong, rhythmic strokes, always alert to where she was so that she didn't go out too far, and staying well clear of the rocks. She turned, swam across the bay again, and did that several times before her limbs started to feel tired and the cold water had numbed her skin.

She waded back to the shore and dried her face with her towel. Then she grabbed a drink from her bag, shading her eyes from the setting sun as she squinted towards the horizon. She needed to go back and call her mother. That was the adult thing to do. She couldn't put it off any longer.

There was no point in beating herself up. No point in wasting time on regrets. What's done was done. What she had to do now was deal with the fallout.

With a sigh she put her drink back into her bag and picked up her towel again.

She glanced at the young family and saw the mother bent over the baby, presumably changing a nappy. The little girl had wandered to the water's edge and Abby frowned.

The waves were bigger than they'd been half an hour before.

She glanced at the mother again, wondering if she was aware that her other child was by the water. Should she say something? No. She shouldn't interfere. It would make her look judgy. After all, what did she know? She didn't even have children.

She glanced back at the water again, sure she was overreacting. The little girl was gone.

Abby's pulse doubled. Gone where? Was she by the rocks playing hide-and-seek? She'd been there just a moment ago. She couldn't have gone far.

The two teenagers nearby were chatting and lazing on the sand and didn't appear to have seen anything out of the ordinary.

And then Abby saw the briefest flash of pink bobbing in the water close to the rocks.

Her heart almost stopped.

And then she ran, scooping up one of the bodyboards from the two boys as she raced across the sand. "Call 911!"

It was only as her feet hit the water that she realised it wasn't 911 here. It was 999. She hoped the boys had the sense to figure that out.

A panicked scream came from behind her as the mother realised what had happened.

"Holly!! Oh my God, Holly! *Help*, someone help."

Abby fixed her gaze on the spot by the rocks where she'd seen the child, gripped the board and plunged into the water.

The current grabbed her instantly and it was immediately clear to her how the child could have got into trouble that quickly. It tugged at Abby, pulling, and she swam with the board to the rocks, scanning the surface for more signs of pink.

Nothing. There was nothing, and the waves pummelled her relentlessly, pushing her onto the rocks.

Her heart was pounding and she forced aside panic and tried to think clearly. Was the child under the water? Had she been dragged down? She hauled the board onto the rocks so that it didn't float away, wincing as a jagged edge ripped at her skin. Then she dived under the water. She surfaced, gasping for breath, and then dived again and each time she came up for air she scanned the surface.

There was no sign of the child. Nothing. And the foaming white waves were making it hard to spot anything.

She was about to paddle further out to sea when she saw the briefest flash of pink a short distance away from her. Had she imagined it? Was it wishful thinking?

No, she'd definitely seen something.

Keeping her focus on the exact spot she grabbed the board and swam towards it. A wave crashed over her head and she spluttered and gasped, barely catching her breath before it happened again. Where had she seen the pink? It was here. She was sure she was in the right place. But maybe the child had been swept further out.

Feeling a mix of desperation and despair, she looked around her. She saw a crowd forming on the beach and a vehicle crossing the sand.

The relief she felt in knowing that help was on its way lasted only seconds. By the time they made it into the water it would be too late.

She trod water, increasingly tired, and then she saw pink again, just a few strokes from her current position.

She dived towards it and grabbed it, screaming in frustration as it disappeared under the water out of her reach.

She wrapped the cord from the board around her wrist and dived down, stretching out her arms, searching. Water slid through her fingers. Water and more water and then finally when her lungs were bursting for air and she was about to give up, her fingers brushed against something and she grabbed fabric and then a limb. She held on with grim determination, pumping her legs hard to bring herself and the child back to the surface.

Her lungs were bursting and for a moment she was disorientated. All she could see were waves. She had no idea where the shore was.

She grabbed the edge of the board and heaved the child onto it, lying her on her stomach, gripping her firmly.

Her limbs were exhausted and her eyes were stinging from the constant onslaught of salt water but somehow she figured out which way the waves were going and angled the board so that it was pointing towards the beach.

She picked up a wave and was swept towards the shore at the same time two lifeguards prepared to enter the water.

The mother was standing at the edge of the water, holding the baby who was crying as hysterically as she was.

Abby finally felt sand under her feet and then the lifeguards scooped up the child, laid her on her back on the sand and started resuscitation just as a helicopter landed on the beach.

Relieved to have someone else take responsibility, Abby plopped down on the sand, but she didn't take her eyes off the child.

Breathe. Breathe.

It was painful to watch the mother's distress and Abby looked away for a moment, her own problems as miniscule as a grain of sand in comparison to the woman's agonising grief.

What did it matter? All this stuff she worried about. What did any of it matter really?

It wasn't important, was it? How had she lost sight of that?

She felt humbled and ashamed that she'd allowed herself to treat something trivial as the end of the world. It could be fixed. And even if it couldn't be fixed, it would work out in some way and she'd handle it. But if this woman lost her child . . .

She heard a thready cough, then choking, and the little girl vomited seawater everywhere.

The mother burst into sobs of relief and Abby was close to joining her.

Thank God.

After that everything happened in a whirl of activity. Abby watched as the paramedics scooped the child into the helicopter, then she felt a hand on her shoulder.

One of the teenagers stood next to her. His limbs were lanky and long, his hair mussed by the sea. He gave her an awkward smile and offered her a can of drink.

"In case you swallowed seawater."

"I did." She gave a grateful smile and took the drink. "Thanks. And sorry for stealing your board without asking."

"It was cool. What you did was cool." The boy frowned. "You're bleeding."

"Am I?" She glanced down and saw the ugly gash on her leg. Blood mingled with seawater. "It was probably the rocks. It's only a scratch. It's not important. Was it you who called the coastguard?"

"Yeah." He grinned. "It's 999 over here by the way, in case you're planning on saving anyone else while you're staying."

She gave a near hysterical laugh. "That was my first and last rescue."

She glanced across the beach. There was no sign of the mother or baby. Presumably they'd gone in the air ambulance.

One of the lifeguards approached her with a first aid bag. "Let me deal with that cut. You did well to grab the board. Bystander rescues don't usually end well."

"I'm aware. But what was I supposed to do? There was no one else around." Although she hadn't really thought it through that carefully, had she? She hadn't weighed options. She'd seen the child disappear and reacted. But now the immediate adrenaline rush had receded, the horror of it seeped into her. It could have ended badly. Her teeth were chattering which made no sense because it wasn't even cold. Maybe she was still feeling the effects of her overindulgence the night before. "I couldn't stand there and let a child drown. I'd had a bad day. I didn't want it to end that way."

He cleaned the cut. "You saved a life. A child's life. I'd say a person's day couldn't get much better than that. You don't need stitches, but you're going to need to change that dressing tomorrow and if the wound looks red get it checked." He glanced up as someone else arrived. "Hey, Tris. Are you okay?"

Tris? Oh no, no, no. That was the last thing she needed.

Unfortunately, although her memory of the night before was a little hazy, she had a clear memory of her time on the beach with Tristan. She'd propositioned him and he'd turned her down. He'd all but carried her from the beach to her bed, but she didn't remember much about that part. Embarrassing didn't begin to describe it. And then there was the fact he'd overheard the message she'd left for her mother.

Currently he knew more about her than any other person in this village.

"I heard someone went into the water after a child. Anything I can do? Use the pub, if you need to. We have food and dry clothing."

"Thanks, but it's all under control. The air ambulance has taken the child to hospital, but it seems she's going to be okay. As is our rescuer."

She wished she could melt into the sand, but there was no chance of that.

"Abby?" Surprise in his voice, Tristan dropped to his haunches. "What the—?"

"You know each other? Your friend is the hero of the hour. She's definitely earned herself a free drink. Fortunately for that family she's a strong swimmer," the lifeguard said. "Hell of a strong swimmer. If you ever want a job, let us know."

Abby thought about Evie and the rest of the team at The Alexandra, Cornwall. She thought about the conversation she still had to have with her mother.

She might well need another job very soon, but it was going to be a long way from here.

"As long as that little girl is okay, that's all that matters." She didn't look at Tristan. She kept her attention on her leg as the lifeguard finished dressing it.

"It was clever of you to grab the board before going into the water. Most people plunge in and then they're in trouble, too." He straightened. "Given that you know each other, I'll leave her in your capable hands, Tris."

She didn't want to be left with Tristan.

"I'm okay. I don't need anyone's help." Determined to prove it, she scrambled to her feet but her legs gave way and Tristan grabbed her.

"You're right. You don't need my help at all."

She ignored that. "My legs are tired, that's all."

"I can imagine. What were you doing on the beach this late anyway?"

"It's not that late. And I was swimming. Swimming is a good way of getting rid of stress. What are you doing here?"

"I was behind the bar when someone said a child had drowned."

Abby shook her head and stroked her hair out of her eyes. It was still wet and matted with seawater. Her eyes stung. "It was a little girl. She was paddling, but fell over and got swept out. I hope she's going to be okay."

"The lifeguards seemed to think she would be, thanks to you." Tristan muttered something and pulled her against him, rubbing his hands down her back. "You're shivering. You're cold. We need to get you warmed up."

She had a powerful urge to lean into him and let him hold her, but she resisted.

"I'm okay." She pulled away and forced her limbs to walk the short distance to her things. She realised how far the tide had come in since the adventure had started. She tugged her sweatshirt out of her bag and pulled it over her head, welcoming the soft warmth. "You don't need to do anything. I can sort myself out."

He picked up her bag. "I don't doubt that, but smart people know when to accept help."

"Are you trying to scare me?"

"Just stating the truth." He glanced at the ocean and then back at her. "I can't believe you went into the water. Do you know how many people drown each year trying to rescue people in trouble in the water?"

"Not the exact figure, but I know it's a thing. Which is why I grabbed the board from those teenagers. I was lucky they were there."

"Still, you should have—"

"Should have what, Tristan?" She pulled up the hood of her sweatshirt. "Left a child to drown? I know you have a low opinion of me, but even I'm not that bad. And honestly after the day I've had, I don't have the energy for this conversation. And before you ask, yes, I told Evie the truth. I have apologised to the people I needed to apologise to, so you can let it go."

She forced her wobbly weak legs forward.

It wasn't far. She could make it without leaning on him.

She could see a small crowd gathered at the harbour.

She tugged her hood further over her head. "What are they doing there?"

"They were watching the helicopter. It's a change from watching seagulls." He put his arm round her and urged her through the crowd. "Keep walking."

"I'm doing my best." She was shivering badly now, and he sent her a concerned look as they headed across the street to the pub.

A man stopped him. "Hey, Tris, everyone okay?"

"Everyone is fine. All good, thanks, Jim." Without pausing for conversation, he propelled her up the stairs and into her room.

Closing the door behind them he strode to the bathroom and turned on the shower.

"You need to warm up."

She waited for him to leave and when he didn't, she sighed.

"I'm not undressing in front of you."

"That's not what you said last night." There was humour in his eyes, and she gave him a look.

"You could have ignored that. You could have not mentioned it. That would have been the kind thing to do." Past caring what he thought, she slid off her shoes. "Obviously I will never be drinking again."

"Why not? It was a fun evening. You're a great piano player. And a sexy dancer. And, it turns out, a strong swimmer. Which is something we are all grateful for, Chrissy most of all."

"You knew the family?" She was halfway through removing her sweatshirt, and paused. "Chrissy. Holly." She nodded. "Of course. I thought she looked familiar, but I couldn't place her. I met her the first day I arrived at the hotel. Evie was talking to her. How do you know her?"

"Her husband comes in here for a drink occasionally at weekends. Spends most of it on the phone wheeling and dealing. Rich city type. He'll probably give you a reward."

"The only thing I want is for my headache to go away."

She saw him raise an eyebrow and knew he was thinking of the night before. And she was thinking of it too, even though she was trying not to.

"Get in the shower, Abby," he muttered. "You're freezing."

She threw her damp sweatshirt over the chair. "I will. When you've gone."

He hesitated. "Okay. I'm going to get you a bowl of soup. I'll be back."

"Don't bother." But she was talking to herself because he'd already left the room.

Too tired to care too much what he thought about her, she undressed. She was tempted to flop onto the bed and skip the shower part, but he was right about her being cold.

She needed that hot shower.

She stripped off and headed to the bathroom. It was already steamy and she stepped into the shower and closed her eyes. Instantly her head was filled with images. The mother screaming. The flash of pink. She kept visualising a scenario where she hadn't been able to find the child. And another where the child couldn't be resuscitated.

Trying to block it out, she shampooed her hair to remove the salt and seawater and stood under the hot jet of water for another five minutes.

"Abby?" His voice came through the door and she sighed and turned off the water.

He was persistent, she had to give him that.

"I'm fine." She dried herself and rubbed at her hair, then pulled on the white dressing gown that hung on the back of the door, taking her time in the hope that he'd be gone by the time she came out.

No such luck.

When she stepped out of the bathroom Tristan was standing by her little table, unloading food from a tray.

"I brought you a small bowl of soup, and some toast. Did you swallow a lot of seawater?"

"Some." She sat down at the table. "I'm not hungry. I just want to sleep."

"Just a few mouthfuls."

Deciding that the sooner she ate something, the sooner he'd be gone, she picked up the spoon but her hand was shaking badly and she put it down again.

"I keep reliving it," she muttered. "I couldn't see her at first. Couldn't find her. There was a flash of pink and then nothing. And the waves were getting bigger and she was so tiny—" Her voice broke. "It would make me happy if you'd leave me alone."

"Why would I want to make you happy? Turns out I like annoying you." His voice was rough. "Thanks to you the whole incident had a happy ending. Try and focus on that."

Tears spilled down her cheeks and she covered her face with her hands.

"What if I hadn't decided to go for a swim? It was a last-minute decision." She was sure the two teenage boys wouldn't even have noticed what had happened.

He gave a soft curse and pulled her into his arms.

She tensed for a moment and then buried her face in his shoulder. "If you tell anyone you saw me cry, I'll kill you."

"Why? You've had a pretty traumatic couple of hours. What's wrong with showing emotion?"

She knew she should pull away but his shirt was soft, he smelled delicious and for a moment it felt good to lean on someone.

"It's not something I do, that's all."

"Another first."

"Oh stop." She sniffed and pulled away. "You should have left me to find my own way off the beach. Why didn't you?"

"The tide was coming in. It's bad for tourism if someone drowns. Puts people off coming here."

Despite everything, it made her smile.

"Okay. I get that. But I'm alive, so you don't need to hang around."

"Maybe I want to hang around."

She felt something inside her soften but she ignored it. She was exhausted, still a little hungover, guilty and drained from her conversation with Evie and shaken up by what had so nearly been a tragedy. This wasn't a time to follow her instincts. Of course she wanted to cling to him. It was a human response to feeling vulnerable. All the more reason for him to leave.

"That's a rapid turnaround, don't you think? I've been here for almost a month and up until yesterday you've barely spoken to me. You called me Robot Girl."

"Because you were frosty, invulnerable and untouchable. And now you're warm, vulnerable and human. I prefer this side of you, by the way."

It seemed he wasn't going to leave, so maybe she should get another of her apologies out of the way. Then there was just her mother left.

"I'm sorry about last night. My memories are hazy, but obviously I'm never drinking wine again, ever."

He smiled. "You're interesting when you drink."

Her memory might be hazy, but she clearly remembered the part where he'd rejected her.

"I saw your note when I woke up." Thinking of it reminded her that she still had to call her mother. "I talked to Evie this morning. I told her everything. Naturally she was upset. It was a horrible conversation."

And that was the worst part of all of it. For the first time in her working career she'd felt as if she had a connection with someone. She'd loved every moment of working with Evie.

He nodded and stroked his fingers through her hair. "You've had a hell of a day, haven't you?"

"Not the best. Why are you still sitting here? I hurt your friend and you don't even like me."

"Oh, I like you. I like you a lot."

"You didn't seem to like me when I tried to remove your shirt last night."

A smile spread slowly across his face. "That's because you'd drunk a few glasses of wine. If you want to try it again, that's fine with me."

Her heart thudded a little harder. It was typical, she thought, that she finally met a man she was interested in and couldn't do anything about it.

"I'm not in a sound emotional state. Also you think I'm a terrible person because I lied to your friend. I admire your loyalty, by the way. Evie is lucky having a friend like you."

"I think you're a person who has been dealing with a difficult situation." He reached for the bowl of soup and pulled it closer. "Did I think you should tell Ev the truth? Yes. But am I judging you for what you did? No. I know what it's like trying to please a demanding parent. I know better than anyone what parental pressure feels like. For the record, I definitely don't think you're terrible. I think you're brave, and not only because you jumped into the water to save a child."

"If I was brave, I would have told my mother no when she asked me to go under-cover." She picked up a piece of toast and nibbled the corner.

"Decisions are rarely as easy as they seem to other people."

The last thing she'd expected was empathy. "I try and please her. I always want to please her."

He nodded. "Because it's work as well as personal. Everyone wants to please their boss. When family ties are involved—it becomes a step more complicated. I could bore you for hours with some of the dilemmas I've faced. Have you always worked with her?"

"Yes. It was just the two of us and I don't remember a time when she didn't talk to me about the business."

"She has built an impressive company." He handed her the spoon. "Eat a little soup. A couple of mouthfuls."

She didn't have the energy to fight him so she took the spoon and tried a mouthful of soup. And then another. "It's good."

"All our food is good. Not Luca's standard of course, but wholesome and comforting."

"Your fish pie is the best I've tasted anywhere." She ate half the soup and then put the spoon down. "I still have to call my mother back."

"Can't it wait until tomorrow?"

"I'm not in a habit of putting off difficult and uncomfortable tasks. It's not responsible."

"Says the woman who dived into the ocean known for its rip tides." He shrugged. "My point is that the right decision isn't always the one that is the most responsible."

"If I don't call her, she'll be displeased."

"Maybe that will be a first for her. And it's good for people to experience firsts."

Even the way she was feeling, he could still make her laugh.

"She's already displeased, so it won't make much difference, will it? You're right. I'm going to switch my phone off and I'll call her tomorrow in my lunch hour. That's if Evie still wants me to work at the hotel. I suppose today might have been my last day."

"Evie told me she'd give you a job if she could, so I would think the job is yours for as long as you want it." He loaded the bowl back onto the tray. "Will your mother want you to go straight back to Boston?"

"I have no idea." The thought of it depressed her more than it should.

He stood up and picked up the tray. "If you decide to hang

around here for the summer you can stay here. Maybe take some time to decide what *you* want for once."

His offer surprised her and also touched her.

What did she want?

She had no idea. It wasn't a question she asked herself.

But she was asking it now.

16

★★★★★

Evie

"I feel terrible." Evie scrolled through the report on her laptop. Beyond her kitchen window the sun was setting over the cliffs, but for once she wasn't looking. She'd had one of the worst days at work she could ever remember having, and it showed no signs of improving. Even the glass of red wine by her laptop wasn't helping. "I feel officially terrible."

"Why?" Luca put a pizza on the table between them, along with a couple of plates.

She glanced at it and then at him.

"Pizza?"

It wasn't true to say the day had been all bad. Luca had insisted on coming home with her and making her dinner. Pizza. Her favourite comfort food.

"I can't believe you made that out of what I had in the fridge."

"I didn't. I went to the shop for ingredients." He sliced the pizza. "You were engrossed in that report and didn't notice."

"You went to the shop? The local shop?"

"They have excellent mozzarella and surprisingly good tomatoes."

"Was it Richard or his daughter Alice serving?"

"Both of them."

Her heart sank. "And no doubt they asked what you were cooking, because they always do. When I was growing up they always knew what Dad and I were having for dinner. It was unsettling."

"They did ask."

Of course they did. "And you told them to mind their own business? You said you were making yourself a lonely mozzarella and tomato salad for one, which you were planning to eat while staring out of the window of your equally lonely apartment?"

"No. I told them that I was making you a pizza in your house. We agreed that the contents of your fridge isn't reliable." He put a slice of pizza on her plate. "Nice people. Excellent quality produce. They welcomed me to the village and suggested I call into the bakery tomorrow and pick up something for breakfast. They also told me to buy a couple of coffees because you never have milk in the fridge. Apparently the bakery is owned by a family member. I forget the name."

"Lucy," Evie said faintly. "She's Alice's cousin."

"That's it. Lucy." He sat down opposite her. "They said cinnamon swirls are your favourite. I said they sounded perfect because we'd be using up a lot of calories tonight that would need replenishing."

"You said *what*? Are you serious? I'm going to have to move." She put her hands over her face and then let them drop. "You do realise you're going to have to wear a disguise and leave before dawn, don't you?"

"I won't be wearing a disguise. And I plan on occupying your bed right until the last possible moment. And then I'll buy cinnamon swirls and probably go out into the street and perhaps sing and dance, so that no one misses the fact that I'm leaving your cottage wearing the same clothes I arrived in tonight."

"Are you trying to make some sort of point?"

"Yes. I'm showing you that I'm comfortable with the whole world knowing I'm making you pizza and then hanging around to make you breakfast."

Something shifted inside her. She felt a swell of emotion. Part of her was appalled but another part of her, the larger part, was touched. He was showing her that he was relaxed about the whole thing.

"You're going to regret this."

"No, I won't." He sounded sure. "You don't have to creep around looking over your shoulder for my benefit, and if someone knocks on your door I will not be hiding in the cupboard or climbing out of your window naked."

She didn't know whether to laugh or cry. To cover her emotion, she kept it light.

"I've seen you naked. The locals are missing out. Wait—" She stared at him suspiciously as something dawned on her. "You're saying all this to distract me, aren't you?"

"Yes. You're upset and I thought you needed to focus on something other than your crappy day."

"So none of the above is true?"

"Oh, it's all true." He helped himself to pizza. "I'm distracting you by telling you the truth. Are you going to eat this? Because I don't want to have to tell Alice that you didn't like her tomatoes."

She reached for the slice he'd given her. "Fine, but you are responsible for what happens next. Don't come complaining to me when the whole village wants regular updates on our relationship journey."

"I won't be complaining. I thought I might start a blog. It might save time." He took a bite of pizza. "I'm still waiting for you to tell me why you feel officially terrible."

"Because I was angry with Abby. When she said she'd been sending reports to her mother, I was furious. It felt like such a betrayal." Evie rubbed her forehead. "I felt exposed and defensive, and I assumed—"

"You assumed she'd said bad things about you."

"Not only me. The whole team. But the team is my responsibility so in a way yes, me. It all reflects on me." She took a bite of pizza and moaned. "Oh my—how did you—this is—"

"This is comfort food. You looked as if you needed comfort food." He put another slice on her plate. "I'm guessing from your sudden bout of self-flagellation that she hasn't said bad things?"

"No. Far from it. It's better than any end of year school report I ever had. They always read *Evie would do better if she talked less*." She ate the second slice of pizza. "This is delicious. You truly are a genius. I can't believe you made it in my kitchen."

"A pizza oven would have been better, but this is still better than those frozen abominations you buy. Can I read what she said?"

"No! It's embarrassing."

"I thought you said it was good."

"It is good. Embarrassingly good. Letting you read it will feel like boasting."

He shook his head. "Just give me the laptop."

She pushed the laptop towards him and focused on the pizza, trying not to feel self-conscious.

"*Evie has done an extraordinarily good job under challenging circumstances and without support from management*," he read. "*Despite a lack of experience she demonstrates excellent leadership and communication skills and her ideas are—*"

"Maybe don't read it aloud. I'm blushing."

He scanned the rest quickly and looked up. "This is glowing."

"Yes. And there's plenty more like that. I honestly thought she'd been digging for dirt. Trying to find reasons to justify to the company—which turns out to be her mother—to shut us down or sell us to Weasel features." Evie took another slice of pizza. "I should call her and apologise."

"You'll see her tomorrow."

"I handled it badly. I don't think I can wait until tomorrow. I was in the wrong and I need to fix it." She grabbed her phone and dialled, taking a deep breath. "No answer. Do you think she's ignoring me? Or maybe I've upset her horribly and she's crying in bed."

"Maybe her phone is switched off."

"But why? It's not that late, is it? I'll call again and leave a message." She dialled and waited. "Hi, Abby, it's Evie. Thanks for sending the reports through. I—they're really good and not what I expected. I owe you an apology, and I didn't want to wait until tomorrow. Anyway, you're not picking up but if you want to call me back then do, otherwise I'll see you at the hotel in the morning. And again, I'm sorry. We're going to figure this out. Please don't leave."

Luca watched her. "Why are you being hard on yourself? She did lie to you, Evie."

"I know. But she was obviously navigating a complicated situation with her mother who is also her boss. That can't be easy. Weird that she works with her mother, and I work with my dad." She helped herself to another slice of pizza. "Now I think about it she did ask me some questions about how I found it working with Dad. But it's not the same, is it? My dad isn't the boss of the whole company."

"Close your laptop now. It's time to relax and stop chewing on it."

"Are you using food analogies to comment on my stressful situation?"

He topped up her wine glass. "Food is all I know."

"I wouldn't say that—" She studied him across the table. "I'd say you know a few other things, too. Do you want me to describe them in more detail on your blog?"

He put the bottle down slowly. "I do, but we both know the only reason you're interested in me is because I can make pizza that makes you forget all the pizzas you have ever eaten before."

"That's true, but not entirely. There are other things I like about you. For example, your eyelashes."

"My eyelashes?"

"Yes. Most women would kill to have eyelashes like yours."

"So if I burn my eyelashes off while cooking your pizza in a hot oven, that's the end of our relationship?"

He knew she was feeling bad and he'd made her pizza, and now he was doing everything he could to make her laugh and distract her. She liked him. She liked him so much she should probably be terrified.

And at least this game of verbal tennis took her mind off how bad she felt.

"It depends—would the pizza be burned too?"

He opened his mouth to respond but then her phone rang.

She assumed it was Abby and grabbed it, but then saw it was the night manager at the hotel.

"Oh please. Now what? There should be a limit to how much crap each day can deliver, don't you think?" She took a breath and answered it. "Rick? Is everything okay?" She listened. "She what? Are you serious? I'll go to the hospital—are you sure? Well, if she calls you, give her my number."

Luca frowned. "Hospital?"

"Okay. I'll see you tomorrow. And thanks, Rick." She ended the call. "Chrissy Robinson took the kids to the beach this afternoon. Late afternoon. Holly got caught in a rip current. Sorry, I forget you don't know the guests as well as I do. Holly is—"

"Her eldest. I know. She loves my fish goujons." Luca's expression was grim. "Tell me she's okay."

"She almost drowned, but fortunately she was rescued and now she's in hospital." Evie couldn't begin to imagine how terrifying that must have been for Chrissy. "They're keeping her in overnight and Chrissy and the baby are staying with her."

"Thank goodness for lifeguards."

"Well, that's the thing—" Evie still couldn't quite believe what she'd heard. "There are no lifeguards on that beach after 4 p.m. It was Abby who rescued her."

"Abby?"

"Yes. Rick heard it from Jim, who witnessed it from the harbour. Maybe that's why she's not answering." She picked up her phone and called Tristan. He answered immediately and she listened while he gave her a summary of what had happened. "She's in bed now? Okay, well I don't want to wake her, so I'll see her tomorrow."

She ended the call and stared at Luca. "Tristan says she's okay apart from a cut on her leg. He said she was tired, but that was partly stress and partly a hangover—literally—from last night. Do you think I should go to the hospital to check on Chrissy?"

"Where's her husband?"

"He's in London. Rick said Chrissy called him but as it seems Holly is going to be okay he decided to carry on with the meetings he has planned for tomorrow and come up for the weekend as planned. What a total b—" She stopped herself in time but Luca nodded.

"I agree. I was thinking the same thing, only in Italian."

"Who does that? She needs his support. She's on her own

with a baby and a sick child. He's probably staying with his girlfriend or something, do you think?" She felt awful for Chrissy. "I think I should go to the hospital. Will you hate me if I desert you? Sorry."

"Why are you apologising? I agree we should go to the hospital."

"You don't have to come."

"I do. I don't want them feeding Holly any old rubbish. She's particular about what she eats, and food is an important part of recovery."

Evie grabbed a few things she thought Chrissy might find useful and stuffed them into a bag. "I had a glass of wine. We'd better call a taxi."

"I didn't drink. I'll drive. My car is parked up the road next to yours."

"Why didn't you drink?"

He flashed her a wicked smile. "I didn't want to risk impairing my performance later."

Her insides melted and she grabbed the front of his shirt and tugged him towards her. "There's something I need to tell you. Right now."

"Could you tell me without tearing my shirt? I don't think Chrissy wants to see me bare-chested." But he slid his arms round her and pulled her close. "What did you want to tell me?"

She lifted herself on her toes until her mouth was a breath away from his. "I like you. I really like you. And not only because you can make pizza and have eyelashes like Bambi."

"Good." He lowered his mouth to hers, his kiss swift but devastating in its impact. "Because I really like you, too."

She sighed against his mouth and reluctantly pulled away from him. "And now we really have to go."

"We really do."

"But we'll come back here after."

"We definitely will."

She scooped up the bag and her house keys and then paused. "Wait—fish goujons?"

"Excuse me?"

"You said you make Holly fish goujons, but they're not on the menu."

"I know they're not on the menu. I make them just for her. She was going through a fussy eating stage when she arrived a month ago, sending everything back to the kitchen, so she and I had a heart-to-heart about what she might enjoy. She was clear. Nothing slimy, nothing yucky, nothing smelly. My niece likes my fish goujons, so I tried those. Holly loves them. She also loves my peanut chicken wings."

"Aren't they smelly?"

"They're a good smell apparently."

"And they're also not on the menu."

He shrugged. "I want happy diners, and Holly knows what she likes. She might be a restaurant critic one day."

He'd talked to a five-year-old girl about what she wanted to eat. He'd been making her food that wasn't on the menu.

As they left the house it occurred to her that there was a strong chance that she more than liked him.

She might be falling in love with him.

17

★★★★★

Abby

Abby wasn't sure what to expect when she arrived at work the next morning, but it certainly wasn't Donna pouncing on her the moment she arrived.

"You need to see this—" She thrust a piece of paper into Abby's hand.

"What is it?"

"It's the memo Evie sent when she stepped up into the role, telling us her ideas for improving the place."

"Yes, I've—"

"She's a star is our Evie."

"I know that, and—"

"And if people don't listen to her, then that's on us. And it's going to change. Evie called everyone together. She levelled with them. Told the truth about the fact that the hotel isn't doing as well as it should, and that we need to find ways to do better. Bit of a shock to hear it to be honest, but everyone is on board. We're going to make this work. So you can tell the boss, or your mother or whatever you call her at work, not to write off The Alexandra, Cornwall just yet. Wait—what did you just say?"

"I said I know she's a star. My mother also knows she's a star. It was in my reports. And no one has written off the hotel, Donna."

"Oh." Donna looked thrown. "Right. Well, good. But still, you should read the memo. You probably think you already know it all, but she has some good ideas."

"Yes, I've—"

"Wait a moment—" Donna interrupted her and smiled as a woman walked past. "Good morning, Mrs Beresford. How was your breakfast?"

"It was delicious, Donna."

"That's because Chef is a genius and he buys all the food locally. Those eggs came from our own hens. Can I tempt you and Mr Beresford to afternoon tea later? It's going to be a beautiful day, and I can reserve you the best table on the terrace. Think about it—the strawberry jam is homemade from our own home-grown strawberries, chef's scones are the best you will ever have tasted and don't start me on the clotted cream."

Mrs Beresford was almost drooling. "I'm sure it's delicious, but I'm trying to be good—"

"You could always order a nice pot of Earl Grey and enjoy the view. But you're on holiday. Good is for when you're home."

The woman caved in. "You're right, of course. Do book us a table, Donna. Thank you."

"You're welcome. Have a happy day." Donna waited for her to walk away and then looked at Abby, pride in her eyes.

"There you go. Upselling. Point number two on the memo Evie sent."

"You were good at it," Abby said faintly. "I almost wanted you to book me a table, too."

"You're staff. No sitting down for you," Donna said. "I had no idea that would be so much fun. Gerald never used to let us suggest anything. He said it was wrong to put any pressure on guests. But I didn't strap her to the chair and force-feed her scones, did I? She could have said no, but she didn't. Next I'll persuade her to book a session at the spa."

Abby laughed. "Go for it." She handed the memo back. "I don't need this, Donna. I've already seen it."

"You have?"

"Yes. And sent it to the boss."

"Right. Well, that's good." Donna straightened her uniform. "So you'll tell us if there's anything else we can do to impress her. And in the meantime, Mandy wants to know if you're still available to clean the odd bathroom, or are you above all that now?"

Abby felt emotion build in her chest. "I wasn't sure any of you would want to work with me again after Evie told you who I was."

"You saved little Holly, so that gives you pretty much a free pass."

"You know about that?"

Donna gave her a pitying look. "You've been here almost a month and you have to ask that question? Everyone knows, Abby. Chrissy is on her way back with the children now. Edward has gone to collect her from the hospital because her no-good husband is still prioritising his work, and we thought a familiar figure might be comforting. You were brave."

"I was in the right place at the right time." Abby felt a lump build in her throat. "I thought you'd all be mad at me. You have a right to be mad with me."

"If we hadn't worked with you, we might have been mad, but we've seen you getting stuck in like the rest of us. You're one of the team. Should you have told us who you were? Maybe, but if you'd done that, we wouldn't have dared ask you to scrub a toilet, so in the end it was probably for the best. Now I have to go. We have guests checking in and I want to try and persuade them that they can upgrade to our finest suite for a small fee. Evie has just finished walking round the dining room charming everyone, so you'll probably find her in her office."

She walked away and Abby headed to Evie's office.

After that encounter with Donna she wasn't sure what to expect.

Evie was on the phone. "If you definitely saw him then yes, it's time we intervened. He can't keep showing up here . . . right . . . okay, well, let me know. And let me know when Chrissy and the girls get back." She put the phone down and saw Abby and immediately rushed across the room. "I can't believe what happened. If you hadn't been there—you saved Holly. I couldn't sleep last night imagining different scenarios. I'm so sorry about what I said to you yesterday."

She hugged Abby and Abby hugged her back.

"You have nothing to apologise for. What I did was inexcusable."

"It was completely excusable. You were in an impossible position. I should understand that better than anyone because I also work with a parent and it's complicated! I saw that once I calmed down. I hope you'll forgive me. I should have calmed down first and then reacted. I'm working on that." Evie stepped back and sniffed. "Whatever I said, nothing changes the fact that I've loved working with you."

"Me, too. I meant it when I said this has been my happiest time at work ever." It was a struggle to keep her emotions in check. She'd expected this to be difficult. She hadn't expected such warmth from Donna and now Evie. "On the phone just now you were saying someone kept showing up. Is it our weasel man again?" She was still part of the team. If they had a problem, then she had a problem.

"Yes." Evie pulled a face. "One of the gardeners just saw him a moment ago loitering at the edge of the terrace. It's creepy."

"I'm going to call my mother and I'll ask her about it." In a way it was a relief to no longer have to pretend. "I'm confident she doesn't know he's still sniffing around the place. She'll speak to the lawyers and deal with it."

"Right. That would be good." Evie gave a weak smile. "I suppose it could be a good thing that you have the ear of the boss."

"Don't overestimate my influence. She doesn't pay much attention to me, but I can make sure she's informed." She stopped as there was a knock on the door.

Sylvie who dealt with procurement staggered in with a massive basket filled with toys and snacks. "This was the best we could do at short notice."

"It's great, Sylvie. You're a star." Evie took a closer look. "Holly will love this."

"Edward called to say they're five minutes away. I'm going to get this into their suite and then see what Chrissy needs. We were going to do a welcoming committee but then we thought Holly might not like the fuss."

"I think you're right," Evie said. "I'll give them time to get settled and then I'll go up to the room and see what we can do for them."

Sylvie smiled at Abby. "You're the one who did the most for them. You're a hero around here." She left the room and Evie smiled.

"She's right. You are a hero."

"I feel like a fraud. I was in the right place at the right time, that's all."

"That's not the way Chrissy tells it."

"You've seen her?"

"Luca and I went to the hospital last night as soon as we heard. We took snacks and stuff for the baby and things we thought Chrissy might need."

"You and Luca?"

Evie grinned. "I may be in trouble. But that's a conversation to have another time."

"How about this evening? We could—" She broke off as Evie's door opened again.

It was Donna again. "Someone to see you, Abby."

Chrissy walked into the room carrying the toddler and holding Holly's hand. "I hope we're not disturbing you, but Holly painted a picture for Abby and she wanted to give it to her." She let go of Holly's hand and the little girl walked shyly to Abby.

"This is for you. Thank you for saving me." She handed over the picture and Abby dropped into a crouch next to her.

"You did this?" She studied it and then pointed. "Is that me?"

"Yes. And that's me in the water, and that's Mummy."

"I can see that. It's a great picture." Abby pointed to the sea of blue. "And what's that, poking up through the water? Is it a rock?" She had a brief flashback of the rocks. Of feeling the sudden splitting pain in her leg and the panicked feeling that she wasn't going to find the child.

"It's not a rock. It's a shark." Holly frowned at the picture as if it was obvious. "That's his fin."

"Oh! I didn't see that. Did you see a shark?"

"No, but it might have been watching."

"Right." Abby held back laughter. And she'd thought the rocks were bad. "Can I keep this?" She took it carefully. "I'd like to put it on my wall."

"It's all sharks and dinosaurs at the moment," Chrissy said. "How is your leg, Abby?"

"It's nothing. A scratch. I'm just relieved Holly is okay."

Chrissy's eyes filled. "I don't know what to say—"

Abby could see how shaken up she was and didn't know what to say either. If she was having flashbacks, she could imagine what Chrissy's were like. It could have been an emotional moment but fortunately Evie stepped in.

"Just make sure you give us a good review, Chrissy. Top marks for customer service."

Chrissy gave a laugh that was close to hysterical. "I think it's fair to say you went above and beyond in this case."

"Now what can we do for you?" Evie was brisk and professional, sensing that was best for everyone. "I expect you want a quiet day."

"Actually, I think the best idea is to keep things as normal for the girls as possible. I thought we might even go to the beach later." She pinned a brave smile to her face. "Build sandcastles. Maybe paddle in the water."

Holly buried her face in Chrissy's leg. "I don't want to go in the water."

"We won't be swimming, not today. Just a paddle. And ice cream, of course."

"Ice cream?" Holly lifted her head. "With sprinkles?"

"With hundreds of sprinkles."

"Now I'm envious," Evie said. "Would you like someone with you? Kristina finishes her shift at two, and I know she has babysat for you a couple of times."

"She has. The girls love Kristina. Thank you, but no. We

can do this." Chrissy breathed. "And my husband should be here soon. He managed to get an earlier train."

"That's great." Evie's smile didn't falter. "If you change your mind about having company on that beach trip, let us know. You have my number. Call anytime."

They waited until the door was closed and then exchanged looks.

"She wants to get Holly straight back in the water," Abby said. "I wish she'd said yes when you suggested Kristina go with her."

"Maybe her husband will get here before she goes. I'm glad he decided to get an earlier train," Evie said. "Maybe he felt the strength of our judgement and disapproval. Now tell me the truth. Is your leg really okay?"

"Truth? No, it's agony. But hey, at least there wasn't a shark!"

"You probably shouldn't be walking around on it. You should have a day off."

"I don't want a day off. Honestly, I'd rather work, Evie. And then I want us to have dinner in your garden so you can tell me about Luca."

"On one condition—"

"Which is?"

"That you tell me about Tristan. And don't say there's nothing to tell because Tristan messaged me last night and—" She broke off as the door opened again. "Maybe Chrissy has changed her mind about needing help—"

But it wasn't Chrissy. It was Donna, and she wasn't smiling.

"Sorry to interrupt again but there's someone to see you. In the circumstances I thought maybe your office was the best place to bring her, Evie."

"What circumstances? Who wants to see me?"

"Not you." Donna turned to Abby. "Your mother is here."

"My mother? Here? No, that isn't possible. She would

never—" She was about to say that her mother would never come in person, when her mother walked into the room.

"Abby." She nodded and then turned to Donna. "Thank you. I'd appreciate that cup of coffee you so kindly offered."

"Coming right up." Donna virtually bowed her way out of the room, which would have been comical if Abby hadn't been focused on her mother's unexpected arrival.

"I didn't know—you should have called—"

"I did call. After I received your message, but you didn't call me back—" she gave Abby a pointed look "—and I decided it would be better to come in person."

Did her mother know she'd been putting off the call? Probably. But what Abby couldn't understand was why one drunken message would induce her mother to get on a plane and come to a hotel she'd been avoiding for the best part of her adult life.

"But—"

"You must be Evie." Her mother gave Evie a rare smile and extended her hand. "I'm Alexandra Strong. Abby tells me you've been doing excellent work here. We're going to have a talk, you and I. But for now I wonder if you'd be kind enough to—"

"—leave you and Abby alone. Of course." Evie grabbed a couple of things from her desk. "Use my office. Take as long as you need. I'll—" There was a commotion outside the door and Evie sighed.

"I'm sorry. I've never known a morning as crazy as this one. Whatever this is, I'll deal with it and give you time together."

Voices were raised and they could hear Donna saying, "You cannot go in there without an appointment," followed by "I'm going to call security" and then the door flew open and a man stood there.

Abby had only seen him at a distance before, but she knew

who he was because of Evie's description which, it turned out, was uncannily accurate. The weasel.

"Finally," he said, jerking his arm away from Donna who had clearly been trying to pull him back.

He adjusted his jacket and looked round the room. "Busy in here today, isn't it?"

"I'm calling security, Evie," Donna yelled as she headed back down the corridor. "And the police."

"No need for all that drama," the man said. "I tried asking nicely and that didn't work, so I thought I'd take a more opportunistic approach. You're a hard person to get a meeting with."

Evie's mouth tightened. "I don't think . . ."

"Not you." He jerked his head at Alexandra. "Her. It's easier to see the King of England."

Abby expected her mother to cut him down in a few well-chosen words that would have him backing out of the door as quickly as he'd walked through it.

But she was silent. She looked unusually tired, and Abby felt a stab of guilt. Was she the cause of that? Had her drunken phone call upset her mother so much she'd jumped on a plane and flown here instead of simply calling?

Evie stepped towards him. "You can't just walk in here." Her voice was cool and calm. "If you want to make an appointment, I'd ask that you go through the proper channels."

"I tried the proper channels. I even put in an offer on this damn crumbling hotel in an attempt to force a meeting, but that didn't work either." His eyes were on Alexandra. "So now I'm trying the improper channels. How are you, Lexy? It's been a while. Done okay for yourself, haven't you?"

Lexy?

Abby couldn't ever remember anyone calling her mother Lexy before.

And finally her mother spoke. “I have nothing to say to you.” The words were coated in ice. “Leave now.”

“Leave? That’s all you’ve got to say after all these years? You used to be a loving little thing. A real daddy’s girl. So come on—” He held out his arms and winked at her. “Give your old dad a hug.”

18

★★★★★

Alexandra

This wasn't happening. This couldn't be happening.

Give your dad a hug?

Was he serious or had he said that to throw her off balance?

In the end it didn't matter.

His arrogance shook her. The fact that he stood here with his chin up when he should have had his head bowed in shame. The fact that he'd forced his way into her place of business, into her life, when he'd walked away without a backward glance.

What was he doing here? What possible reason could he have for pursuing her like this after all this time?

She was so angry she was surprised that the windows didn't shatter with the force of it.

The past churned inside her, threatening to swamp the control she kept over her emotions.

She was grateful for the years she'd dedicated to learning

how to hide her feelings. She wasn't going to give him the satisfaction of knowing how deeply his sudden reappearance affected her.

"I didn't reply to your emails because I had nothing to say to you, and that hasn't changed."

"Maybe, but it's been a while. I thought it was time we reconnected."

"A while." She stayed still. Stayed calm. "I last saw you when I was eleven years old. I'd say that's more than a while."

"Yeah, so maybe time has slipped past a bit, but all the more reason to fix that now."

She'd learned the advantage of silence in a conversation and she used it now.

He waited, and when she didn't respond he frowned slightly, as if he was trying to reconcile this self-contained woman with the sobbing child he'd left behind.

"I mean, family is family, right?" He gave a dismissive shrug. "You're still my child."

Anger raced through her, driven by the deep pain she felt and also her sense of injustice.

She remembered the day Abby was born. Her child. She'd been devoured by love. Filled to the brim with it. And it had shaken her, because she hadn't known it was possible to feel so intensely. She'd been desperate to do everything right, to be the perfect mother, and even though she knew that wasn't possible because of course all parents made mistakes, she also knew that she would never knowingly bring harm to her daughter, that she would die for her child if necessary, and she'd wondered what her father had lacked that he hadn't felt the same visceral protectiveness towards her.

Those feelings came back to her now.

"You're not my family."

"Yeah, I am. I messed a few things up back then—I'm willing to admit that." He eyed her, expecting at least an acknowledgment of that admission. "I made a few mistakes. But it was a long time ago. What happened between us—water under the bridge. Time to move on. Put it behind us."

Water under the bridge.

The words jarred because for her the love she felt for her child was more like a river bursting its banks. It flooded into every part of her and filled every crack. There were times when it felt deep enough to drown her. It would never flow comfortably under a bridge.

She thought of her poor mother, her gentle and loving mother, hurting both physically and mentally. She thought about the days and nights that she'd spent caring for her, trying desperately to put back together the pieces that he'd broken, scared of what lay ahead of them and the weight on her shoulders. She remembered the devastation and disbelief that her father, her hero, had done this. It had been beyond the comprehension of a girl who still believed in fairy tales and happy endings. Who believed that love was about sticking together through thick and thin. But she was older now, and life had made her wiser.

What did a blood connection excuse? How much were you supposed to forgive before you said *no more*?

Giving herself permission to finally move on she broke that connection, snipping through those wires as if defusing a bomb.

"I'm still not clear why you're here, but let me clarify what I believe you've already been told by my very capable lawyers—I won't be selling this hotel. Not now. Not ever. We have nothing more to say to each other."

"And that being the case, I think we're done here." Evie stepped forward decisively and for a moment he was distracted.

"And who are you?"

"I'm the general manager of the hotel. And I'd like you to leave." Evie was poised and calm and Alexandra felt a flicker of surprise and also admiration. She'd seen gentle when she first arrived but now she saw steel. And she was grateful for it. Another layer stepping between her and the past. Another barrier. She'd gladly take them all.

"That's not your decision. This isn't professional, it's personal." He turned back to Alexandra. "I'm your dad. You at least owe me a conversation."

"I owe you nothing." She was dimly aware of Evie moving to her desk and making a call, her voice a quiet murmur in the background.

"Maybe you don't want anything to do with me, but I have a right to get to know my granddaughter."

Something sparked inside her.

"You have no rights. And why would you want to? It's a little late for emotional reunions, don't you think?"

"That isn't your decision to make, is it, Lexy? She's an adult. She can decide." He turned to Abby. "I bet your mother hasn't told you much about me, has she? We'll have to remedy that. You've got your grandmother's eyes."

That was the comment that broke her. Hearing him talk so casually about her beloved mother was too much for her self-control.

She didn't want to feel this way.

She didn't want him to be able to affect her like this.

He was nothing, and yet she was responding as if he was something.

Was it because for the first few years she'd dreamed of this exact scenario? Dreamed of him walking through the door he'd walked out of without a backward glance and saying he was sorry. Making it up to them. Reforming the family he'd left shattered and bent out of shape. Even when she'd long decided she would never forgive him even if he did show up, she'd kept up the pretence for her mother. Night after night her mother had sobbed, *he's going to come back. One day he'll come back*, and Alexandra had held her and soothed and said *yes of course he will*, because that was what her mother had needed to hear. When she'd died, a part of Alexandra had died, too. She'd hoped he would attend the funeral because there were things she wanted to say to him, but of course he hadn't. He'd been no more present in death than he'd been in life.

And yet here he was.

She felt something falter inside her. She had no doubts about her own feelings, but it was true that technically he was Abby's family. Also true that Alexandra had never discussed him with her daughter apart from delivering the bare facts of his betrayal. He'd demonstrated clearly that she had no place in his life so she'd been careful not to allow him a place in hers.

But Abby was an adult now. Lately she'd been asking a great number of questions about her past. There was a chance she would welcome the opportunity to learn more now that she knew she had a grandfather living.

Horror sank its claws into her. Was that what would happen? If so, she'd be forced to support Abby's choice because there was nothing she wouldn't do for her daughter, even when the idea of it half killed her.

But if Abby was feeling even a flicker of sentiment, it didn't show.

Instead she crossed the room and stood next to her mother.

"You're wrong if you think I don't know about you." Her voice was steady. "I know you left my mother when she was eleven years old and never got in touch again. I know you've been hanging around this place and lying to the staff about who you are. I don't need to know more than that. You're not someone I want, or need, in my life."

Alexandra felt a rush of emotion and knew she needed him gone. She couldn't hold it together for much longer.

"What do you want, really? Why are you here?"

He paused and then gave a little shrug. "I'm having a bit of a downturn in business as it happens. The economy isn't what it was. You seem to be doing brilliantly. You have an eye for a deal. Thought we could have a chat."

She almost laughed.

Money. Of course. He was here because he wanted money. That should have been the first thing that came to mind when she'd been searching for a reason for his persistence.

"I see. So this emotional reunion isn't about sentiment, it's about finance."

It was a relief. That unsettling moment where she'd been afraid she might break down passed. This was business, and she was comfortable with business.

"I do have an eye for a deal. And I won't be doing a deal with you."

The door opened and Alexandra glanced across the room, desperately hoping that it was security.

Edward stood there and her heart gave an extra bump.

Edward.

Just when she thought she had her emotions back under control, this happened.

It was too much for one day.

His gaze met hers briefly but then shifted to her father who was frowning.

"Now what?"

"I'm here to escort you from the premises."

"I don't need escorting. I know my way out." He frowned at Alexandra. "I'm your dad. You owe me."

"I owe you nothing."

"This is all because you bear a grudge because I left you?"

"No." She could hardly speak. "I stopped caring about that a long time ago. I stopped caring about you. But I didn't forget, I can never forget, what you did to my mother."

"Look, you were a kid. I don't expect you to understand, but it was tough after her accident. Tough on me, too. She needed almost full-time care, and—"

"Accident? *Accident?*" Alexandra lost the last of her cool and he looked startled.

"Of course it was an accident. She was hit by a car."

"A car that you were driving."

He rocked on his feet, as if he'd taken a blow. "I don't know what—"

"You didn't know that I knew? I've always known. I saw it happen. She begged me not to tell anyone and I honoured that for her sake, but I always knew. I know all of it. I know that she ran out to beg you not to take the car when you'd been drinking but you were already past paying attention. I know that you hit her with that car, and you drove off without even knowing she was tangled under the wheels." She had to pause to breathe and to push aside memories she'd worked hard to bury. For years she'd had flashbacks and for a brief moment the horror of that moment returned, along with the awful feeling of helplessness. "I was the one who called the ambulance. I was the one who went to the hospital with her. And I was the one who pretended not to know what had happened even though I saw it all from my bedroom window."

His gaze shifted away from hers. "It was a tragic accident."

It took all her willpower not to strike him.

"Drunk driving is not a tragic accident. It's a serious crime. And you had to face what you'd done every day, didn't you? First we thought she was going to die, and then when she didn't die you had to face the fact that she was going to need long-term care and that shattered her because the life she'd known was over. And you were the one who had taken it from her." And he'd taken it from her, too, because her childhood had ended on that night. "The least you could have done was stayed and cared and loved her despite everything—in sickness and in health, right? But you couldn't stand it, could you? So you left."

She was dimly aware of Abby putting an arm round her. Dimly aware that her daughter was holding her. Supporting her.

Normally she would have hated the idea that she needed support from anyone, but she knew she needed it now if she was to finish this.

And she needed to finish it.

She lifted her chin and looked her father in the eye. "You wrecked her life physically and then you walked out and wrecked her mentally. So don't ever tell me that I owe you anything, and don't try and pretend that we are anything other than two people who once had the misfortune to cross paths. Now get out of my hotel, and if you come near my daughter again, or near me, or any of my properties or the team who work here, I'll be getting the police involved. And this time I won't hesitate."

Her father stepped forward but Edward moved quickly, inserting himself between the two of them, his broad shoulders blocking her view of the man who had cast such a long shadow over her life.

"The door is behind you," he said. "And you're going to walk through it."

He gave her father no choice in the matter and then the man she hadn't set eyes on for decades slunk out of the office without a backward glance, the same way he'd slunk away from her all those years before.

He hadn't looked back then, either.

The door closed and Alexandra felt something wash out of her. Some long-held stress. There had been so many things unsaid but now they'd been said and she felt, finally, as if something ugly that had been trapped inside her had finally burned itself out.

"Mom, you need to sit down. Evie—can you grab a chair—" Abby was holding her, guiding her, and then she was sitting and Abby was on her knees beside her, chafing her hands.

"I'm sorry—" Alexandra forced the words out. "I didn't want you to witness that."

"Why? None of this is your fault." There were tears on Abby's cheeks. "I didn't know. You didn't tell me that he caused—"

"I didn't want you to know. I didn't want you to have to carry any of that." Alexandra closed her eyes, trying to drag herself back from the past to the present. "I would appreciate a glass of water."

One was pressed into her hand, and she took a shaky sip and then let her daughter take the glass.

"There's a lot I haven't told you."

"Yes. And it's okay. I know now, and—"

"No. There's a lot I still haven't told you." And it was time. If she could summon the energy, then this was the right time.

"Oh—" Abby put the glass down on the desk. "You don't have to tell me anything you don't want to."

"Yes, I do. I probably should have done it before. I thought I was protecting you, but maybe I was protecting myself. I'm not even sure anymore." The room was swirling. "I'm not feeling too good. I didn't sleep on the flight and I think maybe—"

"It's okay, Mom. I've got you." Abby's arms came around her and held her tightly. "I've got you."

19

★★★★★

Evie

Evie went in search of her father and found him helping a family of four with their bikes.

She felt shaken and unsettled, and not only because of the drama that had played out in her office.

She watched as her father patiently adjusted the seat for the youngest child in the group and helped her steady the bike as she got used to it.

"There you go," he said. "You're getting the hang of it. Well done."

It stirred memories. Happy ones. She remembered him doing the same for her when she was six. She'd learned to ride in the grounds of the hotel, with half the staff ready and waiting to catch her if she fell. She thought about Abby, who had never had a father ready to catch her. Never had a father ready to put himself between his daughter and the rest of the world.

She waited as he waved them off on their trip. They were

kitted out with puncture kits, picnics and big wide smiles. The happy family scene was the perfect antidote to the tension of the past few hours.

He turned and saw her. "Is everything okay?" He frowned. "I walked him off the premises and I made it clear we didn't want to see him on the property again. I think he got the message."

"Let's hope so."

He glanced back at the family, his eyes on the youngest. "How is Alexandra doing?"

She noticed the shift in his tone. "I left her with Abby in my office. She didn't look too good, so I thought I'd give them space."

He nodded. "Let me know if they need anything."

That was it? That was all he was going to say?

She hovered, feeling awkward, unsure how best to ask the questions she wanted to ask. She should probably walk away but she couldn't. She needed to know.

He watched as the family cycled away, the youngest gaining confidence as she got used to the bike. "There she goes. She's got it." He smiled as the wobbling stopped and the little girl's feet worked harder on the pedals. "That child reminds me of you at the same age."

She didn't tell him that she'd been having the same thoughts. "Are you getting nostalgic on me?"

"Maybe I am."

"Talking of the past, I have questions."

She expected him to ask her what questions or at least give her some sort of prompt, but he said nothing. Instead he kept his gaze fixed firmly on the family cycling away from them.

Never before in her life had she felt there was something she couldn't ask him, but she felt it now. As if she was stepping somewhere she shouldn't be stepping.

"Dad?"

"We're at work, Evie."

"I know, but—" Yes, she should probably wait, but she couldn't. Not after what she'd seen. Part of her knew she shouldn't be asking, but another part of her had to. "You know her, don't you?"

"Know who?"

"The boss. Alexandra."

He didn't respond. The family rounded the corner and headed the cycle path that wound its way cross-country and then down to the coast. Another couple of minutes and finally they were out of sight.

Only then did he turn to look at her.

"What makes you think I know her?"

"Oh, come on, Dad! I was there. I saw the two of you. You have oil on your fingers, by the way."

"I had to fix the chain." He pulled a cloth from his pocket and scrubbed at the oil on his fingers. "What do you think you saw?"

She thought about that look. That single burning look that had lasted less than a couple of seconds but communicated a depth of emotion and intimacy that had made her catch her breath. She'd felt as if she was watching something she shouldn't be watching. As if she was somehow intruding. "I saw the way you looked at each other. I'm not imagining it, but if you don't want to tell me then I'll respect that. But—" She sighed. "I'm being selfish, I know, making this about me. What about you? I assume you weren't expecting to see her?"

He scrubbed at a stubborn oil stain. "No," he said finally. "I wasn't."

He was shaken, she could see that now. And she was shaken too, because this was her dad and she'd naïvely thought she knew everything there was to know about him. She'd thought they had no secrets (although now she thought about it she was keeping a fair few herself). And now she was seeing him differently. Not as her dad, but as a man with a past and a life lived. A past full of details of which she knew nothing. A man with his own life and his own secrets.

"I didn't know you knew her. You never said anything."

She stepped closer and touched his arm, conscious that although there was no one close by, they were still in public, still at work.

And it wasn't only intimacy she'd seen, it was protectiveness. Of course her dad was a born protector, but this was something different.

"You care about her."

"I owe her a lot."

"Owe her? How?"

He folded the cloth he'd been using. "Things were tough when you were born. I was struggling to cope with the shocking loss of your mother, and I had to care for a newborn. That included earning a living. I had to be everything, and I couldn't see a way to do that. You'd lost your mother and I wanted to be there for you, but the teaching job I was doing didn't allow for that."

"And that's when you took a job at the hotel." She knew that part of the story. He'd told her many times that it had been the best move he'd ever made.

"I've always made it sound easy, haven't I? As if switching was simply a matter of stepping off one path and onto another." He gave a wry smile. "It was a little more complicated than that. I was a mess—not exactly the type of reliable worker people were queuing up to hire. I wanted to be a good father—and I knew that's what Phoebe would have wanted. She was excited about being a mother and the fact that she never managed to do that—" He paused. "I had to work, but I wanted something flexible that would let me fit around your needs. It—I was struggling."

He'd never talked about this part of his life. He'd never talked about how he'd coped. He brushed over it, told her she was the best thing that had ever happened to him, that having her to care for had helped him heal. And it was true, but now for the first time she was seeing the true hardship of that time. The struggle. And she felt ashamed that she hadn't asked him more about it. Encouraged him to talk. He'd always seemed capable and in control. Even though she'd known he was devastated by the loss of the woman he'd loved, she'd never pictured him struggling.

"It must have been hard," she murmured, knowing that was an understatement. "How did you manage? Who helped?"

"Plenty of people helped, but no one was able to help with the employment side of things. No one would hire me. Or at least, not under terms I could live with. And then I tried the hotel. Alexandra had been there for a couple of years by then. I had to take you to the interview because at that stage I wasn't ready to leave you with anyone."

"I was at your interview?"

"Yes, and there was a great deal riding on that interview—I was desperate and ready to do anything. Afterwards, I told myself that was probably why."

"Why what?"

"Why I embarrassed myself. I intended to go in there and impress her with my knowledge of local history and legend. I intended to show her I was confident and personable and exactly the person she was looking for to deal with the needs of the guests. Instead of which—" he ran his hand over the back of his neck "—all these years later it still embarrasses me to remember it."

"Remember what?"

"I cried." He let his hand drop. "And I don't mean slightly watering eyes. I sobbed."

She stopped breathing. Her heart felt as if it was being squeezed. "Oh, Dad—"

"She stood up and I thought she was going to leave me to pull myself together, but instead she picked up the phone and ordered two cups of strong coffee, and when they arrived she met the person at the door to take the tray, so that they didn't see me."

Now she was the one with tears in her eyes. "That was thoughtful."

"Yes. She put the coffee in front of me, along with a plate full of chocolate biscuits and said she knew what it was like trying to get through a day while dealing with grief and sleepless nights. That's when I found out she had a daughter, too. Madeleine. She was two years old." He stared into the distance. "We talked about the pressure of being a single parent. She told me she'd lost someone she loved, too, in difficult circumstances. She was easy to talk to and a good listener."

"And what happened then?"

He shifted and looked at her. "I thanked her for the coffee and her kindness and apologised again for losing control. Then I stood up to leave. She stopped me. Asked me where I was going. I said I assumed the interview was over. Who would employ someone struggling as much as I was? I wanted to spare us both the awkwardness."

"But she didn't let you leave?"

"No. And I remember exactly what happened next. What she said, word for word." His voice was rough with emotion. "I said something like, you're looking at a man on the edge, and she said *I'm looking at a man who cares. A man who is com-*

mitted to his family. And that was it. She gave me the job. She told me not to worry about juggling work with parenthood because we'd make it work somehow."

Evie's eyes burned with tears. "She said that?"

"Yes. And you started to cry at that point—I had to take you to the interview—and her little girl arrived and was intrigued by you. You liked her and you stopped crying. I remember she gave you her toy giraffe to hold and you wouldn't let go of it."

"And that was Madeleine? But—" she broke off "—wait—if she was two and I was a baby—" And then she remembered what Abby had told her. "Abby is Madeleine?"

"Yes. Madeleine Abigail. Back then I just knew her as Maddy. We all did. Alexandra started using her middle name when they moved to Boston. I suppose she wanted to leave it all behind."

"So you knew Abby?"

"Well, she was two years old," he said dryly, "so I wouldn't exactly say I knew her. Alexandra was living in the hotel at the time and she had a nanny for Maddy. Abby," he corrected himself. "She let me share the nanny whenever I needed to. That extra flexibility was exactly what I needed."

Evie blinked to clear her vision. "So she helped you."

"More than that. She saved me at the lowest point of my life. I owe her everything. She enabled me to work and still be there for you. She gave me hope."

Was that what she'd seen in that look they'd exchanged? Gratitude? A debt never forgotten?

No, it was more. Something deeper, she was sure of it.

"If you worked together for a couple of years, you must have got to know her."

It was a moment before he answered.

“Yes,” he said finally. “I knew her well. In the end we were friends.”

Friends?

“Did you know about her dad?”

“She told me the story. That he left when she was eleven. I knew how badly it affected her, but it happened long before we met. When I first saw that man loitering around the hotel it didn’t cross my mind there could be more to it than a developer deciding whether he was interested or not.”

“Will you be spending some time with her now she’s here?”

“I don’t know. That’s up to her.” He turned away and smiled at a woman who was approaching. “Mrs Slater. Are you off to lunch? I called the restaurant to confirm, and your table is all booked for midday and it’s the one by the window as you requested.”

“Edward, what would I do without you?”

They chatted for a moment and Evie waited. Out of the corner of her eye she saw Abby and her mother walking across the driveway towards a taxi.

Abby spotted her and waved and Evie sprinted across to her.

“I’m sorry to ask this,” Abby said, “but would you mind if I took a few hours with my mother? It’s been a rough morning, and—”

“It’s fine,” Evie said. “Of course. What do you need? Can I get you anything?”

Her head was still reeling from the revelations, so she couldn’t imagine how Abby must be feeling. Her grandfather turning up out of nowhere was enough of a shock without the discovery that he’d caused the accident that had injured her grandmother. And then there was the stress of her mother turning up unannounced when Abby was already exhausted after her dramatic rescue of little Holly.

It was enough to make anyone want to lie down in a dark room.

"Nothing, thanks. We're going for a walk. Fresh air would be good, I think. It has been a bit of a difficult morning." Abby glanced towards the car where her mother was waiting, her head turned away.

Evie touched her arm, wanting to offer support. "How are you doing?"

"Me? Oh, I'm fine." She smiled at Evie. "An eventful week. Thanks, Evie. We'll talk properly soon." As always Abby was poised and in control.

Evie knew that if she'd been in the same position she would have been an emotional wreck.

There was so much she wanted to say, but didn't know where to start and anyway this wasn't the time because Abby was already walking towards the car.

Did Abby know that they'd once shared a nanny? That Abby had once shared her toy giraffe with Evie? Was it fanciful to think that they'd had a bond even back then?

As the car pulled away Evie turned to where her father had been standing but there was no sign of him.

She suppressed the feeling of disappointment. That was another conversation that was going to have to wait until later.

And in the meantime, she still had a hotel to run.

She walked back through the front door and past reception where she heard Donna enthusiastically selling the benefits of the special wellness package that the spa was offering.

Smiling, she headed back to her office and closed the door.

She checked her email and saw that the hotel in London had invited her for a face-to-face interview. The last stage in the process.

She felt a surge of elation that she'd got through to the final stage. They'd told her the position was competitive (had she known just how competitive at the beginning she probably wouldn't have had the nerve to apply) so the fact that she'd made it to the final hurdle was dizzying. It was a brilliant job, and would give her exactly the type of experience she needed.

She sat down in her chair and stared at the screen.

London.

At least there wouldn't be seagulls trying to steal her ice cream.

20

★★★★★

Abby

"Are you sure a walk is a good idea? We could find a room, or even go back to the pub." She'd never seen her mother vulnerable before, and it was an unsettling experience. Her mother was always in control, and she had answers to every problem. Abby had never seen her shaken out of her usual state of cool, until now. "The Lookout where I'm staying is cosy and we wouldn't be disturbed."

The taxi had dropped them at the top of the hill and they'd walked down the steep cobbled street to the harbour. It was buzzing with people. Abby didn't think it was the best place for a conversation, but her mother seemed to have other ideas.

"I'm fine, Abby. Don't read too much into my dizzy moment in the hotel. I'd come off a long flight where I foolishly worked instead of sleeping. I drank too much coffee and skipped breakfast. A series of bad decisions on my part. The croissant your chef made was exactly what I needed. And you're right.

He's good." She frowned, considering. "We need to talk about how we can allow him greater freedom to create an exceptional culinary experience for our guests."

Seriously? Her mother had been through what had to be a traumatic experience and she was focusing on how to maximise Luca's potential?

"Mom—"

"Stop looking at me as if I might collapse. I'd like to walk. I walked all the time when I lived here. It was when I did my best thinking." She eyed the path that led up onto the coast path. "That was the walk I did almost every day."

"I love it, too." It felt odd to think she and her mother might have walked the same route and stared out across the same views. "Do you want to stop and change your shoes or anything?"

"No. We won't be walking far." She shaded her eyes. "Just to the top of the path. Is there still a seat there?"

"Yes. It's positioned to make the most of the view."

"If I recall correctly, it's a little set back from the path. That's where we'll go."

"Are you sure? Because—"

"I'm sure. You of all people should know I don't say things I don't mean."

"But seeing—"

"Seeing that man must have been hard? It wasn't pleasant, but it wasn't as hard as I'd imagined it would be if I ever saw him again. Which surprises me as much as it probably surprises you. Let's walk, shall we?"

Was that really it? All she was going to say?

Abby had been frightened to see her mother so vulnerable for those brief moments, but now she was scared that her mother might withdraw to her usual impenetrable self before they could have a proper conversation.

She was brimming with questions, but she followed her

mother's lead and they headed up the coast path that was now so familiar.

Luckily for them the seat was empty, and they sat down.

"I missed this view."

"Yes." Abby found the view breathtaking, but right now she wouldn't have cared if they'd been staring at a brick wall.

"I want to talk to you, and this feels as good a place to do it as any."

Abby relaxed a little. At least they weren't going to push it aside and pretend it had never happened.

"I'm here for you." She put her hand on her mother's arm. "I hope you know that. I'm not surprised you want to talk."

"Oh, I don't want to talk about *him*." She covered Abby's hand with her own. "You're kind, but what you need to understand is that he'd already taken so much from me. He robbed me of my childhood, of my mother, and also my childish beliefs that a father was someone to depend on, to trust. Perhaps if he'd walked into that room showing remorse and eager to make up for all our missed years that might have been harder to handle, but it was obvious to me that he hadn't changed at all. Not one bit. And I will not let him steal a moment more of my time or my thoughts. So yes, I really am fine." She gave Abby's hand a gentle squeeze and then let go. "Why do you think I changed my surname to Strong? At the time it was both a goal and a reminder of who and what I wanted to be. I wanted nothing to do with him, or his name. That hasn't changed. And now, unless you have more questions, I think it's time we put him in the past."

"But you said you wanted to talk."

"Not about my father. It's your father I want to talk about."

"*My* father?"

"Yes. You have questions. It's a shame you had to get drunk before you could tell me how strongly you were feeling."

Abby felt the colour woosh into her cheeks. "I never like to ask because I know it upsets you. You hate talking about the past."

"It's more that I see no point in it. What does it achieve apart from making you dwell on a time you've worked hard to forget?" Her mother stared out across the ocean. "But the real reason I didn't tell you the detail is because I was protecting you. I didn't want you growing up feeling the way I did. I didn't want you growing up with all that baggage. Taking all that into your interactions with other people. Having it infect every aspect of your life, the way it infected mine."

"I don't understand. I can imagine it was very hard for you after he died. You were pregnant and alone—"

"Yes, it was hard after he died," her mother said. "But it was even harder before he died."

Abby waited, her heart thudding hard. She was consumed by a sense of foreboding. "Tell me."

"You grew up knowing your father died before you were born, but what you didn't know was that we weren't together when he had the accident." There was a long pause. "He'd left me. Us."

She absorbed that. "You mean he walked out?" She felt her mother take her hand again.

"I met him when I was eighteen. I was young. I'd recently lost my own mother and I was derailed by grief. You probably can't imagine that. You see me as calm and always in control, but it has taken many years of hard work to reach that point."

She did see her mother that way. Until today she'd never been able to imagine any situation in which she'd feel out of control, but now she could. Today had shown her that her mother was as human as anyone else. And as vulnerable. It was a strange, slightly unsettling realisation. She'd seen her as a rock, but even rocks could be changed and reshaped by the world around them.

"Tell me what happened."

"I'd been working at the hotel for years by then and I'd seen him around occasionally. Bryan. He owned the hotel. He was older, of course. Much older. Did that have something to do with the attraction?" She shrugged. "Maybe. Probably. He was a competent, successful man, or so I thought. When I was with him I didn't think about the future, just the present. He was also attentive and kind and looked after me. It had been a long time since anyone had looked after me. Usually, I was the one doing the looking after. It was novel. It felt like a rest. I'm not making excuses. I'm telling you how it was."

"Excuses?" Abby had to stop herself from asking a million questions. She knew she had to let her mother tell the story in her own way. "Why would you need to make excuses for your choices? You mean because of the age difference?"

Her father had left them. *He'd left them*.

"No, not that. Bryan was married. And before you ask, yes, he told me. He also told me they were separated, that the marriage was over. A lie as old as time, of course. Would it have made a difference if I'd known he was lying?" Her mother paused. "I don't know. Maybe. Maybe not. I enjoyed our time together and I'd learned by then that life was messy and complicated. I told myself it was okay to snatch a little happiness when it came my way. I didn't see him as often as I would have liked. He was often travelling, but he came back to Cornwall whenever he could."

"How old were you then?"

"I was nineteen. Our affair lasted eight months. Until the day I told him I was pregnant."

That statement landed like a punch.

Abby swallowed. "I take it he wasn't pleased."

"That's an understatement. He didn't want me to be pregnant. He was furious. He thought I'd done it to trap him. I hadn't, as it happens. It was an accident, and one he was very much a part of." She reached for Abby's hand. "But I was thrilled. And he saw how thrilled I was and assumed I'd done it on purpose."

"So he left because of me."

"No." Alexandra squeezed her hand tightly. "You were the excuse. He would have left anyway. He was that kind of man. But that assumption is *exactly* why I didn't tell you. He was a different man from my father, but they did have one thing in common—they both shied away from responsibility. The degree to which he did that only emerged after he was killed."

"It was a road accident? That part was true?"

"Yes. He was driving away from me. Upset, no doubt. Panicking. Afraid of what I might do."

"What did he think you were going to do?"

"Tell his wife, I assume. I knew none of this at the time. I wasn't his next of kin, so I wasn't even informed of his death. It started as a rumour around the hotel. Then his wife turned up looking for me."

"Oh no."

"It came as a shock when she introduced herself." Her mother gave a tired smile. "As you can imagine, it wasn't the most comfortable encounter. It turned out he was more married than he'd claimed to be. His wife was as shocked to hear that they were supposedly estranged as I was to hear that they weren't. It was an enlightening conversation."

"That must have been awful for you." Abby thought about her mother, her trust already broken by the behaviour of her father. "It must have taken a lot for you to trust someone again, and he let you down badly. What a horrible situation."

"Yes, and for her, although she handled it with great dignity. I wasn't his first affair."

"But—" Abby frowned. "He left you the hotel. That was how you got started. I know it was in trouble, but—"

"He left me nothing." Her mother's voice was flat. "He left you nothing. It was his wife who gave me the hotel."

"His *wife*?"

"Yes. I'm not even sure what she did or how she did it, but she spoke to lawyers and then came and spoke to me. She didn't feel it was right that he'd left you with no support, and nor did she want to hold on to a hotel that she would associate with his infidelity. She wanted a fresh start. And she warned me that the hotel was something of a poisoned chalice because it wasn't doing well, but I didn't care about that. I knew I could turn it around."

Abby was silent for a moment, absorbing that new piece of information.

"I can't believe she did that—"

"It was unbelievably generous. *She* was generous. She had every right to punish me and turn away, but she didn't. She gave me a helping hand, and I never forgot that."

Abby swallowed the lump in her throat. "Did you stay in touch?"

"No." Her mother gave a humourless laugh. "She didn't want the reminders. And I wouldn't have wanted them, either."

"Did she have children herself?"

"No. They'd decided together that they didn't want children, which also explained why he panicked. Anyway, last thing I heard—which was many years ago—she'd moved to Australia. I hope she built a good life for herself. She deserved that."

Abby sat for a moment, absorbing this information. As a child, she'd occasionally imagined wistfully how it might have been to have her father in her life, but the scenarios she'd conjured in her young brain all had a fairy-tale quality to them. Her father teaching her to ride a bike. Her father cheering her on in a swimming competition or listening intently as she played the piano. It was funny how when you yearned for something, you assumed you'd get the best possible version. *Be careful what you wish for.*

Abby was silent for a moment, digesting the enormity of it and trying to put herself in her mother's shoes. "Who was with you when I was born?"

"I was alone, but I had a kind midwife."

Picturing it, Abby felt her eyes sting. She thought she knew something about loneliness but her experience paled into insignificance compared with her mother's. Her heart ached for her, but at the same time she felt a flicker of awe and admiration.

"I can't bear to think about you dealing with all that by yourself. It breaks my heart."

Her mother smiled. "I wasn't by myself. I had you, and you were everything. I didn't need anyone else. I'd learned by then that I was better on my own. Life was more stable. Both the men in my life had proved unreliable. I knew I had to learn to rely on myself. For my sake, but also for yours. I was the only person I trusted to build a life for the two of us. In those early days I learned to be my own best friend. No one knew me better than I did. No one knew what I needed better than I did. And yes, those early years were hard because I was trying to care for you and turn the hotel around, but they were also surprisingly happy—again, mostly because of you."

"But I must have been an extra burden for you at a time when you were trying to make the hotel work."

Her mother let go of her hand and shifted so that she could look at her.

"You were a joy. Right from the moment you were born.

You gave me purpose, but more than that you made me happy. And it reminded me of the early years of my own childhood, and it made me determined that you would never, ever feel the same rejection I'd felt. That drove everything I did."

And it had driven the way she'd chosen to parent her only child. Abby saw it clearly now. Her mother's seemingly impossibly high expectations had come from a fierce desire to do her best for her daughter. To give her the tools to deal with adversity. To prepare her for the world. And her reluctance to talk about the past, which had frustrated Abby on many occasions, had also come from a desire to shield her daughter.

Abby felt a warmth spread through her. Her mother, who had been hurt badly herself, had been determined to protect her. "You're a wonderful mother. I'm lucky."

"In some ways you are lucky, and in other ways you're not. But that's true of life in general, I suppose."

"How did you do it?" She blurted out the words. "Through all that loneliness, hurt and disappointment. How did you keep going?"

"Because the alternative to keeping going is giving up, and I'm not the giving up type. Also, I had you." Her mother lifted her hand and stroked Abby's cheek. "I love you very much. I don't tell you often enough, but I hope you know."

She'd never seen her mother this way before. She'd never guessed how much was going on beneath the surface. How much she'd had to deal with. How had she managed it all? How had she built the life she'd built from the rubble of her past?

Abby's eyes filled and tears spilled down her cheeks. "I love you, too. And I'm pleased you're here now, and that you've told me everything."

Her mother let her hand drop.

"Not quite everything. In one of your phone calls you asked me about Edward. You noticed that the dates of his employment were wrong."

"You know each other." It confirmed what she already suspected. "I saw that the moment he walked into the room and dealt with the weasel."

"The weasel?"

"That's what Evie calls him."

Her mother smiled. "Evie is remarkably perceptive. It's a perfect description."

"Edward was protective." She trod carefully. She didn't want her mother to talk about anything she didn't want to talk about, but at the same time she was enjoying this new connection. For the first time she had a glimpse of the person, and not just the successful businesswoman.

"Yes. We were friends. The hotel had been mine for two years when Edward applied for the role of concierge. He'd lost his wife and had a newborn. He needed someone to give him a break, and I was able to do that. He brought the baby to work when he needed to and your nanny cared for both of you. It helped him get back on his feet."

"The baby?" Abby frowned. "You mean Evie?"

"Yes, Evie. You've known her longer than you think. You treated her like a little sister. You missed her when we moved to Boston. It took a while for you to forget. I felt guilty about that."

Evie.

"That day in the boardroom, when you were staring at one page of the report. I couldn't work out what had caught your attention. Was it Edward?" Things fell into place. Things that hadn't made sense, now made sense.

"Yes. It gave me a jolt to see his name there after all these years. I stayed away, you see. I thought it was easier that way."

Easier? Abby was increasingly convinced that they'd had a relationship. She was dying to ask but it didn't feel appropriate. No doubt her mother would tell her if and when she wanted to.

"You never did intend to sell the place, did you?"

"No. This place saved me. I would never sell it."

Abby was confused. "So why did you send me here? I never really understood that."

There was a long silence.

"You were the only person I *could* send." Her mother turned to look back across the ocean. "I didn't want to come here myself, and I didn't trust Jack—he's gone by the way—so you were the obvious person. You've always had a gift for getting straight to the heart of what is wrong with a hotel, and what it needs. Your reports were helpful. Astute. It has been interesting reading them."

"I was a little overenthusiastic in the most recent ones. You prefer facts, I know."

"Your reports were illuminating." There was a pause. "You seem to have enjoyed yourself."

"They're wonderful people." Abby stopped herself. "I mean, they're good at their jobs and they create a warm and welcoming guest experience that—"

"Abby—" Her mother stopped her. "I agree they're wonderful people."

"Right. Good. But you should also know that Evie is a brilliant manager. She has all the right qualities to be running the hotel. I don't know what is happening with Gerald, but we should consider making her position permanent."

Her mother looked at her. "I was thinking that—"

"I mean it, Mom." The words rushed out of her. "I feel it really strongly. I know she's young and not hugely experienced, but she's brilliant. An asset to the hotel and to the business."

"I think that maybe—"

"She was the one who appointed Luca, and he has transformed the dining experience. Then there's—"

"Abby!" Her mother's voice held a note of frustration and Abby immediately stopped talking.

But then she saw that her mother was smiling.

Her mother never smiled in conversations about the business.

"Sorry."

"If you give me time to speak, I'm trying to tell you that I agree with everything you're saying. Evie is excellent, and I've made a point in my life never to waste talent. I will be talking to her."

"Oh. Good." Abby frowned as her mother's words caught up with her. "Wait—did you say Jack had gone? You fired him?"

"I didn't need to. Fortunately, he made the decision himself. I suspect he'll be moving to Scotland. Either way that chapter is closed."

Abby wasn't sorry to hear it.

But the position would need to be filled, and she thought about that for a moment. "We need someone good to take over," she said. "Someone who can genuinely offer support where it's needed."

"I agree." Her mother paused. "Perhaps it's something we can talk about in more detail at some point. I value your opinion. You're an excellent judge of people."

Her mother praised sparingly, but that made it all the more precious when it happened.

Abby hugged the feeling close. "So what happens now?" She looked at her mother. "How long will you stay?"

"As long as I feel it's necessary to be here."

Abby wondered what that meant for her.

She'd expected to be here for the whole summer. Her brief had been to learn what she could about the hotel while under-cover and she'd done that. Her job was done, wasn't it? So now what? She hadn't anticipated leaving this place so soon.

She thought of her evenings spent with Evie. Running along the coast path. Eating supper in her pretty garden. The laughs she shared with her colleagues. Playing the piano in the pub. And she thought about Tristan—

There was a hollow feeling inside her. A strange ache she couldn't quite identify.

She wanted to say something to her mother, but what could she say?

Her mother's focus was the business, and Abby was her successor. The next thing on their list was to replace Jack. Then there would be something else, and something else—

"I love it here," she said quietly, and her mother smiled.

"Even as a child, you used to love the beach. We used to build sandcastles together."

"I wish I could remember that." Abby pondered. "Did I ever go to a party with balloons? I had this weird flashback when we were setting up for a party and I didn't understand it, but now I'm wondering."

"It could have been your fourth birthday party. The staff filled the place with balloons for you. It was a few weeks before we moved to Boston."

It was odd to think she had ties to the hotel that went right back to childhood. Were those ties the reason she was feeling disappointment at the thought of going back to her old life?

No. She knew it was more complicated than that.

"I'm tired," her mother said. "I hate admitting it, but I really am tired."

"After all that stress and emotion it's hardly surprising. You need to sleep." Abby stood up. "I'll take you back to the hotel."

Her mother stood up, too. "You need to get back to work.

You're needed there and it isn't fair on Evie that I've taken you away."

"We can have dinner later? We can eat in the restaurant if you like."

"Not tonight. I have paperwork to catch up on, and there's something I need to do. I hope you're not offended."

"Of course not." She hesitated. Normally at this point she would back off and respect her mother's wish for privacy, but the last few hours had changed everything. "I know you keep saying that you're fine, but this is a lot to deal with. Telling me must have been hard. I want you to know that you can talk to me, anytime. About anything." She held her breath, nervous of the reaction her words might elicit, but her mother's expression softened.

"Thank you."

"I'm serious. You've protected me all your life, but I'm an adult now. You don't need to protect me anymore. These are such deeply personal things there probably aren't many people you can share your feelings with. I want you to know that you can share them with me." She saw her mother's eyes glisten.

"I'll remember that." Her mother took her hand. "I'm not the only one who has had an emotional day. You have, too. Are you sure *you're* all right?"

Her mother rarely asked her that, but in the last few hours it felt as if their whole relationship had shifted.

"Yes, I am. I'm glad I know it all." And she needed to process it. Was it wrong that she felt a little relieved that her mother wanted to be by herself this evening? It would give Abby the space she needed to think through everything that had happened.

A chance to get her head around the fact she'd be leaving Cornwall soon.

Instead of returning to the harbour, they took the footpath that led across the fields to the hotel.

Abby glanced at her mother. There was something softer about her. Something different.

"Are you sure you'll be okay this evening?"

"Definitely." They'd reached the hotel and she surprised Abby by stepping forward and giving her a hug. In public.

Abby hugged her back, her throat thickening. "I love you, Mom."

"I love you, too. You've been the most important thing in my life since the moment you were born. Anyway, that's more than enough sentiment for one day. It's emotionally exhausting and I'm out of practice." Her mother stepped back but there was a sparkle in her eyes. "If you'll excuse me, I'm going to take a proper look at my first hotel. It has been a while."

"Of course. Call if you need me."

Abby watched as her mother walked away from her and was surprised again when she turned and gave a small wave.

It had been an emotional day, that was true, but it was worth it to feel this new level of connection with her mother.

21

★★★★★

Alexandra

She was exhausted but her brain was racing and she knew there was no way she'd sleep, so she lay on the bed, her mind travelling back to the beginning.

There was a delicious irony to the fact that she was staying in a room she'd once cleaned, although it was barely recognisable from those days so long ago.

As she'd scrubbed bathrooms, changed bed linen, filled bowls with fruit and vases with flowers, it had seemed to her that some people had everything while others had nothing and it made no sense. She'd started looking at the guests with fevered curiosity, wondering what they did to earn the money that allowed them to spend a week in a sea view suite ordering room service and expensive bottles of wine. Mostly she'd envied the families who spent whole weeks together and enjoyed each other's company.

It had seemed to her that life was a lottery and when Bryan

came into her life she'd felt, for a moment at least, as if maybe it was her turn and she was holding a winning ticket. She'd been in love for the first time, and that feeling of connection after years of loneliness had been more precious than anything.

When he'd let her down as badly as her father had she'd decided that although there were plenty of things in life over which you had no control, there were things you could control. For the sake of her daughter she was determined to focus on what she could control. And part of that was relying only on herself. No more hoping that a man might live up to her expectations. She was going to live up to her own expectations.

It was a long time ago and yet some of the memories were uncomfortably clear.

She stood up and opened the doors that led onto a balcony. Flowers spilled and tumbled from pots and a small table with two chairs was strategically positioned to take advantage of the spectacular sea view.

When Bryan's wife had left her the hotel she'd been given a chance, and she'd taken it.

She might have been content with this one hotel, but her hard work and creativity had caught the eye of an investor. He'd seen her potential, and from there the business had taken off.

She'd made choices, difficult choices, and she hadn't allowed herself to question them until recently when her past had slipped into her present, forcing her to confront things she'd avoided.

Given that her entire life had been ripped open in the past few hours, there was one more thing she had to do.

Turning away from the balcony, she took a shower and dressed in a cool linen shift dress. She took time over her hair and make-up before heading back down to the village as late afternoon turned to evening.

The narrow streets were busy. Families were returning from

a day at the beach, parents loaded down with damp towels and picnic rugs. Tired children with sandy feet clutched fishing nets and buckets.

The smell of the sea hovered in the air, that tangy salt scent that she'd breathed daily and only now realised she missed.

It was crowded, but she knew where she was going. Even after all these years her sense of direction didn't falter.

She turned off the crowded main street and onto a narrow lane which was home to a row of whitewashed fisherman's cottages. They were well tended, the doors painted in soft pastel shades. Colourful plants spilled out of pots and tubs that lined the cobbled street.

A few tourists were sneaking photos, apparently indifferent to the privacy of the people who lived there.

Alexandra turned away from them, wondering at people's obsession with seeing the world through a camera lens. She preferred to store images in her head, where she could access them anytime she wanted to.

Like now, for example. She had clear memories of standing outside this same door.

She hadn't planned to do this, but now it felt like the right thing to do. And if it turned out to be a mistake, then she'd live with it.

That's what she told herself as she knocked on the door and waited, her heart hammering against her chest. She felt nervous, and she couldn't remember the last time she'd felt nervous about anything.

The door opened and he stood there, familiar and yet unfamiliar.

She hadn't had time to focus on him properly when she'd seen him earlier, but she focused on him now. His hair was still dark, although now there were faint hints of silver. His eyes were the same washed green that had always made her think of the ocean. Outwardly he didn't seem to have changed much, but she knew he had. They both had.

"Ms Strong."

"Really?" She tilted her head, raised an eyebrow and saw him smile.

"Alex." He opened the door wider. "Come in."

She hesitated. She was always sure of herself, but not right at this moment. Not with this man. "I probably should have called. I wasn't sure you'd want me here." And that was why she hadn't called, of course. She'd wanted to see him, and she'd been afraid he might refuse to see her if she'd given him the option.

"I was hoping you'd come."

Her heart lifted and she followed him inside. The house was exactly as she remembered it, only back then it had been crammed with baby paraphernalia. Her place had been the same and she'd been relieved to be able to pass some of Abby's things on to him for Evie.

Sounds of the sea wafted through the open windows, along with a welcome cool breeze.

"Have you eaten?"

"No, but I'm not hungry. It has been a long day."

"You always went off food when you were stressed, and after today you must be stressed. You need to eat. You always get shaky if you don't eat." He walked to the kitchen and she followed him.

"You remember that about me?"

"I remember all of it." He took eggs from the fridge and picked herbs from pots that flourished on the windowsill. "There's wine in the fridge. Why don't you pour us both a glass."

"The glasses—"

"They're in the same place."

She found them, and the wine. It was like travelling back in time.

"You were always a good cook."

"I had a child and I didn't want her raised on chicken nuggets." He whisked the eggs to a froth and tipped them into a hot pan. Then he grated cheese and chopped baby spinach leaves. "If I'd known you were coming, I could have made something special."

"I'm not here for the food, although you're probably right that I should eat. And I didn't know I was coming."

"When did you make the decision?" He added the cheese and wilted the spinach. "Just as a matter of interest?"

"A few hours ago. I tried to rest, but I couldn't."

"Not surprising, after what happened with your father. I assume you didn't know?"

"I had no idea he was going to turn up today, but he has been emailing me." She took a sip of wine. "The first email came a couple of months ago." She watched as he slid a perfect omelette onto a plate.

"That must have given you a shock, and not a pleasant one."

"To begin with I assumed it was a hoax. Forty years, Eddie. I hadn't heard from him in forty years, and then suddenly he lands in my email." Embarrassed, she gave an apologetic smile. "Sorry. I haven't seen you in a long time and here I am dropping all my problems onto you. Believe it or not, I didn't come here for sympathy."

"You don't have to tell me that. I know you, remember? You never did look for sympathy. Empathy? That's different. Personally, I'm feeling inclined to punch something. I'm proud I managed not to do him physical damage when I escorted him from the property."

She felt something soften inside her. "What did you say to him?"

"You don't need the detail. But I don't think you'll be hearing from him again."

"Edward." She said his name softly. "Still my hero."

His gaze lingered on hers for a moment and then he grabbed forks and handed them to her. "Let's take this outside." His voice was roughened. "Evie is out, so no chance of her overhearing us if we're talking in the garden. She lives next door."

"In your mother's house?"

"Yes, although you wouldn't recognise the place. It looks like the inside of a beach hut. Turns out Evie has an eye for colour and design. I try and remember to wear sunglasses whenever I visit."

She laughed. "And presumably you visit often as you're next door. And you can keep an eye on her."

"I'm discreet about that part. Mostly I just enjoy her company. There's no rule that says you can't enjoy the company of your own children."

"True." She thought about Abby and how much she'd missed her over the month she'd been away. "Evie is an impressive young woman. You must be proud."

"I am proud, although I'm not sure how many of her qualities are down to me. I see more of her mother in her."

"You don't give yourself enough credit, but you never did. You were always a wonderful father. A wonderful man. You restored my faith in human nature." She settled herself at the little table and listened to the sounds of the sea. "It has barely changed. We used to sit here and let the girls play. You had a sandpit and a paddling pool back then."

"I remember. The sandpit went to a good home a long time ago, and the paddling pool developed a leak. I seem to recall

Evie pierced it with a toy dinosaur." He put the plate in the middle of the table, divided the omelette and handed her a fork. "I should have picked up an extra plate while I was in the kitchen."

"Don't bother. It won't be the first time we've shared food from the same plate." She took the fork and ate some of the omelette and he did the same.

She couldn't quite believe they were sitting here sharing food and chatting comfortably when so much time had passed. It seemed impossibly intimate for two people who hadn't seen each other for almost three decades. But it didn't feel that long. The connection was still there, as powerful as ever.

"I told Abby everything."

He sat back, his eyes narrowed. "Everything?"

Understanding the question he wasn't asking, she gave a tiny shrug. "All right, not quite everything. I told her about my father, about what he did to my mother. And I told her about her own father. And I should probably be feeling guilty that I didn't tell her the truth about him a long time ago, but I don't." She paused. "When that man walked into the room today, I felt—"

"Vulnerable?"

"Yes. For a moment I was eleven years old again and feeling worthless. I had no idea that seeing him would have such an effect on me. Fortunately, it was a mercifully short moment, but I'm glad it happened because it confirmed that I made the right decision not to tell Abby about her father when she was a child."

"We talked about that at the time, but I wasn't sure if you'd changed your mind as she grew up."

"I didn't. I suppose I thought that maybe I'd tell her one day, but it never felt like the right time. At what age do you tell a child her father didn't want her? That she wasn't important? I wanted her to be confident and secure. I wanted her to know she was loved and wanted, because she was. I didn't want her to spend her life trying to prove herself."

"As you did."

She nodded. "I grew up fighting a constant battle between what he made me feel about myself and what I wanted to feel about myself. You know that." She ate another piece of omelette and then put her fork down. "The crazy thing is that for a moment when he walked into that room, I thought maybe he wanted to apologise. I thought maybe the way he treated us had been on his mind and he wanted to clear his conscience. But he wanted money."

He sighed. "I'm sorry."

"Don't be. It made it easier. And it proved that people don't always change. They don't always see the error of their ways. Sometimes they stay as bad as you always thought they were. And in a way that makes it easier to deal with."

"You do seem remarkably relaxed."

"Because seeing him felt like closure." She leaned back and smiled, slightly stunned by that realisation. "Listen to me! Until this moment I didn't even know I needed closure."

"So you also told Abby about her own father? You've had quite a day."

"She took it surprisingly well. She seemed more concerned about me than herself. They have no relationship of course, and I gave her enough of the truth growing up to make sure she didn't harbour any fairy-tale illusions about her grandfather. Hearing the truth about her own father would have been much harder, I'm sure. She'll have questions when she has had time to think about it."

"From what I've seen she's a kind, steady and level-headed person. I'm sure she'll handle it."

It warmed her to hear him praise her daughter. "You think you know your own child, and then suddenly you look at them and realise they are adults and they have qualities you haven't noticed before."

He looked at her with interest. "Like what?"

"I never knew what a good listener she was before today. Probably because I've never confided in her before. Today, I was the one supposed to be supporting her and in the end she was the one supporting me." She felt pressure in her chest as she remembered Abby's hand on hers and the look in her eyes. "And you're right, she's kind. I used to worry that was a weakness, a vulnerability that people could exploit, but in Abby I've seen it is possible to be both strong and kind. She has none of my hard edges."

"Because she has never had to deal with the things you dealt with. You protected her. And you're kind, too."

"I don't think I am."

"Try telling that to the man you helped all those years ago."

"I was lucky to be in a position to help."

"Not everyone would have done it, even if they could. But you did."

And it had felt good to be able to ease someone else's burden, even if only by a small amount.

Alexandra smiled at him. "Abby told me how helpful you've been since she arrived. Did you know who she was, despite the name?"

"Yes. She has your eyes."

"But you didn't tell anyone."

Edward sat back in his chair. "I assumed there was a reason you didn't want her to reveal her identity."

"There was." She paused. "The official reason was that I needed her to get close to the staff. To get a true picture of what was going on in the hotel. People knowing who she was would have altered the dynamic. She was uncomfortable with the idea."

"I can imagine. She seems a straightforward and honest person."

"She is, but she's also astute about the business and she could see there was truth in what I was saying."

His gaze was steady. "You said that was the official reason. What was the real reason?"

"That's more complicated." It didn't come naturally to her to confide in people, but this was Edward. "If I tell you this, it mustn't go any further."

"I've kept our secret for thirty years, Alex. I think I can be trusted with this one."

She nodded. "I did it for her. She isn't happy at work. Oh, she works hard and she's successful and there is no one who understands the business as well as she does. I have no doubt that she loves the work and she has a gift for curating an exceptional guest experience, but the team don't include her." It stressed her to talk about it, just as it had stressed her to watch it over the years. "There are times when they actively exclude her, because of who she is."

"The boss's daughter."

"Yes. It's a hindrance, not a help. They keep her at a distance. She pretends it doesn't hurt, but I can see it does. And it hurts me, too. I don't show it, of course, but it keeps me awake at night. I've felt helpless." She took a deep breath and flashed him a smile. "And that's something I wouldn't admit to anyone but you."

"Welcome to parenthood."

"Yes. Watching your child suffer is the ultimate form of torture, even when they're adults."

"True. If anything, it's harder when they're adults." He pushed the plate towards her. "Eat a little more."

"I'm not very—"

"Eat. For me."

She sighed and took another mouthful of food. "It is good."

"Finish it."

"Eddie—" She started to object but then decided it would be easier to do as he wanted. "No one usually cares whether I eat or not."

"I care." He watched while she cleared the plate and then nodded approval. "So back to Abby. You must have been tempted to fire your entire executive team."

"Believe me, I considered it."

He nodded. "But instead, you sent her here."

"This place is special, we both know that. I thought if she was able to join as part of the team, as herself and not as my daughter, hopefully make friends and have a couple of months here over the summer, it might be exactly what she needed. And at the least it would give her a break from office politics. I knew it would be problematic when the truth finally came out, but I was hoping that by then she would have made sufficient connections to be able to weather it. I probably didn't think that part through well enough. I let emotions drive my decision making, which is a first for me."

"It worked out fine in the end. She and Evie have a bond."

It pleased her to hear it. "They always did, even as children."

He nodded. "Evie has gained some confidence working with Abby, and Abby has definitely relaxed since the day she arrived. And she's something of a local hero since her dramatic rescue yesterday evening. I assume she told you about that?"

"Rescue? No." She listened while he filled her in, feeling pride as he described her daughter's bravery and then laughing as he filled her in on Abby's moment of fame playing piano in the pub. "That doesn't sound like her."

"If your objective was to send her here so that she could let her hair down and live life a little, I'd say you've achieved that."

"I'm glad. And I'm looking forward to hearing more about it."

He finished his wine. "So you engineered this whole thing for her. And she doesn't know?"

"I hope not. She'd be mortified. She's independent and self-reliant."

"No need to ask who she gets that from."

"Indeed. But there's no rule that says a mother can't give her child a helping hand occasionally, even if that child is a fully functioning adult. Also, I had to give a reason to the executive group. I couldn't exactly tell them I was sending her over here for a break from them." She gave a faint smile. "Don't tell anyone. I prefer people to think I don't have a heart."

He put his glass down slowly, his gaze fixed on hers. "I've never thought that."

She swallowed. "Not even when I moved to Boston?"

"You were as heartbroken as I was."

It was true. It had been one of the most difficult decisions of her life.

"I loved you," she said softly. "Very much."

"I know you did. And I loved you back. I also understood why you needed to go."

And that was one of the reasons she'd loved him. "Those first few months were hard. You have no idea how many times I wanted to book a flight back to you."

He held her gaze. "And you have no idea how many hours I spent hoping that you would."

She felt a pang. No matter how much she disciplined herself not to, it was impossible to not occasionally ask the *what if* question.

"It wouldn't have been fair. Not on either of us. I'd made a decision, and I stuck to it."

"But you never came back. Never visited."

"I was busy." She paused. They'd never lied to each other, and she wasn't going to start now. "But that wasn't it. I had a vision for the future and a purpose. I didn't want anything to derail that. After feeling helpless and powerless for most of my life, suddenly I saw a route where I was the one in control. I was given the opportunity to build the business, and I wanted to do that. I wanted to build a secure future for my daughter and I wanted—no, I *needed*—to prove myself."

"And you've done that."

"Yes, I suppose I have." She finished her drink. "We've talked enough about me. Tell me about you. I know you love your work, and I know you love this community. Did you marry?" She had no right to ask, but she needed to know.

"No. I found love twice in a lifetime. That's more than most. You?"

She shook her head. "There was no one after you. No one important." How could there be? Five minutes in his company was enough to remind her why she'd never been interested in anyone else. "Abby has started asking questions about us."

"So has Evie."

"What did you tell her?"

"Nothing. You?"

"Nothing."

He toyed with his empty glass. "So what happens next?"

It was the question she should have been asking herself but she hadn't wanted to.

"I'm not sure. I have a couple of people to see tomorrow and then I need to think."

"I wasn't talking about the business."

"Oh." And now they came to the awkward part. He was going to ask her what she was doing here, visiting him, and she didn't even know.

"You said you felt a sense of closure from seeing your father. Is that why you knocked on my door? Closure?"

"No. That wasn't why." This was ridiculous. At her age, with her level of competence, she shouldn't be sitting here feeling like a flustered teenager on a first date.

He studied her for a long moment. "When are you flying back?"

"I don't know. When my business here is concluded, I suppose."

"Can I persuade you to take some time for yourself while you're here?"

"You mean a vacation?"

"I assume you're allowed time off. You are the boss."

The way he said it made her smile. "That's right. I am." Her smile faded. "But we can't turn the clock back."

"I'm not suggesting that we do. I'm a big believer in living life forwards."

"We're different people now, Eddie."

"No, we're not. We're the same people but in a different place. Possibly a better place. We no longer have the responsibilities we once had. And you've proved whatever it was you needed to prove. We don't owe anybody anything. Perhaps it's time to focus on ourselves."

Her heart was thudding. He was every bit as charismatic as she remembered. "I'm still not sure what you're suggesting."

"I'm suggesting exactly what you think I'm suggesting."

The steady thud turned into a swooping flutter. "We're a little old for romance, don't you think?"

"I do not think that. And neither do you. Love is a feeling, not a fashion trend. You don't have to be a certain age to wear it."

He'd always had the ability to unsettle her. "It has been a long time, Eddie."

“Exactly. Enough time wasted, I’d say.” He stood up and held out his hand.

She hesitated and then took it and felt his fingers close over hers, his grip firm. “What about the plate and the glasses? We should at least tidy up.”

“Tidying up is for responsible adults and tonight that’s not us. We’ll clear them up in the morning.”

22

Abby

A short distance away Abby sat on the beach with Tristan, staring out across the ocean. It was late and apart from a few stray couples in the distance and one lonely runner, they had the place to themselves.

After the turmoil of the morning and the conversation with her mother, she'd somehow made it through the day and then she'd grabbed her towel and headed straight to the beach to indulge in her new favourite pastime. Swimming in the sea.

She'd swum until her limbs were as tired as the rest of her, until her skin felt salty and tight. She thought how much she preferred swimming in the sea to the sanitised, thermoregulated indoor pool in her apartment building back home. It was like comparing cycling outdoors with an exercise bike. The real thing versus a poor imitation.

Tristan had insisted on joining her, shadowing her with his powerful crawl even though she kept telling him she was fine in the water. But she was pleased he was with her. His presence brought her a comfort she hadn't even known she needed.

Now they were sitting on a small curve of sand sheltered by rocks, not quite a cave but offering enough privacy for their conversation.

"That's quite a story," Tristan said when she finished telling him what had happened. "I'm not sure which part to react to first."

"I feel the same way." She rubbed her damp hair with a towel. "You know they always say be careful what you wish for? I really wanted to know more about my past, and now I know and honestly, I'm not sure that I wouldn't have preferred to carry on in blissful ignorance."

"You're not upset that your mother didn't tell you sooner?"

She draped the towel around her shoulders. "No. I'm grateful to her. Thanks to her I didn't grow up with a ton of psychological baggage that would have cost me a fortune in therapy." And even now it hadn't really sunk in. All those revelations were balanced on the surface of her, not sinking deep. The whole story felt detached from her, and in a way it was, of course. It hadn't been part of her life. Until now.

"Still, it's a lot to deal with."

"Yes." She couldn't believe what she'd witnessed in Evie's office that morning, and she couldn't believe all the things her mother had told her. "It turns out I'm descended from a series of truly pathetic men. Ugh."

"If you want to cry on my shoulder, feel free."

"Cry? Why would I cry? That would make *me* pathetic."

He cleared his throat. "I was assuming that with all those pathetic genes swirling around inside you, you might—"

"Fortunately for me I also inherited my mother's genes. They are dominant. So no, I won't be crying on your shoulder anytime soon."

"Right. Good to know. I'll just have to find another reason to get you to lean on my shoulder."

She turned to look at him.

"I did that the other night, remember? You weren't receptive."

His gaze held hers. "That's not quite how I remember it."

Drops of water clung to his broad shoulders and his chest. His legs were as sandy as hers.

"Men have selective memories."

"We're poorly designed creatures, there's no doubt about that."

"Some more than others." She thought of her grandfather, and also her father. "And some are plain faulty. The sort you'd take back for a refund if they were a kettle or a toaster."

"Hopefully in time, AI will invent a better model, then you won't need us at all."

"Interesting idea. As long as no one trains the AI model using the characteristics of the males in my family." They were bantering, lobbing words back and forth, while underneath something deeper shimmered. Something delicious and dangerous.

Unsettled, she tugged the damp towel from her shoulders and folded it. "Do you think her father felt even a flicker of remorse at the way he behaved?"

"You mean your grandfather?"

"There is nothing grand about him, and he wasn't much of a father either so no." She shrugged. "I can't think of him as my grandfather. Family is important, I've always believed that, but so is self-preservation."

"From what you've told me there didn't seem to be remorse. Denial, maybe. You don't think your mother intends to stay in touch with him then?"

"No." She was absolutely sure about that and once again she admired her mother's strength.

He sat up and put his hand on her shoulder. "Do you want to go back? Take a shower and grab some dinner?"

If she did that the evening would be over and she didn't want it to be over. She wanted to stay here, with him, staring out across the sea. She could happily have stayed like this for the rest of her life.

"No, I'm too wound up. My head is racing. And anyway, I like being by the ocean. I find it soothing."

"You live by the ocean."

"It's not like this." She sat up and looped her arms round her knees, gazing out across the sea as the setting sun sent orange and red streaks across the sky.

She felt his shoulder brush against hers and she turned to look at him.

"You don't have to stay. I'm sure you have things to do. More important things than playing lifeguard."

"That's not why I'm here. And if you're staying, I'm staying."

I'm staying.

It could have been just kindness of course, but she knew it was more than that. And he knew it, too. She could see it in his eyes.

The strength of their attraction was something she hadn't ever felt before. She was careful and thoughtful in her decision making but with him she wanted to abandon both care and thought.

She felt shaky and strange, unbalanced by all the revelations about her life. It all seemed unreal, but this—*he*—felt real.

"How was your day? I haven't even asked."

"It was less eventful than yours." He wiped a droplet of water away from her face with the tip of his finger. "Fairly typical day. My dad went for physio which means he was cranky and needed someone to take it out on."

"Ouch."

"But despite that, he's improving. He even admitted it."

"That's good. Does that mean he'll eventually come back to work?"

"I don't think so. He was aiming for that but today he almost admitted that he's enjoying living life at a slower pace."

"So what does that mean for you?"

"I guess it means I'll be hanging around here for the foreseeable future," he said. "How about you? Now that you're no longer under-cover, does this mean you're going back? You won't be staying for the whole summer?"

There was a strange feeling inside her. That was another thing she hadn't allowed herself to consider, but sooner or later she was going to have to.

"I assume so. My mother sent me here for a specific purpose and that's no longer needed, so yes—I'll be going back."

There was a long pause.

"And how do you feel about that?"

It was a good question.

She felt as if she was balanced between two versions of her life. Until a few weeks ago she hadn't even known there was another version. She hadn't had the wit to imagine it, and yet here she was not only imagining it but living it.

She could go back, she *would* go back, but that didn't mean things would be the same. Things would never be the same. It was as if someone had cut her strings, the strings that had tethered her to the life she was living and now she was floating free.

"I don't want to leave, that's the truth. But I have a whole life there, and this was only ever supposed to be for the summer season."

"Summer is great here, but winter is even better. More locals. We're a tight-knit community. Wild cliff walks, hot chocolate in front of a roaring log fire."

"Stop! We're in the middle of a heatwave and I can't think about log fires and hot chocolate." But she felt a yearning inside her that she didn't fully understand. "But you'll be staying? I thought you couldn't wait to get away?"

"I thought the same thing, but now I don't." He stared across the beach. In the far distance a dog hurtled after a ball, came to a skidding halt and then raced back to its owner. "I suppose sometimes what we want changes. Life changes, and we change with it. It's logical if you think about it. We don't stay the same, so how can what we want stay the same?"

"Good point." She definitely felt different. She wasn't sure how that was possible after just a few weeks, but it was true. Her whole future had been mapped out, but now that future seemed blurry. She couldn't distinguish between what was expected and what she wanted.

He rubbed sand from his leg. "Just in case you feel it's time for a change, there's a vacancy here for a part-time piano player if you're interested."

Her heart bumped against her chest. She turned to look at him. "Is the pay good, or are you going to pay in wine?"

"I couldn't afford to pay you in wine. The pub would go out of business in a week."

She laughed. "That was a one-off. You'd have yourself a bargain if you paid me in wine. I'm a one-glass-only person, remember?"

"I only remember the three-glass person, probably because she was a lot of fun. But seriously—if you wanted to stay, you could."

It was a tempting thought, but it wasn't real. She knew it wasn't possible. It was all too complicated. She was her mother's successor. They had their weekly meetings. She was the one who knew everything about the company, including her mother's plans for the future. She was part of that.

"The hotel is Evie's domain. And she's good at it. Better than I would ever be. Let's not think about it now." For now, she wanted to stay in the present. Enjoy this moment with the sky turning orange and this man by her side. "Where will you live if you stay?"

"I'm pretty settled in the apartment above the pub. I might choose to move out one day, but for now it works. It's convenient, cosy and my commute to work is a few flights of stairs."

"I've never seen your apartment."

"It's nothing fancy. Probably nothing like your place in Boston."

"You're doing it again. Making judgements." She thought about her apartment in Boston with its acres of glass and views over the water. Her mother had suggested she live in Back Bay, but she'd chosen a modern apartment near the waterfront. "Does your apartment have a bed?"

"A bed?" He frowned. "Of course it has a bed. Why?"

"Just checking."

"Well, now you're making me doubt myself." He stood up and dragged her to her feet.

"What are you doing? Where are we going?" She watched as he gathered up their things.

"We're going to check whether I have a bed. In case I'm not remembering clearly."

"And why does it matter?"

"Because I'm not making love to you on the floor. For a start it's an old building and the floors slope, and they also creak. Probably been walked on by too many smugglers. We need a bed. I'm pretty sure I have one. And it's large."

She caught her breath, dazzled by the look in his eyes. "But—"

"Can we stop talking about my bed?" He pulled her against

him and kissed her and his mouth was warm and skilled and tasted of sunshine and salt water.

She melted into him, and her surroundings disappeared.

When she eventually eased away, her heart was pounding.

"I thought you weren't interested."

"I wasn't interested in having sex with a woman who had drunk three glasses of wine in quick succession and couldn't stand up straight. This is different."

His gaze was on her mouth, the sexual tension between them so vivid she felt that everyone else on the beach must surely be able to feel it, too.

"You definitely weren't interested in a one-night stand."

He gave a slow smile and cupped her face in his hands. "Who said anything about a one-night stand?"

23

★★★★★

Alexandra

Alexandra was eating breakfast on the balcony when there was a tap on the door and her daughter stepped into the room.

She put her coffee cup down. "Come on in. I'm enjoying the sun and the breeze. It's a perfect combination."

"You're eating breakfast?" Abby stepped onto the balcony. "You never eat breakfast."

That was true. Alexandra glanced at the few flakes of croissant left on the plate. She'd pulled off a corner intending to sample it and somehow ended up eating the whole thing.

"I could tell you that I'm sampling Chef's handiwork, but I'd be lying. I'm eating breakfast because I'm hungry and the rumours about Luca's skills are all true. I was surprised to find him making breakfast."

"We have an excellent breakfast chef, but Luca is in overall charge obviously and he believes it's important to work with all members of the kitchen staff. And he has introduced a new breakfast menu. We're offering brioche and granita for our more adventurous guests."

"I approve." Alexandra caught sight of the undisturbed bed and wished she'd had the foresight to rumple the sheets a little. "How was your evening?"

Abby flushed. "It was good. Thanks."

The flush interested her. She remembered something Edward had mentioned the night before about the man whose family owned the pub. Tristan?

She'd never asked her daughter about her relationships before, instead accepting what she was told and never delving deeper. So why was she suddenly desperate to know more?

It wasn't her business. Her daughter was allowed to have secrets.

But she wanted to share them. They'd shared so many other things since she'd arrived, why not this?

She stood there feeling clumsy and inept. She had no intention of betraying a confidence, which meant she needed to find another way to coax her daughter to tell her about it.

"I was thinking that maybe later we could—"

"Mom!" Abby blurted out the words. "I need to talk to you. About work."

Work.

She felt a flicker of disappointment, although she knew that was unreasonable. Work was invariably the focus of their conversation. Up until this moment it had been the way she preferred it, but that was because she'd had so much to hide. So much she hadn't wanted to talk about.

Now that everything was out in the open, there was no reason for their conversation topics to be constrained or restricted.

But maybe it was going to take a while to change that.

Sharing with her daughter was something she needed to learn how to do, and she would.

And in the meantime, she'd listen.

"Why don't you sit down? Have you had breakfast?"

"No, but I—I'm not hungry." Abby sat. She perched on the edge of her seat, her back straight. "Do you have a replacement in mind for Jack?"

Alexandra finished her coffee and put the cup down. "It's something I've been thinking about," she said carefully. "Why? Do you have someone in mind?"

"Yes." Abby looked at her. "Me."

"You?"

"I know you probably don't think it's the best thing for me professionally—"

"I think the job would be perfect for you," Alexandra said. "And I think you'd be perfect for the job."

Abby stared at her. "You do?"

"Of course. I'm your biggest supporter. Surely you know that by now."

"I thought you might—"

"Want to keep you in Boston?" Of course, selfishly, it was what she'd like. Her daughter was the most precious thing in her life. Which was why she would let her go with a smile, at least on the outside. That was what parenting was all about, wasn't it? You taught them to fly, and when they eventually flew you felt equal amounts of pride and loss. "I want you to be happy, Abby. And you look happy."

"I am. These last few weeks have been the happiest of my working life."

It was a relief to hear it because there had been moments when she'd doubted her decision, mostly when Abby had protested at the idea of being under-cover.

"You like the people."

"The people, the place—" Abby glanced out towards the ocean "—all of it."

"I thought maybe you'd want to be general manager."

"No." Abby turned her head back to her mother. "That's Evie's role. And she'll be great at it."

But did she want it?

Alexandra thought about the call she'd had from one of her contacts who worked at a rival establishment in London. It had been good to catch up after all this time. And it had been an interesting conversation.

Evie had told no one, she thought. Not Abby, who she'd become close to. And not her father. And Alexandra didn't mention it now. If Evie had wanted people to know she was thinking of leaving, she would have told them. Alexandra believed if someone wanted to keep something to themselves, they should be allowed to do it.

"You're sure you wouldn't want it?"

"General manager? No. I'm more interested in being UK manager. We have six hotels here and it's obvious they haven't been getting the support they deserve. I think I'd be good at that side of things. I have the experience to—"

"Abby," Alexandra interrupted her, her voice gentle. "This isn't an interview. You don't have to sell yourself to me. No one knows your qualities better than I do. The job is yours if you want it. Where will you base yourself?"

"I thought that to begin with I'd stay here. It's easy enough to travel around, and I can give Evie moral support. And it means I can carry on doing the things I've been enjoying—running on the coast path, swimming in the sea—" Abby looked at her and gave a half laugh. "You know, don't you? Well, of course you do. You've been here for twenty-four hours which is more than enough time for the gossip drums to beat. Or are you going to tell me you never listen to gossip?"

"Not at all. I love gossip, but people rarely include me. It's a shame, because one learns a great deal. I'm looking forward to meeting this man you seem to have formed a bond with. Tristan, is it?"

"What exactly have you been told?"

"Not much," Alexandra said. "But I see a change in you that's not all down to fresh salt air and stimulating employment."

"I like him. He has been—" Abby paused. "A good friend to me."

Alexandra was sure it wasn't the "friend" side of things that was responsible for the healthy glow on her daughter's cheeks, but she was happy not to delve into the details.

"One good friend is worth a thousand acquaintances."

"True. So what happens now?"

Good question, and one she'd been asking herself since she'd woken up in Edward's bed that morning.

She pushed that romantic detail aside. "We'll need to finalise details for the job here. You'll fly back to Boston once a month or so. You'll need somewhere to stay so I assume you'll keep the apartment."

"I'll rent it out. I can stay with you if I'm in the city." Abby reached out across the table. "I'll miss you, Mom."

The unexpected declaration caught the back of her throat.

"I'll miss you, too." She was surprised how easy it was to say it, and she squeezed her daughter's hand. "But we'll be seeing plenty of each other so I'm not too worried about that. As well as seeing you in Boston, I plan on spending more time here."

It was something she'd decided that morning, as she'd watched the sunrise from the protective circle of Edward's arms. The bedroom window had been open and she'd breathed in the sea air and wondered how she could have forgotten all that was good about this place. A cloud had hovered over it, but now that cloud had cleared.

Abby was watching her closely. "You'll spend more time here because of the hotel?"

Alexandra thought about everything that had happened the night before. Her own bed might be smooth and pristine, but if anyone had taken the time to glance into Edward's bedroom they would have found the sheets decidedly rumpled.

"Partly, but not entirely."

Abby gave a wide smile. "Are you going to give me detail, or do I have to go and eat fish and chips and ask Meg?"

"There's nothing to tell." *Yet.*

But there could be. And she was sure that there would be. And that was as much a surprise to her as it would no doubt be to her daughter.

"He's a special man," Abby said softly, and Alexandra nodded.

He was, but still it hadn't occurred to her that anything might happen. She'd considered their relationship to be in the past. But Edward had made it clear that the past was behind them, and she would be the first to agree with that. What they had now was the present and the future.

She was looking forward to both.

24

★★★★★

Evie

Evie walked through the reception area and found it buzzing.

"How was your stay?" Donna was charming a couple as they checked out. "If you want to book your stay for next year we have an early bird offer."

The woman glanced at her partner. "Tempting."

"Why don't I hold the room for you until tomorrow? Give you time to think it over." Donna focused on the computer for a moment and then smiled. "All done. If you're interested, then call us back by the end of tomorrow. Otherwise the booking will automatically lapse. I hope you have a smooth journey home."

They walked towards the entrance and Evie exchanged a few words with them and stepped up to the desk.

"Nice work, Donna."

"I'm getting the hang of it. It's fun."

Evie decided to exploit the moment. That was what Abby would do.

"I was thinking," she said, "we sometimes give welcome baskets when people arrive. Why not offer a Cornish farewell gift? We could bundle up fudge and clotted cream biscuits, a jar of Chef's strawberry jam, maybe include a voucher with a discount for a future stay if they book within a month of leaving."

"You suggested that a year ago, didn't you? I remember the meeting."

"Yes. Gerald didn't like the idea."

"That's right." Donna nodded. "But you're in charge now and I think it's a great idea. We can partner up with some local companies. And the ones that offer mail order would continue to benefit. We could commission eco-friendly bags—*take the taste of Cornwall home with you*. That sort of thing. I'll do some research. It will be fun. I'll make a list and you can reach out to them."

"You should do that. You're great at making connections, and you've always been brilliant at choosing the perfect gift."

Donna seemed to grow in height. "You think so?"

"Yes. It's your superpower."

"My superpower." Donna looked happy. "I'll start right away."

"Perfect."

Evie's mood lifted. She felt a fizz of optimism. It occurred to her that far from being a disadvantage that she knew the staff well, it could be an advantage. She knew their strengths and weaknesses. She knew what drove them and inspired them. "Thanks, Donna."

"I'm the one who should be thanking you for making the job more exciting." Donna paused. "He's a good man, Gerald, but he wasn't good at delegating, and he didn't like to change anything."

"I suppose most of us are afraid of change to some extent."

"You're not." Donna was about to say something else but then she caught sight of someone over Evie's shoulder and straightened. "It's the boss. How does she look groomed and elegant in this heat? I'm wilting."

"Good morning, Donna." Alexandra greeted the receptionist warmly. "Thank you for arranging breakfast. It was excellent."

"You're welcome. I'll pass your compliments to the kitchen team."

Alexandra turned to Evie. "Shall we talk in your office? Is now a good time?"

"Of course." As if she was going to say no! Evie found it impossible not to be intimidated by Abby's mother. Her poise and composure explained a great deal about the way Abby was.

Still, she'd learned a lot from Abby and she was sure she could learn a great deal from this woman, too.

Braced for a difficult conversation, she closed her office door.

Alexandra sat down at the table in the corner of Evie's office and gestured for her to join her.

"I'll come straight to the point. I've spoken to Gerald. We had a long talk. Much as he loves this place, he has decided to enjoy his retirement. He won't be coming back. Which means I'll need someone to fill the position of general manager on a permanent basis."

Evie's heart gave a bump.

Here we go, she thought. This was the moment she'd been dreading. The moment the boss was going to tell her she didn't have enough experience.

"Right."

"You applied for a new job. In London."

Taken by surprise, Evie was at a loss for words. She felt the colour rush into her cheeks.

"How did you—" She stumbled over the right response. "I told no one. Not even my father."

"I've been in the business a long time, and I know many people. Someone from the hotel you applied to called me, asking about you. Before we talk about that, can I ask why you chose to apply? You've lived here all your life and worked here for your whole career."

How honest should she be?

Deciding she didn't have anything to lose given that Alexandra already seemed to know most of it, Evie told the truth.

She talked about the difficulties she'd had persuading staff to see her in a more senior role, about the problems she had instigating any sort of change, about her own challenges in managing people.

"I'm ambitious, and I thought moving away might be the answer. A fresh start."

Alexandra proved to be a surprisingly good listener. "I can understand that. I did the same thing myself."

"And it was the right thing to do."

"Overall, yes, although I wouldn't romanticise it. Making a big change is never easy. You gain some things, and you lose others. Only you can weigh up the things that matter most to you. When is your final interview?"

"I withdrew my application."

"Ah. That I didn't know." Alexandra's expression was neutral. "Can I ask why?"

"It was partly because of Abby."

"Abby?"

"Yes. I know she hasn't been here for that long, but in that time I've learned a lot by watching her handle people. She has a way of getting people to do what she wants them to do. But not in a dictatorial way. She makes people *want* to do what she's suggesting. She makes them feel competent and—special. Usually they end up thinking it was their idea in the first place. And she's direct." Evie gave a rueful smile. "I've always had a problem with being direct, I suppose because I've known many of the staff forever, but I've tried following her lead and already things feel a little different."

"And the other reason?"

"What you just said about weighing up what's most important to you." Evie stood up and walked to the window of her office and gazed out over the fields to the sea. "I love this place, but I was feeling stifled. There is barely a single thing in my life that the villagers don't know. And that has occasionally been awkward. Not only at work, but socially. It was frustrating."

"You thought it would be good to get away."

"Yes. But I didn't really think through the reality of it. What leaving would mean. It's easy to think you want to leave, easy to see all the positives when it's just an idea—a theory. But then I had that invitation for a final interview and suddenly it all felt real. For the first time I properly imagined not living here anymore. And I realised how much I love being part of this community." Thinking about it now she wondered how she could ever have thought of leaving. She belonged here, in this beautiful place, with these special people. Full of emotion, Evie turned to look at her. "And the hotel is part of that community. And frustrating though people can sometimes be, I realised that I love them. I love living in a place where I know everyone. It gives me a sense of belonging. In a way they're my family. They've been my family since I was born. And yes, if I moved to London I'd be able to walk down a street without everyone stopping me to catch up on gossip, but I realised that I don't want that. I don't want anonymity.

I like the fact that everyone looks out for each other. And it's true that in London no one would notice or care if I arrived home early in the morning wearing the same clothes I went out in the night before, but I decided I didn't want that either. I didn't want to be one of those people whose body was discovered a month after I'd been murdered because no one noticed I hadn't left my flat." She suddenly remembered this was Abby's mother and her boss she was talking to, but Alexandra's eyes were alight with humour.

"That would indeed be a sad end."

Evie returned to the table and sat down, determined to be professional. "I know you'll be looking for a new general manager now that Gerald definitely isn't coming back, but even if it means going back to my old role or even something different, I still want to stay here, if you'll have me. I want to be part of what we're doing here. I really think I can make a difference. I want to make a difference."

Alexandra gave a rare smile. "Why would I look for a new general manager when the best person for the job is sitting right in front of me? If you're sure it's what you want, then we'll make it official. And I'll match the salary you were being offered in London."

Evie knew she should probably play it cool, but she found it impossible.

"Seriously?"

"I never joke about business. Abby will confirm that, I'm sure. It's a big job, Evie, and it comes with a great deal of responsibility. I expect a great deal from you. It's right that you should be paid accordingly. I've always believed a person should be paid what they're worth, not what a company can get away with." There was a gleam in her eyes. "There is something else I'd like to say. I'm pleased that you've found it useful to watch Abby, but it's important to understand that we all have different styles, and different gifts. There are different ways to motivate a team. You have warmth and empathy and those are important qualities for someone in a leadership position. Don't underestimate the importance of that. I spent some time talking to the staff yesterday and it's clear they have great respect for you."

Evie swallowed. "I'm thirty years of age, and they still make me a chocolate cake with chocolate buttons for my birthday."

Alexandra smiled. "It always was your favourite. You should have seen the mess you made of eating it when you were two years old. It took us an hour to clean you up." She stood up. "I'm delighted you'll be taking the job. I feel fortunate to have you at the helm of my most important hotel. I'll make the announcement immediately. I'm sure there will be celebrations. Possibly even chocolate cake."

Evie laughed but she also felt a quake of nerves. She hoped she was worthy of the faith Alexandra seemed to have in her.

"Thank you."

"I should also praise your decision to reach out when you saw the place was in trouble. That was the right thing to do. I apologise for the fact that you didn't receive support when you asked for it. That won't happen again."

"Is there someone specific I should contact?"

"Yes, Abby. She will be the new UK manager, covering all our hotels here." Her phone buzzed and Alexandra reached into her bag and silenced it. "I'm sure that will be welcome news. And of course you can always reach out to me directly, at any time either at the office or at home." She hesitated. "Your father has my number."

He did? What did that mean exactly?

There was more that Evie wanted to say. Questions she wanted to ask, but it didn't feel appropriate to ask them. At least, not at this moment. She had no idea what exactly was happening between Alexandra and her father, but no doubt she'd find out in time.

It could be nothing, but she hoped it was something.

In the meantime, she had a hotel to run.

After Alexandra left she dealt with a couple of mundane problems and then had a message from Donna saying that there was an issue with the King Arthur suite.

Given that they had new guests arriving in under four hours normally she would have felt stressed, but today nothing could stress her. She all but floated up the stairs. Whatever state the previous guests had left the place in, they'd deal with it somehow.

Braced for disaster, she pushed open the door and saw Donna and Abby studying the carpet.

"What is it?"

"It looks like sheep droppings."

"I think we'd know if someone had brought a sheep into the hotel."

"You never know," Donna said darkly. "People are weird. Someone once sneaked in their pet rabbit. We spent two hours trying to coax it out from under the bed. It ignored carrots, but in the end it was tempted by dandelions."

"I think it could be chocolate." Abby glanced up and saw Evie. She sprang to her feet. "It's the boss, Donna. Stand up. Show some respect."

"I have creaky limbs," Donna said. "It takes me longer than you. If I jump the way you did I'll dislocate something and that wouldn't be fun for anyone. Pull me up, there's a lamb." But she was smiling as Abby tugged her upright. "Congratulations. We just heard."

"Thank you." Evie was both delighted and embarrassed. "I'm very happy. And surprised."

"I don't know why you're surprised. You've had us running around after you since you were a baby so nothing much has changed there." But Donna crossed the room and gave her a great big hug. "That's my girl."

Evie felt a lump build in her throat and Donna gave her a pat and released her.

"Right. Well, I need to get something to remove those sheep droppings, or whatever they are. I'll leave you two here for a minute." She left the room and Evie turned to Abby.

"You're staying! You have no idea how thrilled I am. I hope you'll spend as much time in Cornwall as you can. I'm sure the rest of the hotels can take care of themselves."

"I intend to spend plenty of time here. And congratulations."

"I was surprised when she offered me the job."

"Why? My mother makes a point of never losing good people, and you're a good person in every way."

"She's impressive." Evie wondered how honest to be. "I applied for a new job. In London. They invited me to interview. Somehow, your mother knew. I have no idea how." She looked at Abby. "You don't look surprised."

"I'm not. My mother knows everything. She's well connected." Abby took a breath. "I'm glad you didn't go for that interview."

"I probably wouldn't have got it."

"You would have got it," Abby said softly. "I'm glad you've chosen to stay."

Evie's phone buzzed and she checked it. "We're needed downstairs in my office. Both of us. Is this something to do with your mother?"

"I have no idea."

They headed downstairs and Evie noticed that there was no one at reception, and that there was no sign of her father either.

Where was everyone?

She pushed open the door to her office and was met with a sea of people and a chorus of cheers.

While she'd been talking to Donna and Abby, they'd decorated her office.

There were balloons, and a banner that read *Evie—Five Star Boss.*

Evie felt her eyes fill. "Oh." Someone pressed a glass into her hand, and she noticed then that Alexandra was also there, looking relaxed.

Was she the one who had arranged this?

She tapped the side of her glass and said a few words, praising Evie but also the whole team, and Evie stood in a daze, enjoying the moment but also excited about the future.

There were so many things she wanted to do. Ideas she wanted to try.

And she'd be doing it right here, in the place she loved with the people she loved.

And talking of people she loved—

Everyone moved aside and there, in the middle of her desk, was a large chocolate cake covered in chocolate buttons and Luca was standing next to it, a grin on his face.

He winked at her and Donna leaned in.

"Just because we're being discreet," she muttered, "don't think we don't know that you're having a wild affair with Luca. You've been spotted."

"Now, why doesn't that surprise me?" Evie laughed. It was good to know that some things never changed.

But other things would. And that would be good.

She turned to Abby, who was by her side. "Now that you're not rushing off anywhere, does that mean you'll be free for a run on the coast path tomorrow night?"

"Yes. And for supper in your garden after." Abby looked at

her. "I thought we could ask Luca and Tris to join us for that part. If that works for you. Of course that means we won't be able to gossip about them and exchange intimate details that would totally horrify both of them."

"We can do that another time. I like your plan. It works." Evie thought of everything that lay ahead and smiled. "It definitely works."

★★★★★

ACKNOWLEDGMENTS

★★★★★

Whenever I start a book I'm never entirely sure I'm going to make it to the end until I get there, so it's always something of a relief to reach the point where I need to start thanking people.

As always there are many people on the list, starting with the team at MIRA Books in the US, particularly Margaret Marbury, Susan Swinwood and Michele Bidelspach. I feel privileged that our partnership has lasted for so long and I'm grateful for all you do to bring my books to a wider audience.

In the UK, Lisa Milton, Manpreet Grewal and the rest of the talented HQ Stories team constantly impress me with their enthusiasm and creativity. Working with them is a joy, and something I never take for granted. Thank you for all you do, and for always making me feel part of the team even when I'm working alone in my garden office.

I'm grateful to my fantastic editor, Flo, for her editorial brilliance—fortunately for me, she is not only a book genius but also great fun to work with. Every author should be so lucky.

My fabulous agent, Susan Ginsburg, and her brilliant assistant, Catherine Bradshaw, are always by my side (figuratively, not literally, or we'd never get any work done) and for that I'm more than grateful.

To my amazing family, who know to give me a wide berth if a book is going badly and understand the importance of delivering chocolate and coffee at the right moment. Also for showing endless patience when I comment on plot, dialogue and character whenever we watch a movie together. I know it's annoying. Sorry.

I'm grateful to all the booksellers, book bloggers, and reviewers who so generously talk about my books (and books generally) and encourage people to pick them up. We need books and stories more than ever and you play such an important role.

To my readers—whether this is the first book of mine you've picked up or one of many—thank you. With so many books to choose from, I'm honoured that you've chosen mine.

Turn the page for a sneak peek at Sarah Morgan's next Christmas novel, *The Best Christmas Ever*, coming this fall!

1

★★★★★

Mabel

"A fierce storm is bearing down on the East Coast of America, bringing with it record-breaking snowfall, hurricane-force winds and freezing temperatures. Forecasters are predicting this could be the worst storm since records began. A state of emergency has been declared, and people are urged to seek shelter. Not the Christmas gift all of you were hoping for, I know, but stay home and stay safe."

Mabel Anne Miller turned off the radio and looked at the sleek black cat who was watching her from his favourite place by the window. "Did you hear that? That's going to ruin our plans for a last-minute trip to Manhattan to see the Christmas lights and take in a show. I hope you're not disappointed. No partying for us this Christmas, Crumpet."

The cat purred, sprang down from his perch by the window and rubbed himself against her legs. There were days when Mabel was sure he understood every word she said.

She bent down and stroked behind his ears. "I agree. We should stay home in front of the fire with a good book, which is what we would have been doing anyway." It had been at least a decade since she'd been to Manhattan and even longer since she'd been to a show. It would be as alien as a trip to the moon.

Her world had shrunk to this one small corner of Vermont, her house and her pretty woodland garden with its stream that in summer was home to kingfishers and warblers. The stream was now frozen, and the kingfishers long gone in search of less icy climes. But they'd be back, she knew that. Ice melted and the world kept turning.

Another of her cats padded into the kitchen, and she fussed over him as she would have done a child. For a moment she remembered when she had fussed over a child, and she was swamped by a wave of regret so powerful, it rocked her on her feet.

She grabbed the edge of the table for support and sat down hard on the nearest chair.

Crumpet immediately jumped onto her lap, pressing against her, kneading her leg with his paws.

She stroked him gratefully. He always sensed when she was having a low moment. He was always there for her. Cats were complicated creatures, but in her experience far less complicated than humans.

He looked up at her with eyes that were a startling shade of green.

"I know," she said. "You're right of course. It doesn't make any difference to us if it's Christmas, does it?"

There was a time when it would have made a difference. A time when she would have been decorating the house and filling the kitchen with scents of cinnamon and spice and peering anxiously through the window while she awaited visitors.

Walter would have been preparing drinks, wearing the shirt he only wore at Thanksgiving and Christmas. He'd always been more sociable than her. Welcome, welcome, he'd say, opening up his heart and the door of their home to whoever happened to visit. It was because of Walter that they'd never been short of cheerful company.

But that was a long time ago and many things had changed since then. For a start there was no Walter.

She blinked several times, bringing herself back to the present.

"It's just us," she told the cats, "but that's the way we like it, isn't it? We're used to spending Christmas on our own. It isn't as if we haven't had plenty of practice. And what a relief not to have to do all that baking and decorating, and I've never been good at wrapping presents. All that work just for one day—" Her voice gave a little hitch and Crumpet yawned and looked up at her. "I'm fine, really. I'm fine."

Fine, apart from the fact that her house was currently under siege from the weather. The kitchen windows rattled in their frames and snow swirled beyond the glass. The wind kicked angrily at the building, thumping against windows and pounding the roof like a toddler in the throes of a tantrum. It screamed and howled, the noise so loud that for a moment she pictured the wind blowing the house clean away.

She reminded herself that the house had survived storms before and would no doubt survive this one. Not that she was one of those people who underestimated the force and power of nature. Far from it. She remembered a winter when tiles had been ripped from the roof by the wind, and a winter when they'd been snowed in for two full weeks. That one had been bad. Bad enough that Walter had questioned their decision to live just outside the village, particularly as reaching civilisation would inevitably become more challenging as they aged.

As it happened, that hadn't been a problem for him. In theory it could be a problem for her in future, but she didn't see it as a problem.

She had no need to reach the village and she didn't mind storms. They made her aware of how small she was in comparison. How fragile life was against the force of nature and how little control humans had, really. The storm would come when it wanted to come, and it would wreck what it wanted to wreck, and humans would be left to pick up the pieces. Fighting it was a waste of energy. All you could do in the end was protect yourself.

She'd lived long enough to know that not all storms were produced by a collision of cold dry air with warm moist air. A low-pressure system drawing air from the northeast. Sometimes a storm could be inside you. A collision of hope, fear and bitter regret.

The wind would huff and puff like something out of a children's story, but it wouldn't blow her house down. And life could huff and puff and threaten to knock her off her feet, but she would stay standing.

Her cats depended on her, and she wasn't going to let them down.

"Black cats are supposed to be lucky and I have four of you so we'll be fine. We'll make it through Christmas the way we always do," she said. "And we won't be the only ones not travelling anywhere. Everyone with any sense will stay indoors. Only a fool would be on the road on a night like this."

2

★★★★★

Izzy

Izzy fidgeted, her gaze sliding to the windows where outside the storm was building with frightening speed.

This wasn't good. She needed to get out of here. She needed to get out of here right now. It might already be too late. She loved her job, but not enough to die doing it.

"It's incredible. I never realised it could look like this. Never pictured it." The man gazed at his newly staged home in awe, oblivious to the snow that pirouetted and twirled beyond his windows. He saw only the visible evidence of his success. "I almost want to hold on to it myself. Great job. The place is going to sell for top dollar. Your company said you were the best and you are. And I'm not easy to please."

No kidding.

Izzy kept a polite smile pinned to her face. The man had complained, demanded and changed his mind a thousand times over the past few weeks. She'd been ready to dig a hole and bury him somewhere in the fifty-two acres of land that surrounded his property. But it had also been a challenge, and she loved a challenge. Exceeding expectations gave her a buzz.

"I'm pleased you're pleased."

And she was relieved the job was finally done, not least because the weather was worsening by the second.

Behind her client a wall of glass should have offered breathtaking views across the Green Mountain Range and the National Forest, but the only thing visible was swirling snow. It was like standing in a snow globe after someone had shaken it hard.

Everyone else with any sense was already heading home to snuggle safely in the warm. At this rate Izzy was going to be the last person on the roads.

She eyed the snow uneasily. She was a confident driver, but she was also a sensible person and she knew that driving in this wasn't sensible.

They'd been predicting this storm for days, which was why Izzy had tried to persuade the client to postpone the final staging of his property until the New Year, but he'd refused to budge. Like so many wealthy people, he wanted what he wanted, and he wanted it right now. And her company wanted to retain him as a client, which was why her boss had also dismissed her suggestion that they postpone until after the holidays.

It's just a little snow and wind, Izzy. You'll be fine.

So here she was, three days before Christmas, in a glass-fronted mansion that would have housed an entire basketball team and all their supporters, with a man who had more money than he knew what to do with and the storm of the century building outside.

Maybe he could use some of his wealth to pay for her funeral, she thought, because at this rate she was going to need one.

On the positive side, if she was buried in a snowdrift then at least she would be spared the misery of spending Christmas alone in the soulless studio apartment she was renting.

Most of her belongings were still in boxes in the middle of the floor. Since picking up the keys, she'd been too busy to even hang a painting on the wall. It was ironic that she staged houses for a living and yet her own apartment had all the charm of a filing cabinet.

Still, she'd rather be alone in her bare depressing apartment than here with him. There was something about him that made her uneasy. Yes, he was rich and would probably be considered handsome by some, but he was also a little creepy. Whichever room she was in, he was there too. He kept looking at her, and every time she started to gather her things together he engaged her in conversation.

Relieved that she wasn't alone with him, she glanced across the room to where her colleague Jason was carefully packing up his camera and the rest of the equipment. He wasn't technically her colleague because he was freelance, but they'd worked together on the last eight assignments and so she thought of him that way. And freelance or not, she was pleased he was here, and not just because she'd had a wild crush on him since the day he'd stepped into the office to discuss working with them on some of their biggest clients.

He's expensive, but he's good, her boss had said, and her friend Chloe had muttered that she was sure he was worth every cent and that maybe he was on the wrong end of the camera.

His photos had an artistic brilliance that had undoubtedly contributed to the fact that most of the properties he photographed sold for more than their original valuation, but that wasn't why Izzy liked him. She liked the way he stayed calm when everyone around him was panicking, and she liked the way he paid attention. This shoot was another example of that. Whichever room Izzy had been in, Jason had been there too, and now she was wondering if that had been intentional on his part. Whether he'd also noticed the almost oppressive presence of their demanding client.

He sent a quick glance in her direction and gave a quick nod to indicate that he was ready.

The client stepped closer. "How about a Christmas drink to celebrate?"

"Thanks, but it's getting late and I really should get on the road." This time Izzy was firm. Yes, he was an important client, but it didn't mean she couldn't have boundaries. She'd done the work. As far as she was concerned, that was the end of it.

"One little drink isn't going to hurt."

Jason slung one bag onto his shoulder. "Weather's closing in and we have to stop at the office on the way back." His tone was easy and friendly as he picked up the remaining bags in one hand. "I need to sort through these images and pick the best."

"You go ahead." The client gestured to the door. "Izzy will follow."

Jason didn't budge. "We came together. She's with me."

If only.

Izzy felt a momentary swoop of her stomach and then realised that he wasn't being romantic or protective. He was simply telling the truth. They'd driven up from Boston in the same car. His car. It was a statement of fact, that was all.

And thank goodness they had come together, Izzy thought. It gave her the excuse she needed to get out of here.

And then she caught a glimpse of something in the man's eyes. An emotion she recognised, and she realised in that moment that all he really wanted was company. The reason he didn't want her to leave wasn't because he had nefarious intentions, but because he didn't want to be alone. All that money and a big empty house. But loneliness, she knew, burrowed inside you and chilled you from the inside out. It had nothing to do with where you were living.

She thought about the day her life had changed shape. The day she'd experienced the true meaning of loneliness. Her father had married her stepmother and from the moment they'd said "I do," Izzy had found herself pushed out of a space where once she'd belonged. She'd had no idea a person could be fired from their own family, but that was how it had felt. There was no place for her in the new world they'd created for themselves. All she was to her father was a reminder of bad times. *I can't look at you without thinking of your mother.*

Thinking back, she realised that in all the many visits she'd made to this client, the place had either been empty, or he'd been alone. Normally when she staged a house, she had to remove a myriad of personal items. In this house there had been very few personal items. No photographs, no memorabilia, nothing to suggest this man had a life outside his work. Instead of decluttering, her role had been to inject warmth into a living space that was startlingly sterile.

Maybe that was the reason he now liked the place. She'd turned his huge, silent mausoleum of a house into an inviting home. There were even photographs, chosen by her. Prospective buyers would look at those photographs and picture themselves raising a family here, celebrating with friends and enjoying all the outdoors had to offer.

She felt a stab of sympathy, thinking of him alone here. When they walked out and closed that enormous front door of his behind them, what would he do? Would he spend the holidays sitting in an echoey silence? Drink champagne by himself? She was so horrified by the thought of it she almost offered to stay awhile and have that drink after all.

She wanted to say something comforting, but what could

she say? She knew nothing about his personal circumstances other than the fact that he was wealthy.

She could feel her phone buzzing in the pocket of her jacket. She ignored it. It would be her boss, asking her how it was going for the millionth time. It would have gone faster if she hadn't kept having to stop and answer his calls.

"You've turned the place into a home." The client took a slow look round his newly staged living room. "I was planning to spend Christmas at my lodge in Aspen, but now I'm wondering if I might just stay here."

Aspen? How was he planning to get to Aspen? The snow was piling up and at this rate they wouldn't make it to the end of his drive.

Unless she started her journey in the next few minutes, they'd all be spending Christmas here. And although she sympathised with the man, her sympathy didn't extend to spending the holidays with him, snowed in. She'd definitely kill him, and presumably a dead body wasn't what Santa wanted to find waiting for him when he squeezed himself down the chimney.

Her phone buzzed again. She kept her focus on the client. "I'm happy you're happy. And hopefully now the buyer will be better able to picture themselves living here."

"It's going to make all the difference. Maybe we should even be raising the asking price." He turned to Jason. "Did you get good shots?"

Izzy winced. It wasn't the question to ask Jason, who was considered one of the best photographers in the business.

Still, she took advantage of the brief interlude to finally check her phone.

She had fourteen messages.

One was from Chloe, her closest friend who also happened to be her colleague.

You've seen the severe weather warning? I hope you've already left, but if you haven't get on the road right now or you'll be spending Christmas with that creep.

And also from her boss, Howard.

Is he happy? I'd like an update before I leave the office. I'm counting on you to bring this home.

She managed not to roll her eyes. Good to know her boss was concerned for her welfare. Not.

There was a message on the whole company messaging loop.

Christmas drinks cancelled because of the weather. We'll do something in January.

Thank goodness for that, Izzy thought. The last thing she'd wanted to do was stand around making stilted conversation over cheap fizz or disgusting egg-nogg with Howard and the rest of the senior leadership team.

She messaged Howard first. Just finishing up here. Will call from the car. All good!

Then she replied to the work loop. Such a shame! Happy Holidays to all.

She grinned as she sent it, well able to imagine Chloe's expression as she read it.

Chloe messaged her back immediately. Shame? I'm celebrating. How is sexy Jason? Is he making you reconsider dating again after that cheat Darren. Why do you always pick guys who are so obviously wrong for you?

That was far too complicated a question to be answered in a message.

She wasn't good at relationships and it was her fault. She

knew it was her fault. Darren's words still echoed in her head. *You're not capable of commitment. You broke my heart, Izzy. I wish I'd never met you.*

Those words had settled inside her. Yes, he was the one who had cheated but she'd hurt him, and she didn't want to risk hurting anyone else. She definitely wasn't going to inflict herself on Jason.

She'd given up on relationships for the time being, but that didn't mean she couldn't fantasise.

Checking quickly that Jason was still in conversation with their client, Izzy replied. Jason still sexy last time I looked—which was five seconds ago. With luck we'll be caught in a snowdrift on the way home and he'll be forced to warm my naked body with his. Or maybe not. He's so hot he'd probably melt all the snow.

She wasn't serious of course. Jason seemed like an all-around good guy. He was the sort who did everything well, and that probably included relationships. He didn't need someone like her messing up his life.

She pressed Send on the message.

Jason's phone buzzed and she saw him reach for it at the same moment Chloe messaged her back.

You sent that last message to the whole group! Delete! Delete!

What? No, surely not. That couldn't be right.

Her heart rate accelerated. Panic made her hands slippery on the phone and it took her a few precious seconds to see that she had indeed sent that message to the whole work loop rather than Chloe as intended.

No, no no!

Face burning, she hit "delete for everyone" and hoped that

most people were too busy navigating their way home in a snowstorm to read their messages.

But what if someone had read it? What if Jason had read it? He'd definitely looked at his phone, but he could have been reading the messages about Christmas drinks.

Please let him have been reading the messages about Christmas drinks.

Turning away to hide her flaming face, she packed the last of her bags and then sneaked a glance at him.

"Happy Holidays," he said to the client. "We should get on the road, or we'll be stuck in a snowdrift."

Stuck in a snowdrift?

Was that phrase a coincidence or was he subtly letting her know he'd read the message that wasn't intended for him?

She suppressed a whimper and for a moment wished she'd brought her own car. But she hadn't, which meant she was going to be trapped with Jason for the whole drive back to Boston. Which, in this weather, could take a while.

Awkward didn't begin to describe it.

This was all her boss's fault. If he hadn't insisted on her taking this trip to the client's house, she wouldn't be in this situation. She'd be at home, safe and warm and unpacking boxes in an attempt to make her place look vaguely inhabitable. She'd be decorating her houseplant and watching Christmas movies and trying not to compare those happy, smiling people and their perfect candy cane life with her soulless, Santa-free existence.

Still, at least the roads would be empty for their journey.

No one else would be mad enough to be travelling in this weather.